ECHOED DEFIANCE

JACKY LEON BOOK FOUR

K.N. BANET

1

CHAPTER ONE

JUNE 8TH, 2020

Someone who shouldn't have been outside my house woke me up when I had no need to be up at seven in the morning, only four short hours after I got to sleep. It was a warm June morning in East Texas, humid to the point sweat formed at just the thought of going outside. It wasn't unusual for the area. Muggy, hot days were common as spring gave way to the blistering summer to come. It didn't make me excited to go outside, knowing it would leave me gross and needing another shower.

But my werecat magic was telling me I had a visitor, so I got dressed in shorts and a tank, the most comfortable things I could find. Anything more would have been sweltering if I was going to be outside, and that wouldn't do.

Not that he's going to mind my state of dress.

I walked out the front door and smiled as I leaned against a column on my patio.

"Good morning, Heath," I said as he came into view.

Walking in from the trail that connected my home to the rest of the world, he didn't say anything as he drew closer. I watched his every step, taking in how he was dressed. He'd been out for a run—a human run. His shorts only made it halfway down his muscular thighs, and the luxury running shoes probably cost him two to three hundred dollars, if not more. His expensive tastes were matched with an old concert tee, though I didn't know the band.

"Good morning, Jacky," he greeted, coming up the three steps in one small jump. There was something hot in his eyes, and I knew what was coming. This little discussion was only perfunctory. "I was out for a run and decided to stop by."

"Must have been a long run," I commented as he snaked an arm around my waist and brought our bodies together. He lived all the way in Tyler, toward the edge of my territory. If he ran it human, he was a fool.

Or a showoff, but considering the heat this morning, fool is definitely the one I'm going to go with.

Heath Everson, a werewolf Alpha, living in the territory of a werecat was the most unusual setup we could have possibly come up with. Werewolves and werecats didn't get along on the best of days, and they went to war with each other during the not-so-good times. There was an ancient and bitter rivalry between the two, which infested everything, creating deep-seated hatred between the two species. It came up in everything —how werewolves and werecats lived very different lives, how they Changed people using a different protocol. Werecats generally looked at werewolves as overbreeding, irresponsible nightmares who were dangerous to everyone around them and callous with human life. Werewolves thought werecats were pretentious hypocrites with no social skills and a power complex.

Heath and I had found something different from what our predecessors believed. We were brought together by his daughter. He'd never met me, but one day his daughter had shown up at the back door of my bar, calling on the old supernatural Law which called werecats to Duty. It was essentially bodyguard work, and its very existence was the solution to a particular problem from before my time when werecats and werewolves were at war.

Being called to Duty had driven me to lengths I hadn't realized I would go, sent me to places I never thought I would see—such as the den of a strong pack of werewolves in the middle of a civil war.

And into the life of a werewolf who just wanted to retire from a position that made being a father hard.

At the time, I was certain neither of us ever expected a tenuous bond through a precocious human girl to bring us here. Carey was his only daughter, and I could never get between them. She was something I needed in my life, and I was something she needed, and he could never get between us.

So here we were, an Alpha werewolf without a pack, living in my werecat territory.

That wasn't the only social convention we were tossing to the wayside, though. His arm held me in place, and I made no move to get away.

Maybe we're both fools.

He only chuckled at my comment about the long run, as he leaned in to capture my mouth in a passionate good morning kiss that betrayed emotions we both tried desperately to pretend we didn't have. The kiss felt like a reunion even though it had only been a few days since I last saw him. The full moon had passed over the weekend, and we never spent time together when it was near. It was too volatile, too dangerous for us and everyone within a twenty-mile radius. He stayed in his corner of my territory, and I stayed clear of him. It was the safest way.

I tried to step back, but he followed until my back was against my front door, and he was in every inch of my space. He propped an arm on the door over me, closing me in, while his other hand held me to him. I was strong enough to break free since I was the dominant predator here—one werecat could always handle one werewolf.

I just didn't want to. Wrapping my arms around his neck, I encouraged him to continue.

The kiss grew more possessive. He ran that hand down my back, over the curve of my hip to my thigh, lifting it to wrap around his waist.

Feeling the urge to reach for the door and invite him in, I knew it was time to stop. I pulled my head back as much as I could, letting it knock my front door, an obvious sign to him we needed to break this up.

"You need to run home," I whispered, trying to control my breathing and my pulse. "It's a school day."

"School ended like two weeks ago," he said with a growl, leaning in further to kiss my jaw, then ducked down to kiss my neck. "I wanted to see you."

Shit.

"You can come in and have coffee, but the paws need to come off and kept to yourself. We've never even been on a date." I was looking for excuses, really. I wasn't ready to jump into bed with Heath Everson, no matter how good his mouth felt on my neck.

His heavy sigh was humorously overdone. Slowly releasing me, he made it apparent he didn't want to, but when his grey-blue eyes met mine, I knew he understood.

"I wish it wasn't like this," he murmured, leaning in. This time he just touched his forehead to mine and gave me a stare that threatened to send me to my knees. There was an intensity to Heath which had become stronger over the last few months—animal magnetism he had been holding back to appear to be a nice, normal human-like man. That pretense, though, was long gone between us.

"We're taking enough risks. Why add one more?" I asked, swallowing my own want. "This just...It puts everyone at risk, Heath."

"I know."

That was my logical excuse and a good reason not to crawl under the covers with the Alpha wolf who threatened to send me up in flames with just the simplest of touches.

I had several illogical excuses I was never stupid enough to tell him. I hadn't had sex in over a decade. Since before my fiancé died, a man who had loved me and wanted to spend the rest of his life with me. I wasn't even sure I had moved on from Shane, and kissing another man made me think about it more. Beyond

Shane, I wasn't sure if I wanted Heath because I wanted *him*, if it was the taboo that drew me in, or he was just the first man to show me any interest since I lost my human life.

I didn't know enough about myself to know how I felt about anything anymore. I knew I liked kissing Heath. I loved hanging out with him and his family. They filled a void in my life I didn't know I had until they strolled into it.

He finally left my personal bubble, and I was able to fumble my way into my own house. He didn't reach out to help, and the sexual tension was still thick on the air. Honestly, I was glad he didn't help.

"How did you end up running here this early in the morning?" I asked, looking over my shoulder as I walked into the kitchen. I started a pot of coffee while he looked at my things. I kept everything relatively clean, so I wasn't worried about anything embarrassing, and he'd already been this far into my house—no further, though. He never left the public spaces, and he had certainly never been in my house with me alone. We always had Carey around to keep us honest. I needed her to keep me honest. She had no idea I was kissing her father, and I didn't want to give that dangerous secret to a thirteen-year-old girl who already had enough pressure in her life.

I turned to him after I was done setting up the coffee and realized he never answered while I was lost in thought.

"Heath?"

"Hm?"

"How did you end up running all the way out here?" I asked again, frowning at him.

"I caught your scent on one of my running trails and just followed it...Well, the wolf followed it," he admitted softly. And it was a secret to admit. We were predators, werewolves and werecats. If we were wild and uncivilized, or if our animals took control for a minute—which happened more frequently than some would want to admit—there weren't many reasons to hunt a particular scent. Either his wolf wanted to *hunt* me, or his wolf wanted to *mate* me.

Six months ago, I would have assumed hunt. Now, I didn't. The only reason he had caught my scent on his human running trail was my cat had gone to sniff out his running trails over the last full moon—two sides of the same coin, Heath and I.

Normally, the divide between person and animal was clear for the moon-cursed species. Humans were always in control. Heath and I were human first. Personally, I only gave in to the instinctual urges of the cat on full moons. Most of the time, she and I were in complete agreement about everything happening around us, and it was a background idea we were two separate pieces of the same mind. It sounded like a second personality, but it was just a clear divide between the animalistic nature of the mind and the logical or rational human one. Sometimes, those two sides got into very real arguments. Hence why many spoke of the animal as 'other.'

"Did the wolf get what he wanted?" I leaned on the counter, watching Heath. His eyes turned from soft grey-blue to hard ice-blue.

"Not particularly," he answered. I kept my eyes locked on his, refusing to look down. Seeing what I knew was there would only make this more awkward.

"This is the first time your wolf has led you here," I whispered, letting the idea sink in. Attachments could be good things, but they could quickly spiral out of control. I was a werecat and had to be very careful. We were possessive and dangerous animals. I worked hard to not get too attached to Heath and failed every time. All the werecats I knew and spoke to called him my werewolf. It was a joke, playing on the fact he lived in my territory, but it freaked me out because I knew just how right they were.

"It won't be the last," he said carefully. "Hopefully, no one thinks too much about it if they come visit you or me. This is your territory, and I'm an Alpha wolf. We need to be able to talk to each other, and hopefully, that keeps them from getting curious."

"They'll smell what we can smell right now, Heath. There's no hiding we turn each other on. Well...*you* can hide it, I can't." I straightened up and yawned. His ability to mask his scent was remarkable. "And holy shit, it's early in the morning. How long have you been out running?"

"I woke up at five and needed to clear my head. Had some..." He chuckled. "You know...dreams."

That made my face warm. Heath was the type of man who was honest about this sort of thing. Once he'd freely revealed his attraction to me, there was no avoiding it, and he refused to let me avoid it, not that I had been trying *that* hard.

"Then you caught my scent," I said, seeing how easy it would have been for the wolf's instincts to override the man. It helped me understand the passion behind the kiss, too. Plus, it was easier to talk about the instinctual behavior than it was to talk about what his subconscious was showing him at night.

"Yeah. It wasn't just that, but you probably don't want the recent werewolf news," he said, pulling out his phone to check something. For a moment, I saw how bothered he was by something before it was forgotten, and his phone was put away again.

"I wouldn't mind hearing about it," I said softly. He seemed surprised. Normally, I didn't want to hear anything, but I just wanted to hear him talk. I wanted to know what would bother him. Something had to be if he was going on exhaustingly long runs, even for a werewolf.

"There's some tension with an *old* pack in Russia. Since that pack doesn't really talk to anyone, we can only watch the news and try to put it together. Recently, a young female was taken to Mygi Hospital with injuries that concerned a lot of us. She won't talk to anyone, though. Nothing we can do unless she speaks out."

"How old?" I asked softly.

"The girl or the pack?" Something dark flashed in Heath's eyes.

"Both."

"Our best guess? She's in her early twenties. No idea how long she's been a werewolf. As for the pack? It's had the same Alpha for a thousand years, and most of his inner circle are just as old. I don't know his exact age.

Somewhere around fifteen hundred, but I could be wrong."

My eyes went wide, then refocused on the coffee. At my expression, Heath must have realized that was all I needed or wanted to know.

We were quiet until the coffee finished, and I led us back onto my patio, trying to get back into the clear air. We sat together and looked over my woods.

"Work on Kick Shot is coming along nicely," he said, obviously trying to have a normal conversation after a very not-normal start to our day. "Remember, there's a meeting on Friday to finalize your design ideas. You'll be back up and running by the end of July if everything stays on schedule."

"That's wonderful. I miss it, and I'm paying two employees who don't work."

"Dirk and Oliver..." Heath let his head fall back. "Oliver keeps sending in new requests, and I've told him he needs to clear them with you."

"He's sending them to you because I keep telling him no," I whispered. Dirk and Oliver were a recent addition to my life and to the lives of those in my territory. Dirk was the adopted human son of my werecat brother, Nikolaus, Niko for short. Dirk was an enigma wrapped in a cloak of anger and refusal to meet the expectations of his father, not that Niko had many for him—get an education, a good job, and stay out of trouble. Dirk had turned down being Changed into a werecat, which felt right. He was in his mid-twenties and didn't *feel* like someone who should or could be a werecat, happily living a solitary lifestyle. Instead, he rebelled against his adoptive father in every way—he refused to go to college, became a bartender, and got into a fight that drove Niko to send him out of his territory to restart and get his head together.

So, now Dirk was the bartender for Kick Shot, which was funny because not long after he arrived, the bar burned down. Now he was just getting a paycheck. I had a sneaking suspicion he was moonlighting in a bar outside my territory without my permission. I had no intention of calling him out on it, though.

"Oliver...he's a sneaky one." I shook my head a little at the ingenuity of my manager, the young man from London. He was also optimistic, bright, youthful, intelligent, and had the self-esteem of a small child who was told he was stupid all the time. He'd shown up the same day as Dirk, all smiles and not a drop of fear or distrust in him. He had been, and still was, a people pleaser to the nth degree. He would do anything to prove his worth, and sometimes, that grated on the people around him. He constantly went behind my back to Heath to try to get upgrades to Kick Shot's new building, so he could expand my business and prove his worth as a successful restaurant and bar manager. It all boiled down to what he most craved in life, something I gleaned from discussions with Zuri and Davor—his father's approval.

"Carey tries the same thing, you know," Heath finally said, giving me a chagrined smile.

"Oh, I know. I normally let her do something since I know it wasn't what you wanted." I grinned. "It's always harmless."

"Undermining my authority," he mumbled, but I saw a hint of a smile. "She loves you."

"I love her. That's why she gets everything she wants out of me." I was half-joking. Carey could ask for the moon, and I would buy her a moon rock. I wasn't *too* gullible.

"So, that's the secret," he said with a pondering nature, giving me a side-eye glance. "I just need to steal your heart, and suddenly, I'll get everything I want."

"Heath..."

"Don't worry, it'll always be harmless."

My chair wasn't far enough away from him, and I certainly didn't react in time. His lips found mine, the slow kiss tasting like bad coffee and worse decisions, need, flirtation, and forgotten boundaries.

It tasted wonderful. He always did.

It was interrupted by his phone going off, and the groan he gave was comical.

"Never get a break," he muttered as he pulled it out. "This son of mine never gives me a real moment to do anything by myself anymore." It went to his ear, and I heard the growl on the other end. "Yes, Landon?"

"You know you have a meeting in thirty minutes, right? You've been out running for nearly two-and-a-half hours. They're going to be here soon, and you know they won't like it if it's only Carey and me. Are you trying to get us in trouble?"

I watched Heath pale, not a sight I believed I had ever seen before.

"I'll be right home. I'm sorry. If they show up, tell them

I had a meeting conflict, and it won't happen again." Heath hung up on his son and jumped up, shoving his cell phone back into his pocket. "Sorry, Jacky. I need to go—"

"What's wrong? What's this meeting?" I straightened but didn't stand. "Are other supernaturals coming into my territory? I'll need to know—"

"No, they're humans," he said softly, looking away. "This is just about something..."

"About what?" I frowned, watching my werewolf pull off his shirt. If he had to get back in less than thirty minutes, he was going to have to *run*—not on two feet but four.

"It's..." He sighed, sagging for a moment. "It's nothing, Jacky. Don't worry too much about it. Your secret is safe, and there are no supernaturals coming into your territory."

He finished throwing the rest of his clothes into my yard and Changed. His wolf form looked huge when I was human, downright massive. He cast me a glance and picked up his shorts, leaving the rest.

"I'll run everything through the wash and bring them over later," I said, waving. I knew how much of a pain it was to carry so much clothing. He was only taking the shorts because his cell phone and wallet were in them. It looked somewhat comical, seeing the shorts dangle from his mouth.

He nodded his big head and took off into the trees. Once he was gone, I sighed heavily.

"What a way for the morning to go," I mumbled, going out to get his sweaty clothes. As I picked them up, I got curious. What meeting with humans could possibly give Heath a cold sweat?

I threw the clothes into my washing machine, pondering it. I knew better than to go to the house if I got curious. For all I knew, this was werewolf business, and the humans would know of me. The last thing I needed was to draw attention to myself.

It was just another way Heath and I were so different. He'd come to my small corner of the world, but it wasn't his entire world like it was mine. I didn't need to deal with humans knowing who or what I was. I didn't need to deal with higher powers outside of Hasan, my werecat father. Heath was a recognized face of the werewolves who once dealt with human governments about werewolf rights and businesses. He was more than a little famous, or used to be.

Once I sat down in the kitchen, I realized there was no getting back to sleep, but I had options.

2

CHAPTER TWO

Trying to put Heath out of my mind was difficult. I hadn't heard from him as I pulled into the driveway of the small house I recently purchased only fifteen minutes from Kick Shot and my primary residence. It was already nine, and I still had no idea what sort of meeting could have driven the werewolf Alpha who let nothing bother him to go pale and run off my property like a fire was blazing at his house, not even giving me a real explanation as to what it was.

I mean, there're a few options why he might have gotten all freaked out, but none of them really fit. What would Heath have to be scared of?

Before I had the chance to get out of my little hatchback, Oliver was coming outside.

"Good morning, Miss Jacky!" the young Londoner called, waving. "Would you care for some breakfast?"

I got out of the car slowly, amazed at the young man's innate ability to know if I was coming over or not.

"How did you know it was me?" I asked loudly,

locking up and walking toward him. "And I'll have a coffee."

"You haven't checked in with us since before the full moon," he answered, smiling. His bright face was pleasant, always open and giving. He was the type who screamed 'good boy who never gets into trouble,' which made him trustworthy and sweet.

Oliver was with me, though. For a lot of reasons, I was the oddball of my werecat family. Jacky Leon, the American, the baby of the family, the one with no ambitions or drive to take over the world or do more than I wanted. Oliver was an oddball, too, but in a lot of different ways—too driven and too much for a lot of people, at least in personality. Part of me never wanted to send the sweet young man back because of that. We could be the weird ones in my corner of the world.

"How's Dirk?" I asked as I followed him inside. "And how's the house? I know I ask all the time, but I didn't have it built, so who knows what might be wrong with it—"

"We had a plumber out yesterday for a clog in the sink I refused to let Dirk try to fix, but it's fine." Oliver smiled as he locked the front door again, something I was glad he made a habit. His introduction to living in a werecat territory had been an eventful one, with my territory being invaded by a group of werecats looking to overthrow my family from the position of power it had built over the centuries.

"Well...if you ever want me to hire someone for a complete rebuild, let me know." I didn't like that I had to buy them a house built in the eighties just to find them a place to live. They had been planning on just getting little apartments, but that had been completely out of the question to me, and there hadn't been time to build them something new.

"You've already given us so much," Oliver said, smiling. "My parents are jealous."

"Yeah, well…they can take up their living arrangements with Davor and Zuri," I deflected, not wanting to discuss how much I spoiled Oliver and Dirk. I knew why his parents were probably jealous. Most employees earned their paycheck, then went home to the house they had to buy, the house they had to pay for. Since I only had two human employees and probably wouldn't get any more who had been introduced to the supernatural world for a very long time, I was spoiling them. It was my secret, though. I didn't want my family to think it was okay to just send me their troublemakers and their misfits.

To me, it was totally reasonable to make sure they both had fake U.S. identities and driver's licenses. To me, it made sense to buy Oliver a car, so Dirk didn't have to drive him around. While I hadn't accepted their presence fast enough to buy Dirk his truck, I had at least gotten Oliver what he needed.

Plus, Dirk would have been pissed if I bought him the truck. He's that type. I'm family, and he hates accepting gifts from Niko, which probably carries over to me. If his own adoptive father pisses him off, why wouldn't his kind of aunt?

He was the harder of the two to convince to live in a house I bought for them. I finally stomped my foot and said it was a safety issue. That got him to relent and move but had pissed him off for about three days because he had to accept something for free from me. Niko had a laugh when I had told him about the entire ordeal, but in the end, Dirk wasn't living in a motel, and I knew he was safe.

I sat down at the small breakfast table off the kitchen, nestled in a nook with a view of their back property. Of course, I didn't put them in the middle of Jacksonville. I needed to be able to get to their house in werecat form without neighbors wondering what I was at two in the morning.

"Kick Shot should be back up and running by the end of July," I told my young manager as he put a coffee in front of me. "Once the date is confirmed, we can talk about reopening plans. You'll want to throw a party, I'm guessing."

"I will, and I want us to hire more bartenders and staff," he said, smiling as he sat down. "They don't need to be paid as much as Dirk and me, of course, but you're going to need more hands. I'm going to market Kick Shot heavily and hope to double or triple your clientele."

"You're insane," I smirked. "I'll hire two extra bartenders to work the patio bar on rotation. That's all. That's what you get, Oliver. We've talked about this. Dirk and I will be rotating the main bar and together on busy nights."

"But—"

I leveled him with a stare, and he didn't continue with that 'but,' which was good for him. Maybe one day, I'd open a location he could do more with, but as it was, I missed my job. Having my bar had been a simple pleasure in my life.

"It's too close to my home to get too big," I said finally. "Bar, pool tables, poker nights...that's all."

"We put in that wonderful kitchen," he moaned, sitting across from me with a precious pout I was certain worked on his mother, Zuri, and every other woman in his life.

I saw Carey at least once a week, so it didn't work on me. Not as well as Oliver was probably accustomed to, anyway.

"We put in that wonderful kitchen, I'm certain we can find a use for...like hosting events, occasionally. Renting out the bar for parties and the kitchen to catering companies." I had been thinking about it for months. I didn't want a large, permanent staff, but this could be the compromise I needed to give Oliver. The way his eyes lit up, I realized I had been right.

"Oh," was all he said.

I sipped my coffee as heavy footsteps started overhead, then came down the stairs.

Dirk eyed me hard as he passed into the kitchen, confusion written all over his face as he poured himself a coffee and made himself a plate of eggs and bacon.

"Oliver, have you fed her yet?" Dirk asked softly, pointedly looking at his roommate and not me when he sat down.

"She only wanted coffee."

Dirk turned back on me, frowning.

"I've been awake for a couple of hours now, already ate," I said, trying to be light. This wasn't my first time visiting, but I had to be careful. Dirk was wary of being smothered, which was an appropriate thing to feel because he was raised by a werecat. Niko never admitted it, but I knew for a fact he probably suffocated Dirk, which every werecat parent accidentally did until they were forced to stop. Hasan smothered me until I left. I was certain he still would if I ever gave him the chance. "With the full moon past, I just wanted to check in."

"You don't need to get paranoid. We're fine," Dirk said, looking away and starting in on his breakfast.

Well, just call me out, why don't you?

"I'm not paranoid," I muttered.

"Yeah, you are. You check in before and after every full moon, and I know it's not because Niko wants reports. He emails me just fine to bother the hell out of me, demanding to know how life is here in America *because* you won't tell him anything. Plus, he's still with... Hasan. I think it's driving him crazy."

"It is." I already knew the crazy part. Niko was around eight hundred years old and was being smothered by our shared father since his injuries back in February. His back had been broken, and Hasan had no intention of letting him leave the island until he was certain Niko could handle anything life threw at him. "He'll probably be there for a year before Hasan is ready to let him go."

"Good. He shouldn't have gotten so fucking hurt," Dirk said angrily, but I knew there was some care in those words. They had an antagonistic relationship, but Niko and Dirk cared for each other the same way any rebellious son and smothering father did.

"I'll tell him you said that," I said with a bit of

mischief. That comment earned me a glare from the young man.

"Don't bother, I already have."

I tried not to smile.

"You know, my parents tried to get me to go back to London after what happened," Oliver said, looking between us. "They thought working for you was too dangerous. They told..."

"With me, you can just call them by their names, Davor and Zuri. They're my siblings, not royalty."

"Yeah..." He was obviously uncomfortable, but I wanted him to get over the strange hero worship he had. My siblings had egos; I didn't. The only way to get Oliver more comfortable with me was to get him more comfortable with the entire family. "They told Davor and Zuri they wanted me back home in London, or they would quit their jobs."

"I know."

"I chose to stay." Oliver smiled. I smiled in return, grateful he trusted me so much even though we hadn't known each other for very long. I knew the rest of the story that he didn't. His parents had threatened to quit, ranted, raved, and stomped their feet at Davor and Zuri.

Zuri tried to talk to them because she could be deadly and cool, but she had once been a mother, and I was certain she took that into consideration when approached with two scared human parents. Davor had no such heart and started calling his assistants to have the positions opened up for interviews.

Both of his parents backed down, their bluff called. By the time Oliver got ahold of them again and told them he wanted to stay here with me, they were more inclined to agree.

They had made the mistake of insulting my ability to protect their son, and my siblings had made them realize that wouldn't be tolerated. Truthfully, I thought I had done fairly well, keeping Dirk and Oliver out of harm's way. They never saw a bit of action and mostly stayed hidden with Heath and his family during the entire thing.

The conversation died off, and I just took up space at their table as they ate and cleaned up afterward. Dirk didn't know what to do with me sitting there, so he quickly escaped, changed his clothes, then called out he was leaving. I waved as he left, then turned back to Oliver for an explanation. It was only ten in the morning. If Dirk was moonlighting, he certainly wasn't doing it this early in the morning.

"He doesn't stay here all day. He likes getting out and going to see places around town," Oliver explained, reading my expression. "He normally waits until you've left. You know, he acts weird with you."

"He's different with just you?"

"Yeah. He's a good guy, but whenever you're around, he closes up a lot."

"Ah." I finished my coffee, which was cold. "Well, I should get out of your hair. If you need anything, you have my number. And if you go out, drive safe."

"Okay!"

Standing to take my cup to the sink for Oliver, I felt movement through my magic. My wolves were moving. Landon and Heath were heading away from home, and since it was both of them, I had to assume Carey was with them.

They're probably heading out to get lunch together. They don't sit in their house all day, either.

After the morning with Heath, I felt strange about it, though. I waved to Oliver as I walked out. Getting in my car, I tracked the wolves as they turned. They were in a vehicle together, their signatures on my mental map nearly on top of each other, and their movement wasn't organic. Normally, they sat in the back of my mind, their presence a part of my daily life and unbothersome. It had taken over a year, but my instincts had finally decided neither wolf was a threat to be attentive about.

But Heath had a meeting that had made him pale. *Pale.* There was something about it I couldn't shake.

My phone went off as I turned the key to get the little Nissan Versa started. I checked it and cursed.

LANDON: We're heading over to Kick Shot. People want to meet you. They're from Child Protective Services and the Bureau of Supernatural Affairs.

CPS AND BSA? Jesus, Heath, you could have warned me shit was fucking going on. God damn it.

I peeled out of the driveway too fast and hit the gas. I would beat them to Kick Shot, but my mind was reeling. Was I dressed well enough to meet people from either organization? Was there anything in my house that could give me away as a supernatural? Or, worse, cause them to think Carey wasn't safe?

I flew into my parking lot and started running for my house. Not that I wanted to bring them back here, but I would concede to it if it was necessary. They would wonder why I put it out in the woods with no proper trail, but that was something I would just have to take.

As I got into my house and started looking for things that were too dangerous to leave out, I kept mental track of Landon and Heath. They were getting closer, but were coming from Tyler and following the speed limit. I had time. Not a lot of time, but enough. I grabbed the sketchbook Jabari had given me over a year ago and shoved it into a drawer. There was no way I could leave a book full of runes of power out. I had started practicing them again after the incident with Lani and the other werecats; not that the runes could have helped me then.

Once the sketchbook was out of sight, I looked up, remembering there were some things I couldn't hide. Jabari and I had carved runes into the very walls of the house. There were a few over my front door on the inside, and I could only hope no one noticed them or knew what they were. I checked for any mess, glad I didn't keep anything stupid like pictures of my werecat family in public. I had a couple of me and Hasan tucked away in my master bedroom closet, but nothing else.

I looked out the window right as my phone buzzed. They were nearly at Kick Shot. I tried to fix my hair, tightening the ponytail holding my mass of reddish-brown hair. My clothes were clean, but the jeans had holes in the knees. It was Texas, and I owned a bar, so I hoped that would shield me. I didn't have time to put on a pair of slacks or anything.

I checked my phone as I walked back through the woods.

LANDON: We're nearly there. The story is you and Father met after we moved here. Carey really liked you, and we needed a helping hand since we don't have a pack anymore to support us, so you stepped up. You and Carey are very close. You're human.

WELL, no shit, of course I'm human, Landon. If they knew I was anything else, there would be hell to pay.

I wasn't mad at Landon. I was worried because I had never had to play being a human like this before—not to government agents who were probably trained to find supernaturals. It didn't help while werewolves had been out in the open for a couple of decades, werecats were very much still in hiding. Fae and witches were somewhat exposed, but really, everyone looked at the werewolves as the dose of supernatural they needed in their lives, and half the time, they didn't even want the werewolves.

Humans could only handle so much, and no one wanted to push the luck the supernaturals had so far with being found out. We didn't want to overdo it.

3

CHAPTER THREE

I walked around the nearly finished new building for Kick Shot as they pulled into the parking lot. Leaning on the wall, I watched them park. There were three vehicles—Heath, Landon, and Carey in Heath's truck; behind them a black SUV; then a small, kind of dinky sedan.

Werewolves, BSA, CPS...in that order.

My werewolves were a little stiff getting out of the truck, Landon especially, but it was the look on Heath's face while the humans couldn't see him that surprised me. He was *pissed*. Carey looked a little worried, but I watched her face brighten when she saw me.

"Jacky!" she called out, waving. Heath waved her to go, and I grabbed the thirteen-year-old as she launched herself into me for a hug.

"Hey, kid," I said, running a hand over the top of her head. "Hope you're having a good day."

Her face screwed up as she turned to glare at the black SUV. I watched the same vehicle. No one from either agency had come out of their rides yet. I knew we were being watched.

They wanted to see before they jumped into questions.

Control yourself, Jacky. Now isn't the time to be flashing gold cat eyes at people.

It took a moment, but Heath and Landon came to stand next to us, and the feds finally got out of their car, two self-assured men in navy-blue business suits and one woman in a navy-blue pencil skirt with a white blouse. Was navy-blue their work color? I purposefully ignored the BSA for my own self-preservation. Humans didn't know much about the organization formed by the U.S. government, and too much knowledge on my part would be suspicious.

The woman from CPS was the most cautious, getting out even slower, but she followed the lead set by the feds. As they drew closer, she walked behind them. One of the men held back and stood at her side.

Ah, so they bring numbers in case werewolf parents get pissy about their kids possibly being taken away. I'll bet my bar they're all armed.

"Agents, this is Jacky Leon. She owns the bar currently being remodeled behind us," Heath said, positioning himself in the middle of the pack. "Jacky, this is Agent Robinson, Agent Taylor, and Agent Smith from the BSA. Hiding in the back is Miss Davis from CPS."

"We heard there was a bar fire down here a few months ago. Would that be this one?" the female agent asked, giving my bar the once over, then turning on me.

"Yeah, electrical issue," I answered. "No one was in

the building. It was closed for repairs and maintenance, anyway. It was a very old building, and the contractor I had previously hired missed a wiring issue." That was the official story. It had cost me a pretty penny to bribe and rewrite the records. They had wanted it written up as arson and to go after whoever set it up in flames. I couldn't tell them the person was already dead.

More specifically, I couldn't have them look into her because I had killed her.

"Do you have a better contractor now?" she asked, a small smile forming.

"I would hope so. He's a werewolf," I said, tilting my head to the side to stare at her. Not just a friendly, human stare, but a real stare to make her uncomfortable. It was a ballsy thing to do, but she was asking stuff that wasn't her business. I figured she had already made up her mind about me.

She turned to Heath, her eyes narrowing. While her attention was diverted, I took the liberty to look at the delicate silver necklace she wore. I knew it was silver because I could smell it. The reason for the metal choice was obvious, but the symbol wasn't.

It was a rune of power. One I couldn't identify off the top of my head. I tried to dedicate the shape of it to memory to look up later.

"You're helping her rebuild her business?" Agent Robinson seemed curious. "That's very kind of you. She watches your daughter, and you rebuild her entire business." The way her gaze fell back on me made the hair on the back of my neck stand up.

"I'm a paying client," I said tightly. I didn't like what she was implying.

"Why don't we see where you and Carey hang out?" Miss Davis asked politely. "We're not here to get into anything but Carey's wellbeing and safety, Agent Robinson."

"Of course, my apologies." There was nothing sorry about the agent, but the lip service would have to do. "Where do you live? Why did we meet you at the bar?" Those were once again directed at me.

"I live in the woods behind the bar. It's a short walk, and the trail is well worn. Normally, I have a dirt bike to make the trip back and forth, but with so many of you, we'll be walking."

"You don't have a driveway or a garage?" That made one of the male agents curious now. I made a mental note, it was Agent Smith.

"No, I use the bar for my car, the little Versa over there." I pointed out my little blue car with a smile. "I like the seclusion, and when I had the house built, there wasn't a reason for anything more. When Carey comes over, we walk it together. I've been considering putting down a concrete or stone path for the last few months, but I need to get Kick Shot back up and running." Now I was paying lip service. I had no intention of putting a visible path through the woods that led directly to my house. People could walk.

"It's a really pretty house," Carey said, her voice soft. "Prettier than Dad's."

"Thanks. Let's show them." I chuckled, keeping an

arm over her shoulder as we started walking. Heath and Landon fell in behind us and behind them, the agents.

I heard someone mumble a curse as they tripped over a tree root, one of the men. The two women were much more careful. When we reached the clearing, I heard a low whistle.

"Now, this is a nice place," Agent Taylor exclaimed in a hushed way. "How much did something like this cost you?"

Ah shit. I own a bar and have a forest home that looks like it came out of some fancy architecture magazine. I didn't think about that.

"Not an amount I like talking about," I answered, smiling tightly, crossing my arms as I turned to them. The feds and the woman from CPS stayed in a little pack. Carey ran up the steps, and I heard but didn't see Carey go inside, and Landon followed her. Only Heath stayed with me. "I came out here after a family tragedy. I wanted to get away and had the means to do it. I've tried to enjoy a simpler life since then. It's worked for me so far."

"I didn't have you pegged as someone with money, but everyone has their surprises and secrets," Agent Robinson said with a thin smile. "Can we get the grand tour?"

"Certainly." I turned on my heel, sending Heath a glare as my eyes passed over him. He winced. There would be words about this invasion of my privacy later.

I didn't give them a real tour, tell them about the place, or explain the design choices. Those were my business, not theirs. Instead, I led them in, walked into the kitchen to find Carey and Landon already having their way with my stuff, and took a seat at the kitchen island on a swivel bar stool I had installed for Carey to watch me while I cooked or help me when she wanted.

"Serve me, bartender," I ordered, looking at the old werewolf standing on the other side of the island. The look on Landon's face wasn't amused, but it wasn't pissed off, either. Somewhere in the middle of those two emotions? Definitely.

"Where are we allowed to go, and where would you like us to stay out of?" Miss Davis asked softly, coming to stand next to me.

"Carey doesn't go upstairs. We do everything down here. Keep it down here." I turned to her and sighed. "I wasn't expecting company today and also think there's no reason for anyone to see my private bedroom. That crosses a line for me. If you feel the need, I'm going to have to disappoint."

"Oh, no, it's fine." The cautious, somewhat scared woman gave me a little smile. "Mister Everson said Carey only does day trips to spend time with you while he and his son get some work done in the after-school hours. I'm certain there's no need to go through anything but the public spaces."

"Thank you." I tried to smile back. This was already way too far for me—too many people I didn't know or trust in my house, the center of my territory, my sanctuary.

Doing it for Carey. Just survive it for Carey. Then scrub the house down and erase every bit of evidence they ever came from existence.

Heath was surprisingly quiet as he walked around

with the agents, taking in my house as much as they were. I could see him, thanks to the semi-open floor plan in the living room. I wasn't bothered until I saw the female agent's head tilt back, and her body stiffen. I could smell a trace of fear in the air as I stood up and started walking closer.

"Can I speak to Miss Leon alone?" she asked before she realized I was nearly right behind her.

"Sure, we can talk outside. It's too hot to send everyone else out," I said softly. That made her jump. Heath had a momentary look of panic as the agent walked around me and back out the front door. I shrugged. I had never had to handle something like this before, but I figured I could manage. I found Agent Robinson standing in the grass about ten feet from the house by the time I made it outside.

"You are *not* human," she snapped, glaring at me.

"Why do you say that?" I asked innocently, pushing my hands into my pockets, working to keep my breathing even. I couldn't get pissed off now. If I slipped and my eyes changed, I was made, and there would be problems. I'd probably have to leave the country until this woman grew old and died. I certainly couldn't stick around near Carey, Heath, and Landon. I'd probably have to go back to Hasan until he could erase me from existence again and help me set up in a different country. The Eversons would have to move, too, or they'd be harassed about me until the end of time.

"Those runes carved—"

"Those runes are old superstition, just like the one around your neck. Or are you trying to tell me you aren't human?" I frowned. "I don't like being accused of something I'm not, and I'm certain you probably don't either. So, let's not jump to conclusions."

"I..." She reached up and touched her necklace, frowning, the anger still in her eyes. "You aren't what I expected when Alpha Everson mentioned you."

"I'm never what anyone expects," I mumbled, looking away, annoyed. When I looked back at her, I sighed. "Look, I get you're here to make sure Carey is a well-adjusted kid. I'm just trying to help my friends by letting you come here. She spends time here. I watch out for her and trust her father and brother. They make sure she does her homework every day, and she gets good grades. My life, however, isn't your business. The way I live my life isn't your business. My beliefs aren't your business."

Her mouth thinned. I knew of the BSA but had no experience with the organization. It was overseen by a congressional committee, which meant it probably had an agenda. I didn't know what that agenda was. I never wanted to know what that agenda was.

"What do they do?" she asked, crossing her arms.

"The runes? I've heard they're supposed to ward off evil. Obviously, they don't work." I shrugged.

"Why? Because they let the werewolves walk right into your house?"

The werewolves. There was a detachment that bothered me, and I finally saw enough of this woman to know exactly why Heath hadn't been comfortable with this meeting in the morning.

"No." I worked *so hard* not to get snappy with her. It took every ounce of my self-control not to teach this woman there were things more dangerous than the wolves. Things willing to kill for these wolves specifically. "Do you have a problem with werewolves?"

"They're dangerous. I'm amazed you feel safe living out here with them so close." She seemed so sure of herself. I wished desperately for the right and ability to knock her down a few pegs. "You don't seem concerned at all for Miss Everson's safety or worried her mother isn't around."

"Heath's romantic life or lack thereof is none of my business. From what I know, it was a short liaison that accidentally led to a kid. Carey's mother didn't want to be tied to a werewolf or to raise one, so she left Carey with Heath and ran off. I feel bad for Carey not having a mom, but that's the only opinion I have on the matter."

Agent Robinson must have realized we stood on opposite sides of this one. She obviously wanted me to slip up and make Heath look bad. I was doing my best not to let that happen while protecting my own secrets.

"Well..." I turned back to the house. "Are you coming back inside, or are you going to sit out here and create a bunch of conspiracy theories about what is a harmless situation? First, I'm not human, and now you think Heath must have done something to Carey's mother. What else are you going to come up with?"

"There's nothing harmless when werewolves are involved," the woman hissed softly. "You'll learn when they go wild and betray or hurt her. Or, worse, turn one of you." The hate I could smell off this woman was threatening to choke me. She'd hoped to find an ally in me? Or maybe she was just pissed because she knew she wouldn't get what she wanted out of this little visit. Heath's life was too respectable, and Carey was so perfect, no one would dare take her away from her family.

"I didn't think the BSA would hire people like you, but you asked why I didn't think those runes worked. It's because they let someone like *you* into my house. You should go before I call your superiors and tell them some hateful bitch was harassing good people." I was glad I wasn't looking at her. I heard her stutter as I started walking.

"Traitor!" she called out as I slammed my door. Everyone turned to me as I walked into the kitchen, rubbing my eyes to cover them, hoping they weren't gold.

"She's mad because I don't think werewolves are evil," I explained as Heath stepped to my side. "She's a mean little thing." Taking a deep breath, I pulled my feelings back and tried to control them. I turned to him first, so he could check my eyes. His were ice-blue, but that wasn't a problem for him.

"This is the first time I've met her," he told me. "Though I expected she was anti-werewolf. I figured that would piss you off more if she tried to play it with you."

That was what I needed to hear. I wasn't pissed off enough, so my eyes were still a safe human hazel. I turned around and leaned on the counter. The other two agents were wary, but not angry or upset.

"Did she say anything, miss?" Agent Taylor asked. "This is her first time doing one of these house calls."

"First, she accused me of being not human. Then she implied Heath must have done something to Carey's mother."

That made Heath growl. Landon reached out and grabbed his father's shoulder, pulling him from the kitchen.

"Then she was just mean. You need to talk to someone about making sure unbiased people are making these visits. I might be human, but that doesn't mean I tolerate that sort of bullshit in my home or on my property." I glared at the agents, then turned to the woman from CPS.

"Have you seen everything you need to see? I'm going to take this nice family out to lunch once you're gone. They deserve it after putting up with this rude invasion into their lives."

"Oh, yes, we're done," the woman practically squeaked. "Heath's an amazing father, and I'm really glad to see Carey has a new positive female role model in her life. I was concerned she might not with her mother's absence. It's been a pleasure. You have a lovely home. Have a nice day."

She practically ran out of the room. One of the agents chuckled. If he had long hair, I could imagine it falling over his eyes in some roguish manner. This one wasn't so bad.

"She's not scared of you or them. She's just sensitive. She doesn't like hurting people or making them feel uncomfortable," Agent Smith explained. "We'll get out of your hair now. Um...tell Alpha Everson we apologize for this intrusion. We're required to come by at least once a year, and normally, it goes smoothly. The parents are never comfortable, of course, but we try to make it easy on everyone involved."

"Why?" I demanded. "Why do you need to come out once a year? Doesn't my government trust werewolves to be decent parents?"

"Yes and no. We want to make sure the children are getting the right education and will have a choice to follow their parents or not without being pressured. It's invasive, for sure, but we've actually saved a few kids. Some were being treated like they were werewolves already, which you can imagine, is a much harder lifestyle."

That would be a rough way to treat a human child. A werewolf youth could handle getting snapped at or getting roughed up a little. It was expected, a necessary lesson in dominance and controlling the animal instincts to learn how to behave, like a wild animal teaching its young. Human kids didn't need those lessons.

I nodded slowly. "Well, Heath doesn't do that," I promised. I'd kill him if I ever caught teeth marks on Carey's arms, and no amount of feeling I had for him would stop me.

"Of course. You have a nice day." Agent Taylor bowed his head a little and walked out. I went to a window and watched them disappear down the trail. The woman was already gone, hopefully having headed back to their vehicle with Miss Davis.

Carey was the first person to come up to me.

"There's always one mean person in the group," she whispered. "Always. It's never the same one, but there's always one who tries to make Dad and Landon feel bad for being werewolves. They always try to make me say stuff that will make Dad look bad."

"Why didn't you ever tell me about this?" I asked gently, looking down at her. "Carey..."

"Because it embarrasses Dad. It embarrasses me. It's like how my school counselor always pulls me into her office, just for a 'quick chat,' so I never bring it up. They just don't understand, and they never will. Why talk about it all the time when there's no way to change it?"

There was a naïve and sad wisdom to those words. Why, indeed?

I hadn't known about the school counselor. That bothered me, but I figured it was best not to bring it up—definitely not today—but maybe another time when my sweet girl wasn't feeling so obviously bruised.

"How did they only just find out about me?" I crossed my arms. "And why didn't I see them last year?" This was their second summer in my territory. If this happened yearly, they should have already wanted to meet me.

"Oh, they didn't visit last year. They talked a lot with Dad after he left the Dallas pack—"

"They wanted to give us time to settle in a new place," Heath said, cutting off his daughter as he walked back in. "This is the first time I've seen them since. This was why I had to run out on you this morning."

"Ah." I looked over his face and saw what Carey mentioned. There was shame in his eyes. Something weighed down his normally proud posture, all that powerful Alpha in him crippled by the idea someone thought he wasn't a good enough father or even safe to be around his daughter.

We stared at each other over her head. I wanted to strangle him because I'd just had to expose myself to government agencies. They would come back and ask more questions. My life now had a giant spotlight on it.

"You might want to tell your family this happened," he whispered.

"Oh, I plan to," I snapped. "Damn it, Heath. You could have told me something like this was coming up. I could have prepared something, anything that might have made this go a little smoother. Instead, I was blindsided and didn't know what I was dealing with. The BSA is out of my league. I can barely handle secret supernatural shit, and now the people who like to expose people like me have been *in my house*."

He looked down at Carey, then back up at me. I put my hands over her ears and felt her sigh.

"Don't get high and mighty with me right now," I growled. "She can handle a couple of bad words. What I can't handle is being the person who..." I stopped and inhaled sharply. "Is there a chance they bugged my house?"

"No. They never have before, and they can't start now. That's something the North American Werewolf Council fought with them about a decade ago. They can't secretly spy on us like that. Since you're 'human,' they have even less right or reason to."

"Good, then I'll continue. What I can't handle is being the person who might expose werecats to the United States government. Slip ups might happen, but if they start thinking I'm a supernatural, I'll have to leave the country. You'll probably have to leave, too. No one wants that, right?"

"Right," he agreed softly. I deflated at the defeat in his voice.

"I'm sorry. I'm pissed, but..." I let go of Carey and started to walk out of the kitchen.

"You have every right to be." I stopped at his words, leaning over to let my forehead touch the frame of the doorway I was in. "I should have mentioned it this morning, should have mentioned it before the last full moon, should have mentioned they might want to meet you because Carey spends so much time with you. I should have mentioned all of that. It's not easy being looked at like I'm a danger to my own family, and I was too much of a coward to bring it up. I never wanted to tell you about it when we moved in, and then we became friends, and I...was too ashamed."

"Well, now I know, and we can work with this," I said softly. "Let me take you three out to lunch."

"Let me buy." I opened my mouth to turn him down, but he lifted a hand and kept talking. "As an apology and a thank you for your involvement today. You did great, by the way. None of them really believed you weren't human. A highly opinionated human is what they're probably going to write down."

"Fine," I sighed. "But you and I need to talk privately later, away from prying ears."

Carey's long, drawn-out sigh told me she knew exactly who I was talking about.

Before we left, I grabbed the sketchbook Jabari left me and threw it into a bag. Heath and I had a lot to talk about.

4

CHAPTER FOUR

Lunch went as smoothly as it could with me angry at Heath, while Landon and Carey tried to ignore it. Heath took me and his family out for pizza, something easy and fast because the tension was probably too much to deal with. I had to be angry with him, but I didn't want to be. There was a difference. He spent the morning kissing me and couldn't bother to tell me the BSA was coming into my territory. I already knew I had to tell Hasan, and that wasn't going to go over well.

Once Carey was done eating, Landon took her somewhere in Heath's truck. I had to ignore her vocal protest. In some ways, she knew more about the world of werewolves and humans than I did because she lived in it while I was an outsider. In other ways, I knew much more about the supernatural world at large, and there were things I knew Heath kept from his daughter.

Even though I knew a lot more than Carey, I barely knew anything myself. Every day, that became clearer, especially when I spent time talking to my family, who were so deep into the supernatural world, I was certain they barely knew what it meant to be human in this day and age.

Heath and I went into his home, in a sense the only neutral ground, both my and Heath's territory. We walked into his office, me trying to continue to ignore his bad design choices with all the brown furniture. I couldn't get over that I really didn't like his favorite colors. Being internally distraught by his interior design helped me ignore the long, drawn-out silence between us.

He locked his office door as I sat down on a small loveseat. I could smell Landon the most, and picturing the scene in my head was easy. Heath would sit behind his desk, facing the door with the large window behind him. Landon would sit here, and they would talk about the family, things that needed to be done, or possibly me. Landon might even relax for just a moment, something I didn't think I'd ever witnessed. This room was his father's office, and he could probably be a son, not a werewolf, a second in command, or the older brother. He could just be Heath's son.

The idea of that image resonated with me because I had done the same thing when I lived with Hasan. I would sit in his office and read a book on a similar couch while he worked. For a moment, I wanted that again. I wanted to visit Hasan and just sit in his office, a refuge where I knew he would protect me from the outside world and let me clear my head.

"You look like you're thinking about something

important," Heath commented, sitting beside me. "Care to tell me?"

"This couch smells like Landon. There's a couch in Hasan's office I'm certain smells like Niko right now. It probably smelled like me for a few years. Hasan would let me hide in his office if I needed to. I want to right now," I explained, not looking at my werewolf. "I don't like attention, Heath, and you put a giant spotlight on me."

"You've had a lot of attention since we met. I figured you would almost be used to it by now." There was a bite of annoyance to his words, which pissed me off.

"Getting used to it and liking it are two very different things. Carey is used to you serving her lima beans at dinner, but she absolutely hates eating them." I growled softly. "Even then, it's one thing to expose me further to the supernatural world and another to expose me to the *human* one. The supernatural world knows what I am, who I am. I'm a werecat, and there's an expectation I'm left alone. Humans? Heath, exposing me to humans could expose werecats to humans. I'm fairly certain neither of us wants to be the reason that happens."

A small growl told me Heath was listening but frustrated.

"I already apologized," he said stiffly. "I'm *sorry*. How much more do you want from me, Jacky? Do you want me to deny the BSA and CPS visitation with Carey? Because that will get her taken away faster than you and I could blink. It would be a firestorm. Imagine the headlines? 'Werewolf Alpha has a human daughter taken from him over safety concerns.' Or 'Werewolf Alpha resists human government's efforts to protect a human girl.' I'm *sorry* you were brought up, and they wanted to meet you. I am. I understand the reason why you're upset. I just..." He stood up and ran his hand through his hair. "There's nothing I can do. This is out of my control."

It hit me that Heath's problems and his annoyance had nothing to do with me, and my anger eased. He was right; he couldn't do anything. For a dominant creature like Heath Everson, it was eating him up. His apology was sincere.

"What else don't I know?" I asked softly, trying not to sound angry with him anymore. He was making it a point to beat himself up more than I could, and I regretted my initial outburst. "If there's anything..."

"Jacky, the depth of supernatural knowledge you don't know would take years to teach," he said, sagging back into the seat next to me. "Years. You don't even get the simplest of magics others use in their daily lives. You don't have fae contacts or know a local vampire nest, and I know you chose this region because many of those things aren't close by. You don't know what other supernaturals run in the area around you, in the major cities."

"I knew about you," I snapped, angry he thought I was so ignorant. "I knew about the Dallas pack and know about the Houston pack and the fucking Austin pack and the New Orleans pack." I knew where all the werewolves who could possibly be a threat lived.

"Why did you know about me? Why did you know about the Dallas pack, Jacky?" He leaned back, shifting his body, so his chest was toward me. His legs outstretched, and I found myself thinking about the moment I met Heath Everson in the back of a pack SUV.

"Because..." I looked away. "Hasan taught me to know where werewolf packs were located near me, so I could keep an eye out for trouble."

"Did he tell you how to get to the Market? Do you even know what the Market *is*? Or the Mygi Corporation and Foundation? The hospital where your family took Niko and Zuri after that explosion? You know just as well as I do, in some ways, you are just as ignorant as my daughter when it comes to the supernatural world."

I leaned over and rubbed my temples.

"Are you saying I need to start learning?" I didn't *want* to. I liked my home. I liked my simple life, even as it tried to grow more complicated.

"I'm saying you should think carefully when you ask what else don't you know," he clarified. "If you want to keep the illusion you live a simple life, you need to ask questions like that with much more care. I can teach you. Jacky, I can expand your worldview, but you might hate me for it...and I don't want that," he ended in a whisper. I saw his hand come into view before it dipped down and grabbed my chin. I didn't fight as he lifted my head, so he could stare into my eyes. His grey-blue eyes looked a little scared, a little hurt, very sad. "I don't want that."

"You said, years." I licked my lips. "Would about six years cover it?"

"Yeah? Maybe? Why six?" He frowned. I turned, breaking his hold.

"I left home too early. There was a lot Hasan still wanted to teach me. Ten years is the accepted amount of time for a new werecat to live with their...parent. I left his home and protection after four years. If you think I don't know how ignorant I am, you are sorely mistaken." I sighed, staring at the far wall. "But that's not the point. What I was trying to ask...Is there anything about you and your family I need to know? Is there anything you've kept from me like today that could put me or my kind at risk?"

"I..." He trailed off, a look of concentration coming over his face. "I don't know, actually. Nothing off the top of my head."

"Good. Since we're on the topic, and because you owe me for today...is there anything you think I should know, even if it has nothing to do with today?" I narrowed my eyes on him, waiting and wondering what his answer would be.

"There are...some things I might be able to help you with," he said carefully as if he was trying not to upset me. "But you could ask them of Hasan or any of your siblings, I bet. With Hasan's connection and position with the Tribunal, I'm sure he knows even more than me."

"I'm *not* asking him, though. What's wrong with you telling me?"

"Jacky, there have always been a couple of things I wished you did to protect yourself and Carey—always—but I never brought them up and don't want to bring them up because I know how you would react." He seemed so uncomfortable. "If I had told you a year ago, you would have stomped your foot and said I was trying to be your Alpha."

I flinched. He was right, I would have. I would have

been pissed. Now, I was pissed I didn't know things—not that I had ever wanted to know any of it—but now it seemed like the safest thing. Better to live with knowledge I didn't need than continue to be ignorant. It was a lesson that should have sunk in years before, but I had gotten complacent. I had successfully lived with the limited knowledge I had. With the BSA sniffing around my territory, I had the foreboding sensation I couldn't live like that any longer.

"Jacky?" Heath's voice was so gentle and soft. There wasn't any dominance or indication the man beside me was a werewolf Alpha, based on the way he said my name.

"Sorry, I got lost in thought. You're right. I wouldn't have liked you telling me how to do anything, especially if it meant reaching out to other supernaturals or doing something different than I have for years," I said, sighing heavily.

"I know today really bothered you, but what else is going on?" He shifted closer, an arm going around my shoulders, not touching me, but over the back of the couch. It was such a startling change from the passion we had this morning.

I didn't like it.

I leaned into him, smelling how shocked that made him. For a moment, I wished we were human, and this could be normal. It wasn't and would never be normal, though. Nothing in our lives was.

With my head on his chest, I pointed at the bag I had dragged into his house.

"She was wearing a necklace with a rune of power," I

whispered. "And it's making me...paranoid. She hated you, Heath. Hates werewolves. Tried to convince me or see if I did, too." I shook my head. "Yet she was wearing a rune of power. I don't know which one. I still haven't looked it up. I think...not knowing BSA would take an interest in your family and my life and her...it just freaked me out. I don't like having the spotlight on me, but it's here and...I don't know how to really protect myself from it. Maybe it's time I learned."

"Don't give up what you love and who you are because you're scared." His words were warm as his breath drifted over my ear. "The BSA is my problem. I don't want you to change or be forced to change because of my problems."

I turned a little and smiled sadly.

"Heath, it's not just about them," I said softly, moving so my lips grazed against his. Heat built as I searched for comfort. His breath was heavier as I spoke. "What about us? We have this secret and..." If anyone found out, we were dead. Not even my relationship with Hasan would save me. My siblings, as much as they might care in their own way, wouldn't be able to save me. Part of me wasn't certain they would try. Maybe Hisao would be the one who did me in.

"I know," he murmured. He was the one who leaned in as though I was some sort of magnet, and he couldn't resist.

Our lips met in a slow kiss, one that reminded both of us exactly what the problem was.

We shouldn't have these feelings. They're going to get us killed.

When the kiss ended, I sighed.

"Anything I can do that can keep protecting all of us is stuff I need to learn," I said, showing him just how freaked out the BSA visit left me. "This is my territory, and I swore to you I would protect you."

"You swore to protect Carey," he corrected. "I'll never ask you to protect me. I've been doing that pretty well for about two hundred and fifty years. I'm not a young werewolf. Neither is Landon."

"You live in my territory."

"So? I didn't move here expecting you to give your life for me. I didn't move here, expecting this." He lifted a hand and gently grazed the tips of his fingers over my cheek, the line of my jaw, and down my neck. Without warning, he gently tugged the collar of my shirt and revealed an old gunshot scar on my shoulder. "You have suffered enough for me. I really am sorry for today."

I pulled his hand away. The scars didn't bother me, not really. They weren't disfiguring, so I ignored them on most days.

"You mentioned one of the BSA has a rune of power on her necklace. The little mean one, Agent Robinson?" He didn't move, but he changed the topic so swiftly, I was nearly thrown off from shock.

"Yeah." I moved off the couch and grabbed my bag, digging to grab the sketchbook. "I should recognize it if I see it again, but some of these are so similar. Like, one line is tilted in a slightly different way similar." I sat on the floor, my back to the couch, and stretched my legs out with the sketchbook on my lap.

"Oh, that's going to make this hard." He slid down to

sit next to me, shoulder to shoulder. "I saw the necklace, but I didn't think anything of it. People like obscure jewelry."

We started flipping through the pages. I knew Heath wouldn't be too helpful, but I enjoyed his company. I was rattled, but the anger was gone. The further I was away from what happened, the less likely I found it to be a problem. The BSA could look into me all they wanted. All they would find is a carefully crafted fake life and a series of lawyers to stop them at every turn, courtesy of Hasan.

"This?" I said, pointing a finger to a page, frowning. "No...It's got a second line here. I don't think the one she was wearing did."

"What's this one do?" he asked, leaning over, his dark hair blocking my view somewhat. "Conceal? That's all it says."

"I'd need to ask Jabari or Zuri. The descriptions in this thing don't make a lot of sense." I sighed and flipped another page. Then stopped, growling softly. "Fuck, if it was that one, that may mean she was concealed from magic. What if she..." I took a deep, angry breath. "I need to go. I need to take this to Jabari and Zuri now."

"She smelled human, and there wasn't a lick of magic to her scent. I don't think she was a witch," Heath said, moving back again and giving me the space to get to my feet.

"I'll let them know. She smelled human to me, too, and didn't register as a supernatural in my territory, but I need to make sure." I closed the book and shoved it into my bag. By the time the bag was over my shoulder, I was ready to go, and Heath was back on his feet as well. Before I could get out of the room, his arm wrapped around my waist and held me pressed against him.

"Are we okay?" he asked softly, his grey-blue eyes searching my face.

"We're fine. I'll figure this out, and we'll go from there." I chewed the inside of my lip, staring at his eyes, then dipped to stare at his lips. I leaned in and kissed him softly, letting him know everything was okay.

"I promise not to spring anything like this on you again," he whispered. When I pulled away, he held me in place.

"I believe you."

He wrapped a hand around my neck and held me close. Once again, I had no desire to move away. There was something heady about the way Heath liked to handle people, me especially. Even though the morning had shaken him as much as it had shaken me, he held me with confidence. A small arrogant smile crossed over his face as his fingers began to trace small lines on the back of my neck.

"Landon took Carey shopping," he murmured. "And your siblings are probably busy."

"They probably are," I agreed. Considering the time, it was their business hours, including Hisao's, even though it would be incredibly late at night or early in the morning for him. He was in Japan, so there was a chance it was already the next day for him, though I couldn't guess exactly because I was bad with time zones.

When his mouth returned to mine, I gave in, knowing we didn't have many moments like this. We barely found ourselves alone once a day, much less twice, and there was no denying I loved the way he kissed me. His hand on my hip began to push up my shirt, making his intentions clear. Obviously, he wanted to make the best of this sudden alone time, even more than I did. Maybe it was an apology for the bad morning. As my shirt went up and uncovered my ribs, a bolt of indecision ran through me, like it always did. I didn't know how to stomp it out. I wasn't sure I should.

What if I'm just doing this because I'm lonely? What if he's just bored with werewolves and humans? What if I'm just a shiny toy to play with? What if we're only doing this because it's dangerous?

'What if' was a dangerous question, and the weight of it made me stop his hand and shake my head. He didn't make a sound, his lips not leaving mine, but his hand trailed back down to my hip, letting my shirt fall.

I slowly pulled away from him as his phone picked the opportune time to begin buzzing, drawing a long, slow groan from the Alpha.

"That's probably more news about werewolf stuff you don't want to know about," he said as he reached into his pocket to check.

"Saved by the bell?" I grinned and darted for the door, making it out before he could catch me.

I heard him chuckle behind me as I made it to my Nissan. He leaned in the door as I got into my car, smiling at me. I waved, then drove off, not looking back.

5

CHAPTER FIVE

When I got home, I tried calling my family. Thankfully, a couple of them picked up.

I should have counted on Hasan always taking my calls.

"Jacqueline, it's good to hear from you," he greeted, smiling in that kind fatherly way he did when he was in a good mood.

"Hey, Father," I greeted in return, still testing the word. I'd used it consistently for months since I had been taken and beaten, since we fought together. I still slipped into calling him Hasan sometimes, and in my head, he still was just Hasan, but there was something more between us now. For the first time in over a decade, I really looked at him as my parental figure—a source of guidance and refuge. Today had nailed home how much I really appreciated him. Even though I was less worried than I had been hours before, I still wished I could hide in his office and pretend like nothing bad was happening, like the world couldn't get me.

"You seem concerned," he said gently as another video feed booted up, and Davor appeared.

"Ah, fuck. What have you gotten into this time?" he grumbled. I saw his eyes roll and worried they weren't going to come back down for a moment. The only person I knew with an eye roll that impressive was Carey.

"Davor," Hasan snapped. "We just started the call. Why don't you sit quietly and listen?"

"Yes, sir." Davor's feed had a little mute symbol come up. It was probably for the best. The man had no filter. If he said anything, at least no one would hear it.

"Today, I learned the hard way the American BSA regularly checks in with werewolves...particularly those with human children. Along with CPS, which I mean isn't the problem," I started, sighing. I wasn't really sure how to phrase it all as Zuri jumped onto the family call.

"The BSA? An American organization, I'm assuming?" Hasan was frowning, and that reminded me he wasn't a local. He had territory in New York, but he didn't live there. He was so ancient, most things didn't faze him. On top of that, I figured he was too busy with the Tribunal and the werecats to be bothered by one government's organization to deal with public werewolves and the secretive witches and fae.

"Yeah. The BSA is the Bureau of Supernatural Affairs, and CPS is Child Protective Services. What I'm trying to get to is, I met some agents from the BSA today."

"No worries," Zuri said, chuckling a little. "I rushed to take this phone call?" She seemed a little incredulous. "This must be your first time. We've all had run-ins with human governments at some point or another. Kind of you to let us know, but it shouldn't be a problem."

"Really? I'm not even done—"

"You have a legally impenetrable identity," Hasan said kindly, and I caught the small smile he wore. "There's nothing to worry about."

"No, you don't—" I growled softly. It was good of them to think so, but that only helped so much. Getting cut off repeatedly was fucking annoying.

"Really? This is what we get emergency calls about now?" Davor snorted. "So what if they sniffed around? You have werewolves nearby. That was bound to happen. It's going to. Just keep saying you're human, and they won't figure it out. Eventually, you'll have to move on since you don't age, and that will be that."

"She was wearing a rune of power! An agent of the BSA came into my territory wearing a rune of power," I snarled, finally getting the unconcerned smiles to go away.

"Which one?" Zuri asked carefully. "Was she human?"

"Of course, she was human. If she had been a supernatural, I would have already mentioned that, but you all keep cutting me off." I groaned and ran my hand over my face. "I don't know which one. I can try to sketch it and send it over to everyone—"

"Send it to me," Zuri said with a snap. "If I don't know it, I know who to ask. No reason to drag the entire family into this."

"Your mother doesn't even know all of them," Hasan said, serious as well. "Even if this rune of power was a problem, though, and not some sort of protection spell or meaningless, I still don't think there's a reason to worry about the BSA, Jacky. Now, you mentioned CPS is...child protective services? Why were they there?"

"Yeah...Heath never mentioned it, and I had never heard of it, but apparently, the U.S. government tracks werewolves with human children and makes routine visits to decide whether the parent is fit to raise a human child." I rubbed my arms, goosebumps forming as the very idea made me ill. It was discriminatory at best and wasn't public knowledge. I might have kept my head down for years, but I was pretty sure I would have caught an article or something about it at some point. I never had, and of course, werewolf parents weren't going to embarrass themselves and bring it up to the press. "The BSA, I think, just backs up CPS in case the werewolves give them a hard time.

"The only reason I got pulled into the visit was because Carey accidentally brought me up. They wanted to know about the new adult who hung out with her, which is...reasonable, I guess. There was a really hateful bitch, the one wearing the rune. She noticed the ones Jabari and I drew around my house. She obviously knows what they might be. I played it off like I was just another human with my own superstitions."

"Good thinking," Hasan said, nodding slowly. "I think you're fine. The werewolves are very good at covering for everyone, not just themselves. They know it's a Tribunal matter if they accidentally or purposefully expose another species, and it would be an ugly thing to happen.

Alpha Everson has always seemed like a smart man. I don't think you're at risk."

"I just wanted to make sure." I was already feeling better. I grabbed a piece of paper and drew the little symbol the human had been wearing, then took a picture and texted it to Zuri. "There you go, sis. You can figure that out."

"Thank you," she said, smiling again. "I'm glad you trusted us to call," she said softly. "I like when you call with questions."

"Do I want to ask?" I asked and rubbed my face, trying not to acknowledge the heat of my cheeks and the redness that was probably taking over.

"I like you finally trust us," she explained, her smile unfading. "Is there anything else you want to talk about?"

I shook my head as I leaned back in my chair. I caught her looking at her phone and frowning.

"I don't immediately recognize it. It looks like an incorrect concealment rune," she murmured, mostly to herself, her head tilted to the side, causing her long braids to fall over her shoulder. "If it was a correct concealment rune, we'd have a problem, but this would be powerless if that was the effect intended."

"Really?" That made me curious, but not worried. If the rune had no power, then I had nothing to worry about. I was curious what the concealment rune did, though.

"A concealment rune would have hidden a supernatural from your territory's notice," she said with a small growl. "It's a problem if she had a real one. She wouldn't have fooled your nose, but you wouldn't have known what she was until you caught her scent."

"She smelled human. So, in theory, if she had the correct rune, she could have been a witch."

"Yes, though you might have smelled magic on her as well. A werewolf would have picked it up without a problem, even if you couldn't." She finally put her phone down and looked back to her camera. "There's nothing to worry about with the concealment rune, though, or we would have warned you about it ages ago. First, not many know the runes of power, and most have been too butchered by humans over the centuries to have a place in modern magics. Even if someone did use it, it would only get them so far. Second, not many want to toy with werecats. There are people who work for the Tribunal who don't want to toy with even the youngest of our kind." She gave me a pointed look I could have assumed was directed at anyone else, but I wasn't an idiot. She was making sure that sank in with me. "I also can't think of a reason a witch would target you specifically. Jabari and me? We have history with them, but that was thousands of years ago."

"So, this human probably had some bogus reason she thought the rune would help her, but it's powerless. Seen it before, will see it again," Davor said, nonchalant and dismissive. Bored. There was something bored in his tone. "Are we done?"

"You can go," Hasan said, his words only betraying the barest hint of annoyance. Davor disconnected without another word. I kept my mouth firmly shut. I would not ask Hasan for the hundredth time why he thought Davor was worth the trouble. Knowing my werecat father, he would only remind me Davor often asked the same question about me.

"He can be such a petulant boy," Zuri commented, chuckling. "Don't mind him, Jacky."

"I wasn't minding him," I said with a stiffness that betrayed me.

"I can't smell the lie, but I can see it on your face," she retorted. "Before we go, since it's just us and Father, I feel like I should say something."

I noted Hasan's face didn't change at all. At this point, it seemed like he was waiting on the sidelines like a referee, ready to break up his children if needed.

"Say whatever you want," I said, killing the silence Zuri had left in her wake. "You know you can text or call me any time."

"Well, this is just something I've been thinking about, and now seems like a good time to bring it up after your brush with human authorities. Jacky, the best way to avoid being exposed is to close your circle of friends. It would be safer for you to distance yourself from the wolves...and from Carey. When this all started, none of us knew human authorities might take an interest in a werewolf father and his human daughter, but they do, so it's time to consider taking a step back from them. It would be safer in the end, at least until Carey is an adult. You've done a lot for them, and I'm certain they're friends, but..." She trailed off with a look of 'you know what I'm saying.' I totally understood every word that came out of her mouth, comprehended the sentiment, and I couldn't refute it.

It would be safer if I never saw the werewolves again.

She doesn't even know how deep it goes.

"I swore an oath to Heath when he asked to move his family into my territory to protect Carey for as long as she lived here. Or something like that. I don't remember exactly what I said," I explained, swallowing. There was no reason to bring up that I was intensely attracted to the Alpha, or that he had the insane ability to make me want more than I had wanted in over a decade. No reason to bring up that I was risking everything to dabble in the taboo of getting physical with our mortal enemy.

No reason at all.

"I'm certain he would understand needing more space for your safety and the necessary secrecy of your life," she said with a motherly sternness that made me a little more worried. There was a hardness to her stare that made me want to squirm.

There was no way she knew, I was certain of it, but the rush of fear in the back of my mind and the tightness in my chest were instinctive reactions.

"I'll take it into consideration," I promised, looking away. "It won't be easy, though. They're friends, and I love Carey. I really do. It would be hard losing her in my life. She's so young, and she wouldn't really understand..."

"Just think about it," Zuri whispered, her stare too intense for me to be comfortable.

"I will," I said with more conviction.

She disconnected first, and I rushed to cut off whatever Hasan opened his mouth to say. I stared at the screen for what felt like an eternity.

Zuri's advice rang in my ears like some sort of

condemnation. Distancing myself from the wolves was smart. Distancing myself from Heath was potentially lifesaving.

Zuri always gives out good advice, I'll give her that.

I just have no intention of listening to it.

With my mind made up, I felt more resolve. I could keep my fling with the local werewolf a secret until I figured out exactly what I wanted out of Heath Everson.

"Well, at least they aren't worried about my little run-in with the United States government," I mumbled, finally closing my laptop and standing.

Taking a deep breath, I set myself to an evening of cleaning. I could still smell the human scents lingering in my space, humans I didn't know and didn't trust. There was no way I was going to leave them to dissipate naturally. They had to go.

6

CHAPTER SIX

The week flew by on me. It was astounding, really. When I first started to relinquish control of Kick Shot, I had been at a loss what to do. I still was most of the time, but I was getting better at finding small things to do. Since the bar had been burned down and rebuilding took time, I had dedicated myself to new skills. I had always felt wholly ill-unequipped for my position as Hasan's representative, and nothing was going to change that, due to my age and lack of experience, but all my free time was giving me a chance to try to make up for both of those things.

So, I was teaching myself languages. Thanks to my location, I decided the first had to be Spanish. I did quizzes, used apps and programs, and I was coming along. I still wasn't very good, but it killed time. I was beginning to realize how my siblings knew so much. When there was only free time, learning something kept you sane.

I was finishing up my daily lesson when my phone

started to ding with an alarm. Already knowing what it was, I silenced it without reading the notification. I had a meeting at Kick Shot about the interior design, a meeting I was thankful was just going to be me, Heath, and his favorite designer, who already knew the look I wanted. We just needed to finalize the pieces and colors.

I left my computer and dressed in something sensible. I spent my days in shorts and tank tops, thanks to the overbearing heat, not my usual jeans and band t-shirts. It wasn't just the heat, though. I didn't need to worry about dressing for work because I had none.

I didn't move quickly. The meeting was at the bar, so the walk from my house was my only commute, something I had to fight for since the rebuilding process had begun. I was the one who paid for the trailer sitting in the parking lot because it had been my demand. Heath had tried to convince me to make the drive to his home for meetings. He wasn't surprised when I had put my foot down on that idea.

As I walked around the building, I smiled at the sight of him, leaning on the hood of his truck. I had known he was there. The smile didn't last long as the designer burst out of the trailer, blonde, her bone straight hair getting caught in the wind. She looked like a movie star, dressed to walk into the homes of the rich and belong there. Her blue eyes caught the sun and shone like stars.

"Finally! I've been here for an hour!" she declared, looking between Heath and me.

"You getting here early is not the client's problem," Heath said with a bite, his gaze shifting over to her. "You know that."

The exaggerated sigh of the designer, Miss Lucille Ralston, was every stereotype I could think of. She was privileged and wealthy, from the moment she had been born with the typical silver spoon in her mouth. She was a good designer, but Heath had made sure to tell me everything about her, like the fact her grandfather was the werewolf Alpha of New York. Her business had boomed thanks to the silent, steady support of the pack. Now, she designed homes for the rich and famous. Heath had told me when he asked to hire her, he and the Alpha of Los Angeles were only tentative allies, both serving on the North American Werewolf Council. That rubbed off between Heath and Lucille, who tentatively worked together. He had made it clear to me Lucille was great at her job, but not the easiest for him to work with. He'd made it sound like a warning.

Sure enough, every time I was in the same area as both, there was friction. I'd grown used to it.

"You're lucky you pay so well, considering the heat of this blasted place," she snapped at Heath. "I can't believe you moved out—"

I growled softly, getting her attention.

"Be nice in my territory," I reminded her softly. She knew I wasn't human. There was no way the granddaughter of a werewolf Alpha didn't know what I was. I never outright confirmed it, but the knowledge was there when she looked at me.

"My apologies. It's nice to see you, Miss Leon. I hope you're doing well this afternoon," she said, her eyes dropping. She even held the door open for both me and Heath when we made it to the trailer at the same time.

"This should be a quick meeting. We're just confirming one final time. The floors and paint come first, then we're going to get in the light fixtures...You probably don't need all the little details."

"It's fine, and I'm doing pretty okay, thank you. Please feel free to tell me whatever you think I need to know. I'm okay with knowing all the little details," I said, smiling kindly as I sat down at the small table in the trailer. I could see the pictures of everything I had chosen and started going through them. "I'm happy with everything so far. With an entire rebuild, there's no way to keep the charm of the old building, but I'm glad you found ways to keep the feel of the old place."

"I'm glad." Lucille sat across from me.

Heath, in his Alpha way, said nothing as he moved to a small kitchenette and began making coffee. Making coffee probably didn't seem like a very Alpha thing to do, but I knew what he was doing. He was hovering without getting involved. He wanted me to finalize everything and was just there to make sure I didn't get run over. It had nearly happened a couple of times over the course of the rebuild, thanks to the strong personalities he liked to hire. Lucille was just one of them.

"This doesn't need to be a long meeting," Lucille continued, not noticing Heath or not appearing to. "We're going to sign some confirmation documents, just so everything is in writing about the final decisions. Thank you for meeting me. I like to have a paper trail."

"I bet," I said with a chuckle. "How many times did you have people get angry because they didn't like the end result?" It wasn't a question of her ability to do her job or her eye for interior design. People could be fickle. It was a conversation she and I had to have before, more than once.

"Let's just say you are one of my most consistent clients. You knew what you wanted from the start, and that's always a treat to work with." Her smile was genuine. I didn't dislike Lucille, but her strong personality rubbed me wrong sometimes, especially when she turned it on Heath. She didn't make the mistake of turning it on me, which was a plus. I knew it was familiarity that caused her to do it with Heath, but my possessiveness over the werewolf made it a dangerous thing for her to do.

Not that she knew or understood, or that I could tell her.

"Hey, don't be rude to Alpha Everson. I'm kissing him when no one is watching him, and I'm prone to killing people who are mean to people I think are mine." Yup, that would go over well.

I signed the papers, noting exactly which pieces of furniture and fixtures I wanted in what colors. I signed off on the photos of them as well, just to make sure there was no mix-up.

It was over and done with as quickly as it had started, Lucille smiling the entire time. As she left, there was no barbed comment to Heath, who had stayed silent the entire time.

"It's always interesting seeing her," I said lightly. "Do you think her grandfather told her about me?"

"I'm certain she knows everything there is to know about you and your place in the supernatural community," he said, chuckling as he sat down in her spot. "Are you excited for Kick Shot to be open again?"

"I really am," I said, groaning at the end. "I'm so bored, I've decided to learn languages."

"I know. About time you started picking up new skills." He was teasing, but he wasn't the first person to say it to me. "Speaking of new things, we had a talk on Monday. I thought about it all week. Do you really want me to start telling you more about the supernatural world?"

"I mean..." With my anger gone, it didn't seem like much of a priority. The family thought I was fine, so it seemed as if I could continue to get away with my ignorant life. I had barely thought about it all week.

"I knew it." His smile was all the 'I told you so' necessary. "Well, I was thinking, just to help with some things, of getting you some simple security measures."

"Like?" I leaned back in my seat, wondering what he could possibly want to do to make my territory any more secure than I could.

"Have you ever heard of fae charms? There's a popular one, everyone uses it, that's called a Look Away charm. It stops humans from looking too closely at something and makes them unable to concentrate when they look at it. It's used on cars a lot, so we can get away with driving too fast, things like that."

"I have heard of that," I said, snapping my fingers and smiling. "Yeah, Davor told me a little about it when we were trying to get to the hospital."

"Well, to help you avoid prying human eyes, you should invest in it. It's a simple, easy introduction to getting supernatural work done. I never did them to my vehicles, but I got half my pack in touch with fae in Dallas to get their vehicles done." Heath gave me a semi-guilty look. "It's actually something I was surprised to find you didn't already have. It barely works with supernaturals, but it really helps with humans."

"I'll consider it," I said, shrugging. "It doesn't sound like a terrible idea."

"You asked," he said.

I should have known he would pick up on my sudden reluctance to the idea of more magic in my life. I liked my life of minimal magic.

"I did," I said with a groan, throwing my arms up in defeat. "And when I was pissed off at you, it made sense, but I really like keeping my life simple. Now that I've talked to my family, and it's been a few days..."

"I'll make you a deal. I'll do it. You don't have to worry about a thing. You can decide to come with me one day and see who and how it's done, or you can just let me take your car and get it done without you. I'll even pay." He leaned in and grabbed my chin, using a thumb to trace the outline of my lips. "Please?"

I narrowed my eyes. I knew what this was—Heath was finding a way to be an Alpha. Aside from the way he was making the offer, it was tempting.

"It would keep me safe and secret, wouldn't it?" I asked, trying to ignore the way his warm, calloused finger moved as I talked.

"It would help keep Carey safe, too," he murmured, his eyes dipping to my lips now.

"How long have you sat in silence, wondering if I would get it done?"

"Ages. I tried not to think about it after a while. It took a month for me to realize you just never would unless I said something, but by then, I'd already figured out you wouldn't want me to bring it up."

"And now? Alpha werewolf needs to make sure everyone is protected? He'll even do it himself to make sure it's done?"

"No. Boyfriend werewolf wants to do something nice for you and, in turn, appease the need to protect his daughter. If you don't want it, I won't make you. An Alpha werewolf would try to make you."

I coughed, pulling away to cover my mouth as the word 'boyfriend' finally registered. It was like the air had stopped in my lungs, deciding at that moment, I needed to pass out and stop breathing. Heath reached out, nearly coming over the table to rub my back. I could hear him asking what was wrong, but I didn't respond as I hit my chest, trying to get my lungs to stop seizing.

"Boyfriend?" I asked as I remembered how to breathe. "That's what you think you are?"

"I thought it was the best way to describe our relationship," he said, his face closing off and his scent dying. It was a funny sensation. One moment, I could smell him and how he worried about my sudden fit. The next moment, that flavor in his scent was gone, sucked out of the air with no indication that it ever existed.

I stopped coughing, rubbing my chest to help with the ache the coughing fit had given me.

"Don't do that," I whispered. "Please?"

"If you don't want—"

"We're not dating, Heath. Boyfriend..." I scrunched up my face as I said the word, which probably wasn't the most tactful thing to do. Heath's blank face told me enough. I had hurt him. At the same time, I had to make my own feelings known about the designation. "We can't have a relationship. Not like *that*."

"Is it the relationship you have a problem with? Or the word?" he asked. "Because we're barely able to keep our hands off each other when people aren't looking. There's something between us, Jacky. There has been for *months*."

"I don't know," I admitted softly.

He stood up quickly and walked toward the door. He didn't leave, standing there, staring at the doorknob like it was the most interesting thing in the world. His scent was still locked up tight, leaving me in the dark of exactly what he was feeling.

"Carey wanted you to come over for dinner," he said, looking back at me and leaning on the door. "Do you think it would be possible? She's wanted to see you all week."

"Yeah, she texted me yesterday." I kept my voice soft, looking away from him. He looked too good there, leaning on the door in the most casual way but somehow commanding the room. "Heath, I don't know what we are. I know what we *can't* be. You know that, and I don't understand why—"

"We'll play it by ear," he whispered. "I guess I was hoping you and I were more than casual. I feel like a boy in the fields again." He started to chuckle. "Kissing the farmer's daughter when the boss isn't looking." There was a sadness underneath his words, something deep.

"How did that end up for you?" I asked, looking back at him again. "Kissing the farmer's daughter."

"I married her, and she gave me my first son, who would stay by my side for two hundred and fifty years," he answered. I saw the pain, could smell the pain now. It went on and on.

It made me think of Shane and how much I missed that man. How much I had wanted to spend my life with him and how much it had destroyed me to lose him. I had buried it, hiding it under the need to survive and learn to be a werecat, but it had always been there. It would always be there. The same way Heath buried his pain under being a werewolf and a father, focusing on everything else except the loss he had suffered.

"I'm sorry," I murmured. "I just need time. This is... this is new to me. I haven't been with anyone in over a *decade,* then we kiss, but I'm not sure what that makes us, then there's what we *are*..."

"I know. I shouldn't have assumed there was more between us than what we have." It looked as if it was hard for him to say those words, the way his muscles tensed, and his jaw was clenched.

"I would love to come over for dinner," I whispered, looking down to avoid his intense grey-blue stare that was beginning to lighten up to ice-blue, his wolf eyes. "And you can take my car to whatever fae you want for that spell thing. For Carey's protection, of course."

"And *now* she learns how to bargain and bribe with an Alpha werewolf," he mumbled, a rueful expression on his face when I looked up at him. "Let's go. Bring your hatchback over, and I'll drive you home after dinner." When he realized I was watching him again, he smiled. "Do you think I could convince you to join me on the trip, and we can have a not-date?"

"We'll talk about it," I said, chuckling. The question made me realize we were fine. At least for the moment.

7

CHAPTER SEVEN

Carey ran to my car when I arrived at the Everson house. A picturesque thing with a wraparound porch, it was a beautiful home. Not that I had a moment to appreciate it since I got out of the car and was attacked by a thirteen-year-old.

"Dad beat you and told me you were coming!" she declared, grinning. "He said you were right behind him, but that was like an hour ago."

"I wanted to clean up," I said, giving her the hug I knew she wanted. We walked to the door together, my arm over her shoulder and hers around my waist. "I know we text, but you never told me how you were doing after Monday. Want to say something before we go inside?"

"Not really. They come, they leave. Everything goes back to normal. Dad would never let them take me, and I know you wouldn't either." Her nonchalant words carried more weight than I figured the young teen realized.

The loyalty and faith she had in us was heartwarming...and correct. There was nothing on this earth that could take her away from Heath Everson, who loved his daughter more than the sun.

And there was no one who could take her away from me. The world had tried that once before, when I had just met her, and nearly succeeded. I would never allow it again.

"Well, if you ever want to talk about it, you know you can, right?" I stopped her before we got to the door and turned, so we were face to face again. "I know it's hard having people look too closely at your life and judging you for things that shouldn't be their business. If you ever feel like you can't talk to your dad or brother, you can talk to me."

"Yeah, I know." Her one-shoulder shrug told me she wasn't taking this nearly as seriously as I was. Or she wanted to avoid talking about it in general. Carey was much like her family of werewolves. If topics were too emotional or vulnerable, they weren't going to bring it up and made it seem like whatever it was didn't matter. I was used to the act and had seen it falter on many occasions, but I never tried to force it. Not with brute force, at least. I knew how to fool Carey into talking to me.

"Fine, don't talk to me," I replied, lifting my hands up in defeat.

"Jacky!" The whine nearly made me chuckle. "It's not easy. All the kids at school know I was raised by werewolves, and now, a lot of them know what happened in Dallas. Like, it's not hard to search for me on the internet, and *everyone* has the internet. Some have really mean parents too and..." Her face screwed up into a pout, something I thought she had outgrown. Turning away, she looked to the street and kicked a small rock off the concrete walkway to the front door. "And they don't even know about the people who come here and make Dad feel bad or worry Landon. I hear them talk! I hear how other people talk about us all the time..."

I glanced at the door, particularly at the windows on either side of it, seeing Heath and Landon each hanging out in one. They could hear her, definitely eavesdropping on the conversation. I narrowed my eyes, and Heath was the first one to notice he'd been caught. I watched him tap Landon, and they moved away from the windows. Once they were gone, I turned my attention back on Carey.

"I can't imagine how hard it is for you—"

"It's harder because I don't have a mom," she mumbled. "They all notice that, too. It's whatever, though."

Yes, you do. It's not whatever, Carey. I'm right here.

My heart clenched. *No.* I couldn't try to fill that role. I wasn't her mother. I couldn't be her mother. I could be a fun aunt or a friend, but I wasn't her mother. The woman who had that responsibility was gone and had never come back. Heath had never lied about it, and she had never reached out to Carey as far as I knew.

Fucking bitch doesn't know what she's missing.

"What can I do?" I asked gently, squatting to be on her level. "Do you want me to help out?"

Her eyes went big...very big.

"Do you think you could...come to my school stuff?"

"Um...not parent-teacher conferences—"

"No, like the science fair!" She reached out and hit my

arm. I pretended it hurt and rubbed the spot, but in reality, I had barely felt it. "Don't be dumb. Or like...I want to start playing soccer in school or maybe softball. Or volleyball! I'm human, so they can't stop me. You could come to my games! Last year, I didn't do anything because Dad and I didn't know anyone, and the year before that, I missed like half the school year, but this year, I'm going to do a lot. I'm going into the eighth grade. I need to start worrying about college."

I tried my best not to be surprised by her ideas of college already. She was thirteen. I didn't start worrying about college until I was sixteen. Then I remembered my twin. She started worrying about college when she came out of the womb.

If anything, Carey's a good middle ground.

"I can definitely go to those," I promised. Then I had to deliver the bad news to her plan. "Carey, it might not help with the fact your dad is a werewolf Alpha. Me showing up...To everyone here, I just own a bar. That might not have the effect you want."

She shrugged even more. Somehow, only Carey could make one shrug seem even more impactful than the last. It was an entire language done with one simple movement of her shoulders.

"I know I'll outgrow a lot of this stuff. I'll get out of school and go to college. Maybe no one will know where I came from or who I'm related to at college."

Unlikely.

"But maybe they'll be cool with it if they do know. Right now, it's just..." She sighed. "I'm fine, I really am, Jacky. It's always been like this. It sucks, but I'm going to be okay. As long as I have you, Dad, and Landon, and no one is getting hurt, I really like my life, and everyone else sucks. It's their problem, not mine. That's what all the other human kids used to say. They said when they got out of high school, it all changed. College was way easier."

"Okay, then." I smiled and straightened up, looking to the door. The father in question was back at the window and gave me a weak smile before disappearing again.

Nosy wolf. He's so protective but tries so hard to give her space.

I somehow got her through the door, and she went toward the kitchen. I turned to see Heath hiding behind the door as I closed it.

"Does she...talk to other kids like her?" I asked softly.

"Regularly," he said with a tight smile. "She still messages friends she grew up with from the Dallas pack. Once she turned thirteen, I was *ordered* to create an account on some social media thing for her, so she could talk to them more. She never told you?"

"Nope." I shrugged this time. "It's not really my business, though, is it?" I chewed the inside of my lip, something about her having a social media account bothering me. "You monitor her online, right?"

"Me and Landon," he answered, his tight smile becoming more genuine and relaxed. "Yeah, we would never let her talk to strangers on the internet. We don't hover, but she knows we know her logins, just to make sure. And when strangers try to add her, we run a quick background check on them just in case, block them from her account, or monitor them other ways."

"Wow. Okay." I wasn't expecting all that. My parents hadn't monitored my sister and me on the internet. We were a little older when it became available to us, and no one really understood the dangers of it yet. Somehow, I had half-expected Heath not to understand either, though it was a stupid assumption. He wasn't one of those ancients who was behind the times. He stayed up to date, just like my werecat family, and took advantage of everything new technologies made possible.

"I noticed when I looked into you years ago, your human accounts were still active," he said slyly. "There are a lot of old pictures of you still on the web."

"Yeah..." I sighed. "Hasan and I left them because of my human family. If I had suddenly disconnected everything, they would have noticed. Instead, I've let them go dead, killing them off slowly through the years. What about you?"

"Hmm, that makes sense." He nodded slowly, then looked in the direction Carey had run off to. "Landon and I don't have them. We can because people know what we are and all of that, but it's never seemed safe when it comes to werewolves, so I had a blanket ban on werewolves in the Dallas pack. Carey is human. Imposing my personal ideas of werewolves and the internet on her didn't seem fair."

"Makes sense. Let's go before they get suspicious."

"Oh, Landon will keep her busy for however long is necessary," he murmured, leaning in to kiss me. "He's got us figured out."

"Of course he does," I mumbled, stepping back and

heading for the kitchen. "Doesn't mean I'm going to give you what you want every time you want it."

The growl I got in response made shivers run down my spine, but I didn't stop moving. I went into the kitchen and started helping with dinner until Landon stole a spoon from me and silently pointed for me to leave. Carey's laughter followed me out.

"Come on. We can hang out on the back porch while those two destroy my house," Heath whispered, leading me away.

"I can never do anything here." With an eye roll, I obliged, heading into the backyard. As I did, I decided to strike up a normal conversation. It was better than playing with fire while Carey was just inside. "If you don't mind me asking, how's the werewolf doing? The female from Russia?" I found my favorite seat on his back porch as he grabbed two drinks from a new mini-fridge. He was obviously setting up his backyard for future barbecues. With who, I had no idea, but he had the entire set up built-in now.

"She passed away Tuesday morning," he answered, sighing heavily. My gut twisted. That wasn't the news I had expected. I had been hoping to hear a story about how she was recovering. "Last night, a submissive member of the pack stabbed the Alpha. Silver knife, to the heart, human form. He's not dead, but he was flown into Mygi for emergency surgery."

"Shit," I breathed out. "That's..."

"Yeah, it's not looking good for Alpha..." Heath growled softly as he held out the drink. "I shouldn't be telling you any of this."

"I would never tell my family what you tell me," I reminded him. "I'm sorry you lost her." I didn't reach for the soda, watching him as he finally gave in, put it on the small table between us, and sat down.

"He probably deserved getting that knife," Heath said, the animalistic growl still in his voice. "That knife should have killed him, but since they could stabilize him and get him to the hospital here in the States, he'll probably make it. A good surgeon and some magic can fix fucking anything."

"You hate him," I whispered. "Heath, did that Alpha kill the female?"

"If he didn't, he allowed it to happen." Heath turned his drink around in his hands. "An Alpha sets the tone and pace for the pack. If my pack had seen me hitting Landon to put him into place, they would assume it's okay for them to hit their werewolf children or possibly any wolf not as dominant. If they saw me hitting Carey? They would hopefully report me to the NAWC, but the bad apples would possibly..."

"Hit their own kids," I finished, letting a harsh breath out. "And you think the Alpha..."

"The Alpha is not a good man. He never has been. It seems like things are finally boiling over with that pack, and it's going to destabilize the entire region."

"Don't think I don't notice you won't tell me his name," I murmured, narrowing my eyes.

"Don't think I'm foolish enough to think you would stay out of it," he replied softly. "You have dangerous siblings, and if you go back to Hisao and say, 'This Russian werewolf Alpha is abusing his submissive wolves,' I don't know what your brother would do. That's scary."

I nodded, grabbed my drink, cracked it open, then put it back down, a little frustrated.

"Fine, you're right. If I thought...He probably wouldn't. My family doesn't get into werewolf affairs—"

"No, but you don't see her as just some werewolf who died, do you?" he asked, pointing at me. "You see a woman who died, and you're hoping that Alpha doesn't survive. I don't blame you. In fact, I respect the hell out of you, Jacky. But you're a werecat, and we both know how ugly things get when your kind sticks its nose into werewolf affairs. Generally, with you nearly being executed."

I winced. He was right.

"It sucks," I mumbled, "that there's nothing we can do."

"It's not our business. The only reason I know what's going on is I'm still a recognized Alpha, pack or no pack. They'll keep me up to date because there might come a point...If the Russian pack falls apart, there are a lot of wolves who will need new homes," he finished, sipping his drink. "I wouldn't bring them here, but there's a chance I might need to help some."

"You don't sound too upset about that." He didn't seem to think of it as a burden or a potential problem, just acknowledged the possibility as if it was Carey coming home with a project from school, a thing that happened.

"I'm not. I would keep them outside your territory, help them recover, then find them a new home. It would be a temporary thing. I don't want a pack yet, not for another decade, at least. I'm enjoying this life where there aren't fifty-plus werewolves needing me every moment of the day. For the first time in Carey's entire life, I'm home when she's back from school almost every day. I won't give that up for anyone or anything." He looked at his drink, took another sip, and smiled. "I won't give up on this either." He waved a finger between us. "Bringing in a lot of wolves, starting a new pack..."

"You don't need to finish that thought. I know."

A new pack would mean he and I would have to distance ourselves from each other. There would be no more dinners at the Everson household, no more Mondays with Carey, no more stolen kisses when no one was watching. Neither of us wanted to stop whatever it was we were doing, but a full pack of werewolves would make everything too dangerous.

He didn't continue, and neither did I. We enjoyed our drinks, and I thought about a young female werewolf dying in a hospital. I tried not to, but there was a processing time. I wasn't sure why it stuck out to me. People died every day, and I had killed my fair share of werewolves, werecats, and vampires, but this one bothered me a lot.

"Is there really nothing the North American werewolves can do?" I asked softly, looking over the backyard. I heard Carey's pony nicker in the barn, and my eyes flicked to it, instincts immediately perking up. I pushed them aside, ignoring the way my stomach growled. I avoided the horse for this very reason.

"Yes and no. We brought up the female to the

Tribunal werewolves. They rule all of us and keep the peace between different councils. If they want to do something about the Russian pack which is way too big for its own good, they will. The European Werewolf Council is closer and might have more sway on the matter, and they have older wolves in that part of the world. Not much older, but older. If there was a need for a hostile takeover, the Tribunal would call on those packs. It would destabilize the entire region, though. A massive pack that covers most of Russia would have to be broken up. Alphas would need to step in and take in all of those wolves and relocate them to new areas or move to Russia."

None of that sounded pleasant. I was about to say so when the door opened, and Landon stepped out.

8

CHAPTER EIGHT

"Lasagna is in the oven, and Carey is coming out to check on the pony. Might want to drop the conversation about Russia," Landon informed us, grabbing a third chair from beside the house and pulling it closer. Heath and I nodded as Carey walked out, waved at us, then ran to the small barn. We watched her in silence as she disappeared inside.

"There. She won't be able to hear now," Landon said softly. "I didn't know we were okay with telling Jacky about the Russia thing." He pointed at his father but didn't seem upset, just curious.

"I'm not going to do anything," I said, hoping to ease his fears.

"She's fine," Heath tried to say at the same time.

"I know. Well, since you and Father are now an item-

"We're not an item," I cut in, but my protest was ignored. Heath's shoulder shook with silent laughter.

"Which I figured was going to happen, I'll tell you how I feel. The Russian pack situation is..." Landon growled. "I hate that Alpha. When I heard he got stabbed, I nearly celebrated."

That shocked me. Landon never seemed celebratory, and with that statement, I was certain he hit his talking quota for the day.

"Have you met him, or do you hate him from afar, based on rumors?"

"I hate him very up close and personal," Landon said with a snap of his teeth. "Being Father's second, sometimes I have run-ins with other Alphas. Some try to sway me into their packs, some try to kill me when no one is watching. Some just call me a few derogatory names behind my back and play nice to my face. Alpha Vasiliev is the type who isn't afraid to call me the 'n' word because he's smart enough to know America's history with it. Or a faggot. Not that he's unusual for our community. I've gotten it a lot over my years. He's just particularly venomous."

I glanced at Heath and noticed how dark his eyes were as though he was ready to murder whoever would dare hurt his son. It didn't matter that Landon was a powerful werewolf in his own right, Heath wanted to kill anyone who walked over his son.

And he's judging me right now. He wants to know if I'm going to accidentally hurt his son.

"She doesn't know, Landon," Heath said softly, his eyes lightening a little. "I never told her."

"It's not my business," I said quickly. The last thing I wanted was to shove my foot in my mouth. "You don't—"

"You never told her I was gay?" Landon huffed like an exasperated wolf, then turned to me again. "Well, now you know. That's beside the point. Alpha Vasiliev is a piece of work, who needs to be put down like a rabid dog. He's known among the submissive wolves for being cruel, even to those outside his pack. He tends to think of women as his playthings and his submissive wolves as whipping boys for his temper. Anyone who doesn't fit into his narrowly defined view of what a good wolf is doesn't survive in his pack for long, but he has a stranglehold on Russia. If a werewolf is Changed or born in that area of the world, he makes it a point to keep them. It's ballooned the size of his pack, and that's how he gets away with what he is."

I had never heard Landon talk so much, especially not so passionately. I was pretty certain my eyes were the size of dinner plates by the time he was done. When he noticed, he gave me the exact same smirk as his father, and the relationship they shared was never clearer.

"Father, I broke your cat." I had never heard someone joking and annoyed at the same time until that moment.

"I see," Heath murmured, amused.

"I didn't know you could talk so much," I said, trying not to give a weak laugh.

"I don't trust many," Landon softly reminded me, leaning forward. "I can't, being a gay, black werewolf. We've had people challenge me for my position, try to kill me on principle when I visited other packs. It's gotten better over the years, but it's taught me to take my time with people." He looked me over. "But you're good." He nodded as he came to some sort of decision. "You would have made a good werewolf."

"Ah, you missed the chance by a few years," I said, smiling. "Just missed it."

Twenty minutes later, after a round of chuckles and jokes between father and son, Carey came out of the barn, dirty and grinning. Heath followed her in, and I was left with Landon. I didn't miss how Heath had gently patted his son's shoulder before leaving him alone with me.

"I'm sorry I was so off-putting for so long," the werewolf said as I stood to head inside as well. "It wasn't polite, and I never made a good impression."

"It's fine. You never hurt my feelings." I had joked about Landon's distrust of me, but I had never let it hurt me.

"I wanted to hate you for killing Richard. He understood me and taught me it was okay to be who I needed to be. He protected me when I was young when people tried to hurt me before I could defend myself. He was everything a good older brother was supposed to be. And then you killed him." He sighed, shaking his head. For a moment, I saw the weight he carried. I wanted to say it was okay if he did, but he continued talking before I had the chance. "But...Carey loves you, and my father..." A small smile formed. "It's idiotic what you two are doing. One day, Carey will find out, and I don't know how she'll react."

"Or the rest of the world," I commented under my breath.

"Hm." He nodded slowly. "But it's okay. I know what it means to be with someone the world tells me I shouldn't. What I want to say, though...I *don't* hate you for killing

Richard. I respect you, Jacky. You protected my family from a threat we weren't prepared for. He betrayed us. Father and I were too blinded to see what was happening, and Carey was too young. I don't hate you for killing him. I hope we continue to prove to be as good allies to you as you have been to us."

"Landon?" I almost touched his arm as he stood up but pulled away at the last moment. He looked down at me, curious. "Um...thank you."

He nodded, then left me on the back porch by myself, following his family inside. A moment later, Heath walked back out, smiling.

"He's been preparing that speech for a few months," he explained, leaning down to kiss me. "He finally realized it was time to let you in."

"I wasn't prepared to have a deep conversation today, much less with Landon."

The Alpha only chuckled as he kissed me again.

"Let's go in and eat dinner," he murmured on my lips. "Let's stop talking about Russia for the evening. There's nothing we can do. Better minds are working on it."

"Of course."

We went inside together, and I helped Carey set the table, my little rebellion. Heath made his displeasure known with good humor, and Landon went back to his quiet self as he worked on a side dish for dinner.

It felt like a home.

By the time dinner was on the table, we were all ready, finding our seats and digging in without preamble.

"Landon, teach me this recipe," I said, pointing at the serving on my plate. "I've never had lasagna this good."

"I can do that," he agreed, smiling when I caught him looking up from his plate. "If—"

A phone started going off, and for a moment, I sat confused as both the wolves checked theirs and frowned as the blaring, repeated noise continued. It took four rings for me to realize it was my phone. It was the ringtone I set for any werecats who weren't my family.

"Shit. I'll be outside," I said, jumping up and pulling my phone out as I went. I answered before I made it out the door and was able to shut it before the person calling me could respond.

"Jacky speaking."

"Jacqueline, this is Everett. We spoke before, after..."

"You're the werecat in Minnesota. What can I do for you?"

"I need you to come up here. Bring your wolf. I'll see you—"

"Wait. Why? Everett, what's going on?"

"I was called to Duty, but it's more complicated than that. The human is *lying*, but I don't know what she's lying *about*. She *reeks* of werewolf and blood. I figured your wolf should come up here to help...I don't know, but this seems like it's going to get me killed."

"If she's lying..."

"She has no right to my protection," he finished for me. "Jacqueline, this human *asked for you,* and I think you should come. I *can't* tell you more on the phone. It might not be safe."

My heart skipped a beat. If that wasn't a sign I needed to get on a plane, I didn't know what was.

"Okay. I'll head out now and catch the first flight available. I don't have access to a private—"

"Figure it out because I'm not keeping this human beyond dawn tomorrow. I want her out of my territory, in your custody or not. I'm calling you instead of Hasan out of courtesy. If you're not here when I throw her ass out of my territory, I'll call him." He hung up on me.

I was shell shocked for a second before heading back inside.

"I have to leave," I announced. "There's something going on, and another werecat wants me there and..."

"Carey, will you step out? Finish dinner in your room, please." Heath's request was in the tone of an order. Carey stood, cast a worried glance, then walked out of the room with her plate.

"Jacky?" Heath stood up slowly.

"I don't know. I was asked, and it seems like I need to go up there, but I don't know what's going on. There's a human lying to a werecat, trying to get protection. This human asked for me."

Right on cue, Landon and Heath's phones started going off. I watched as they answered them, and Heath's eyes went dark while Landon got a vicious smile.

"What is it?" I asked, swallowing. Minnesota. Everett was in Minnesota. I tried to make a mental map. Was he the closest werecat to...

"Alpha Vasiliev died in surgery," Heath answered in a whisper. "From what Alpha Harrison said, he's been dead for an hour, but the Russians don't want to announce. A werewolf loyal to us found out at the hospital and spread the word."

"Everett, a werecat, is in Minnesota with a human asking for protection," I repeated to myself, things beginning to click, puzzle pieces falling into place. "She smells like werewolf and blood. What if she was part of the surgery team?"

"Oh, hell," Landon growled. "Father—"

"He asked me to go up and take her off his hands. He also wanted you to come." I wrung my hands. "I wasn't going to ask..."

"I'm going," he growled softly. "If the Russians think she or anyone on the surgery team killed their Alpha, there's not a pack close by strong enough to stop them from killing a lot of innocent people. If there's a werecat involved, we could be—"

"Looking at war if they move on him," I cut in, nodding. "This is our job, isn't it? Stopping things like this before they get out of control?"

"We've never done it before, but...from my understanding, yes," he said, nodding. "I agreed to be a go-between for werewolves and werecats because of my association with you. You work for Hasan and represent his interests and the interests of all werecats in this part of the world. If we're going to use our connection for anything, why shouldn't it be this?"

"Okay." I nodded in return. "Let's go to Minnesota and find my werecat and whoever this human is. The sooner we get answers, the better."

"I'll start calling around to see if the hospital is willing to release the identities of the surgery team," Landon said sharply. "Once I know who they are, I'll send them your way."

"Try. They probably won't, but please try," Heath said. That made me curious, but I resolved myself to ask in the car. Heath grabbed a light jacket and walked out, talking over his shoulder as he went. "Let's take my truck. I'm grabbing a go-bag. Do you have one at home you want to pick up?"

"Yeah," I answered, calling after him as he disappeared from view. I turned to Landon and sighed. "Sorry I keep getting your father into sticky situations. Are you going to be okay alone with Carey again?"

Landon looked up from his phone and nodded. "We'll be fine. Just don't bring the Russians down this way. If push comes to shove, I'll take her, Dirk, and Oliver to my safehouse, where they'll never be able to find us."

"If you need any help, those two will help you," I reminded him. I didn't question that he had a safehouse or that he could hide all of them indefinitely. "They work for me and are quick learners. Plus, they need something to do."

"I know. If it would make you more comfortable, you might want to tell them to come here and stay in our guest rooms while you're gone. Or I can check up on them every day with Carey."

"Check up on them. I don't want to rip them from their house just yet." Heath walked back into the room as I spoke, and I waved at Landon before joining his father. "Carey—"

"I said goodbye to her from both of us," he said simply. "She understands."

Once we were in his truck, I turned to him. There was

more I wanted to ask him, but I hadn't wanted to get caught up talking before we were on the move.

"Why wouldn't the hospital tell us who worked on the surgery team?" I demanded. "We can—"

"Because of cases like this," he answered. "If I were in that hospital, they wouldn't tell Landon or Carey who was working on me. If I die, people are at risk of angry supernaturals lashing out at them. No one is at risk of failing if my son didn't know who they were. Normally, once someone is out of surgery, the team will meet the family, but why would they risk someone taking revenge if someone died?"

All of that made sense. I hadn't paid attention while I was there with my family, too consumed with everything happening to ask many questions. Though there was a case that Hasan being the werecat Tribunal member had different privileges than the average Alpha werewolf.

"Why are the Russians trying to keep it a secret?" I couldn't stop asking questions. This was a new puzzle, and I didn't know enough to draw the right conclusions or any conclusions, really. What I did know, I wanted Heath's confirmation.

"Alpha died. The pack is technically gone. They need to get ahold of the second, deal with challenges, probably a small civil war in their territory. The loyalists are going to put that off for as long as they can to maintain control and figure out which one of them will continue in Alpha Vasiliev's stead."

"Because he didn't die in a challenge..." I realized what Heath was trying to say. "He died due a knife wound from a submissive in the pack who could never take over."

"Exactly. We might be looking at the complete collapse of the Russian werewolf pack. They're going to be violent and angry. It's likely the hospital is already worried about the pack lashing out."

"And somewhere in the middle of this is a werecat with a human who smells like werewolf and blood," I said, taking a deep breath. "This wasn't how I expected today to go."

"I don't think this is how anyone expected this to play out. At least we haven't been completely blindsided."

"No, but Everett has been. I don't think he follows werewolf politics. He probably doesn't know what kind of bomb he's sitting on. There are so many ifs. If Everett has a human who was involved with Vasiliev's surgery and if the werewolves from Russia find out, there's a chance they'll go after her. Everett is already at odds. He's guarding her until we get there, but he doesn't want to keep her. Apparently, she lied to him when she called him to Duty."

"What could this human be lying about?" Heath asked, frowning.

"I have no idea, but we're not required to protect humans who are lying. At the same time, we're not going to let a pack of werewolves kill her when a failed surgery wasn't her fault." I groaned and hit the door in frustration. "We don't know enough, and I feel like we're walking into a war zone."

"I'm right there with you," he said, his eyes trained on the road.

We made it to my home in record time. I ran for my pack and made it back to the truck in less than ten minutes, tossing it into the back with his.

Then we sped off for Dallas, resolved to figure out what exactly was going on.

9

CHAPTER NINE

"What if there's no flights?" I asked as we parked at the airport.

"Don't worry," he said sharply. "I'm about to call in a favor, and we'll just hope it works."

"Okay..."

We left his truck together. It was already seven in the evening. A straight flight to Rochester, Minnesota wasn't common. We had used private planes when Niko and Zuri had been hurt, but I didn't keep one of the family's planes in Dallas.

I'm beginning to think I should. Whatever happened to my quiet life in Texas, where no one bothered me, and I went nowhere?

When we entered the airport, I caught the scent of another werewolf and was surprised to see an old face as I turned to track the scent—Ranger, a werewolf I had worked somewhat closely with over a year and a half ago when I was initially pulled into the lives of the Everson family. It felt like an eternity, and everything had changed since then. Sheila came up next to him, another familiar face.

Neither of them looked excited to see me, though.

"Don't worry," Heath whispered. "They're here because I texted them while you were getting your bag."

"What favor did you ask for?" I growled softly.

"To use the pack plane." There was nothing repentant on his face. "We're pressed for time, and I don't think we should waste it looking for a ride and getting caught up in layovers. The pack has a plane to use for the Alpha and inner circle."

"And you think..." I sighed as Heath looked over my head at the two werewolves.

"Ranger. Sheila. It's been a long time," he said tightly. I knew his current status with the Dallas pack was tenuous and dangerous. He was their old Alpha, and that caused tensions I hadn't considered. He'd explained, but it boiled down to he abandoned them, and they didn't know if he would ever come back and take over again. A level of distrust had formed over time and distance since he had stepped down.

Sheila cast an uneasy look at Ranger. Neither of them spoke, and locals in the airport were starting to take notice of the werewolves. Heath had one of those faces people didn't forget. Mostly because it looked too good, too classically beautiful. His five o'clock shadow didn't detract from it either.

"Call me Heath, if that's what you're thinking about," my werewolf said softly, stepping around me and putting himself between them and me. I raised an eyebrow. They weren't a threat to me. "Tywin knew I was coming through."

"He sent us to tell you the last time he saw you pass through Dallas, there was an incident in another area of the States. He's not sure why he should let you through, or why you think you can ask for the plane," Ranger said with the same stiffness as Heath.

"Fine. Heath, I'll find us flights." I started walking away.

"Excuse me, Miss Leon—"

"Jacqueline, daughter of Hasan," I corrected, turning to the two wolves. "Tywin and I had this conversation once before. He can't tell me where I can and cannot go. The airport is neutral territory in every city. If he wants to change that, he'll be opening a can of worms he and the Dallas pack are ill-equipped to handle."

Ranger met my gaze, then dropped his eyes. Sheila sighed.

"We're flying you both," Ranger said softly, "with conditions."

"Let's hear them." Heath crossed his arms, eyeing both wolves. "I bet I'll love this."

"Tywin is worried about you living so close by, Heath..." Sheila groaned. "This is childish. He's worried. He's still a new Alpha, and no one really knows the protocol with an old Alpha who didn't leave because of a fight or get thrown out of the pack. He was also mumbling about something going on in Russia. He wants to make sure you aren't going to stir that pot and is under orders from the council to keep an eye on you when you try to leave the state through Dallas. From my understanding, the other Alphas are too."

"Let's take this conversation somewhere private," I casually ordered. I couldn't talk to them openly, and while standing in the middle of an airport, discussing this might be safe for them, it was dangerous for me. Ranger nodded and led us to a staff entrance, past security, and outside. We walked for what felt like an hour to a hangar where a small private plane was parked.

"This work?" he asked me.

I looked around, sniffing the air, and checking for humans. They could have cameras and listening devices, but there wasn't much I could do about that.

"Yeah, this will have to do," I said, not really liking it, but it was better than a crowded airport ticket area. "He's not stirring the pot. I'm going to see a werecat who is requesting my assistance because werewolves might be involved with the situation," I explained. "I figured a werewolf might be good to help me sort it out."

"Oh." Sheila seemed surprised, looking between us. "Ranger?"

"You want a flight to Rochester," the male said tightly. "Where we all know—"

"The location of the werecat isn't your business," I snapped, feeling protective. Everett was one of mine, and anything to do with him was my business, not a wolf pack's. "He's not going to see the Russian werewolves. He's coming with me to handle something else." I wasn't lying, not really, just omitting that the two incidents were most likely related, but since I had no hard evidence, there was no way of knowing either way. Not that Ranger or Sheila had the right to that information. I was under no obligation to tell anyone what I knew from Everett, except Hasan.

I'll need to bring him into the loop, eventually. I'll get stock of everything in Minnesota before I drag him in if he doesn't reach out before then.

Neither wolf looked happy. Beside me, Heath smelled confident as if I had already won the argument, and we would be in the air soon. He knew these werewolves better than me. I had worked with them for only a handful of days while he had spent years as their Alpha.

"Let's go," Ranger said, defeated.

"I can buy other tickets," I said softly. "I don't need this ride."

"Just get in," the wolf grumbled.

Ranger and Sheila went to get the plane ready and left me with Heath, standing in the hangar bay.

"When you said they weren't your friends anymore, I didn't realize you were serious," I muttered, looking back at him. "I figured a few would still be..."

"Members of the pack might still like me, but Tywin is a new Alpha, and he's paranoid. Ranger and Sheila probably just don't want to be caught in the middle. On top of that, you're a werecat, and I'm convincing them to help you."

"I've helped this pack," I reminded him.

"I know, and I reminded Tywin of that. He wouldn't have a pack today if it weren't for you helping us. What's one quick plane ride for that?" Heath gave me a small smile. "I'm more dominant. I was when I ran this pack, and I *still* am. I'm the most dominant wolf in the state of

Texas, and probably in the top three in the United States. He was going to listen. He's going to be pissy about it, but he listened."

I didn't reply, thinking about what he said about how dominant he was. I had never really considered Heath's power in the general scheme of things. He always played off his power by saying there were others above him. I had never really considered how many, rather, how few, werewolves were above him.

Something about his casual declaration and ability to use that dominance when it suited him showed he wasn't just being boastful. He had held onto that information for a long time, which he could have told me over a year ago. It was something to think about.

My phone buzzed, and I checked the text to see if it was from Everett. I had sent him a text, asking for his address, and he sent it back over an hour later. I quickly updated him, telling him we were about to jump on a plane and head his way. Hopefully, this was something we could clean up easily and wasn't as bad as it felt.

"Would the Tribunal werewolves tell Hasan about the Russian werewolves?" I asked my partner quietly. "They might be able to put their feet down and stop anything before it happens."

"No. It would make them look vulnerable. I bet Hasan has his sources, just like they would, but..." Heath seemed thoughtful. "They didn't take advantage of what your family went through in February, so I don't see Hasan using this to take advantage of them."

"But they won't talk to each other. They keep their distance, just in case."

"Just in case," Heath agreed. "It's safer that way. No one likes when other species get involved with their affairs."

"Yet..." I lifted my hands and gave him a hard look. I got what I wanted, a masculine chuckle.

"Yes, yes, I know. Werewolves and other supernaturals successfully pull you werecats into things that shouldn't be your business. Take that up with Hasan. He's the one who decided someone needed to protect the human aspect of the supernatural world and that werecats should do that," Heath said, smiling. "You are one of the few people who can talk to him about it."

"Yeah..." I stared at the plane. "You think we'll be able to leave soon?"

Right after I said that, Ranger walked out of the plane again and waved us to board.

"Well, never mind." I started walking, chuckling a little. Heath ignored the wolf as we boarded, but I stopped. "Thank you for doing this."

"Yeah, sure." He was curt and stiff, not that I could blame him. I moved into the main cabin of the little luxury private plane and sat as far from Heath as I could. When he looked back at me, I really tried to convey the reason through the look on my face.

There was no way in hell we could sit together for this flight. The risk of seeming cozy was too high.

He shrugged and turned around again, looking toward the front.

We settled in for the flight. Sheila went through the safety procedure, then went back into the cockpit with Ranger, locking us out.

I ignored Heath as we entered the air, turning my thoughts onto the situation in Minnesota. I had no real idea what I was walking into, which disturbed me. The last time I left my territory on a plane with Heath, I had no idea what I would find. It made me uncomfortable last time, but now, I knew to fear the possibilities.

Not that my territory was much safer last winter. The other werecats pushed me into running and...

I banished the memories, trying to stay in the present. If I thought about my captivity too much, I knew I would have nightmares for a week.

One Russian werewolf Alpha is dead to a submissive werewolf, who can't take over, which leaves the pack in disarray, and from the sound of it, Everett has a human covered in werewolf blood.

Instinctively, I knew the human wasn't safe. If Heath was right about the Russian werewolf pack, they would go after every human involved with the Alpha's death for revenge. Innocent doctors, nurses, and techs would be killed if they had any reason to think the hospital was responsible for the death of their Alpha.

Heath made it sound like the pack was old and strong, something that made this more complicated. Most wolves in the U.S., from my understanding, were fairly young and not as strong.

About two hours into the flight, I got a text I wasn't expecting.

Dirk: So, you just leave town without telling us now?

. . .

Wincing, I quickly replied.

Jacky: Sorry, it was urgent. Landon is going to check in with you guys while I'm gone. Hopefully, it won't be a long trip. Is that okay with you? Also, please don't tell Niko or anyone else from the family about this.

Dirk: I won't tell them. Oliver doesn't even know you left yet, I haven't told him. Landon gave me a call and let me know, and I've been thinking about how to tell Oliver without scaring him. He's easy to spook.

I frowned and wondered for a moment how Landon had Dirk's number, then decided to ignore it. If Dirk and Landon were friends or could contact each other, that was only a good thing for me.

"Heath, when did Landon and Dirk exchange numbers?" I asked loudly.

"Back in February, I bet. They ran an errand together and probably traded contacts in case they got separated."

"Ah." I nodded slowly and got to work on my response.

Jacky: Stay safe. Thanks for understanding.

Dirk: Will do and no problem, boss.

I chuckled. Dirk, born and raised in Germany, was blending in with America really well. Oliver couldn't completely cover his English heritage, but obviously, Dirk had training in it from Niko. More and more, he came off as a relaxed American guy, an act to get his customers to tip him better.

Putting my phone away, I relaxed for the long flight. I had a feeling it would be the last chance I had for a long time.

10

CHAPTER TEN

When we landed in Rochester, Heath and I quickly thanked Ranger and Sheila.

"Look, just go back to Dallas, okay?" I said, looking between them. "We're not going to ask this of you ever again, I promise." I heard Heath make a noise of disagreement but ignored it. We still needed to rent a car and get to Everett. We could talk about whatever offended him on the drive.

"Good luck with whatever you're into," Sheila said softly. "I hope nothing we've done or said has changed your feelings about the Dallas pack."

Ranger growled softly, and the female werewolf made a face.

"I know this is uncomfortable for your Alpha. Let him know I'm grateful for the assistance, and if there's a time when any of the pack's humans need protection, I will take that Duty without complaint." I bowed my head a little, and without anything left to say, I started the search for a rental company.

Heath caught up with me after only a couple of steps.

"You could have stayed a moment and said a longer goodbye to them," I chastised softly. "They used to be—"

"They used to be my pack, but it's getting more apparent Ranger is growing more dominant. If I haven't lost my touch about these things, he'll be part of Tywin's inner circle before the end of the year. Good for him, but frustrating for me to deal with. He's instinctively hostile to me, therefore you, because he's growing to think less about following pack orders and more independently to protect the pack as a leader."

"Ah." I tried to sound like I understood, but really, I didn't. Werecats didn't have anything like that. We went through a whirlwind of an adjustment period when we first changed, then settled into our lives for the coming centuries. I did, my siblings did, every werecat I ever heard of had. The only time werecats deviated from that path was when other species got involved, wars, and the like.

"You did good, but you offered them a lot." Heath didn't sound pleased.

"I offered them what I thought they deserved—"

"You didn't owe them anything—"

"I don't like unfair politics—"

"And what's going to happen when another human—"

"Heath!" I snapped, tired of cutting each other off. His eyebrows went up when I stepped in front of him and narrowed my eyes. "I'm stressed out, and you involved a pack of werewolves without letting me know, which led to awkward tension that could have been avoided. I understand we're on a time crunch, but you could have run it by me. How I handle it after you drop it on my head is my business, and I don't need the critique."

"I just want to help you," he growled softly. "What's so wrong with that?"

"You're not allowed to, remember?" I hissed.

"You're getting paranoid," he snarled. I watched him, ironically, cast a glance over his shoulder, then survey the rest of the area before continuing. "I have done nothing but help you since we met. When we met, you were woefully bad at politics. You're getting better, and supernaturals know who you are, but that doesn't mean I think you can go without some advice every now and then."

"I am not—"

"You wouldn't even sit beside me on the plane to talk about what we're walking into," he reminded me, then stepped around me and walked off. That didn't bother me. What bothered me was the storm brewing in his eyes as he said it.

I took thirty seconds to sigh and glare at the small plane we were walking away from. Ranger and Sheila were out of sight already.

Am I being paranoid?

Shaking my head, I dismissed the idea.

I caught up to Heath as he entered the airport. He didn't speak to me as he found a rental car company, got keys, and walked back out of the airport. When we were finally seated in the small sedan with our bags, he sighed.

"I know...I know there's a lot between us people can't know about, but that doesn't mean we need to avoid each other. The world knows we're allies. There's no hiding that now and trying to makes us look even more suspicious. As for critiquing you…I'm an Alpha werewolf, and that's hard to turn off. I don't like when I see people I care about get in situations I could have helped them avoid without any fallout. I can be controlling and don't always think things through. I've lived a long time by my own agenda." He turned the car on after his little speech. I wanted him to look at me, but he didn't. "You're good at politics. Maybe it's from bartending or something, but you have a natural knack. I don't agree with offering more to the Dallas pack, but I'm willing to admit I'm on bad terms with them, so I'm biased."

"Why did you even call them?" I asked softly.

"Because I was checking flights, and we might have been too late to get this human before your werecat tossed her out. It's more time-sensitive than the last time we left Texas for Seattle. I didn't think it would be this much of a problem."

Watching him, I read his face as he pulled us out of the parking lot. I punched in the address and settled in, new knowledge bouncing around my head.

He seemed disappointed in himself, another thing I had never seen. I felt foolish for a minute, relating to that. Thinking I was doing the right thing and making an ass of myself.

"Thank you," I whispered, fiddling with the radio, "for trying to help. It worked out in the end."

"Any time," he mumbled, keeping his eyes on the road.

Night had fallen, and we drove on the dark roads

farther and farther out of Rochester. I stayed in contact with Everett, letting him know we were getting close. He kept me up to date on the human, saying the woman had shut down and stopped talking. He couldn't find any injuries on her, which was a positive. He also made sure I knew where his territory line was.

"Stop," I ordered nearly an hour later. Heath slowed down and pulled off the side of the road.

"Stay here," I ordered. "I want to let him know we're here without just busting into his territory. I'll be right back." I jumped out and started to the territory line twenty yards in front of me and walked slowly past the invisible line. The initial reaction was fear and distrust, but I didn't move, waiting for Everett to remember he had called for my help. Sure enough, the feeling of the magic in the air, Everett's mood, shifted to wary but welcoming. He was worried about guests, but he wasn't going to attack unless we did something. I stepped back out of his territory while Heath drove up slowly behind me. When I got back into the car, I chuckled.

"I told you to stay where you were," I reminded him.

"I didn't think you needed to walk all the way back," he countered, a small smile forming.

"Alphas," I groaned, rolling my eyes. "Go slow to start. I'll tell you when you can speed up."

"This is different from when we entered Gaia's territory in Washington," he pointed out as he hit the gas, and the car started rolling into Everett's territory.

"Gaia was dead," I whispered. "Everett is very much alive, and he's five hundred years old. Bigger and badder than both of us. I didn't want us to accidentally upset him by being rude."

I saw him nod out of my peripheral vision.

After a few moments, Heath sped up at my direction, getting back to the speed limit. It was another twenty minutes before we reached the heart of Everett's territory and turned down his long dirt driveway. It wasn't flat, showing signs of neglect as though he never left his home or bothered with it.

Heath parked in the clearing in front of the deceptively small house. I had a sneaking suspicion, it was bigger on the inside, or I couldn't see all of it. Only a single story, I had a feeling it was one of those sprawling homes that looked small from one side.

There were three cars parked in front—a Ford pickup, a sedan I didn't immediately recognize, and a small minivan.

Does this human have children we should worry about? I don't see a werecat of any personality ever driving one of those around...or any sane adult.

Everett was waiting in the dark on the front porch. I didn't notice him at first, but my eyes adjusted quickly when the headlights went off, and I saw his outline. There were no visible lights on in the house. I tried to keep my courage together, but something scared and paranoid ran through me as I saw my first non-family werecat since I had killed Lani. I'd spoken to enough of them on the phone, but no one visited me, and I didn't visit them.

He was a tall, lean man with light brown hair and

chocolate brown eyes. Spectacular for his height, but he screamed stereotypical normal beyond that.

"Jacqueline, daughter of Hasan, be welcomed in my territory," Everett said softly. I heard boards creak as he walked down the wooden porch steps onto the grass where Heath and I stood. "Alpha Heath Everson. Thank you for joining her."

"What's going on, Everett? There was a lot you refused to tell me on the phone."

"Based on her clothing, she's a doctor, and there's a lot of werewolf blood on her. I assume there's something going on at the Mygi Hospital."

"Fuck," Heath muttered. Neither Everett nor I reacted to that.

"You'd be right," I informed him. "How deep do you want to be brought in on this? If you don't want to know everything, you don't need to."

"I don't want to be involved at all. I could and should have turned her away," he reminded me. "She's lying about something, but I don't know what. When she got here, she was rambling and scared. I couldn't put enough of it together to figure out what the lie was."

"Then why did you keep her?" I asked, crossing my arms. "And call me and Heath? You obviously think she needs protection."

"I called because I'm not stupid. She asked for you when I started asking too many questions, and I knew something was up." He gave me a toothy smile, and his eyes began to glow a terrible yellow-gold like my own. "You'll need to see this to believe it."

"Then show me." I waved a hand, hoping he would let

me get to the bottom of his fun little mystery. He turned on his heel and started back up to his house. I followed first, keeping my body between him and Heath, who had returned to complete silence. I knew he wanted more information as well, and we still needed to confirm this was actually connected to the death of the Russian werewolf Alpha.

Once the front door closed, lights began to come on, and footsteps could be heard from the back of the house. My assumptions were right about the home. It was actually a spacious mini-mansion, tucked in the center of the werecat's territory—his home and den, his safest place. I had to tread carefully, but whoever was running around the back of the house toward us was not doing the same. There was either a familiarity to the other person or a lack of respect for Everett's domain.

"Who's there?" a feminine voice called, mature with age and weighted by exhaustion. "Everett, is she here?"

That must be her.

"She's here," he called back. He kept walking, and I followed him, frowning deeply. Heath was like a strung bow behind me, tense and uncomfortable. Having him at my back was one of the few things I was comfortable with, even if we were in a bad position and no way of knowing what was coming.

Everett stopped and turned to the side as the running stopped. We had walked through a wide entryway into a hallway, only five feet from the door.

I wanted to backpedal back through that door and leave.

The human woman was panting from her short run,

her hazel eyes wide in surprise and relief. Her long, chocolate brown hair was just a slightly different shade than my own, had blood in it, and was styled as if she had used that blood to glue it into place by running her hands through it. She had been with Everett for hours and hadn't cleaned up yet.

The blood didn't surprise me. I had known about it.

I hadn't known who the blood would be on—I wasn't ready for the who.

I could have never been ready for the who.

"Do you see? I figured keeping her and calling you as she asked was the only good option," Everett said with a note of fear now. "I wasn't going to turn away—"

"Gwen," I said, letting all the air rush out of my lungs as if I had been hit on my chest.

I was looking at myself, over ten years older. I had stopped aging at twenty-six when I had been Changed. Most guessed my age around thirty now, but most changes in my look were superficial.

But my sister? She was the 'me' I never got to be.

"Jacky," she whispered. "I was hoping you would come."

My world began to crumble around me at her words. Heath put his hand on my back, out of Everett's sight, but I barely registered it was there.

"What?" I tried to form words to ask the questions I needed to ask, but as I stared at her, everything was lost.

No. What does she mean? She...she shouldn't be here.

"I'm going to guess you two *do* know each other," Everett said very carefully as though he was expecting his next words to start violence. "I knew I had a strange doppelgänger situation on my hands, but I didn't think you two had met before."

"She's my twin," Gwen explained, her hazel eyes locked on mine.

Everett's jaw dropped as his eyes swung back to me.

11

CHAPTER ELEVEN

"Do you think the ladies could sit down and talk privately?" Heath asked kindly over my shoulder to Everett. "Obviously, this has come as a shock to...most everyone." He sounded as surprised as I was.

I finally dared to inhale through my nose, taking in every scent, and processing them as quickly as I could. Heath's surprise and confusion was the first thing, thanks to his proximity. Everett's emotions were similar, except there was a touch of fear, though I didn't understand why he was suddenly afraid. I dismissed the other scents of blood and werewolf since they were no use to me yet.

Then there was Gwen. Her scent was close enough to mine, I had missed it walking into the house. It was a tamed version of mine, a little more aged and mortal. There were some differences, but it was like knowing the difference between a name brand perfume and its best knockoff—so close, nearly perfect, but not quite. Just off enough to notice, but similar enough to miss if someone wasn't paying attention.

The complicated mix of her emotions took me the longest to work through. Fear was prominent. She was also hopeful and worried, grateful and upset—so many things to be feeling at once—but there was no confusion, not a single bit in her scent. That was only in everyone else. She was the only person in the room not reeling from this revelation and our reunion.

"How?" I asked softly, not moving my feet.

"How what?" She crossed her arms, mimicking how I did the same thing. She did it more often than me if my memory served me right. She was always the bossier of the two of us, with her crossed arms and pinched stare whenever she wanted to tell me how to live my life.

"How do you know about me? Or...Gwen, I don't understand." I didn't know how to ask such a big thing. It wasn't just me. How did she know about any of this? How in the hell did she find Everett and know to ask for me?

"Let's go talk," she said. "Maybe we should do that."

"You can tell me right here," I said, refusing to budge. "How do you know about *any* of this?"

"I work as a heart surgeon at Mygi Hospital. I was introduced to all of this just over two years ago. You?"

"I was turned into a werecat the day Shane died." One piece of information for another, an even exchange. Her eyes went wide as she counted the years since that happened, and I had cut off all contact from the family. I had disappeared from their lives for a reason, and it hadn't been just because of grief. Grief, in the end, never factored into the matter.

I did the mental math. She would have been working at the supernatural Mygi Hospital only half a year before I had been caught up in the coup in Dallas and needed to protect Carey.

"Really?" she asked, anger entering her scent. I didn't need to smell it to know it was there, though. It was beginning to edge its way into her expression and clear in the tone of her voice. "You've been a werecat for nearly *twelve years*?"

"Yes." I didn't need to beat around the bush. "Let's find somewhere to sit and talk. Then we need to get you out of here. Everett, I'll take over from here."

"I'll be in my office. It's soundproofed, so don't worry about me listening in. Less I know, the better." The tall, lean man walked away, disappearing into a side hall and out of sight. I was grateful for the werecat tendency to run from getting involved. I seemed to be the outlier, or maybe it was my entire family line. Everyone else wanted nothing to do with anyone.

"Gwen, this is werewolf Alpha Heath Everson. Heath, this is Gwen. You've heard of her." I gestured between them. Being active kept me from freaking out, but I wasn't strong enough to know I wouldn't. I just needed to keep the feeling of paralyzing fear at bay until I could be alone, preferably where neither of them would hear me scream. I looked over my sister's face as I gave the introduction, seeing and smelling the distrust she had for my partner. "Heath is here to help because we suspected there might be werewolves involved."

"And how is he supposed to help?" she demanded.

"He's probably just going to hand me over to them. How am I supposed to trust—"

"Heath is trustworthy. For once, I know more about something than you, so listen to me," I snapped, annoyed at her assumption Heath was anything but trustworthy and honorable. I knew for a fact, he was both of those things and would defend him until my last breath. "Been in this world a lot longer than you, so—"

"Sure, whatever," she snapped. "Come on. We can talk in the living room, I guess. It's not my house." She turned on her heel and walked further down the hallway. I followed, growling softly. Heath's hand rubbed slowly, an obvious attempt to support and comfort me, but I walked faster, breaking the contact.

Gwen sat down on the tan couch in the middle of the farmhouse-style living room. There were animal heads on the walls, which were rich reds matched with deep browns, very earthy and warm. It was similar to Heath's home but also foreign. It was dark, even with the lights on. I found an armchair away from my sister while Heath took the matching loveseat.

"I need you to tell me everything," I said, my voice shaking enough to be noticeable to everyone in the room. "I need to know what happened that led you here. I need to know how you knew about Everett. I need to know how you know about *me*. In that order."

Gwen's eyes widened as I put her on the spot. For years, she was the one who controlled every conversation.

"I'll need to break doctor-patient confi—"

"I don't care," I growled softly. "We're past the point of caring about HIPAA."

My sister nodded slowly, rubbing her hands together. "I was part of the surgery team for Alpha Vasiliev. He had a silver dagger to the chest. It had done damage to his heart, and he couldn't heal through it."

"Of course not," Heath said softly. "Remove it, and he would have bled to death because of the trace amounts of silver in his system left behind that would slow healing. Keep it in, and it slowly poisoned him to death, also thanks to the silver. That's why one would use a silver dagger, in case the initial stabbing isn't fatal."

"Exactly," my twin agreed, nodding sagely as though she had heard all of this before and understood the severity of the injury. It only gave me a sense of just how much she knew—enough to be comfortable. "So, they brought him into the hospital. It was a delicate procedure on both ends, with surgery and the magic necessary to help his body correct itself. There are not many who can pull silver from the body of a moon cursed, and they're all fae. Even then, very few fae are capable because it requires a certain amount of power and skill."

"Depends on the bloodlines," Heath added, pointing that information at me. "Trueborn children of Titania and Oberon, some of the different clans have a talent for it."

I nodded. I had it done once. Trace amounts of silver had been pulled from me by a fae named Brin. It felt like an eternity ago. He'd also given me the gift of telepathic communication in my werecat form. I had always figured he was an immensely powerful fae, and now I had another little piece of evidence toward that fact, but that was a rabbit hole I never wanted to go down. Brin was gone, and I was grateful he had never come back in my life to stir up trouble. That was one of the reasons I refused to tell anyone his name. Some believed by saying a fae's name, they could be called to who talked about them, an old superstition I took care of now.

"We were waiting on the fae, but I was called in to get the dagger out of him and quickly do a patch job on his heart to keep him from bleeding out when it was removed. He was at risk of organ failure and more with that much silver in him. Everything was going fine...until it wasn't. He died on the operating table before the fae could make it. We all knew we needed to go on lockdown before his pack decided to take his death out on us. So far as I know, everyone in that operating room left the hospital once we reported the death and went to find our safehouses and shelters."

"The hospital supplies those, though," Heath said, something distrustful in his voice. "Why didn't you go with the others, so the hospital could protect you?"

I was impressed with his knowledge of the matter. He was asking questions I didn't know to ask and filling in gaps my sister didn't think to.

"I know about Jacky. I figured...I could reach out, and she's a werecat and..." Gwen gave me a desperate look. "I learned about you when you came in with the werecat ruling family, Hasan and all his children. A couple of nurses pointed you out when I was in the recovery ward, checking on another patient. I saw you but didn't get the chance to talk to you. You left with someone and never came back. I heard that...you're part of that family now. It was crazy, but when I asked a friend in security to show me the footage...I knew it was true."

I opened and closed my mouth, realizing my sister only knew half the story. I looked at Heath, whose expression was unreadable. When I looked back at Gwen, I took a deep breath, knowing there was no avoiding it.

"I'm part of that family," I confirmed. "Everett knew my number and was able to call me here because I'm a part of that family, Gwen. Hasan, ruler of the werecats and member of the Tribunal, is the werecat who Changed me. Shane and I were in an accident and rolled the car down a hill. Hasan happened to be there. He took a chance and was able to give me a second chance at life. He is, for all intents and purposes, my werecat father." I rubbed my hands together, staring my sister down—hazel eyes to hazel eyes. We were a match in every way but species and age. "To the supernatural world, I'm Jacqueline, daughter of Hasan, and representative of the werecats in the Americas, his eyes and ears in this part of the world, and the voice to the werecats who live here when they need to speak to him."

"You..." Gwen seemed annoyed, but I wasn't sure why. Her scent was a mix of annoyance and a touch of anger. "You disappeared from me to be a werecat. Your *sister*! *Your twin*!"

"I'm also the younger sister of Zuri, the Negotiator, and sister to Mischa, the Rogue, Jabari, the General, Hisao, the Assassin, Davor, the Genius, and Niko, the Traitor. They're my siblings, too, children of Hasan and the werecats I fight beside when others would see us fall."

I was proud of that. For a long time, I hid from my relation to the most powerful werecat and the family around him. For a long time, I had no relationship with my werecat siblings. After Dallas, my life changed and so had my way of thinking. I knew my place in the world and had a large, passionate, and loyal family around me. I still wanted a quiet, peaceful life, but I knew that life came at a cost.

What had Zuri said? We fight to continue the lives we want to have?

“I couldn’t come back to our family. The world doesn’t know about werecats, Gwen.” I shook my head, frustrated she had the gall to be mad at me. “It was to keep you safe. Now, you know, but how did you know about Everett?”

“Everyone at the hospital knows about Everett,” my sister said with a touch of bitterness, which probably had nothing to do with Everett and everything to do with me. “He’s an open secret. The hospital and our bosses don’t brief us on him, but it’s passed.”

“Jacky, can I speak to you privately?” Heath asked suddenly, then got up and walked out of the room. I watched him go, confused and shocked, then took off after him.

“Stay here,” I ordered my twin as I went to find Heath, who had gone all the way back out to the car and sat on the hood, his expression dark.

“What’s going on?”

“Her story doesn’t add up. The hospital gives protection to all staff when they’re involved in this sort of situation. Why come here? Why ask for you?”

“What are you implying?” I demanded. “I know it’s

strange she came here and not to a hospital safe house, but I'm her sister and certain..."

"She knew about you since February," he reminded me. "February. Jacky, it's June. She always knew about Everett. She could have come and visited him and explained she was the human twin of a werecat and wanted to get in touch. She could have made you aware at any point, but she waited until now. Why?"

"Heath, that makes it sound like she was fine not seeing me until she...needed something." It was hard for me to finish.

"I know."

"I don't like that," I growled softly. "I...Are you sure this is what you think it is?"

"I don't know, but—" he stopped as the front door creaked again. "Jacky..."

"I know this is weird!" Gwen called out. "But I don't really want to be alone with Everett anymore. Why don't we find somewhere else to go? Like another safehouse? Or maybe your territory."

I turned and frowned at the sight of her on the front porch in the doorway. Why had she followed?

"Sis, why are you..." I looked back at Heath and saw there was resolve there—he knew my sister was hiding something. I trusted Heath and his instincts—trusted him enough to fall for him when it could get us both killed. We had our differences, but his age and experience was something I tried to never discount.

"Yeah? Look, I know you said wait but—"

"Is there any reason the werewolves would want to kill you?" I asked, meeting her gaze again. The wind picked a good time to pick up and swirl around us. My nostrils flared as I paid attention to what they told me.

"No," she answered, swallowing.

I caught it then—the lie.

"Did you purposefully let Alpha Vasiliev die on the operating table?" Heath asked boldly. I winced at the directness.

"No!" My sister's indignation was false, but the tears in her eyes were very real. The scent of her lie was strong, dominating the world as my sense of smell honed in, and it took over my brain and consumed me, making me ignore how scared she was.

She knows what she did. Oh my God. She murdered a werewolf Alpha.

For the second time that night, I felt as if the air was knocked out of me. I couldn't figure out the best way to respond, so I started to laugh as fear and anger flooded me. No one else moved or said anything as I laughed and turned to lean on the car, covering my face as the laughter turned hysterical. It took a long time, but it finally died down as my laughs became tears.

"Jacky?" Heath's voice was soft.

They're going to execute her. The Tribunal...the werewolves...they're going to execute my sister for murder.

"What's wrong with her?" Gwen was louder, demanding. I heard footsteps coming down the steps, the creak of wood.

"Don't come closer," I growled, lifting up to glare at her. "Did you forget that werewolves and werecats can smell a lie, or did no one ever tell you? Did you really think you could lie to *me*?"

She paled, but her chin went up. How many times had I done that to someone? There was a defiant glint in her eye, captivating and fierce, which reached into me and held me.

"He deserved it," my sister whispered. "I was doing a volunteer ER duty when that poor girl was brought in because another doctor called in sick. We all heard what the werewolves were whispering about. That girl should have lived to tell her story, but someone overdosed her with painkillers." Gwen's face morphed from scared to enraged. "And we were told to keep it quiet because it was her own pack who did it, and that was an Alpha's *right*! I had a chance to stop a *monster*!"

I was quiet as I looked at my sister from a new perspective and knew what I had to do.

There will be consequences. Fuck, I just got my life on track...

I was going to throw it all away.

"Jacky, this complicates...everything," Heath whispered. "Gwen, go back inside. We need to figure—"

"You're just another goddamn werewolf!" Gwen snapped. "I'm not leaving my sister with you. You'll tell her to turn me in, but that fucking werewolf deserved it."

"Go inside," I ordered. I needed to talk to Heath alone. There was a chance he wouldn't understand.

"But he's—"

"Now!" I roared, the snarl at the end of the word making my sister stumble back and hit the porch steps. She fell on her ass and kept backing up, moving toward the door, then disappeared inside.

"Your eyes," Heath hissed. "Jacky, you need to control—"

"I don't need to control myself," I growled. "I need to figure out how to keep my sister alive. You need to go, Heath. The moment they put it together, and they will, everyone near her will be vulnerable. I'm going to keep her safe."

"Do you know what you're getting yourself into?"

"She's right. I know exactly what I'm getting into. Expose the awful things a werewolf Alpha did to his own kind and hold him accountable, while also getting my sister out of a death sentence. I've tumbled with the Tribunal before—"

"And you *lost*, Jacky!" he viciously snapped. "Hasan saved your life by causing trouble and threatening them with using your death to turn the world against other supernaturals. I know this is your sister, but really? She's known about you for months, but now she's in trouble and using you to protect herself. She knows who you are. She knows who *Hasan* is."

"I can't turn her over to die. I can't do it. What she did is...terrible, but..." I was breathing hard as adrenaline started pumping through my veins. I was about to dive headfirst into trouble that would most certainly kill me if I didn't succeed. *Again*. "You and Landon said it yourselves. Alpha Vasiliev was an awful Alpha. He did terrible things. His own submissive wolves turned against him. What my sister did was wrong, but..."

Heath leaned onto the car and bent over, covering his face and blocking my view.

"You're justifying murder," he whispered. "There were better ways."

"I know. You can go. You should. Um...You can drive back to the hospital and tell whoever you want what we just learned. I'm going with her."

He looked up, a deep sadness in his eyes.

"And let you do this alone?" he asked. "Jacky..."

"Carey needs you," I mumbled, tears flooding my eyes. "Right or wrong, I can't leave my sister to die. Like Hasan and my siblings didn't leave me to die."

He straightened and looked down at me, his grey-blue eyes hard.

"And I can't leave you," he said with a bite. "Not again. Not like last time when I did what you asked and took everyone to safety while you were taken, beaten, and had to escape on your own. I left you once before, and you were tortured. I am *not* leaving you alone again. Don't dare think I would."

I had to take a step back. The intensity in his gaze was almost too much for me to keep eye contact. He was exerting his dominance, his sheer force of will, which had a lot of oomph behind it.

"What's the next step in this plan of yours?" he asked softly, his body losing some of the tension.

"We need to get her a change of clothes," I said, swallowing. "Then we need to find a safe place to stay. There's a chance they'll never figure out the death wasn't accidental. We could just ride out the storm."

He nodded slowly, then stepped closer to me.

"Never underestimate how serious I am when it

comes to you," he whispered, then walked around me, heading inside.

I leaned on the car and finally let the air leave my lungs, relaxing my shoulders.

This couldn't have gone more wrong.

12

CHAPTER TWELVE

When Heath and Gwen walked out of Everett's home together, I had a better idea of how this needed to play out. Everett followed them, his eyes locking on mine. As Gwen and Heath climbed into the car, I stepped toward the werecat.

"Your werewolf gave me some very sparse cliff notes and said you two were going to take her somewhere even safer than my territory." He rubbed his jaw as if he was considering what he was about to say. "I won't tell anyone," he promised. "Family for ones like us is more important than all else. Plus, I'm not looking to get on Hasan's radar, not after what happened in February. I'm sure you'll let your father know what's going on when it's needed."

"Thank you." I knew what it could cost Everett if it ever came back to him. "We can leave you out of it if this blows up. I'll say my sister found a way to contact me directly through you, but....Well, it's not lying to say you have no idea what's going on."

"Yeah, exactly." He nodded. "You should get out of here. The less time you spend here, the better it looks for me. And, I guess, you three."

"Thank you—"

"Jacqueline, daughter of Hasan, I want to say one more thing if I can be so bold." His words wavered as though he didn't want to say it, but at the last minute, decided it was right.

I waved him on, curious.

"I learned the hard way it's best to leave your human family in your human life," he said softly. "I know saying that is probably crossing over a line, but I don't think your father and siblings would be too happy if you throw away everything to protect a human—"

"I don't need your opinion on how bad this could get," I hissed. "Unlike you, I know everything that's going on. Stay out of it and keep your head down. If you have any reason to believe werewolves might try to enter your territory, you will call me, and I'll get Heath involved. We're not looking to start a war."

"Of course." He waved and started walking backward. "You have a safe trip and good luck with the...family reunion."

"Yup." I jumped into the car, taking the passenger's seat. Gwen sat in the back, silent, her fear nearly choking me. Heath hit the gas and took us back down the dirt driveway. Once we were out of sight of Everett's home, I turned to my sister.

"Do you realize your actions might start a war the supernaturals tried their best to end eight hundred years ago?" I demanded, glaring at her.

"Excuse me? Are you trying to give me a history lesson?" She huffed. "Yes, Jacky, I do know what the problems are between werecats and werewolves. That relationship and several others are trained into us before we're even allowed to see a patient. I know the fae and vampires have a long, bloody history as well. I know most supernaturals don't like witches because they're pretty much humans. I'm not an idiot." She raised her chin and looked down her nose at me. "I didn't consider that when I went to Everett to get ahold of you. I just knew you would be able to help me."

"Well, damn, and here I thought *I* was the reckless one in the family," I growled.

"You're the one who literally isn't human anymore," my twin retorted. "That's not the point. I thought you would understand. I heard stories, you know. Not many have seen you in person, so only a few people at the hospital knew we looked alike. No one knew we were related when—"

"Not that hard to find out," Heath muttered, shaking his head. "I did seven years ago."

My sister's glare at the back of Heath's head could have killed the man.

"Moving on from that," she snapped. "I did a lot of digging about you, Jacky. I learned about Dallas, Washington, and the incident that brought you into the hospital with...them. You've been putting yourself in situations like mine for at least a year. When this happened, you were the first person I thought to call."

I looked away from her and back to the front, staring out the front window.

My reputation precedes me, I guess. I didn't realize it was so fucking widespread.

"Where do you live?" I asked softly as we left Everett's territory. She rattled off her address, and I punched it into the car's dashboard GPS system. "Where are your kids? Do we need to bring them into custody?"

"You don't know?" Gwen asked with a fair amount of bitterness to throw at me. "Daniel left me three years ago. He has primary custody of the kids because I work such odd and long hours. They're in Minneapolis. So are Mom and Dad, not that you asked about them. They should all be safe, not that you care. I mean, you could have gotten all of that from a quick look at Facebook, but obviously, you don't care enough to do *that*."

"I didn't look into your life, no," I said softly, trying not to be angry. "I don't stalk your social media accounts or theirs."

"Yeah, because you finally found a reason to drop us—"

"No, because I'm going to live for a very long time, potentially forever, and you are all going to die of old age," I snarled. "I am a species of supernatural the world doesn't know about, *can't* know about. Don't get high and mighty with me, Gwen. I'm risking my life and Heath's to keep you from being killed. I don't need the animosity right now."

"Sorry. I just..." She shook her head. "I didn't think about how angry I would be, seeing you for the first time in twelve years. Avoiding me, our parents, not getting involved in the lives of your niece and nephew, and now you've walked in and..." She didn't finish, so I took my chance to say something, hoping to get her to see my side.

"I wasn't going to risk exposing my secret and my species for the love and affection of parents who always made me feel like I was second best," I growled. "I wasn't going to watch them, you, and your kids grow old and die. I had to do what I thought was safer and healthier in the end, and you know it. Don't act like—"

"The werewolves keep their human families, but you cut us out of your life. We couldn't even go to Shane's funeral."

"You never even liked him," I muttered, getting comfortable in my seat. I didn't need to look her in the eye for this discussion. She had always thought Shane was a freeloader, lazy, a deadbeat. He had been looking for what he wanted to do in his life, and we'd had time. We were only in our mid-twenties. We had plenty of time. Now, only I had plenty of time.

Fuck, sometimes I have too much time.

"And we're back to that," Gwen mumbled.

"Why don't you two talk all of this out at a later time and let me drive?" Heath asked patiently.

"I like that idea," I declared, reaching to turn on the radio. I looked back at her for a second and saw her sitting with her arms crossed. It wasn't a pout. It was an act she put on to seem above it as if she knew she was in the right. It was something I was used to seeing since we had our first real fight at fifteen.

Before that, we had been as inseparable as twins people would see in movies. Too bad I didn't remember a good chunk of those years.

We drove back into Rochester to my sister's home. A small two-bedroom, it didn't look like a home for a woman with two kids. Heath didn't stop driving and park in her driveway, though.

"I want to case the neighborhood before I stop," he explained when I gave him a confused look. "I want to make sure no one is watching."

"Well, if they are, they'll be able to see us in this car," I reminded.

"No, they'll be scoping out the house, not random cars driving through the neighborhood. Just let me check. There are a lot of cars parked on the side of the road."

"I'll stay down," Gwen whispered. "Maybe you should too, Jacky."

"If they recognize Heath, they'll know I'm nearby," I told her with a sigh. "The entire world probably knows he and I left Dallas together. Well, all the werewolves, anyway. The Dallas pack flew us up here."

"Why do you run with these werewolves? You were just reminding me that you hate each other."

"I don't hate werewolves," I whispered, looking out the window. *Very much the opposite, in fact.*

"Jacky and I have been allies for over a year. We're... breaking in a new path, I hope, for the rest of our species," Heath clarified. "We're friends, and that friendship is begrudgingly tolerated by the rest of the werewolves and werecats. It's not smiled on, but they have no reason to try to kill us."

"Would they?" she asked.

"Yes," I said in a voice so quiet, I didn't know if she heard me. "If they feel either of us is betraying our own kind to help the other…" I inhaled as that thought ran through me. "Heath."

"I know." He shrugged. "They won't execute me without giving me a chance to explain my side. You know that. If I can explain to them I felt justified that my actions were necessary to stop a small conflict from escalating into an all-out war, I'll be able to walk. I already thought about that. Even if it wasn't your sister, if *any* human went to a werecat, and the Russians decided to ignore that invisible line of protection, a war would start. We both know that. This is part of the reason the other Alphas in North America let me live near you and keep contact, so I can use you to stop conflicts on the same small scale."

"It didn't start when I helped Carey," I reminded him. "The ones who turned against you still tried to kill me, and that didn't almost escalate to a war between species until Hasan threatened to out everyone to avenge me."

"I think the situations are a little different. Carey is a child of a werewolf and specifically, my daughter. Her role in any of these things is expected as the daughter of a werewolf. Gwen is a surgeon at the Mygi Hospital, neutral ground, and shouldn't be at risk to begin with. She's also *your* sister. Let's ignore the familial relationship, though. Let's look at this as if she's any human who worked at the hospital. If the werewolves start killing the hospital employees, they declare their self-interests are more important than the health and wellbeing of *all* supernaturals. *No one* would let that stand, and the werewolves on the Tribunal would have to draw the line. Either leave the Russians to die by the hands of others, step in and protect them, or kill the pack off themselves. All of those situations turn ugly. All of them."

"Oh yeah, that makes a lot of sense." I couldn't disagree. "So, there's a strong chance you don't get killed in all of this by the Tribunal. Like everything in our world, it's politics."

"Yes," he said softly. "It would be better if I told them I was involved, but that risks exposing you and Gwen right now and..." He shook his head as he turned around another block. "I don't want to do that yet. The more time we can steal without anyone knowing about the two of you, the better."

"Definitely," I agreed. "What do you think are my chances?"

"I won't let you die," he said, his jaw tensing and a twitch forming on his neck. "So, the chances don't matter."

"Wow, you two are intense," Gwen said in the back. "More people don't have to die."

"You killed a werewolf Alpha," I reminded her. "More people will die. It's just a matter of time."

"He—"

"Deserved it," Heath growled. "Yes, we know. Heard that speech already. Once we're in a better location, we can discuss your reasoning further."

"Fine."

It took another ten minutes before Heath pulled into Gwen's driveway. We all walked to the front door together, Heath and I keeping our eyes, ears, and noses on alert for anything out of the ordinary for the suburbs. Gwen fumbled with her keys, but once the front door was unlocked and we made it inside, I locked the door again, refusing to leave any possible venue of protection unused. A front door didn't offer much protection, but even the thirty seconds it allowed could be necessary.

Maybe I was just getting paranoid after so many adventures.

"Get something clean on," I ordered. "Don't bother showering. Your home isn't safe to stay in for any length of time."

"Of course," she agreed and ran into the back room.

While she was gone, Heath and I searched the front side of the house, the kitchen, living room, and a small dining area. That was all my sister had.

Heath was checking for intruders, but I was looking at other things—pictures on the walls, framed portraits on the shelves.

I saw my parents. The picture had to be after I Changed. They seemed older. Gwen and I didn't get our hazel eyes from either of them. Our mother had green eyes, and our father had dark brown. Our hazel came from somewhere in the middle, but I wasn't a genetics expert. They both had brown hair, in two different shades. We matched our mother's. We were both taller than her, but not nearly as tall as our dad, who reached over six feet.

I looked away from the picture, feeling the sting as I realized my mom was now fully grey. I had missed over a decade, and they had changed physically. They were doing the very thing I had never wanted to see. They were growing old.

I moved to the next set of pictures—baby pictures, kid pictures, and Daniel.

I can't believe they split up.

It was disheartening. Gwen and Daniel started dating their freshman year of high school and were the couple everyone had wanted to be, even me. Everyone wanted to have their life. He became a fancy lawyer, and she became a doctor, and somehow, they stayed together through all of that and brought two kids into the world.

The fact she still had his picture on the wall made my heart hurt. I couldn't bear to look at Shane. I had lost him, still madly in love until our last breaths. He *left* her, and she tortured herself, looking at his picture.

Finally, I hit one picture I really didn't want to see. The complicated mix of emotions that ran through me as I stared at my face was one I couldn't sort out, not then. She had a few pictures of us together and alone—graduating high school was prominent, one of us as teenagers, each holding a trophy from the county science fair. We were sixteen when that had happened. Gwen's was first place. Mine was third place. She was grinning. I wasn't.

Every kid in the county would have killed for that trophy, but I had known they would talk about Gwen the entire way home. Third place wasn't good enough when the twin was first.

There was even a picture of us from the time I couldn't remember. We couldn't have been more than ten. We were fishing with our dad, who stood over us, beaming at the fish we caught.

"I loved that day," she said behind me. I didn't look at

her as she walked up next to me and sighed happily. "Do you remember? You were so good at fishing, and I was the worst. Couldn't catch anything to save my life until that fish. Once we both had a fish, he asked Mom to take our picture."

"I don't...I don't remember that day." Most of the time, I ignored the missing years, but their absence hit me when Carey brought them up. Every time she asked about those years, I felt the ache of losing them like an old scar. Now, it was like being shot.

"What?" She grabbed my shoulder and turned me to look at her. "You don't remember?"

"Sometimes, when a werecat is Changed, they get blind spots in their memory. Bet it happens to werewolves, too." I didn't see any reason to lie to her. She was a doctor at a supernatural hospital, after all. "There's no real explanation, but I have always wondered if it's because brain cells might die during the Change. My memory loss is a bit worse than most, but I was dying when I was Changed. I had a lot of bad injuries and took some pretty terrible knocks to the head on the way down the cliff. So, I lost...about six years of my long-term memory. I don't remember anything from like six to twelve. I've gotten used to it."

"So..." For the first time since I had seen her in the entry hall at Everett's, she was concerned.

"I know we had a good relationship before we became teenagers, but I don't remember most of it," I said softly, looking back at the picture. "Wish I could, but we only have the hands we're dealt. It's fine."

"Jacky..."

"We're not here to go down memory lane, especially since I can't go with you. Do you have your bag? We need to go." I felt cold and knew I was behaving that way, but I couldn't deal with the emotional load those pictures tried to put on me. I put them behind me and looked for my werewolf. "Heath? We clear to get out of here?"

"We're clear!" he called back, coming out of a small room. "Had to hit the bathroom. You seem preoccupied."

"I bet I did," I mumbled.

I walked out of the house, trying to banish Gwen's face from my mind. She was looking at me as if I had two heads. I was the first to get into the car, and Heath stood with her while she locked up the house. He was ever the gentleman he always was, holding her duffle bag.

Once we were all inside the car, no time was wasted to get away.

"Where are we going?" she asked from the back.

"I don't know," I answered.

13

CHAPTER THIRTEEN

Heath was the one who found us a place to hide in the unfamiliar territory. We had to pull over and do a fast search of realty listings, and he picked a small, abandoned farm outside the city that wouldn't go to auction for another month.

"If there are contractors working there, we'll go to the second place. We'll keep going until we find an empty one," he said as he pointed it out. "Because it's at auction, there probably won't be. They don't flip these houses. They auction them off for as much as they can get to pay the debt on them. The flippers are normally the ones who buy."

"Good idea. And it's not connected to either of us," I pointed out. "There are no favors to call in and give us away."

"Exactly. To cover our tracks, I'll buy it through my company and say it's for Carey when she's old enough to live on her own, get married, or something. I own properties all over the country, so this won't surprise anyone. Plus, it's good to have a place so close to the hospital."

"Why?" Gwen was curious as she leaned through the seats. "I mean, you all have private jets. It's not like it takes any supernatural very long to get to us if they have the right connections."

Heath looked around her at me.

"I get hurt a lot, I know." I tried not to roll my eyes.

"Yes, you do," he murmured. That made Gwen lean back and look between us, but she didn't say anything.

It took us thirty minutes to get to the house, and Heath pulled in when there was no one there. We parked in the back, keeping our car out of sight. If anyone drove by, we wanted them to think the property was abandoned until the auction. We set up in the back bedroom, Heath checking floors before Gwen and I were allowed to walk in.

"So, what's the plan now?" my twin asked, looking around with a bit of disgust for the abandoned, century-old house.

"We wait," I answered, shrugging. "There's a chance this blows over."

"For that to happen, the Russians would need to leave the country." Heath was looking at his phone as he sat down on the floor. "From the looks of it, they've disappeared from the hospital but haven't left the country. The Minneapolis pack is having a hard time tracking them, which doesn't bode well for anyone."

"Do you think they'll give up whatever hunt they're

on and go home? Once they do that, this is over before it even starts." I needed some reassurance from Heath to keep some hope this wouldn't blow up. Sure, I'd already had a bomb dropped on me with Gwen being involved and a murderer, but that was only the tip of the proverbial iceberg. This could get much worse than a simple hide-and-protect plan.

"Depends on what they're looking for, and if they find anything." He kept staring at his phone. "Mind you, I don't have all the information since I'm not considered essential. No one even asked me about what Dallas knows, coming up here to help you with a werecat thing."

"Any chance Tywin is keeping it a secret?"

"To help me? No. To protect himself because he helped us? Definitely," he answered. He shook his head, sighing. "I wish it wasn't like this between us. I naively thought we would remain friends, and I could stay connected to the pack in some way. Only Carey has had a good interaction with them in months."

"I keep hearing about Carey," my sister said, ignoring what we were talking about. "Your daughter, right?"

"That's right." Heath looked up and gave my sister the same distrustful look he had when he first met her. I knew he had problems with how this went down, and I understood them. I just didn't want it to become an argument, not another one.

"How old is she?" Gwen stepped closer, looking at me, then back at Heath. "My oldest is ten."

What's she doing?

"She's thirteen and my youngest," he said.

"How many do you have?" Gwen tilted her head to the side.

"Three...two alive, one dead. My oldest was two hundred and fifty-three when he passed away. My middle child is one hundred and fifty-seven." Heath smirked as he put his phone away. I wanted to laugh when I looked at Gwen and saw her face. "I'm two hundred and eighty. I was Changed during the American Revolution. I was a soldier in Washington's militia. Some advice? It doesn't matter if they're fifteen or two hundred, children never get easier. Not for their parents, at least."

"Well...you would know, wouldn't you," Gwen said, sitting down away from both Heath and me. "Did you Change them?"

"My oldest, Richard. I Changed him because he wanted it when he was old enough to understand what it meant. It was a risk I really didn't understand. I didn't know much about my own kind at that time. My middle boy was born a werewolf because his mother was one. My youngest is human. I'm hoping she chooses to stay that way."

Gwen only nodded, silently considering. I knew the look. She was forming her opinion about him as a werewolf and a father—as a man. I didn't want her judging him or to deal with her possible condemnation of him.

"Ever been married?" she asked, looking up again.

"Gwen," I snapped. "Maybe his personal life isn't your business."

"I'm just asking. I'm hiding from werewolves, and

you...brought one with you. I just want to get to know him."

"Don't you work with some?" Narrowing my eyes, I slid down my wall to find a seat. Four walls in the room and we each claimed one as though it was our territory, our bubble of safety from the others. I didn't like it. I wanted to sit next to Heath, but I didn't know how much I could trust Gwen.

If she learns Heath and I might have some sort of romantic relationship, she'll find even more reasons to judge him and me.

"It's fine, Jacky. Yes, Gwen, I've been married twice. Both have passed on."

"My condolences," she said, chewing the inside of her cheek. I had never realized she had the same bad habit, but the way her jaw was moving, and her cheek looked, it was pretty obvious. "Tell me, Alpha Heath Everson, have you ever beaten a werewolf you were in charge of?"

I hissed, but it was nothing compared to Heath's growl.

"No, and I would appreciate not ever being compared to Alpha Vasiliev, Doctor Guinevere Duray. You have seen the worst of us, and I can see the judgment you're already making. You made it clear the moment you found out who I am and more specifically, what I am. I can only imagine the things you see come and go from that hospital, but let me tell you a little secret. Not every werewolf is a monster, just like every human isn't a racist, a serial killer, or a rapist. We all have our bad ones."

"You're right." She lifted her hands. "My apologies.

I'm stressed and angry. I don't like the idea of hiding here until this blows over. We should be—"

"It's our first and best option," I reminded her. "You don't really understand what's at stake, do you? I hate to say it, sis, but in the eyes of the Tribunal, Alpha Vasiliev's life was worth more than yours. He was an Alpha who was cruel and awful, from what I've heard, but he brought stability to a large group of werewolves, and without him, it seems most of Russia's werewolf population will fall apart. There's a very likely chance they will not care why you killed him, might not even care you did it on purpose, only that he died in your care." I wanted her to understand. Her life depended on her understanding, and for all of our issues, I couldn't live with watching my sister die.

"What happened to the Jacky I knew who stood up against bullies and injustice?" she snapped. "You got kicked out of medical school for punching a guy in the face, so he wouldn't accidentally hurt a patient because he wouldn't listen to you. Don't you want to hear about what I possibly have? What if I can say we can take down that Alpha—"

"He's dead! You killed him! Does it matter anymore?" I couldn't believe it. She wanted to keep trying to get into trouble.

"She wasn't the only one," my sister yelled across the room. It made both Heath and I jump in our skins. "That female werewolf? Her name was Devora. She was forty-five and had been in the Russian pack for twenty years. For many of those years, she tried to keep her head down, but there's an expectation of females in that pack. They're sex objects, to be used whenever a male is..." My sister took a steadying breath. "She was raped, repeatedly. She couldn't freely walk around without putting herself in danger. Eventually, she was picked to become the mate to a male who had impressed Alpha Vasiliev. She didn't choose him, didn't want him. After her mate fell from grace and lost the interest of their Alpha, he beat her. Her complaints and pleas fell on deaf ears. Her Alpha told her that her role in the pack was to keep her mate satisfied by whatever means necessary, just as she had kept all the males satisfied before mating. She killed her mate. In the end, she killed him as he tried to beat her to death. Her pack didn't bring her to the hospital. Oh no, that's the story they wanted to spin after the fact."

"Who took her?" Heath asked, his voice taut.

"A lone male brought her, claiming to be her brother. A true beta werewolf. A submissive who just wanted to make sure his sister lived. She had so much to say..."

"Why didn't she tell any of the American werewolves?" Heath demanded. I knew Heath could get pissed, had seen it a couple of times, but now he was facing an injustice I knew he couldn't tolerate. He was too good a man. He and Landon had told me about Alpha Vasiliev's cruelty, but rumors and evidence were two different things.

"She was scared. I...I volunteer in the ER because my kids and husband are gone, and I have a lot of free time. There are not many heart surgeries needed, you know? She talked to us, but she didn't trust any of the werewolves. She spoke to us humans—not the fae, the vampires, the witches, or any other supernatural. She had only ever been a human and a werewolf. She didn't know them, but she believed the humans in the hospital could help her. The reason you all never knew about the brother was she wanted to protect him. And the Russian werewolves who followed them? They shipped him back to Russia as fast as they could."

"Who else knows about this?" That poor brother was in trouble if he wasn't already dead.

"All employees are sworn to secrecy. We talk amongst ourselves, but we do *not* talk to outsiders. There are a lot of threats and punishments which make it very clear we shouldn't talk to outsiders. If they found out I was telling you any of this for any reason, I would lose my job, probably more, but I'm already in deep because my team and I decided we were finally going to take action. We were done with watching innocent women get treated like Devora."

"How many?" Heath was quiet, his emotions gone. His scent was a blank slate that left a million options, but I had a strong idea he was enraged.

"I've seen three, but it wasn't until this week I learned they were all connected. There are probably six or seven total, in the time I've been at the hospital. One girl even had stories about Vasiliev himself a friend of mine had to listen to. A few days ago, I caught a couple of the werewolves who work with me talking about it. They saw me and explained what they were talking about, both visibly upset, angry, the Tribunal and the North American Werewolf Council hadn't stepped in. Too many bodies were showing up. Russia was already destabilizing, but they couldn't say anything, thanks to the hospital's gag order."

"I wonder what was happening," I mumbled, looking at my werewolf. "Heath?"

"Modern technology and medicine happened," he whispered. "Things were always bad in Russia, but we could never put a finger on how bad and no one in the pack would speak out, not to us. Alpha Vasiliev never let anyone from the NAWC in the country. He let Callahan in..." Heath growled softly. "Corissa has never been to Russia. Callahan would have wanted to protect her."

"What are you talking about?" Gwen sat up a little, her anger written clearly in the lines of her face. My sister hated feeling out of the loop. I remembered her as a teenager, getting annoyed when I talked to my friends about something she didn't hear about.

"Callahan and Corissa are the two most dominant werewolves in the world. They sit on the Tribunal. Callahan has always personally dealt with Alpha Vasiliev, from what I know. I've never heard of Corissa meeting him. I thought if they knew he was a misogynist, Callahan would have never put Corissa in the position to have her position weakened by an asshole like Vasiliev. But that's part of the problem, isn't it? They knew." Heath chuckled darkly. "They put stability in Russia over the lives of potentially dozens of females of their own kind. And if Vasiliev was Changing them personally, the Tribunal would never need to know females were going into the territory. He was picking from the human populations around him, and there were no other packs to call him out."

"Heath, that means he could be into all sorts of shit," I said, swallowing the bile rising up.

"If he's giving females away like prizes, I promise you, he is, and probably his entire inner circle. He wouldn't give anyone less than loyal to the death a seat at the table with him."

"Why wasn't he put down years ago?" Gwen stood up and began to pace. I couldn't really blame her for that question. I was thinking the same thing.

"Because...Russia has hundreds of wolves. Over the centuries, he defeated packs and merged them into his own. There was a time the Tribunal and the councils didn't have as much power. He's still living in those times. Potentially hundreds of werewolves could die if there was an all-out war between the western world and his army." Heath rubbed his face. "I need to walk."

He was on his feet and had walked out before I had the chance to grab him. I was worried about him.

"Heath, wait!" I called out before he could get out of the building. He turned, his eyes full of pain.

"Yes?"

"I'm sorry..." I lost the words I wanted to say. I didn't know how to approach him when he looked like that. "What did you mean by modern technology and medicine?"

"Modern technology is becoming more prevalent in even the most rural areas and more affordable by the day. The females in his pack are probably starting to afford it, and if they have a loving brother or a family member or a friend...they can get out. Modern medicine keeps people alive for longer. With proper care, a wolf can survive the long flight from Russia to the United States, and suddenly, Alpha Vasiliev's problems get a worldwide spotlight. Things we only theorized about are now being proven as true."

"Oh, okay...You can...go for your walk." I waved to him, surprised when he turned back to me, took three easy strides, grabbed my face, and his mouth took mine in a desperate, passionate kiss.

When he pulled away, I was panting.

"I hate all of this," he whispered.

"I know."

"It could be Carey one day." The fear in his eyes told me where his mind went. "And the excuses the hospital werewolves gave your sister? An Alpha's right?" He shook his head slowly. "That's not good enough to excuse this. I can't abide by it."

"You're a good man," I whispered, reaching out to touch the scruff on his jaw. "We will never let that happen to Carey."

He nodded, then kissed my cheeks.

"I'm glad you're in our lives, and you might be the only person I trust to uphold that promise," he murmured before letting go. "I'll be right back. I'm going to see if there's any information I can fish up. I might give Tywin a call too."

"Okay. I'll be here with..." I gestured at the door. He nodded, kissed me one more time like he couldn't resist the urge, then left.

Walking back into the room, I was well and truly alone with my sister again. When it happened at her house, I knew Heath was nearby, but this time, I had no such assurance. I was immediately uncomfortable.

"There's more if you want to hear it," Gwen said as I took my seat again.

"I don't." There was only so much discussion about rape and abuse I could take in one day.

14

CHAPTER FOURTEEN

I stared across the room at her, my eyes on an older body. Twelve years wasn't that long, not in reality, but it took its toll on a person, especially one with a busy life like Gwen's. She had wrinkles I would probably never get, smile lines around her eyes. We were only in our thirties, but it changed the body, and human bodies were so fragile.

"Why did Daniel leave you?" I asked, rubbing my hands together. "I'm sorry, by the way. Um..."

"I worked too much," she answered, looking away. "I was always gone. When he kicked me out, he said...it wouldn't be like I lost any time with the kids...I already barely saw them."

"Ouch." I winced. "Asshole."

"He was right. I still love him. I thought everything was perfect, and he tried to ask me for more time with him and our children, but I never thought it was serious. I was bringing home good money, and my career was really important to me. I was finally done having babies, so I could focus on it. One day, I came home, and our kids weren't there..."

I could smell the tears. We had no lighting in the room or outside, but I didn't need to see them. The smell alone was enough to know how badly my sister hurt.

"He told me...he wanted me to move out. He'd already secured an apartment in Minneapolis and wanted me to move into it. I left, thinking...he'll want me to come back. So, I didn't change. After a year, I went to him and asked, and he just looked at me like I was crazy. I realized then my marriage was *over*. I got an offer to work at Mygi, accepted, and moved out of the city down to Rochester."

"Gwen..."

"He started dating last year," she whispered.

"I'm so sorry." I moved across the room to sit next to her. Wrapping an arm around her shoulder, I pulled her in as she cried for a moment. This was still an open wound for her, and she was still my sister. I couldn't let her bleed this out when I was the one who brought it up. I couldn't remain so detached.

"I was a fool. I was arrogant and selfish." She wiped her face as she pulled away. "And now my kids barely talk to me. I asked for it. I put my job in front of them. I missed their games and everything else. I gave birth to them, then I handed them over for their dad to take care of, so I could get back to work."

"That doesn't sound like you." I knew my sister was driven, but having a family had always been a dream of hers. Always.

"I had them, then I didn't know what to do. After my

daughter, I dealt with postpartum depression. Almost didn't have my son," she explained, looking away now. "Our parents tried to help, but..."

"They're our parents. Mental health doesn't exist. Get up and deal with it like an adult," I whispered.

"Exactly. We're both trained to know otherwise, but the fact of the matter is, that way of thinking is hard to break through. They love their grandchildren. They see them more than I do." She waved a hand, an obvious sign for me to dismiss the topic. "What about you? What's life been like for you for the last twelve years?"

"Very different and very similar to the one I lived as a human," I answered, swallowing. "I own a bar in the middle of my territory with two employees. Heath and his family live toward the edge of my territory, and I see them all the time." Shrugging, I tried to find a way to put my life into words. "Not being human anymore...things are different. I don't have as many friends as I used to. I can't. I've changed a lot. There are some personality traits that werecats can't avoid, just like werewolves. You'll never meet a werewolf who doesn't love to be a part of a big, cohesive pack or community. You'll never meet a werecat who doesn't like having space and alone time, hidden from the rest of the world."

"Why is that?"

"We're not human anymore. When the full moon rises, and the sun falls, I turn into a big cat with five-inch-long fangs. That cat isn't just a physical form I control... she's a piece of me. She's primal urges, something wild that lurks in my mind. She's not something else, she's me.

She's every instinct to hunt and survive. She's the instinct to fight against intruding predators and protect her territory and whatever else may belong to her. It's easier for the human mind to detach from those urges by making it sound like the animal is other, but it's not. Werecats, werewolves, even vampires, any supernatural species that was once human, we're irrevocably changed by what we've become. Something new was added to the equation of our humanity." I pulled my knees up and wrapped my arms around them, rubbing my upper forearms. I wasn't chilled, but I felt the need to warm up.

"I remember when you didn't believe in magic," she whispered. "Not that I ever did, either."

"Easier to do as a human. I've seen things..."

"Me, too. Obviously, I'm still human, but..." Gwen nodded as I chuckled at her response. After a moment of silence, she continued. "You said it was similar, too. How?"

"Oh." Snorting, I shook my head. I had been thinking about how my human family and my werecat family treated me. Hasan and my werecat siblings were getting better, but sometimes I was reminded I was the bad kid, the troublesome sibling. I always had been. "There're some things..."

"Come on, you can tell me. I've kept the supernatural secret for a hospital for two years."

"No, not about this," I declared as I stood. I needed to move and let my feet take me where they wanted, pacing around the room. "It'll drag up stuff I try not to think about."

"Like us? Me, Mom, and Dad?" Gwen sounded hurt. "We were a good family, Jacky. They did their best."

"For you," I whispered as I looked her in the eye.

"Excuse me?" Gwen jerked back, insulted. "They loved us."

"I'm sure," I mumbled, turning away again. "It doesn't matter, Gwen—"

"It does matter. You cut us out of your life, and for what? I didn't cut them out when they disregarded my depression. It was bad, but they were only doing what they thought was—"

"What they thought was best," I finished for her, nodding. I paced once more around the room before propping myself on the far wall again. "Yeah, that's a favorite excuse of parents. From what I've learned, it doesn't matter the species. They'll always do what they think is for the best."

"Then what's—"

"When are you going to understand I couldn't go back? I'm not human anymore, Gwen!"

"I understand you're hiding behind that excuse, but it feels like there's a much deeper reason why you never bothered to pick up a phone and call any of us. Even a token phone call would have been—"

"I didn't *want* to," I growled. "Is that what you want to hear? I didn't want to contact our parents. I didn't want to contact you. I didn't want to be surrounded by reminders of my human life, day in and day out. I didn't want to be reminded Shane was dead, or that I could never live a normal life. I didn't want to scare our family and see how much they hated what I had become. They never liked werewolves. How do you think they would feel about me?"

"You know, those reasons might work if I didn't work with other supernaturals—"

"Do you have a way out?" I demanded. "If you ever wanted to stop working for my world, is that possible?"

"Well, yes. They would transfer me to another great hospital. They would tamper with my memory a little, but there're ways out for humans at the hospital." Gwen's confusion at the turn in the argument was clear.

"I don't," I hissed softly. "There's no leaving for me. Since the day Hasan bit me, since the day he Changed me, there was no turning back. I will always be in this world. You said it earlier. You've heard the stories about me, the rumors about what I've done with my immortality. Do you honestly think it would be smart for me to reach out to my vulnerable human family members? Do you? Between the werewolves, werecats, and fucking vampires, I'm pretty sure I've made enemies I don't even know about." Scoffing, I turned my back on her. I hadn't even brought up my one and only run-in with the fae. "It's not like you tried after you found out what I was, so what does it matter? You've known for a few months that I'm a werecat, and you didn't bother reaching out."

"That..." Gwen never continued that sentence, leaving us standing in silence that threatened to drive me mad.

"It's long past, Gwen. You have your road, and I have mine," I whispered, looking over my shoulder. I couldn't bear the silence anymore, the crushing weight of it as we stood in the same room and couldn't be more different people. "And I liked it that way."

"You always were—"

Gwen stopped as Heath walked back in. As he entered slowly, we both watched him, and she never continued when he came up beside me.

"Jacky, come outside with me for a moment," he said softly as he drew close. I followed him out the backdoor.

"What's wrong?"

"Since the death of Alpha Vasiliev, the hospital has been making regular calls to all of their employees, making them check-in, both verbally and physically at the hospital. An ER nurse didn't check-in. They tried calling her, and no one answered. That was two hours ago," he explained softly. "They reported it to the Tribunal, who had put all werewolves living in the area to finding her."

"The werewolves make sense. You guys find people better than anyone from scent alone, and this could be related to your mess. Where are the Russians?" I crossed my arms, not liking the sinking sensation in my gut.

"The ones everyone knew about left the hospital, but they haven't left the country. As it stands, there's no public reason to believe this ER nurse is connected to Alpha Vasiliev."

"We know better."

"We do," he agreed. "And I promise you, others are thinking the same. My contact with the NAWC made it clear they all feel the Russians are playing a game, but no one really understands what's at stake or what the game even is. Mygi Hospital still refuses to release any information about who treated who and how they might be connected. There's a chance the Russians know more than they're letting on, and the leadership at the hospital is trying to scramble to protect their people from further problems."

"Their silence is becoming detrimental," I growled, talking about the policies at Mygi Hospital. "So, we have no one who can confirm if this ER nurse treated the female werewolf."

"We have one person, but I wanted to talk to you before approaching her."

I sighed, my shoulders sagging. "I don't know," I admitted. "I didn't even think to ask her. I don't want to."

"Why?" He watched me intently as I leaned on the car.

"You said it earlier. I'm already trying to get my sister off for murder. She killed a reportedly awful man and is standing beside that, not that I can blame her. If they never know she's involved, should we go further? If they never rule Alpha Vasiliev's death a murder, does it matter?" Crossing my arms, I looked at my feet. The need to keep my sister out of danger and trouble was one thing, but I didn't want to go after a werewolf pack unless I absolutely had to.

"I understand." Heath leaned on the hood next to me. "And I don't disagree. I don't like her, your sister, but you were right. She's your sister, and you feel you have an obligation. I can't fault you for it. It's the same obligation I feel for any of my family, alive and dead. As for her reasons for killing Alpha Vasiliev...you were also right about that, and I can't fault her reasons. I just wish this didn't land on us to deal with."

"Me neither," I agreed, swallowing that painful pill. "If I had the chance, knowing what he did to women..."

"I know. In that way, you and Gwen really are twins." Heath's words held a note of teasing. I side-eyed him, hoping he would elaborate. "Jacky, I think she's set in her convictions. She's decided the way werewolves have gone about this is wrong. She's done what she felt was right and is obviously willing to stand by it. You do the same thing. You stood in front of the Tribunal and proclaimed all you ever did was uphold your word. You walk your own path. Apparently, so does she."

Nobody had ever said Gwen and I were that much alike. Never. In fact, we had grown up with our differences showcased at every opportunity. She was always smarter, more stable, more obedient.

"How do we get out of this without it blowing up?" I asked, turning to stare at the woodlands around us. This was an old farm, completely overrun by trees and shrubbery. The idea of running through the wilds called to me. Just run from the problems. They were so human, and I was tired of these sorts of dramas playing out in my life. The idea of running was instinctive.

The idea of fighting for my sister was something my humanity wanted.

"We hope the hospital continues to cover for Gwen," he whispered. "Sit here and ride it out. We can't take her back to your territory. That's too suspicious."

"Wouldn't the hospital be doing an investigation of

their own?" I asked, swallowing. "Won't they realize she killed him?"

"Yes." A large, warm hand touched my lower back and began to make circles. "But..."

"But?" I raised an eyebrow as I turned. "They'll turn her in."

"Maybe, but I've been thinking about that. What if you and I reached out to the hospital and tried to broker a deal? What if she was punished internally, and it never went to the Tribunal?"

I stared at him, my eyes narrowing as I considered what my smart Alpha werewolf was thinking.

"Do you think we have enough political power to make that happen?" I considered my question as I asked it. "I'm a daughter of a Tribunal member..."

"I'm just some werewolf, but I wouldn't matter in the end. You do, daughter of Hasan."

Nodding, I accepted that.

"Do you think they might know about our relationship already?" Crossing my arms, I looked toward the back door, thinking about my sister just beyond, tucked away inside and safe. "Do you think they put it together?"

"If they didn't, they're fools," Heath said with a dark chuckle. "You and she look too much alike. She has the age lines of humanity, but you have the same eyes, the same hair. You seem a little more vibrant, but that's the magic of the curse and our immortality. In comparison, she seems dull. She lacks magic. That's all."

"So, the hospital is asking everyone to report in. She obviously hasn't, but they haven't put anyone to finding her yet…" I took a sharp breath. "Do you think they might have guessed I'm here? Or that I would get involved?"

"What would their game be?" he asked, then growled softly. "Blackmail."

I nodded again, very slowly as that piece of the problem fell into place.

We didn't have a chance to continue our conversation, though, as my sister screamed.

15

CHAPTER FIFTEEN

Heath and I nearly took the doors down as we ran inside and found my sister, where we had left her in the dark back room of the abandoned home. The only source of light in the room was the glow of a cell phone screen, illuminating her face and showing the sheer terror there. Her heavy breathing had a soft whimper to it, the moaning of pain and fear. Her scent told the same story.

"What's wrong?" I asked, rushing to her side. "Sis?"

Her hands were shaking, and she dropped the phone as I grabbed her before she could fall. I eased her to the floor, ignoring the phone as Heath grabbed it.

"Talk to me," I pleaded as her mouth hung in shock.

"Fuck," Heath murmured. "Jacky, they know."

"Who knows what?" I demanded, turning to him while keeping my hands on my sister. I couldn't let her go. I wouldn't let her go.

"The Russians," he whispered, turning the phone to me, showing me the gory mess on the screen.

"Oh..."

"That's...that's..." Gwen began to cry, and all I could do was rub her back. Slow and steady, I tried to comfort her. My stomach twisted at what was on the screen. There was a person there, though there was no way of knowing if the person was alive or dead—most likely dead.

Heath was the one who stepped up.

"Gwen, an ER nurse went missing. Is that her? Did this woman work in the ER?" He went to a knee in front of us, his eyes trained on my sister. "Is it?"

She nodded, sobbing as she covered her face and pulled her knees up.

"Did she know what you did and why?" I needed answers. It felt like I was always one step behind. I didn't know who I was dealing with, what their intentions were, nothing.

"Yes," Gwen whispered the word, breaking into another sob. "We were friends."

"Was she one of the nurses who treated—"

"Yes," Gwen repeated. "Sarah. Her name is Sarah. She was involved. She was one of the emergency teams who initially helped Vasiliev when he came in and prepped him for surgery. She saw Devora when she came in as well. She specialized in werewolves and werecats."

Her shaky breath rattled me to the core as I recognized the sound as something I had done before. It was what I did when I knew I needed to focus, even as the world crumbled around me.

"Gwen, what do you want to do?" I knew she was already considering her next move. She was smart enough to know to find Everett to find me. She was smart enough to know she couldn't go back to her home. When she didn't answer, I grabbed her arm, probably more roughly than I should have, and yanked her to pay attention to me. "Gwen, what do you want to do? What's your endgame here?"

When Heath tried to comment before my sister could answer, I waved a hand at him, stopping him from interrupting.

When she looked up, I saw resolve again in her eyes.

"I want to see them fall. We knew killing Alpha Vasiliev would only take out one problem, but his entire inner circle of werewolves…they're all just as bad. We were hoping the infighting after he died would destroy the pack from the inside, but…"

"But what?" I snapped. "We are beyond the point where you needed to tell me fucking everything."

"We…we recorded a full interview from Devora. She said it all. I was there. We didn't know what we were going to do about it because the hospital had already made it clear they wouldn't let us take it to the Tribunal. We're neutral. I've never worked at a hospital where we didn't report abuse, but Mygi Hospital is set on remaining neutral. They won't report *anything*."

"That doesn't answer my question, sis," I growled softly. "Did any of you think this through?"

"No," she admitted softly. "We were thinking about leaking the video, hoping someone would deal with it. Then he came in, attacked by one of his pack. He came in, and we…we were so mad, Jacky. We were so angry, and I was in the right place to do something about it. Why hope someone else can fix it when you have the chance?" The desperate look on her face was seeking validation I wasn't sure I could give her. Not yet, although I wanted to. My heart raced as I considered what I would have done in her shoes. Possibly the same thing if I had a group of people around me who felt the same.

But murdering someone on the operating table was a line I wasn't sure I was willing to cross. Taking justice into my own hands was a terrifying thought.

"And how do you feel now that people are dying?" Heath asked, obviously bordering on anger. The hint of a growl in his words and the lockdown on his scent was what gave him away. It seemed like a reflex to external problems, that quirky ability he had.

My sister summoned a lot of strength at that moment, looked up, and glared at Heath, her hazel eyes catching the light from her cell phone.

"Alpha Vasiliev didn't deserve another day on this planet. If I have to die for that, then so be it. I'll die knowing he's gone and can't hurt anyone else. If I can expose that entire pack before I die, even better."

"Well, obviously the Russians know what the hospital doesn't want them to know," I finally said, trying to put the thoughts out of my head. I wanted to focus on my sister's safety, not the moral quandary of her decision to murder the werewolf Alpha. I would have plenty of time to battle myself over it once everything settled down.

"Yeah," Heath agreed. "We need to stop chatting and think about our next move. You said you have video of Devora's account somewhere? That's good. We can use that. For a long time, we've only had whispers of what might be going on in Russia. We knew it was bad, but we had no idea he was..." Heath growled. "Fuck, I could kill him myself, but..."

"Politics," I murmured, knowing what he was trying to overcome.

"See? Even now, you're both more worried about the political fallout than doing what's right," Gwen snapped as she pushed herself to her feet. "My friend is dead, but I promise you, she didn't care about the politics, not when we had Devora in our care. She wanted to do this just as much as I did. And you two...Jacky, I never expected you to care about politics. What's more important? Politics or the lives of women?"

"Don't you dare," I hissed softly, looking up at her.

"We didn't *know*," Heath snarled. "We had no idea what he was doing to his females. We knew there were some isolated cases, but for all we knew, those could have been from natural pack fighting. We knew Vasiliev had issues, but we didn't know...No one would talk to us..." Heath dropped her cell phone and stomped off, but he didn't leave. The distinct sound of each of his footsteps echoed in the room as he paced. When it stopped, he filled the silence. "You could have sent the video to any werewolf in America, hospital be damned. Who was going to punish you more than for murdering a man? We would have pushed the issue, done *something*. You didn't even give us a chance, and now we're going to see dead bodies who didn't need to die."

"I did what I had to!" Gwen yelled across the room. "Everyone told me he could do whatever he wanted because he was the Alpha! The hospital was adamant that nothing we said was going to work. That no one had the authority."

"And that makes you ignorant," Heath roared back. "The deaths of a lot of people could be on your hands before the end of this. The hospital played you to keep you quiet, so they could maintain their impartial nature."

"I am not some ignorant child—"

"You look like one from where I'm standing."

I closed my eyes, trying to focus. Now, I understood. Heath was angry because he hadn't know what was going on in Russia. He felt guilty, and I was certain when this got out, lots of people would join him. He also didn't like the undercurrent of blame my sister was giving off. I knew Heath. He would have never tolerated the abuse of those females if he had really known what caused it. Never. He would have thrown himself into a battle he'd lose if he had known the true extent of the problem. If he could have helped, he would have.

My sister was carrying a lot of anger, as well. Anger no one had stopped Vasiliev before, and maybe because Heath was right. She could have broken hospital rules a little earlier and got the video out there. That could have stopped people from dying, like her friend, maybe even Devora, since the NAWC would have stepped in and taken custody of the female before the Russians could silence her.

I leaned on the wall, my mind trying to pick it apart. Going to my family for help was out of the question. I couldn't drag Hasan into this without getting him and me into serious trouble with the Tribunal. This wasn't a werecat issue. It was mine because Gwen was my human family.

Russian werewolves, Mygi Hospital, the North American Werewolf Council, my sister, me, Heath—so many things to consider, and I was getting lost in it all.

"Why don't you just admit it?" Gwen finally said, breaking through my thoughts. I had tuned them out and lost track of their argument. "You're only mad because someone called you out, and you're trying to cover your tracks. It's easy to say you would do something in hindsight when the job is already done. It's the politician's response. A lawyer's idea of a defense. It might hold weight in a courtroom, but real people don't believe you and never will."

"I do," I whispered. "I believe him."

Heath chuckled at my sister's shocked face.

"Jacky—" Gwen tried to speak, but I shook my head.

"It doesn't matter. I'm tired, and we have no plan. Someone is dead, and we're too busy arguing with each other." I drummed my fingers on the wood floor. "Heath, if we can get hold of the video, do you think we could send it to someone?"

"I know we could. It wouldn't be hard for me to get it to the Tribunal, actually. Or we can use Gwen's name to send it in to cover up you and me getting too involved. There are lots of options here."

"Good. I'm going to call the hospital. Sis? I need their number."

"Why?" she asked, reaching for her phone.

"I need to talk to them. While I'm doing that, Heath,

do you think you can grill my sister about where we might find it?"

"I can do that. Jacky, are you sure you want to expose yourself to the hospital?"

"Yeah. I need to know at least one side is taken care of."

My sister rambled out a number to her superior, and I punched it into my phone as I walked out of the room, then out the back of the house again.

As it rang, I considered what I would say.

"This is Doctor Jacobs. May I know who is calling?" He sounded like an older gentleman or maybe just a tired man—someone who desperately wanted a nap.

"Hello, I'm Jacqueline, daughter of Hasan. I'm calling to speak about Doctor Duray to someone in charge."

"Oh my God," he said softly. "I..."

"Look, I don't have time to explain. I need to talk to someone in charge."

"Is it true? Are you really her sister?" the man asked as though he hadn't heard what I said.

"I'm her twin. Give me to someone in charge."

"I'll transfer you," he said quickly, and I was put on hold. The line reconnected quickly.

"You call at the worst times, you werecats," a new man said, power exuding from his voice. "It's very early in the morning."

I hadn't been paying attention to the time. It hadn't even crossed my mind it was probably nearing sunrise.

"Do you want me to apologize?" I asked softly. "If so, I'm sorry."

"It's fine. I know why you're calling, Jacqueline, daughter of Hasan. Your sister."

"That's right."

"Do you know where she is?" He seemed curious.

"Yup."

"Ah, so she somehow reached out to you. I'm going to assume you don't care what she did, and you want to protect her. Honorable. There's no reason for you to ask for what you want, I'm pretty sure I can guess. You don't want her implicated in the death of Alpha Vasiliev and punished accordingly. We have been performing interviews with everyone who came into contact with the Russian werewolves, including the rest of her surgery team. She'll be given the same punishment as the rest of them."

"And what's that?" My hand tightened on the cell phone as I began to worry.

"She'll never work in the medical field again."

"You won't have her executed?" I practically lost my balance and fell, I was so relieved. Stumbling, I leaned against the side of the house for a sense of stability.

"Of course not. That would expose us as having a less than perfect record. We can't allow that at Mygi. See our self-interest is in line with your needs. Also, I have no intention of upsetting the daughter of a Tribunal member by killing her human family. If we had known she was your family before we hired her, we wouldn't have brought her on. That's playing with fire and leads to possibly having political ties we don't desire."

I wanted to laugh, an insane bubble rising, I could

barely resist. Something felt comical about this entire conversation.

"So, you...you don't have any intention of hurting her?"

"None at all," he said warmly. "She'll be quietly moved out of the area and told to never try to find work in medicine again. Her life will be ruined, and she'll no longer have a career, but that's a fair trade for what she did."

"What do you think of what she did?" I didn't know why, but I wanted this man's opinion. He was willing to let my sister walk for murder.

"I'm upset because if it gets out, the reputation of the hospital is ruined, but I understand healers can sometimes get wrapped up in their moral righteousness," he said with patience that reminded me of Hasan. "We have this system in place for a reason."

"I just realized, I never caught your name." I had no idea who I was talking to.

"My apologies. I'm Director Johansson. For posterity, since I know you are a werecat, I'm an Immortal," he answered.

"What type of immortal?" Every supernatural was immortal.

"An Immortal." When I didn't respond, I could hear his realization I wasn't getting it. "Ah, you don't understand. My kind, we're just called Immortals. We're humans who don't die. Nothing more, nothing less."

"That's very interesting."

"Hmm, yes. Most never meet one of our kind, and many around me don't understand what I am, but that's not the topic at hand. Is there anything you would like to discuss beyond the fate of your sister?"

I considered that. I had no idea what the agenda would be for an Immortal. Was he like the fae, always making deals and bargains? Or was he more like humans and witches, with a moral code of his own? I didn't know what I was talking to now, and my desperation about Gwen's situation had distracted me when I had started this phone call. Now, I was more wary.

"How would the Russian werewolves find out who was involved with Alpha Vasiliev's care?" I asked. "Has the hospital told anyone?"

"No," he said quickly. "We haven't. We don't intend to, but we have a missing ER nurse."

"I heard," I whispered. I didn't confirm the girl's death. I didn't know this Director Johansson and didn't want him to know exactly what I knew. "She would know."

"Yes, and that makes this world very dangerous for your sister. Jacqueline, it was nice of you to call, and I'm glad you reached out. I'm sorry I can't help more if I wish to maintain the hospital's neutrality in these stressful times. If you need care, please feel comfortable knowing you can come to us at any time. It's my hospital's privilege to serve the family of Hasan and all werecats."

"Have a good morning," I replied, then hung up, sighing. The hospital was out of the way. For a moment, I was relieved. Hopefully, Director Johansson was trustworthy, and I could forget about the hospital while dealing with the werewolves.

As I walked back inside, glad for that news, I heard Heath and my sister continuing their conversation.

"She's good, most of the time. She's had trouble, but I think she's good," Heath was saying.

Stopping at the door, I listened, knowing Heath was talking about me.

"Trouble," Gwen mumbled. "She's always been good at finding it."

"Well, she didn't find it this time. You gave it to her," he said with a sharp tone, only dulled by a touch of humor. "I've seen her in troubling situations a few times, you know. She's only gone looking for it once, and it was sanctioned by her family. We went to Washington to investigate some missing and dead werecats and werewolves. Most of the time, trouble finds her."

I walked in, smiling at the way Heath tried to defend me.

"You weren't telling that story right," I commented, putting my phone in my pocket. "I went to investigate two dead werecats, and I needed you to introduce me to a werewolf Alpha in Seattle, so I could get information. Then we learned about the missing werewolves. Whatever happened to the one who survived?"

"He's recovered as much as he can," Heath said softly, watching me walk across the room to lean on the far wall, away from both of them. "He emailed me once to say thank you, then disappeared into his pack to continue healing." He shifted his weight on his legs, his eyes never leaving me. "How did the call to the hospital go?"

"Good. Director Johansson spoke to me. He knows what his staff did, but it's not going to be a death sentence. Gwen, you'll never practice medicine again, but he has to protect the reputation of the hospital, so he's not going to report you to the Tribunal, the Russian werewolves, or anyone else. Apparently, this has happened before, and this is the hospital's typical response." Her eyes went wider as I explained the outcome of the phone call. Without giving her the opportunity to comment, I continued. "This does a couple of good things for us."

"Yes, it does," Heath agreed. "And we can talk in the car about all of them. Gwen told me where the USB was hidden, and we need to go get it."

Nodding, I followed him out of the house, noticing how quiet my sister was, but didn't let it worry me.

I just told her she has no future in her career. She's going to need a moment to process that.

16

CHAPTER SIXTEEN

"So, the Director wanting to keep the hospital out of it means the Russians only know what they can theorize or get out of the nurse," I explained further as Heath started the car. "They might not have any solid proof of Gwen's or anyone else's involvement in the death of Alpha Vasiliev. Publicly, it's still a surgery gone wrong and hopefully, will remain that way."

"Strange, because if they did have proof, thanks to Sarah, why haven't they taken it public?" Heath hummed as he started down the long dirt drive. "They could go public and get the hospital to hand over the rest of the staff, including calling your sister in to stand trial in front of the Tribunal."

"Well, if we go public with the pack's crimes before they go public with Alpha Vasiliev's murder, we can swing the Tribunal in our favor." I leaned back in my seat, trying to relax. "Let's just get this USB, then go from there. I bet the werewolves don't know the death wasn't accidental, which we can use. No one will ever have to know."

"What about avenging the death of my friend?" Gwen asked. "Are we going to forget those werewolves killed her?"

"No, we won't forget," I answered, only somewhat pissed off my sister needed to nail that morality sword into my back. Of course, I wouldn't forget about the death of an innocent human nurse. Just like I wouldn't forget the death of Devora or countless other female werewolves at the hands of this pack.

"There's not much we can do about it yet," Heath said. "We don't know where the Russians are staying in the United States; no one does. From the sound of it, the werewolves in the area didn't even know how many are here. We also don't have nearly enough of a force to go against them. Not everything can happen right now." Heath looked around at us as he stopped at the end of the drive. "Let's do this one step at a time. We're talking about exposing the Russian werewolf pack for the very criminals everyone has believed they are for years. Step one is getting our evidence. If we can send it in, Gwen never needs to have her memories read by the Tribunal, and they never need to know she killed Alpha Vasiliev. Step two is rounding up the group. We need to crush the pack completely, but at that point, neither of you should be involved. Okay? We'll leave that last part up to the Tribunal werewolves. They'll be forced into action by the public outcry of the Russian's behavior."

"Agreed," I said, nodding. I could accept that. Doing

my part, then letting others more capable finish it was how these things were supposed to work.

"Fine," Gwen said tightly.

Heath punched in an address my sister must have told him and started driving.

"Tell Jacky what you told me," he ordered as we got onto the dark road. The long night felt like it would never end.

I had been at his dinner table the evening before. We had been laughing, and Landon had been opening up to me. Neither of us had expected a two-hour drive to Dallas, a five-hour flight to Rochester, or the last four hours going back and forth with my sister of all people.

Dawn should be in another couple of hours. Right?

"Sarah hid the USB at a hospital safehouse, just in case. Some of the staff volunteer to maintain them instead of doing other jobs. I have an inactive area of medicine when it comes to supernaturals, so I volunteer in the ER. Some doctors volunteer to travel to see patients who pay high prices. Some volunteer to help Mygi Pharmaceuticals. She picked safehouse duty."

"I didn't know the hospital and the pharmaceutical company worked together," Heath said softly. "Didn't Mygi Pharma get into a lot of trouble last summer?"

"They did," she answered.

I looked back at her, frowning. I had only heard of the pharmaceutical company in passing from Hasan and could barely remember what he had said. I didn't move when she gave me a confused look.

"Tell me more, I'm curious," I said with no preamble. "Hasan doesn't tell me about the stuff he sees as a member of the Tribunal, and I don't follow supernatural news."

"From my meager information on the relationship, they started together, then separated about three decades ago. Only recently, the board of the hospital took the pharmaceutical company over again because of the trouble Mygi Pharma got into last year," she explained. "Something about illegal experimentation. I don't know much more. Sorry, sis."

"Heath, what do you know?" I asked, looking at him for more.

"They never went public with a lot of the information. The Tribunal and some of their people handled the entire mess. A lot of people went to prison. Not that we can trust the prison in Arizona to keep them there, considering there was a major outbreak a year and a half ago."

"What?" I sputtered. "How did I not hear about that?"

"Right after, you and I were in Washington, dealing with vampires, and we didn't know each other very well. I think I assumed your family told you, and even when I realized you didn't know, it's not exactly a conversation one has over a beer," he said, smiling at the end. "Do you want me to keep you up to date on supernatural news?"

"I don't know." I shrugged. "I didn't even know there was a supernatural prison," I mumbled, looking out my window. "I really need to start learning about this stuff, don't I?"

"Yes," Gwen said, sounding half amazed. "I mean, you've been a werecat for twelve years, and you're the 'daughter' of a Tribunal member. How do you not know there's a prison?"

"The same way I didn't know there was a hospital until February. I never asked and never needed to know," I retorted.

"And no one in your new family thought to tell you?"

I didn't respond as my mind came up with an answer.

I wouldn't have let them tell me if they tried. And for a long time, they wouldn't have tried.

"Jacky likes living a simple life with very little to complicate it," Heath said pragmatically. "It's admirable how well she stays out of the way in her corner of the world until someone drops trouble on her."

"Seems foolish," my sister mumbled, not directed at anyone.

Holding up a hand to keep Heath from responding, he nodded and focused on the road. It wasn't an argument I wanted to have while we were still in the middle of this Russian werewolf mess.

"So, she stashed the USB with Devora's recording at a safehouse," I said, trying to take the conversation back to the task at hand.

"Yes. She installed a safe in one, and it was always our idea if we needed to hide, we would go there," she said.

"Well, damn." I rubbed my face. "Heath—"

"I'm thinking the same thing," he said softly. "If they took Sarah, then they either had her followed, or they were able to nab her from the hospital. I don't know the circumstances, but I'm certain they tortured her for information once they had her. They wouldn't have killed her without getting every piece of information they could get out of her."

My stomach twisted.

"How can you talk about it so casually?" Gwen sounded as ill as I felt.

"Because it's just a part of our life," I answered. "I've been beaten and starved by Hasan's enemies, other werecats. We've been hunted by vampires who were addicted to getting what's called a death high, and their master who was trying to cover up his negligence. Heath's family has been torn apart and hurt by ambition. We're not being casual. We're being realistic."

Lani's face flashed in my mind. Those damn vampires in Washington. Emma and her mate, Dean, and Richard —they had all done whatever necessary to further their own goals. These werewolves would be no different. If they saw the opportunity to get information, they would take it.

We drove in silence for a long time until the GPS said only ten more minutes until our destination.

"The Russians will know about this place," I said softly.

"Yeah," Heath agreed. "We can only hope we're here first, or they've already left. If I see any evidence of them, I'm not stopping, and we'll find another way to get this done."

"We don't have another way," I countered. "You said it earlier. We're trying to avoid making Gwen testify in front of the Tribunal."

"Why?" Gwen asked from the back, her voice soft and a little weak.

"They'll search your memories to read the truthfulness of your testimony. They'll discover what you did to Alpha Vasiliev," Heath clarified. "They don't do it often if they have enough witnesses, but you'll be speaking out against an entire pack, and you're Jacky's sister. They could see you as trying to ruin a strong werewolf pack in the name of the werecats. We don't need those sorts of conversations coming up."

"Okay, so we *have* to get a copy of Devora's information," she said, sounding stronger. "I get it. Can't go and make more trouble."

"No, Gwen, we can't go make more trouble," I growled back at her. "Can you stop implying we're terrible people because we're looking at the big picture here? It's fucking frustrating. We agree with you. Alpha Vasiliev was a monster who needed to die. We're going to protect you. We agree the crimes of his pack need to be exposed, so more werewolves aren't abused and hurt. We're trying to make that happen. But all of that is worthless if they think this is a werecat plot against the Russian werewolf pack to weaken the werewolves globally. If they think you acted for me or I'm defending you for werecat interests, we're screwed. They won't care about the Russian pack. They'll care about how you killed an Alpha, regardless of the reasons, and how I'm Hasan's daughter, and I'm protecting you from punishment."

"You used to be for justice, no matter the costs," she whispered. "Getting in fights and taking the fall, but always fighting for what you believed in."

I winced. She was right. When I was helping Carey, the ramifications of my decisions had been an afterthought. Now, all I could think about were the ramifications. I wanted to do this right. What was so wrong with trying to do a good thing without hurting the people around me?

Why do I feel like I've sold out?

I couldn't bring myself to speak after that as Heath pulled up to the small house outside of Rochester. At this point, I felt like I had driven around the entire damn city.

"There are no other cars here," I pointed out softly. "Heath, are you okay going first? You have the best nose."

"Definitely." He cut the engine and jumped out of the car, with Gwen and I following much slower. He was ten feet from the car by the time she and I were closing our doors. I grabbed her elbow and kept her at my side, trying to see everything around us. The lightest glow of the coming dawn was finally hitting the eastern sky.

He was at the door before us, where he froze.

I slowed and held Gwen to stop with me as I watched him sniff the air.

"Heath?"

"They've been here," he whispered. "Werewolves."

"How many?" I sniffed the air, but if this was an old scent, there was a chance I wasn't going to pick it up. "I'm not smelling anything."

"I didn't notice it until I caught it on the door," he replied. "The wind would have blown their scents away, but one...no, two of them touched the door. There are no signs of forced entry, though."

"Do you think it's safe?" I asked. I was glad my sister was waiting in silence, trusting us to do this, to judge the situation.

"I don't know, but I'm going in." He instinctively reached for something, then growled softly. "Should have brought a gun."

"Yeah, I'm thinking the same thing," I mumbled, looking around, dreading the possibility I caught glowing eyes in the surrounding darkness. To Gwen, it was probably still pitch black except for the glow of light in the safehouse, and even in the lightest glow of dawn, it was pretty dark. My ability to see at night was damn good, but a good supernatural would know how to hide, using the deep shadows of the night.

He opened the door and stepped in, a growl slipping through his lips.

"I smell blood," he explained, disappearing from view.

Gwen and I followed, my sister grabbing me, locking our arms together instead of my pulling her around.

"Shit," Heath snarled. "There's no one here alive," he called softly.

"What?" Gwen's voice jumped an octave and cracked.

I didn't react in time. My sister broke from my grasp and ran, letting me play catch up. The scent of blood hit my nose as I passed through the threshold, which opened up into a spacious living room, with the kitchen on the other side of the room. Heath stood in the kitchen, looking down at something behind the counters. I caught up to Gwen and stopped her from getting to his side.

"Jacky—"

"Heath, how?" I demanded. I wanted to know what I was about to show my sister.

"Clean," he whispered. "Gunshot...two to the chest."

I released her, letting her go into the kitchen and look down at the body.

"Oh, no," she cried out, falling to her knees. "This was...this was the anesthesiologist. Um...His name is..."

"Breathe," I whispered gently. "Take a deep breath."

She did, her shoulders jerking.

"His name was Carlton," she finally said. "If he's here...his car should be here..."

"The werewolves probably stole it," Heath said, looking around the kitchen. "There aren't any keys anywhere, but I can smell them in here. They probably came in while he was doing something and shot him before he had a chance to be afraid, then took his belongings."

"Gwen, where did Sarah hide the USB?" I asked. "I can let someone at the hospital know we found Carlton here, but I want us to get out of here as quickly as possible. I'm sorry. I know it's a rush, and you don't have any time to grieve, but we have to keep moving."

She nodded, and I helped her back to her feet, trying not to feel like an asshole. It wasn't easy telling her she couldn't do more for him or stay to say goodbye, but it was necessary.

She led the way in silence toward a back room and in the bedroom, pulled back a rug.

"The house is a cover," she mumbled, gesturing at the hatch she uncovered. "This is the real safe house. It would be down here. It's a typical bunker."

"Let's go," I said softly. "Heath, come in here and keep watch?" I didn't need to raise my voice. A second later, my werewolf appeared at the door and nodded.

I went down into the bunker first and stood to the side, taking it all in. The hospital took the safety of its staff seriously. Gwen went through a door into another room of the bunker, and I heard the mechanical noise of a safe pop open. A minute later, she was back, holding a bag.

"I don't know which one it is," she said, opening the bag to reveal several USBs. "I don't understand why there are so many."

I had the sneaking suspicion this Sarah, an innocent ER nurse, was doing more than helping female werewolves from Russia. I had a gut feeling whatever was on all of those USBs could hurt a lot of people.

"I'll carry them, and we'll figure it out. My go-bag has a laptop, and I'm certain Heath was smart enough to bring one as well."

Gwen nodded slowly and handed me the bag. I shook my head as I looked at the dozens of USBs. This had been stupid. Sarah might have felt she was saving a lot of people, but this was plain stupid.

We headed back up where Heath waited patiently. His eyes narrowed on the bag in my hands. I quickly showed him the contents before walking past him.

We moved quickly and got outside, heading directly for our car in silence. We had what we needed, and it was time to go. A conversation could wait.

17

CHAPTER SEVENTEEN

None of us were expecting a black sedan to come down the drive. We ran for the car, and I was able to shove Gwen into the car with the bag as the car got closer, pushing her head down, so her face was obscured by her hair.

"This is bad," I murmured.

"Definitely," Heath agreed, nodding to his left.

I glanced in that direction and saw a large werewolf walk out from the trees. It had been downwind of us, no way of us catching its scent, but it probably caught ours. I cursed under my breath.

"They had a watch on the building we missed. No way we would have known without risking one of us going into the woods, which we didn't have time to do. Very effective." I stood beside Heath, who locked the car, using the key fob. My sister sank into her seat, but the windows weren't tinted enough to block someone from seeing her face.

"They knew someone would come, eventually.

There's probably a second guy out there with a fucking phone who made the call," he agreed. "We don't have time to drive off, and I don't want to risk them opening fire on us. This thing isn't bulletproof, and we have no firepower."

"Agreed."

The sedan stopped with the driver's side toward us. Heath didn't move from my side. The driver stayed in the car, but on the far side of the car, both doors opened, and two large men got out, looking over the roof at us. I used my body to shield Gwen from their view.

"Doctor Duray," one greeted with a nod, directed at me for some reason. I nearly smiled. He thought I was Gwen. A thick Russian accent made it clear we were dealing with the very werewolves we didn't want to be. He wore a suit, a small indicator this was a werewolf with money or power, probably both. "And a werewolf." He sniffed the air and frowned. "Is that a werecat in the car? Did you convince some werecat to protect you? Foolish."

"What do you want, Alexei?" Heath demanded. Now I knew a name for the werewolf in front of me. The other one bared his teeth at Heath's words, but it was the first one who spoke again.

"You know me?" He seemed confused, looking at Heath with new interest.

"You're the fourth of the Russian werewolf pack. What you're doing in Minnesota, I don't know, but I know your name and face, yes," Heath answered.

"How do you know me?" Now there was distrust on Alexei's face. Fourth in the Russian werewolf pack.

Would he know North American werewolves by face and name? How did Heath know who he was?

"That's not the question you should be asking," Heath whispered in a cool voice that made me concerned.

Alexei's eyes narrowed as he took in Heath, then flicked back to me, and his nostrils flared.

"You aren't the doctor…" he realized.

He must have realized I'm not the human scented one. Damn, so much for playing that ruse. Good at a glance, but I should have figured it wouldn't have held up for long.

"No, I'm not," I confirmed. There was no point in lying, they would have caught that immediately.

"How does a werecat take the face of a human?"

"That's for me to know." I wasn't going to confirm a relationship with Gwen. Not yet, anyway.

A click made me glance at the other werewolf, who took a picture of Heath and me, his phone still in position. There was nothing I could have done to stop it, so I didn't let it bother me. He said something in Russian, a language I hadn't attempted to learn yet, then Alexei nodded.

"Well, we'll know who you are soon enough."

"That's fine," I said, shrugging. My mind started kicking into high gear. We needed to leave, which meant we needed to convince these guys to let us do that without bloodshed. "But since there's only a few of you, I think we're going to get in this car and drive away, okay?" I smiled. "Because even with that wolf in the woods, his partner, and you three, all in human form, you can't beat me. I shift a lot faster than you."

"We have guns," he growled, definitely catching my overconfident threat.

"Good for you," I purred. "But killing me won't work in your best interests."

The second werewolf started talking again, showing his phone screen to Alexei, whose eyes went wide. The text must have quickly confirmed who Heath and I were, which was an interesting turn of events. Whoever they were talking to must have recognized our faces.

That's a horrifying problem to consider another time. Werewolf packs making it a priority to know who we are. Great.

"Tell whoever you're talking to, attacking a daughter of Hasan won't work in your favor," I growled as Alexei looked up, his eyes showing me just how furious he was. "Doctor Duray is in my care, and you can ask some of the werewolves on this continent how well it goes when someone tries to take away what's *mine*."

"We're not leaving here without her," Alexei growled. He reached beneath his blazer and pulled out a small handgun. "You, werecat, don't get to shove your nose into werewolf affairs. I don't care who you are."

"Put the gun away, Alexei," Heath said, maintaining a calm approach. "Don't ask for trouble. Your pack will suffer for it."

"Don't tell me what my pack needs. We need that doctor. Let her out of the car and give her to me."

I flicked a glance at Heath, then stepped out of the way of the door.

"Gwen, I'm going to open the door and let you out," I said, a plan coming together. I opened the door, and she came out slowly, lifting her head to see Alexei. I watched his eyes narrow.

"How is this possible?" he asked, looking between us.

"You're right. As a werecat, I can't get into your affairs, but as Doctor Duray's twin sister, there's no such limit to my actions. Gwen, get back in the—"

"Then both of you will come with us," Alexei ordered, the gun in his hand going to my sister. "Now."

I looked at Heath, wishing I could talk to him openly. Since I was in human form, I couldn't telepathically talk to him. *There's no getting out of this, Heath. They aren't going to let us drive away. This is going to get bloody.* That was what I wanted to say.

By the look on his face, I didn't need to say the words. He knew. He had probably figured it since the beginning but, like me, had been trying to find another way—any other way.

"Fine," I agreed, nodding, and lifted both my hands. "Gwen, stay beside me."

"Okay," my sister murmured, sticking to my side.

Alexei gestured for us to walk around the car and come closer, so I walked. Out of the corner of my eye, I saw the werewolf draw closer, another coming out of the woods behind it.

Targets. I needed to know all the targets.

Alexei's comrade was typing on his phone with one hand and had his other hand on a gun at his waist. As I walked, he put the phone away and pulled his gun out, turning it on Heath.

"Don't shoot him," I pleaded softly. "That will get you in trouble with the North American Werewolf Council."

"We'll only shoot him if you try something or he does," Alexei said with a bite. "So, don't try anything."

The werewolves were drawing closer. Alexei grabbed one of my arms and was about to spin when I looked at Heath one more time.

He didn't blink.

"RUN!" I screamed at my sister as I started to move.

In a flurry of action, I twisted my hand from Alexei's grasp and used my other hand to grab the gun by the barrel, shoving it, so it was pointed away from me.

A second later, two gunshots went off. When there was no scream, I prayed that meant no one was hit. My hand burned from the heat of the metal in my hand, but I didn't stop. I kneed Alexei in the groin, causing him to drop the gun. Before he could recover, I grabbed his head on each side and twisted hard.

A snap told me he was down for the count.

I dove for the gun he'd dropped as a werewolf jumped on me, teeth snapping dangerously close to my neck. I held off the teeth as I reached for the gun. Those teeth grazed my cheek as I struggled. My fingers grazed the gun, but my left arm was beginning to tire. The wolf was using its body weight to hold me down. A healthy werewolf could weigh over two hundred and fifty pounds, and some of the biggest could reach four hundred.

A shot rang out, and the wolf over me sagged. Blood began to pour over my face, and I shoved the wolf off me to see Gwen shaking, holding a gun.

I rushed to my feet and gently took it from her. Surveying the area quickly, I saw Heath and someone I didn't recognize fighting in human form over another gun. Alexei's friend was already dead on the ground.

"Where's the last werewolf?" I asked quickly. "Gwen, there were two. Did you see where the last one went?"

"No," she said, shaking her head quickly. "I didn't...I don't know. I have no idea."

"Fuck. Go get in the car and lock the door. I'm going to help Heath."

She nodded and ran for our car. I ran for Heath and his opponent, grabbing the enemy by the back of the shirt and pushing the gun into his spine. Heath didn't realize I was there immediately and gave the werewolf a mean right hook.

"Heath! I'm right here. Be careful," I ordered, looking around the now sagging werewolf.

"Where's the other one?" he asked, coming to his senses. He took in the bodies, and his grey-blue eyes narrowed. "Where's the last one?"

"I don't know, but we need to get out of here. We need to go right now. He probably realized it was a losing fight and went to call for backup."

"Shit." Heath reached out and checked the pulse of the one I was trying to hold up now. "This one is still alive. Should we take him?"

"Yeah. Let's see what they have in their car and hope there's something we can use." I dropped the unconscious werewolf and nodded to the black sedan. "They owe it to us for this fucking bullshit."

Heath nodded, but confusion flashed over his face. "They should have let us go."

"What do you think is going on?"

"They're desperate for your sister. Alexei should have backed off with you and me here. If they had been planning on violence, they would have brought more wolves, but obviously, they just wanted to grab your sister and go." Heath went to the black sedan's driver seat and popped the trunk while I went to a back door and opened it to search the back seat.

"I'm certain they'll be more willing to negotiate once they catch wind of this little scuffle," I said in a huff. "Now they know we're involved, they'll have to. Right? Maybe we can get some fucking answers."

"Hopefully," he agreed. "Found something. They have handcuffs and other shit. Definitely meant for torture and taking captives. They definitely meant your sister harm."

"Didn't need that confirmed," I said with a snap. Heath looked up at me, his gaze severe. "Sorry. This isn't your fault."

"It's been a long night," he whispered. "I understand. Just don't take it out on me. I'm in the middle of this with you."

We handcuffed the werewolf and threw him into our own trunk, which he almost didn't fit in. I checked his pockets and found a cellphone, leaving it behind before closing the trunk on the werewolf. They had my sister's number and could call that if they wanted to talk to anyone. I wasn't going to take a phone I knew they could track. I could only hope they hadn't figured out a way to track my sister's.

"I'm getting the guns," Heath said while I went to check on Gwen again.

"Cool." I opened the back door and slid in beside her. "Sis, answer me truthfully. Were you bitten?"

"No." She looked over her body, shaking her head. "I took cover when it started, then I saw you fighting off that werewolf, grabbed a gun near me, and—"

"That's all I need to know." I was out of the car before she could continue talking and looked for Heath. "We ready?"

"Come help me."

I couldn't see him. I went around the car and saw him checking over the weapons we were taking.

"They weren't using silver," he explained quickly. "They weren't expecting anyone but your sister, which was a good thing, but it's not going to help us."

"Are you really checking all of them before we go? Heath—"

"I wanted to see what we had." He was shoving clips back into guns and held one out to me. "Take it. Keep it on you. It won't kill a werewolf unless you hit the head—"

"And maybe not even then," I muttered. There were humans who could survive a bullet to the head. Crazier shit happened.

"Exactly, but they might have the stopping power to protect us. If we run into any more of them, they might think we're using silver." Before I could step back and head to my side of the car, Heath grabbed me. "Jacky, this is going to get uglier before it gets better. They aren't telling anyone here what they're doing. I promise you, right now, the North American Werewolf Council and the Tribunal have no idea what the Russians are doing."

"I know. I could change that. I could tell Hasan right now what's going on."

"Do you want to?" Heath narrowed his eyes, searching for something, but I wasn't sure what.

"We'll talk about our options in the car. They know you and I are a part of this now. That changes everything."

"It does," he agreed.

18

CHAPTER EIGHTEEN

We drove away from the safehouse, leaving the bodies and the black sedan. My sister was quiet in the back, probably trying to come to terms with how this entire situation was shaking out. I had been there before, with Carey. I had moments where I stopped and was in awe of the violence around me. I was focused on my goal, but I wondered how my life had turned in that direction. One day, I had been innocently living in Texas and running a tiny dive bar with a couple of pool tables. The next day, I was killing werewolves for trying to take someone from me. It took time to process through that, even though it was also a time of split decisions and deciding what convictions I held most dear.

Twenty minutes into the drive, she finally opened up.

"I shot him," she whispered into the silence that surrounded us.

"Yeah, you did. Thank you. You probably saved my life." I tried to sound strong. I was becoming used to the violence, becoming hard to it. This was the world, and I had a place in it. I could help her adjust to her new position.

"I killed him."

"He's the second person you killed," I pointed out, swallowing a lump in my throat. I didn't keep count of how many people I had killed since the violence came crashing into my life.

"He is, isn't he? I didn't think..."

"You would have to kill any more?" I turned back to her. "Gwen, if you come out of this and that's the only time you have to fire a gun, you've gotten out cleaner than so many others. You dipped your toe into fighting for something you believe in, and this world is going to make you fight to the end. Supernaturals aren't like humans."

"What do you mean?" She looked up, and I saw the hollowness of her expression.

"Violence is the exception for most humans," Heath said softly. "It's the rule for supernaturals."

"Let me explain what he's trying to say. From the human perspective, a mob, mafia, or gang? Those are bad, evil, and people who join them are bad, evil...or desperate." Sighing, I tried to resist the truth for a minute, but there was no denying it. "With supernaturals...that's the normal thing. Do you know why I made a splash with supernaturals? Because I tried to be normal for so long. I didn't use my connections, actively avoiding them. I didn't band with the werecat ruling family and take power as soon as I could. I did what very few do."

"And werecats are outliers in general," Heath added.

"Werewolves are big gangs if you think about it. Rogues who live alone are the exception. It's expected to be in a pack and work for the *pack's* benefit. Vampires have nests, where they create communities that work together. Witches make covens where they combine their power to cast spells and do magics they can't do alone. Supernaturals are very community-oriented if you look at the big picture. And communities that have been together for hundreds, if not thousands of years, will kill for each other if threatened or just because it benefits them. We play with deadly forces, so even a small political move could turn violent."

"It would be corruption or an abuse of power for humans," I said, leaning my head on my seat to stare at her. "But in our world..."

"So, everyone bands together into good or bad organizations for...self-preservation, then if that's threatened, or the community is attacked, violence is always the answer."

"Yeah. I wish I could say I was better than that, sis, but I'm not. When my family went to the hospital in February, we were dealing with a band of werecats who wanted to overthrow Hasan and the rest of my family. They came into my territory, as the youngest and weakest, and wanted to use me as a bargaining chip. Things got out of control, but my family? When we got the chance, we killed every one of them. They threatened us, and we *ended* them."

"And you're okay with that?"

"What good is a family if you aren't willing to die for them? What good is loving them if you won't fight for them?" I stared into her hazel eyes. "You loved those female werewolves when they came in. I see it. You saw them, saw their pain, and how badly they were hurt. You aren't a werewolf. You're a woman, just like them. I'm certain, if I had seen them, I would have gone off the deep end, too, and killed a man."

"I'm not like the werewolves," she snapped. I should have been upset she couldn't see the similarities, but I was too glad the fire was coming back to her eyes.

"No, but the instinct is the same. The Russians feel threatened. Something is threatening to destroy the community they built that props them up. So, Gwen, think about that. You killed their leader. Now, I don't think they know it's murder. They would have shot on sight, right, Heath?"

"Yup." The ease in which he answered was impressive. "Which means they think you threaten them in a different way."

"Right," I agreed. "Probably exposing them with all the evidence needed to destroy their entire community, but we'll get to that later." I focused again on my sister. "Gwen, you will be very lucky if you only have to kill two people by the end of this. I promise you, they are willing to kill whoever is necessary. They weren't going to leave Heath alive after taking us. They just weren't going to shoot him before they secured me." I ran a hand over my face. "In the human world, exposing them and watching the world tear them apart socially is enough. In our world, if you want change, you need to be willing to fight for it. Not in a courtroom or in the media, but actually fight for it."

"You were always a fighter, Jacky," she said softly, looking away.

"Obviously, you are, too, because you pulled the trigger." I turned back to the front. "Now, let's figure out what to do next."

"Have you had any thoughts about telling your family what we're into?" Heath asked, jumping to that idea.

"Not really. I know Hasan won't be okay with this. Sadly, I think I can exploit my relation to Gwen, but he can't. He's not related to her. My humans aren't his humans. And he's Tribunal, which complicates everything."

"It could also help us out if we tell them the Russian werewolves are killing human civilians who work for the hospital."

"What do you want me to do? Call Hasan, who will then get Hisao?" I huffed. "Heath, if the Assassin rolls through the Russian pack to protect Gwen and me, werewolves around the world will be forced to retaliate Hasan's aggressive actions, even if they are justified. That's an act of war, regardless of the reason."

"Doesn't that go both ways?" My sister leaned forward. Life was back in her eyes as she put her head between the seats. "Aren't they committing an act of war against the werecats?"

"The powers that be might not agree," Heath replied, sighing. "But they also might. Jacky, we could use that. The Russian pack has murdered the hospital's staff and now tried to take you and your sister into custody."

"The hospital would need to report they believe the

Russian werewolves are killing their employees," I pointed out.

"Call the Director again. Tell him he needs to go see Carlton's dead body."

I liked the idea. We didn't have Sarah's body and no way to prove it was the Russians who did it. It was a theory and most likely right, but Carlton was right where the hospital could find him. Left there, either as a sign or a mistake.

"What are the downsides?" I asked myself, considering the possible moves. I wasn't sure when I grew adept at it, but sticky political situations were becoming easier for me to navigate. With the Russians learning I was with Gwen and related, the idea of using Gwen to expose the pack's crimes was shot. They would just claim it was werecat propaganda to destroy a healthy pack. Heath would be called a traitor to his own kind and discounted because of his connection to me.

"You were always good at this," my sister commented, leaning back again.

"Good at what?" I looked back at her in confusion.

"People," she said without elaborating.

I didn't know what to say, so I went back to looking at my phone.

"If the hospital reports they believe the Russian werewolves killed their people, the Russians come under fire and have to admit why or try to deny it. It makes everything go bad for them—"

Heath's phone started going off, jarring me hard enough to stop talking. I had been thinking out loud. He answered while he drove, and I listened in.

"Heath, just wanted to give you the heads-up the Russians just took off from a private airport in their pack jet," a male said tensely. I didn't recognize the voice. "They came in and took off before anyone could stop them to ask what the hell was going on. They haven't reached out to anyone, but it looks like this situation is finally over. Whatever the hell is going on with them is going back to Russia, and we can all sleep a little easier."

"Did they?" Heath asked rhetorically. "Because it's not over."

"What do you mean?" The suspicion was thick. "What do you know? You're in Texas. Do you have another guy willing to spy for you who knows something the North American Werewolf Council doesn't? Heath, you're well respected and have allies everywhere, but you don't have the clout you had two years ago before that shit with the werecat."

"I don't know what's safe to tell you." Heath side-eyed me, and I shook my head.

"You aren't in Texas, are you? What the fuck are you doing?"

"Helping a friend." Heath hung up. "Jacky, call the Director. There's going to be fallout, but the Russians just left the country, and that's concerning."

I was already hitting call before he finished talking. The number I called this time redirected me straight to the Director.

"I didn't expect another phone call from you," Director Johansson said. "What's wrong?"

"We found a dead human at one of your safehouses.

Gwen called him Carlton. He was part of the surgery team for Alpha Vasiliev—"

"I know," The Director said patiently. "That's what happens when people try to take the law into their own hands."

"Excuse me?" My heart thumped. "You're going to let them get away with it?"

"They called me shortly after you did. They are trying to stop this little rogue band of medical professionals from interfering in their pack. That's the pack's right. Once the team decided to kill Alpha Vasiliev, they lost my protection. If the death had been accidental, I would say something and protect them, but they asked for this trouble, and protecting them puts the hospital and me on a political side. I would have to condemn the Russian werewolf pack and let them expose the pack's secrets. I can't do that."

"Excuse me but—"

"Yes, excuse you. For decades, this hospital has been a haven for those who need care, no matter the circumstances. Your sister and others from my staff decided to breach the sacred trust the supernatural community put in us," the Director snapped with rage. It was the first emotion I had heard from him that felt honest. "And the Russians don't know they did that, but I *do,* and it's *my* hospital. I will not press charges against the Russians over any deaths for my *fired* employees. I feel the Russians are justified. On top of that, I buy the pack's silence by letting them do what they must, and they won't speak out about my remaining staff, and the hospital's neutrality is protected."

"You're a monster," I growled. A sick feeling spread through my gut.

"Funny since many can say the same thing about you and your family, and I'm not only talking about Doctor Duray," he said with an edge of cruelty. "I've treated people who have survived Hisao and people who have run afoul of Hasan. When your family came in, I put all of that aside, and we treated your family. Don't talk to me about monsters. We're *all* monsters. It just depends on what we want to be monstrous about."

He hung up on me.

The sick feeling in my gut was because I knew he was right. I had just been telling Gwen the same thing, yet my human mind still wanted to rage. But he was right.

We were all monsters when the situation called for it.

"What is Director Johansson?" Heath asked. "Maybe we can use something with his species to convince him to go our way with this."

"An Immortal," I answered. "Whatever that is."

"Ah, never mind," Heath muttered, shaking his head. "You'll never convince an Immortal to do something they don't want to."

"I didn't know the Director was supernatural," Gwen mumbled.

"He's just a human who can't or just won't die," Heath said with a sigh. "Origin unknown. They follow their own rules."

"Okay, so the hospital is a bust," I said, flipping my phone around in my hands as I bit the inside of my cheek. "I'll call Hasan. Maybe he can offer some sort of advice. I don't see another option, other than trying to negotiate with the Russians, and I don't..."

"They would make it clear they're going to keep doing everything they're doing," Heath said for me. "I don't think any of us would be okay with that."

"No, we won't," Gwen said from behind me. "They have to go down. Someone has to stop them from hurting more women."

"Even with the threat of death and only two allies left, she's not going to give up on this," I said softly.

"Sounds like someone I know," Heath commented slyly.

Narrowing my eyes on him, I hit Hasan's name in my contacts, then listened to it ring. I tried to do the mental math to figure out what time it was for him, but my brain didn't want to function. It took four rings for him to pick up. I stared out the window, wondering what he could have been doing that distracted him from his phone for that long.

"Jacqueline? What's wrong?"

I heard water in the background, a shower. The mental image came and went without scarring me for life. Hasan naked was something I had seen before. The water cut off quickly enough.

"How do you know something is wrong?" I countered. "Did I interrupt something?"

"You very rarely call me, otherwise," he parried. "And I was in the shower."

"Sorry about the timing. I'm getting better at calling more often, but...you're right. Something is wrong. Like really wrong. I don't even know where to begin wrong."

"Talk to me. We'll figure it out. Are you in danger?"

"I just killed some werewolves, so...probably."

A long silence greeted that. I looked at Heath, who shrugged. I wondered what he would do if he got this sort of call from Carey or Landon.

Hey, Dad. Just killed a man. Need some advice.

Funny enough, I couldn't imagine Landon making that phone call. He was capable. He would know exactly how to manage to hide a body or several. Carey, however, would definitely make the call.

"Hasan?" I said softly, feeling like a child for a moment. His silence was crushing, and I felt smaller by the moment.

"Where are you?" he asked. I heard something creak, but it wasn't the telltale sound of his office chair I recognized well.

"Minnesota, near Rochester."

"Who is with you?"

Shit, am I in trouble, or is he sending help?

"Heath...and my twin sister, Gwen."

"Oh, Jacky," he breathed. "What happened? Are they both okay? Is anyone hurt?"

"No one is hurt yet—"

Another phone started ringing in the car, and my sister started moving around, patting her pockets.

"It's a blocked number," she told us. Heath extended his hand, and she dropped her phone in it.

"Hasan, I'll be right back." Before he could say anything, I hung up and grabbed her phone from Heath, answering without skipping a beat.

"Jacqueline, daughter of Hasan, speaking," I greeted stiffly.

"I was expecting Doctor Duray, considering this is her phone number," a deep male voice said with a slight Russian accent. It was an attractive voice that probably made a woman's toes curl. I took a moment to be grateful I was often exposed to those sorts of men.

"She's not the one you get to negotiate with. Please introduce yourself." I didn't like that he didn't immediately give me his name. Heath kept driving back toward our little hideaway, but now his foot hit the gas as if he felt some urgency to get us into a safe place again.

"No. It won't be necessary for you to know my name yet," the werewolf said. "Tell me, is Doctor Duray related to you? You look remarkably similar."

"We're twins." I wished people would stop asking for that confirmation. I really did. It grew frustrating that every supernatural wanted to know. Were doppelgangers real, and they wanted to make sure she wasn't mine or vice versa? I had no idea, but the repetition was getting annoying.

"Ah. So, you're protected by Law. I was afraid of that, but it's also a good thing. See, you and your sister probably have something I want. Now, I heard you got into a fight with Alexei—"

"I didn't fight him. I killed him. There's a difference," I informed the werewolf. "He didn't get the chance to put up much of a fight."

"Of course. Very typical for your family. The werecat one, at least."

Why are you making that distinction?

"He tried to take my sister and me into custody. I wasn't going to allow that. He should have known better."

"He should have. He's taken recent events hard, and we weren't expecting you. I don't think it would surprise you to learn we had no idea of your relation to Doctor Duray."

"Let's go back to that thing you want," I said, not wanting to get tangled up in weird small talk. "We have several USBs. Am I going to find something on them you don't want the world to see?"

"You will. Sarah Gerber was prolific in her efforts to document things she felt were wrong. After Alpha Vasiliev died, she came to one of my packmates and offered a deal. She would keep the videos private or even destroy them if we made changes after the death of Alpha Vasiliev. She made a mistake, thinking she could dictate the terms." There was a soft chuckle on the other end. "She told us everything she could before the end, but we still couldn't find the evidence she had collected from our werewolves who were patients. Now, we can't let those get into the hands of the Tribunal."

"They don't have to," I agreed. "But you need to do something for me."

"Jacqueline, daughter of Hasan. No, Jacky Leon. Jacky, do not make the mistake of thinking you can dictate the terms. Miss Gerber told us Doctor Duray would be trying to get the videos, and we waited. Alexei didn't know we had a backup plan. He was expendable, and I didn't want him to waste my hand."

"Then what are your terms?" I asked, not liking the

deep darkness opening up in me, an abyss I would fall into. This werewolf was leading me into something.

"You love your family, obviously, since you are willing to go to such lengths to protect your sister. It's honorable, and you should do whatever you can to protect them. Any good person would do anything to protect their family. Elderly parents need strong children. Children need strong parents. Lovers need to be shielded from pain. Families are so important."

"You can't touch Hasan and..." I trailed off, my chest tightening.

"We didn't know they were also your family when we took them," he explained softly. Even soft, I heard the deadly edge, like he was a sharp sword ready to cut me in half. "So, here's the deal I am willing to make. You will give me the evidence Miss Gerber collected against my pack. You and your sister will be magically sworn to secrecy, along with Alpha Everson. Then we will give you your family back."

"And if we don't? Will you kill them?" I swallowed.

Heath sent me a hard glance and took a sharp intake of air. He was listening in. I looked back at Gwen, keeping the phone to my ear. She was the only person in the car who couldn't hear this werewolf, but she listened to me with a concentrated look on her face.

"No. We'll keep them indefinitely. As long as you have the evidence and it stays private, we'll keep your family. If you release it, then they all die. Then we'll come after you and your sister."

"Mutually assured destruction," I whispered.

"Yes. You should hurry, though. It might seem like a

long time away, but...her daughter could make a great werewolf one day. Wouldn't that be interesting? We could test the theory that genetics really do play a part in humans surviving the Change. You know, I've heard of children surviving very young. Maybe we could put *that* to the test."

My blood ran cold. My mind flicked over every possibility. We hand over everything, and I spend an eternity hating myself for only saving my own and leaving countless women to die. It wouldn't get rid of the Russian pack, knowing I'm their enemy, either. I could hold on to the evidence and stay in a cold war against this pack for years, risking their lives every day. I could release the evidence and know my family would be dead long before I could get to Russia to help them. Because he was definitely taking them to Russia. Holding hostages of this magnitude wasn't possible for werewolves outside their territory. It was too bold and too dangerous.

But sneaking them onto a plane and taking them out of the country was fucking easy.

Or I can save my family.

Option four. Don't play by the rules laid out by the Alpha and throw caution to the wind. Go to Russia and take my family back, by any means necessary, then send every one of the werewolves involved straight to hell.

"I don't know your name, werewolf." I tried to be cool as rage threatened to consume me. Not fear, though it was the smart choice. "How can I go into a bargain with someone I don't know?"

"Sergey. I was the second of the Russian werewolf pack. I am now the Alpha by unanimous decision of the inner circle. Well, not quite unanimous. There was one against me, but he's dead now. See? Expendable."

Alexei. He voted against Sergey becoming Alpha and was probably desperate. He knew he needed to please the new guy or lose his position, probably by means of brutal death by the rest of the inner circle. These Russians don't play around.

"I'll call you back after I've discussed it with my sister and Alpha Everson. Please text me a number I can reach."

"Good idea. You have seventy-two hours to make a decision. During that time, I won't touch your family. After that, I make no promises," he said with a glee that made me angrier. He thought he was winning. "Have a good day. I look forward to hearing from you."

When he hung up, I kept the phone to my ear, listening to my heartbeat, listening to Heath's. To Gwen's. The sound of our breathing became the loudest sound in the car.

"What's wrong?" Gwen asked, her voice a deafening roar.

"They have..." *Shit. I didn't ask who. I should have asked who.*

I tried to think about the conversation, replaying it. He talked by leaving clues. He had proven that early, telling me how Sarah was killed, trying to dictate the conversation. He left me clues—elderly parents, children, lovers.

"Jacky, she needs to know," Heath murmured. I knew he wouldn't say it. He would want me to deliver this blow.

"They have our parents...they have your children and Daniel. They have our *family*," I said. "If we release the videos of Devora and other werewolves Sarah interviewed, they will kill them." *Except your daughter, who they'll attempt to Change, which might happen anyway.* "For as long as we keep the videos to ourselves, they will hold our family hostage. In exchange for their freedom, we have to hand over everything Sarah collected and be sworn to secrecy, all three of us. We need to protect the pack in exchange for protecting our family."

"How? When?" Gwen yelled.

"They took them before we even saw Alexei. A backup plan. Alexei was told to grab you and encountered Heath and me. He was on the way out, anyway. If he failed, and he did, then Sergey was—"

"Fucking Sergey. He's lost his mind," Heath muttered, shaking his head. "He can't expect this to go well."

"I think he believes we'll take the deal. He's got an almost iron-tight plan," I countered. "It's our fucking family, and you heard..." I stopped, shaking my head as well, unable to believe the threat Sergey had made against my niece's life. I'd never met her, but my heart was in it—a little girl, Changed. The pain would be horrendous. She would be broken.

My eyesight wavered as my body tried to Change. I was barely holding on to a thread of control. I wanted to taste blood. I wanted to tear Sergey apart, limb by limb.

"Heard what?" Gwen pressed.

"There are some things you don't need to know," Heath said darkly, his anger undisguised. His scent was completely useless, but his face and voice told me everything. "Jacky, they've backed us into a corner."

"They're taking our family to Russia for safekeeping,"

I explained for my sister, flipping my phone around in my hand to keep my hands busy. “They made a mistake.”

“What mistake?” Her voice sounded small and scared.

“They didn’t consider option four.” I bared my teeth as I stared at the road ahead of me. “Heath, take us to the closest airport. We’re going to Russia.”

He turned the car around in the middle of the road.

19

CHAPTER NINETEEN

As we came to the Rochester airport, I let Heath and Gwen go head inside to find us a route into the country. Heath had an intimate knowledge of where the Russian werewolf pack spent most of their time, a large compound deep in the wilds of Siberia. A smart place to go since very few lived out there to get in the way.

But I knew someone.

During the drive, I had debated calling Hasan back. He probably thought I was in danger. I knew once I called Mischa, she would let him know what was happening, but that was good enough for me. I didn't want to test my will to get back at the werewolves against Hasan's will to keep me safe and out of trouble. She could tell him what I was doing without me needing to cross his path again.

I hit her name and dialed her cell phone, wondering if she would have reception where she was. Since I had gotten into regular contact with my family, I noticed Mischa was hit or miss. She would go a few weeks at a time without having reception wherever she was. I think she liked it that way. It was her escape.

"Jacky?" Mischa yawned. "Why are you calling?"

"Hasan hasn't gotten to you?" That was surprising.

"No...should he have?"

"I figured he would. I called him and told him I killed some werewolves, and I'm in Minnesota." I took a deep breath. "I need your help getting to the Russian werewolf pack."

"Why? Jacky, what did you get yourself into? And why am I or anyone just finding out something is happening? You couldn't give anyone a courtesy call before you killed werewolves?"

"It's a long story. I didn't expect to get in this much trouble when Everett called. He had a human show up in his territory. Thanks to Heath, I knew there was something going on with werewolves in the region, and suddenly, everything was connected, and there was no getting out. Not if I wanted to be able to sleep at night, anyway."

"I think I need to hear this story from the beginning."

"Yeah. So..." I launched into the story chronologically —Devora, the events at the hospital, my sister making it to Everett, and Heath and me flying up and getting pulled into everything because the Russians knew we were involved now. "Then the hospital decided they were okay with the Russian werewolves killing the staff as a trade. You know it's blackmail."

"Revenge for silence," Mischa agreed. "When did you finally decide to call Hasan? You should have the moment you realized your...twin was involved."

Something about the way she said twin made it clear she had her opinions about Gwen, and they weren't positive. Was she upset I still had a human family? Was she angry I was risking my life for that human family?

"I called him right after the hospital shut my plan down, and we learned the Russians were leaving the country," I explained. "But we didn't get to finish the call because the new Alpha called us and..." I swallowed. "He took hostages."

"Who and what are his terms?"

"My parents, Gwen's kids, and her ex-husband. They all lived in Minnesota, close by. Gwen was here in Rochester, and the terms are simple. If we release the information on the pack, they kill my family. If I keep it, they keep my family. Or I trade. They get what they want, and I get my family back."

"Your family," she murmured.

"What?"

"What do you need from me?" Her tone was frustrated, angry. Maybe I was used to people being angry at me and took it as a sign she didn't want to help.

"Mischa, he threatened to Change a little girl." I saw red at the thought. No longer physically ill, I only felt rage. I clenched my jaw to keep from Changing to attack whatever I could as my control slipped. "My niece. I need you—"

"I know what the Russian pack does, Jacky. I don't need an explanation. I've known for years. I'm asking you what you need from me to take these motherfuckers down for daring to take humans who belong to you," she ranted, a growl punctuating more than one word.

"Oh. Well, we're headed to Russia. Heath knows the location of their main compound, where they'll probably take my family for safekeeping. I..."

"You need multiple things, then. You need a place to stay, backup, and more information. That compound is their main hub, but they have three small towns around it, all under the radar, where more of their wolves and humans live. Beyond that, they have pockets of population all over the country and several others. Jacky, do you know Genghis Khan?"

"I've read a history book."

"Good. This pack was started by him. It covers most of the ancient area he once ruled. When his human empire failed, the werewolves were still strong, but they went into hiding and worked under the human world like the rest of us. When we were at war with the werewolves, they owned the entire region. It took me four hundred years to convince werecats to move back into the region, and even now, I have to keep them from going too close to the wolves."

The sense of scale I was confronted with almost scared me. It would have if I didn't go into a blind rage every time I thought of my niece. I held onto that anger. I needed the rage.

"So, what else do you know about the pack?"

"I'll text you coordinates where to meet me. They'll probably fly directly into their compound, which puts you behind. Fly to Tokyo and pick up Hisao's jet. It's small, and I have a runway at one of my homes that can support it. I'll meet you there. Hisao can fly, so don't worry about needing a pilot."

"Perfect. What's the travel time?"

"From Tokyo to me will be eight hours. I don't know how long from where you are..." I heard fingers on a keyboard. "If you leave out of Rochester, it's fifteen hours to Tokyo, including layovers...There's a flight you need, leaving in an hour. Talk to me when you get to Tokyo. I need to get moving if I want to meet you and Hisao at my runway."

"Thank you," I said, grateful for such a supportive family. If it weren't for that, Gwen and I would have to take the deal from Sergey and hope he wasn't lying. Thanks to Mischa, I could do what I needed to do.

"Never forget, I would do anything for you. No thanks required, little sister," she said softly, then hung up.

I won't.

I shoved my phone away and ran inside to find Heath and Gwen. They were looking at flights when I caught them at a kiosk.

"We need a route to Tokyo. Mischa says there's something leaving in an hour..." I looked at the flights as Heath pulled out his phone and started searching.

"Did she give a total travel time?" he asked.

"Something like fifteen hours."

"Then we're flying to Chicago first, then to Haneda Airport in Tokyo. That'll have to do."

"What am I buying?" Gwen demanded.

"You aren't paying. Move." I gestured for her to step aside, which thankfully, she did. I found three tickets for the next flight to O'Hare and bought them all. It was still early in the morning, and I jumped on the chance to grab the seats in the empty first class. The flight was just over an hour and would most likely be empty.

"Heath, buy our flights to Tokyo. Gwen, do you have a passport?"

"Yeah. I keep it on me..."

"Good." I grabbed my go-bag off the cart Heath had found and looked through it, making sure I had one of mine—specifically, one that matched the credit cards I was using. "Heath, is anyone going to give you any trouble for leaving the country?"

He looked up from his phone. "Like who?"

"The BSA, the NAWC? CPS?" I rattled off every acronym involved in his life.

"No." He shook his head. "I invest my money all over the world, and before moving into your territory, frequently traveled by myself. The NAWC will find it odd I'm on an international flight with you, but they won't ask. Not immediately, anyway. You worry about you and your sister. I'll worry about the other werewolves."

But I want to worry about you. You're my werewolf. You're only here because I am, and that means so much to me. Let me worry about you.

I kept my eyes on him, wishing I could say what I was thinking, but I couldn't. It was too public, too possible for a supernatural who might catch our scents or recognize us.

Tickets bought, we all raced through security. We would be separated on the flight to Tokyo, but we would at least get first-class together to Chicago.

~

I WAS NEVER someone who enjoyed long flights. There was a reason I never offered or considered visiting my siblings or Hasan once I moved into my own territory. Even as a human, I tolerated flying just to see new places and enjoy a vacation on the rare occasion. As a werecat, they made me itchy. I was getting better each time I got on a plane, but there was something to say about being wealthy. An empty plane was much more relaxing than a crowded one.

After the short flight to Chicago, we quickly found our flight to Tokyo. I didn't ask about our guns, knowing they had been left behind in Rochester. That didn't worry me because both Hisao and Mischa would have small arsenals in their territories.

We didn't speak at all as we got onto the second flight and found our seats, barely able to see each other over the heads of all the humans around us. I looked for my sister, making sure she found a good spot. I was grateful we had time in Rochester to let her wash out her hair and get some of the noticeable blood off her. It was something I hadn't thought about, but Heath had. Now on the second flight, I wished I had let her do more in her own home, like take a proper shower, grab several changes of clothes, and more.

While my sister was behind me, Heath was toward the front of the plane. He had picked the seat, so he could smell any supernaturals coming onto the plane in case someone came after us. He'd be able to warn Gwen and me before there was any chance of an enemy reaching us.

My phone dinged, and I checked it, trying to block the screen from the person beside me.

. . .

Heath: Wish we could sit together. I can smell you up here.

I chuckled softly, shaking my head as a small smile formed.

Jacky: After the night and morning we've had, you pick right now to try to be cute?

Heath: We're stuck on a plane. We have a moment to breathe. There's nothing we can do for anyone until we get to your siblings.

My smile grew a little more. I was lucky enough to get a window seat, so I could lean on the side. It wasn't the most practical seating for safety or danger, but I liked it.

Jacky: Thank you for sticking with me. I couldn't do it without you. I hope this doesn't blow back on Carey or Landon.

Heath: Leaving you to do this on your own wasn't and will never be an option for me.

I played with my phone, then put it away as the plane started to move. He was so committed, and I didn't understand why. He had a family to protect, a reputation, and he was walking a dangerous road, betraying his own species by helping me. Sure, the North American Werewolf Council had given him the token job of working with me when the need arose, but I was pretty certain they never intended it to go this way.

As the plane took off, I looked back at my sister again, making sure she was okay. Pale, she gave me a thumbs up from the back of the cabin. I knew she hated flying even more than me. We didn't grow up traveling the world, and our first flights were in undergraduate school when we went abroad for a week. We went together, but nearly twenty other students had gone on the trip, so we spent most of it hanging out with our own friends. Instead of a normal spring break, we were in Spain on a field trip and ignored each other.

I couldn't remember the fight we'd had that time. It felt like we had always been fighting back then.

An hour into the flight, I pulled my phone back out and took it off airplane mode. I looked at Heath's texts, trying to take my mind off my sister.

JACKY: Why?

HE DIDN'T ANSWER IMMEDIATELY. I looked up to see him looking back at me, a frown on his face, his head tilted to the side in confusion. When he turned away, I knew to expect an answer and looked back down at my phone, hoping he could explain.

. . .

Heath: Your sister admitted to what she did, yet you told me to go because you worried about my family. Your family has been taken, and you're still worried about my family. You've always considered the safety of my children and helped me protect them.

You've taken risk after risk for me. You've tried to give your life for Carey on more than one occasion. You are selflessly driven to do good things and fight for what you love and for what you think is right. It's my honor to help you.

I'm not in the business of breaking my honor by abandoning you to protect your own family.

I held my phone to my chest after reading those words. He was too good a man, Heath Everson. He was going to get himself hurt, and it was going to be my fault. When my phone buzzed on my chest, I pulled it back down.

Heath: And why the hell would I leave a woman to fight on her own when I want to be with her? You convinced me to make that stupid decision before, and it's never going to happen again. I care about you, and there's no reason for you to be alone anymore.

. . .

MY THUMBS HOVERED over the keyboard. How did I reply to any of that? The words touched me and terrified me. I typed out something and stared at it without hitting send.

I CARE ABOUT YOU TOO.

THEN I DELETED it and tried again.

I'M grateful to have you in my life.

DELETE. Type. Delete. I didn't know what to say. After long enough, I put the phone down.

I could have done a number of things to pass the time. I could have tried to contact Sergey about my family, but I didn't want to antagonize him. He gave me seventy-two hours of safety before I had to make a decision. If I called him just to try to talk around his options, he would know I was planning something, and the timeline could accelerate. I knew why he wanted seventy-two hours, or I could reasonably guess. He was also on a plane, heading for Russia, and it would take some time for him to handle pack business once he landed. He knew we would follow him because he could dictate the meeting area and held the more valuable bargaining chip.

I didn't know why I felt so confident in my judgment about Sergey. Something about him seemed just as human as anyone I went to school with. His behavior was logical, I could make sense of it. Just like I could look back at Lani and make sense of her.

"You were always good at this."

"Good at what?"

"People."

Was I? I leaned back in my seat and opened my window shade to stare at the clouds. It was a long flight, and I had time to think.

20

CHAPTER TWENTY

This was my first time in Japan. As the plane landed, I wished I could enjoy it. I wished I was on a family visit to see my enigmatic assassin brother.

Regretfully, that wasn't the case.

I yawned as the plane taxied to its terminal. I had slept on the flight, unable to keep my eyes open after a very long night and morning. I had been lulled into it, and when I woke up, I was grateful to get some sleep while I had the chance.

Heath didn't text me again, and Gwen couldn't since I still had her phone, which was blissfully quiet during the flight. Sergey hadn't reached out, something I was going to take as a good sign for the moment. I had to trust the new Alpha to protect my family from the troubles in his pack. If he let them get hurt, his ability to bargain was gone, and I would make it my personal goal to destroy the entire pack. He seemed like a smart werewolf, so I was certain he knew that was the case.

It took thirty minutes, but I was eventually able to get off the plane and meet Heath at the end of the ramp. Gwen wasn't far behind me.

"Where do we go now?" she asked, looking around. "I've never been to Japan before."

"Neither have I," I said, also searching the surrounding airport.

"Let's go to baggage claim. Maybe Hisao is waiting for us there," Heath said, grabbing Gwen's elbow and leading her. I followed, trying not to stare at where he touched her. It wasn't a danger thing—it was a jealousy thing. He could touch her in public, and no one would blink an eye. She was human.

I scanned the crowds. From what the pilot said, it was nearly three in the afternoon. What made that hard to deal with? It wasn't the same day we left Chicago. What had been a Saturday morning takeoff was a Sunday afternoon landing, and apparently, Sunday afternoon at this airport was insanely busy.

I caught his scent before I saw him and noticed the moment Heath caught it as well. With the crowd, we were both struggling.

It's probably easier for me. He's probably overloaded with scents right now.

Hisao wasn't the tallest man, but when I saw him, I wanted to breathe a sigh of relief. His severe gaze caught mine, and that relief left me as fleetingly as it had come.

"Here," I told my group and started walking, weaving through the crowd to my brother. He didn't move a muscle as I walked toward him. Once I was right in front of him, his eyes left mine, and he looked over at Heath and Gwen behind me.

"Mischa told me what's going on." His words were curt. "Let's go. I've prepared the jet—no need to wait. We can take off in two hours. We'll wait on the plane."

He turned on his heel and walked away. I reached back and grabbed my sister's hand, keeping her close. Heath took the back of the group, and we followed Hisao into the depths of the airport, past security checkpoints not meant for passengers. He didn't look back, talking in Japanese to the staff as he walked. When he gestured back at us, I could only guess he was telling them we were with him.

These people knew him, which made me wonder how often he took the jet. I was privileged to be Changed by an insanely old, wealthy family. From my knowledge, the family owned three private jets. One was maintained by Zuri and Jabari, who used it to hop between their territories in Africa. One was kept here in Japan by Hisao. The last was in Western Europe, shared by Davor and Niko. Hasan rarely left his island by human means, and I had never felt comfortable with the wealth I had, preferring a simple life. Mischa was the enigma. I assumed she didn't have one because of her lifestyle, roaming the continent like she couldn't stop her feet.

"Get on," Hisao ordered in a soft growl when we came to the small jet in the hangar. I jogged up the steps, looking back to make sure my sister and Heath were following. Hisao came up the stairs last and locked us in.

The private jet was simple, understated, luxurious, but not ostentatious. Something about that bothered me.

I was expecting more. This was my first time on one of the family's jets.

"Do you have the evidence Mischa mentioned?" my brother asked, looking down at me as I found a seat.

"Yeah. I was thinking I would go through it while we were flying. Not all of it has to do with the werewolves, so we need to figure out what to do with the rest."

"Of course. Father might not approve, but there could be something we can keep in the family to use at a later time."

"Why? He's got spies," I said with a snort.

"He won't approve how you got this information," he said, sitting across a table from me. Looking away, he eyed Heath. "How did you get pulled into this? Her twin killed someone. That had nothing to do with you."

"When we first learned something happened, we hoped I would be able to keep violence from happening between Jacky and the pack. I know Sergey and a few others from the Russian werewolf pack. If I don't know them personally, I've read the files kept on them by the North American Werewolf Council. My son has probably met them, and I can call him."

"We were hoping this wouldn't become a huge deal," I said softly. "We were hoping we could keep Gwen in secret, but then those fucking werewolves killed a girl and..." I shook my head, thinking about how we found ourselves at this point. "They don't know Gwen killed their Alpha—they can't—but they do know she was with Sarah, trying to expose the abhorrent shit the pack was doing to their females and submissives. That's what they're angry about."

"How did they find out?" Hisao asked, watching me again.

"Sarah played her hand and tried to dictate the terms of the agreement with the Russians in Minnesota. She was an idiot—"

"Jacky!" Gwen's insulted, hurt shout echoed in my ears. Hisao didn't speak loudly, so in comparison, Gwen sounded like she was screaming through a megaphone.

"She was," Hisao agreed. "Humans don't dictate terms to us. We're more powerful in every way. We also have more at stake."

Well, I wasn't going to go that far, Hisao. Shit. I was just going to say she obviously had no experience with negotiating. Hell, even I made a couple of mistakes talking to Sergey.

"Bullshit," Gwen muttered.

"Please, tell me your viewpoint," Hisao said, looking past me. I heard my sister's heartbeat speed up. She was close enough, I caught the hitch in her breathing. She probably hadn't expected Hisao to call her out.

"We have so much to lose. We don't have centuries to live and do whatever we please. We can't spend fifty years or more building wealth to live for five hundred years. Most of the time, we can only struggle every day for what we have. We have to fight for every single day. We have a lot to lose."

"Yes and no," Hisao whispered. "You live in the present, but so do we. Everyone else on this plane lives to see the years pass by, far more than you ever will, but we still live in the present, struggling every day. We make attachments we aren't willing to lose because we've had them for so long, and they should be immortal. You know that one day, your human parents will die of old age. My father is endless, and I will destroy anyone who dares to try to stop his journey through the ages. My siblings are endless, and I would do the same for them. My family has spent centuries building peace after centuries of fighting nearly decimated us. Do not begin to think you have more to lose."

Centuries? The war eight hundred years ago didn't last that long.

"So, your life is worth more than mine?" my sister dared to ask. "Because you've been promised immortality, and someone might dare to change that?"

"No, not worthless. You just made the mistake of thinking we're without feeling. That we build nothing of worth during our years. I wanted to correct that assumption."

"Sure." My sister sounded disbelieving. "Jacky—"

"I'm not getting into a philosophical debate of immortality versus mortality. I'm undecided." I lifted my hands. "There're better things to talk about."

"I can comment," Heath said softly, looking around at us. "I've had and still have both mortal and immortal family members who help me keep perspective. I've lived long enough to understand immortality, long enough to know I should be long dead." He sat across the aisle at a different small table area with four chairs. "They're different. Immortality brings with it long, if sometimes ignored, relationships. There's confidence, but it has to be worked for. There're a lot of immortals who will continue to struggle every day for wealth, just like humans. But wealth isn't the point." He chuckled softly, shaking his head. "Wealth will never be the point.

"Humans love each other for their fragility. One day that person will be gone, and we cherish the mortality for as long as we can, as hard as we can. Immortals form connections based on the endless. Who do we want by our sides for the centuries to come? Forever is a long time when death is only possible in a violent way. Stay out of trouble, and you get forever. That's a massive commitment and not one to be taken lightly. I will love my daughter every day of her mortal life as best I can. I know my son will stay by my side endlessly."

"Yes." Hisao nodded slowly, which made me appreciate my assassin brother more. "I like that way of thinking about it. Very insightful of you, Alpha Everson." My brother wiped his hands, but I didn't know what he was wiping off. Maybe it was the topic. "Now, it's a long flight to Mischa. Please get some rest. She's asking me to take you somewhere that's very special to her, and I might not have the chance to say it later, so I'll say it now. You will *all* be respectful of her home. Under normal circumstances, outsiders aren't permitted. She only keeps a runway and fuel for the plane, when she needs it and for the locals. This isn't a commercial camp that sees many people coming through."

"Anything else?" I leaned back and spread my legs out, a little upset I didn't get much time to properly stretch them out between flights.

"Don't contact the Russians until we've had a chance to confer with her. Feel free to discuss the options and ideas you might have about how to approach this, but we're not confirming anything."

"Should I call Hasan?" I hadn't missed how my werecat father hadn't attempted to call me back.

Something angry flashed in my brother's eyes—something directed at me.

"No, that won't be necessary. He, Mischa, and I have all spoken on it. By the time we land, the entire family will have been briefed. Zuri and Jabari have been off the grid on a long camping trip. We've had to get one of their humans to go find them."

Oh. They're all pissed. I should have expected that.

He stood and walked out of the main cabin into the small cockpit at the front of the plane. After twenty minutes, a human came out and asked us what we wanted to drink. He wasn't Japanese. His accent was close to Russian, but I wasn't proficient in the small nuances of similar accents. He disappeared back into the cockpit once we were served and left us alone.

"I'm always grateful I can hide my emotional scents when I meet your family," Heath whispered, looking across the plane at me.

"He's pretty scary," I agreed. "You know, he once offered to teach me how to endure torture."

"That's..." Heath sipped his drink, not finishing. Then it was like a light bulb went off. "Hasan believes my ability is a real Talent, you know. I don't think I ever told you that. He commented on it when I met him at my safe house in February."

"You didn't," I replied, raising my eyebrows. "How was meeting my entire family in their—"

"They aren't your family," Gwen mumbled behind me.

It felt like an attack.

"Don't ever let one of them hear you say that," Heath cautioned. "In fact, don't ever say it again."

"They're not biologically related to you—"

"Leave it," Heath growled as I sat in silence at my sister's words. "That is not your place."

"Heath, it's okay," I finally forced out, reaching to him and patting his thigh in a friendly way. "It's fine."

"Your family was taken by werewolves," Gwen said boldly. I turned back to her as she raised her chin. "They..."

"What is your problem?" I demanded, keeping the anger and hostility I felt out of my words. Instead, the emotion that clung to those words was my pain. Why was she saying this?

"Nothing. Obviously, I'm the one who doesn't understand anything," she said, looking away.

"I'm here, pissing off the family I've had for over a decade, and not for the first time, to protect and help you. To finish a fight *you* started. What...what do I need to do or say to get you to stop attacking me?" I shook my head, unable to understand her.

"Family doesn't tell you to stay away," she said, looking down at her hands. "You asked why I never reached out? I was angry at you for being a werecat and never coming home. I was also told not to. When they saw I worked at the hospital, they told me not to."

I schooled my face before I could give away anything to Gwen, but Heath picked up every scent. As I turned to look at the front of the plane, his eyes went wide as my fury built and stewed.

Which one did it? Hasan? Zuri? Which one would do that? She knows the secrets of the supernatural world. Why couldn't she reach out to me? Why couldn't I know she was there? Which one of them decided to interfere in my life like that?

21

CHAPTER TWENTY-ONE

Two hours after the plane took off, I tried to get to work. After waving Heath over, I grabbed my bag and took my laptop out. Heath moved next to me, bringing his laptop as well.

"Are we going to sort through the USBs?" he asked softly.

"Yeah," I mumbled.

"Are you okay?" He leaned in, his grey-blue eyes searching my face. "You can...you can talk to me—"

"Not about this." Looking away, I opened my laptop and sighed.

Before continuing, I looked back at my sister and was glad to see her sound asleep. Long hospital hours and traveling long hours were two different beasts. On top of that, she was probably still reeling from the new dangers in her life. She wasn't built like Heath and me. As apex predators, we were built for the fighting and constant go, go, go of the supernatural world. Humans weren't.

When I turned back to Heath, I dared to voice my feelings.

"How could they?"

"They had to have had their reasons," Heath said gently. "I don't think what they did was the right thing, but it does explain your sister. She was desperate and scared, and reaching out to you defied your family."

"Yeah..." I was glad Heath finally had a reason to like my sister. I knew he was still having a hard time trusting her intentions of why she reached out to me. They were valid concerns, and if she was a supernatural, they would most likely be correct.

"Jacky..." My name sounded like a plea when it rolled off his tongue in a hushed whisper. "You were adamant for years about not reaching out to them, for a lot of reasons. Maybe they were just trying to let you maintain the peace you had achieved with being a werecat."

"Would you have done it?" I asked as I logged into my computer. When he didn't reply fast enough, I turned to him again. "Heath?"

Sighing, he shrugged. "Not without telling you. I would probably have told you she was there if I knew and asked you what you wanted to do about it. If you didn't want a relationship, I would have let her know she needed to stop pursuing information about you."

"That's..." I tried to smile. "That's better than what they did. I could have known she was there. I could have..."

"I know."

Shaking my head, I reached into my bag and found the smaller bag full of data. I unzipped it and dropped it on the table, grabbing two—one for me and one for Heath.

"Let's get to work." He only nodded and took his, plugging it into the side of his laptop. Plugging mine in, I clicked through folders. Sarah wasn't the most complicated person by the looks of her file organization. I clicked the first video, and my speakers suddenly roared to life with a video of a young man talking.

"Shit. I need headphones."

Heath held out a pair, and I took them, only a little confused by their sudden and easy appearance.

"They're in the side pockets of the chairs," he explained, then put his back in his ear and went back to whatever he was watching.

I set them up and started the video again, turning my volume down.

The young man talked about a vampire nest that turned him. They had kidnapped him at the age of ten and changed him at only sixteen. Then they drank from him repeatedly to tie his life to theirs. The story made me sick as he described the abuse he went through, thanks to the obsession of the nest's master. He had been a plaything.

I forced myself to stop watching and closed the video. I quickly checked the videos in all the folders. This particular USB was all vampires. I put it aside and went in for another drive.

This one had several humans talking about how they worked for a werewolf pack in Atlanta, and that some of the werewolves were cruel. The Alpha was never told when they tried to report it.

I put that one aside as well, trying not to think about how I had a passing acquaintance with the werewolf Alpha of the Atlanta Pack, Alpha Harrison. He'd been particularly cranky when he found out I was a daughter of Hasan. For a moment, I wondered if he ever discovered his pack was a danger to the humans they employed and were related to.

I put it aside and continued. There were just over a dozen USBs. Some only had one video, some had a string of them, pointing to a problem in the organization they came from.

Heath growled at one point, then put the USB he had been watching between us. When I reached for it to see what was so upsetting, he put his hand over it.

"Let's find the Russians first," he whispered.

Nodding, I went back to searching.

It was the last one because, obviously, I was out of the cosmic luck I normally had.

There were fifteen videos. Swallowing, I started watching the first one, promising myself I was going to watch every single one.

"Did he beat you?" Sarah asked softly. "You can tell me. No one will ever know. We're sworn to secrecy. Just consider me a place to get the pain out of your soul."

"He beat me," the young woman answered. "He beat me when I would serve the other werewolves. He said I was too pretty to go to waste, so he never hit my face. He always let me heal before sending me..."

I winced as tears welled up in my eyes. She had been Changed by Alpha Vasiliev to serve his inner circle as a present for when their mates grew *tiresome*. She talked about Sergey and Alexei. She said other names I didn't recognize.

"I found it," I said, trying to wrangle the storm of emotions brewing. "I found the videos Sarah has of the Russians."

"Let me figure out what my last one is," Heath said in a stiff way, which made me wonder for a moment what was bothering him. The easy guess was the constant bombardment of trauma coming in front of our eyes.

I went to the second video and saw a young male, uninjured. Sarah convinced him it was okay for him to talk to her. Watching this video, I realized none of Sarah's patients knew they had been recorded. She never told him there was a camera, which was cruel, taking down this footage of the pain these people were going through.

This young male was Devora's beta brother. He had a peaceful quality to him, I had only run into once before. He talked about living conditions and how hard it was for him to see his sister. He had been Changed first when the pack came through his neighborhood, looking for possible recruits. They had pinned him as a beta werewolf before he even knew what they wanted. The pack ended up buying both him and his sister from their parents for the price of a new home and a new life in Moscow, somewhere far away and living better. They thought it was an honor for their children to go to the great pack. Surprisingly, Devora's brother had no blame for them. Apparently, the poor people living near the pack had been duped in a great PR play.

The interview was cut off when another werewolf entered the picture and ordered Devora's brother to do something in Russian. By the look on the beta's face, he was in trouble, and he knew it.

I watched because I felt like it was my duty to watch. This was the reason my sister was sacrificing everything. This was why she killed a man, breaking an oath I knew she took seriously. This was why we were on the plane.

Sarah was able to interview another female while her injuries were still apparent. She had been beaten by a mate and couldn't find help. Her father was a member of the pack and was able to escape with her.

One older female said she was the mate of an inner circle werewolf. She didn't look old, but she carried the ages on her shoulders. I recognized age in immortals that old because I saw it in Hasan and most of my siblings. Zuri had shown it to me only back in February. There was a weight they carried once they had seen centuries turn and empires built and crumble.

She was tired. She wanted to leave but knew if she did, her husband would mate their daughter.

I closed my laptop after that, unable to bear anymore.

This is the pack that wants me to hide their crimes. This pack...

I can't do that. I can't let them keep doing this. I'd never be able to sleep again.

"Should I watch it?" Heath asked gently as I took out my headphones.

"No." I shook my head then reconsidered. "Yes. Yeah... You need to watch it." I slid my laptop in front of him, warring between rage and being violently sick. I wanted blood on my hands—their blood. At the same time, I figured the sight and smell of blood would make me puke. I wanted to be furious and scream. I wanted to call my entire family and do to this pack what we had done to Lani's fucking friends. I wanted destruction, and I never wanted to commit another act of violence ever again.

The warring emotions left me paralyzed as Heath watched. I could hear it all because I had nothing else to focus on.

"We'll deal with this," he promised, pulling out the USB. "I swear it, Jacky, we'll deal with this."

"We better," I whispered. "You said you figured Callahan knew…"

"I don't think he knows all of this. If he did, we all would. This is…" By the look on his face, he was worried—sick. His scent was unknown to me, but I didn't fault him for that. I was trying to bury my feelings for him to stop Hisao from picking anything up. He was probably locked down for the same reason.

"They've been keeping their secrets through force, just like they are right now. They own the entire region, and they've crushed disobedience." I could see it—authoritarian rule, dissenters killed. Everyone walking on eggshells, kept poor and desperate, needing to please the Alpha and his inner circle. Middle-rank wolves using their power and rage to subjugate lower werewolves even more.

He only nodded, reaching for the USB he had put down.

"This is about…" Sighing, he put it back down. "This is something recent. A human girl ravaged by a werewolf in an American pack. Apparently, they were attempting to Change her, and the wolf who did it lost control."

"What?" I put a hand over my mouth, considering what he was saying. "Did she live?"

"They rushed her to the hospital where she passed away, probably from a combination of the injuries and the Change trying to take her. There's no real interview. I think Sarah felt it was necessary to secretly tape her treatment and listen to what the pack was saying. Probably a new little fucking side project she wanted to work."

"Which pack?" I asked, knowing I shouldn't. I didn't even understand why he was telling me.

"Dallas," he whispered. "An Alpha should do Changes—all of them. I've Changed over a dozen people, for good and bad, and it weighs on my soul, but I never asked someone else to do it. Some people I denied the chance, and they tried to convince others. In those instances, I had to be the judge, jury, and executioner. This? Either Tywin lost control and killed this girl, proving himself unfit, or he asked someone else to Change her, and it went wrong. Her Change was approved. The werewolves made that very clear when questioned."

"Who else would know about this?"

"The Alphas on the council if anyone reported it to them. The hospital wouldn't have, and Tywin probably didn't."

"What are you thinking, Heath?"

"I don't know yet," he admitted. "But...I left the pack to him."

"There's something going on in Atlanta too," I said, finding that USB for him. "Werewolves are treating humans in the pack unfairly, and in many cases, violently. When it's reported up, someone keeps it from getting to Alpha Harrison, or so the victims believe." I held it out to him, and he took it very slowly from me.

"How many of these do you think she made? Do you think we missed a second stash somewhere?"

"Probably. I can only imagine how many of these 'files' she made," Heath muttered, looking at the two in his hand.

Hisao came out of the cockpit, forcing me to look away from Heath's troubled expression. I couldn't comfort my wolf here or any time soon, so I quickly shoved the idea away.

"What do you need?" I asked my brother as he sat down across from us.

"You've been talking. Even without hearing, it's hard with the plane noise and the thickness of the cockpit door and wall," he explained. "I want to know what you have."

"A lot of blackmail," Heath said softly, leaning back in his seat. "This Sarah person would secretly collect the worst stories from victims, offering therapy help, just someone to talk to, then record the talk without telling the patient."

"Hmm...Normally, when people get into this sort of business, they see a couple of patients come in and start to notice a trend. Then they start recording," my brother said, looking at the different USBs. "Who all can be hurt with this?"

"Two werewolf packs in America, though those aren't as severe as some of the international cases. A vampire nest turning humans young stuck to me in the beginning. They had heavy accents, but I couldn't tell you from where." I shrugged. "I'm not sure what to do with all of this. It's too much...evil."

"There's a lot of evil in everyone. Humans expose great crimes and conspiracies all the time among their own. It happens in our kind as well." Hisao shifted in his seat, appearing to get more comfortable, and crossed his arms. "I can only offer a suggestion."

"Sure." I waved a hand at him, wondering what he could possibly have. He had thousands of years of experience.

"Give them all to Father. He'll decide which ones I should handle. I'm only suggesting this because you found them. They belong to you, and I won't force you to...play a part in their deaths. It's one thing to fight a battle and win. It's another to murder someone who doesn't see you coming. There's a reason only one of us in the family has taken that role."

Is that why you're so cold? Because you made the decision to be that person, so the rest of us could sleep easier?

"I'll...think about it. Thank you for the suggestion." I quickly closed the bag and shoved it away, keeping only the USB the Russians wanted. Then I considered what Hisao had said. "What did you mean by business?"

"Heath called it blackmail, and I'm inclined to think this Sarah wasn't like your twin, who might genuinely care about these victims. If Sarah truly cared, she would have acted much faster or found a way to secret the information out and keep her job. There's always a way.

Nothing is foolproof. You said she died to the Russians, correct?"

"Yeah...Apparently, she tried to dictate the terms..."

"I have a feeling she wasn't trying to help anyone. I bet she was looking for money, and her insurance was someone else exposing them if they didn't pay her what she wanted." Hisao smiled, and it was a mean thing. "Why would someone who cares try to bargain with people they believe are evil?"

I looked at Heath, knowing my eyes were wide.

"Want my timeline?" Hisao asked as I looked back at him. He leaned forward with a strangely cold and amused look on his face, almost mean, vicious. "Because I'm darker than you, I am more likely to see the darkness in others. You went into this thinking everyone your sister knew was honorable, not that it changes anything. I've been thinking about it since I was brought in and still thinking about it when we took off."

"Tell me," I ordered.

"Sarah collected blackmail information over her time at the hospital. Easy money for an ER nurse who saw the worst of the worst come in. She recorded secretly, giving the victims no hope they would ever get justice. She might have done a couple of small ones, extorting men who beat their wives or something, or maybe this was the first time she tried, which is how she got herself killed."

"What gave her the balls to make the jump into something this big?" Heath asked. I could hear the Alpha mind working now in the way he spoke. He was looking at this like a professional, a leader of the supernatural world, who did everything he could to protect his people and defeat his enemies.

"In February, my family visited the hospital, and yes, Jacky, we discovered your sister was working there. Yes, a decision was made that we shouldn't tell you. We can have that discussion in depth once everything else is handled."

"We better," I growled softly. "And you can send that message to Hasan."

"Noted." He took my anger without any indication it mattered to him. "And to answer your question, Heath, it was the hospital discovering Jacky and Doctor Duray were related. See, Jacky didn't go into public, and she's fairly young, so she isn't recognizable the way most of us are. Sarah and Gwen were friends, and now—"

"Sarah had a huge contingency plan. Use Gwen, who truly believed in helping people, to pull Jacky into the fray as protection. Suddenly, the ruling werecat family is dragged in, and things go public." Heath spoke fast. "I knew something was fucking wrong with this. I thought it was Gwen, but it was how Gwen got pulled in. Sarah was running an illegal blackmail operation, and it blew up in her face. That's why Sarah sold out Gwen, but apparently, no one else."

"Shit," was all I could manage. Heath had a point. Carlton died, being in the wrong place at the wrong time. Gwen was being targeted.

"Sarah made trouble for Gwen on purpose," he continued. "Some fucking friend."

"Hmm..." Hisao nodded slowly. "It's the only plausible explanation."

"I'm amazed we haven't woken up Gwen," I said, looking back at her. Heath was practically yelling.

"She won't. Her drink was drugged, so she could sleep on the flight," Hisao admitted. "That way, we could talk about sensitive things."

I tried not to reach across the table and attack him because I knew I would lose, and we were flying. Two powerful werecats fighting in an aluminum death trap was a good way to get everyone killed.

"You have no regard for anyone, do you?" Heath asked, giving my brother a look most people had when they were shocked, disgusted, and disbelieving.

"For her?" He pointed between us at my sister. "I have regard for her. That's why she's *asleep*."

"Hisao?" I didn't like the emphasis he'd put on *asleep*. Even a toddler could figure out he meant asleep instead of dead.

"She roped you into a dangerous situation that could have very well got you killed. She might think we're not family, but I would kill for you, and I *only* kill for my family. I refuse to believe a woman who worked to become a doctor didn't understand just how dangerous this situation could become. She was either willfully ignorant or didn't deserve her medical license." He bared his teeth. "And we are family, Jacky. It hasn't been easy bringing you into the family because of the circumstances around that time, but you *are* my sister. I won't lose another one of those." He got up and adjusted his blazer, his eyes dark, promising violence. "But I also understand that she's your family as well—your twin. Zuri and Jabari made it very clear, while you might be estranged, that bond will never truly be broken. So, she's asleep, instead of any other option I had once she came on my plane."

He walked back into the cockpit.

"He's terrifying." It was really all I could say.

"Yes." Heath didn't add anything. We were in complete agreement about that, at least.

I looked at him, a question on the tip of my tongue I couldn't ask.

A small smile broke out on his face.

"I think someone who cares about you won't let your terrifying people chase them away," he said so quietly, I almost missed it. "Now, we need to talk about how much of this to tell your sister."

"Yes, we do," I mumbled, looking away, trying to control myself. I couldn't become a blushing beauty on my family's plane with a werewolf.

22

CHAPTER TWENTY-TWO

In the end, Heath and I decided not to tell Gwen our main theory about Sarah. It didn't change all that much. The dead human was getting what she wanted. The Russians killed her, and her plan for a little post-mortem revenge through me and my family was happening.

There was no reason for my sister to know she got played, thanks to her good heart and her relation to me.

The landing was rough, but we endured it. From my first time in Japan to my first time in Russia, I wasn't sure how to feel as Hisao and his copilot opened the door. This time, there was no fancy staircase to get on and off of the plane. Instead, something that appeared handmade was brought over. I considered jumping as I saw Hisao and the unnamed copilot leave. It was a small wooden ladder. The jet wasn't very tall, but when Heath coughed behind me, I decided to climb down like my brother.

I took in the scenery as we congregated on the grass strip Mischa called a runway. There were mountains, hills, and trees everywhere. It was so much greener than I expected it to be, but I knew that was because of my own lack of knowledge about the region. People only spoke about Siberia in terms of how cold it was and the permafrost. Part of me had expected a harsh winter landscape in June, which made little sense as I took in the landscape and thought about it. The only thing that turned the wild landscape into anything remotely human was the three small buildings and a cellphone tower at one end of the runway. Humans had brought technology to even this wild place.

"It's a little cold here," Heath said softly.

"It's not so bad. Colder than Texas, sure, but it's an acceptable summer temperature," I countered. I tapped Hisao on the arm. "Where's Mischa?"

"She'll be here," he promised. "It might take a few moments. This is an outpost."

Thinking about the cell tower, I took a moment to check my phone and saw a missed text message. The number wasn't saved, but when I clicked it, it had two messages. One declared it was Sergey speaking, nearly a day ago. Another was only two hours before, telling me I only had forty-eight hours to decide what to do. He had even been nice enough—or cruel enough—to attach a picture of my family. They looked terrified but unharmed.

It was a kick in the gut. I shoved my cellphone back into my pocket, not showing Gwen. She didn't need that on her.

My sister didn't notice, but the two men in our little group did, probably from my scent. Both turned to me, giving me their own version of curiosity and concern. Hisao's was cool as if he didn't understand what my problem was and maybe didn't care. Heath's was genuine, the hurt clear in his eyes as I hid my phone.

"Sergey wanted to remind me time is running out. We spent twenty-four of the seventy-two-hour grace period on planes," I explained. No one needed to see the picture. "Family is unharmed for now."

"Did they send evidence?" Hisao was stupid enough to ask. I glared at him as Gwen grabbed my wrist.

"Did they?" she demanded. "Did they send pictures?"

"Yes," I answered, my jaw tight. "I'm not showing you, Gwen. They're alive and unharmed. You don't need to see them in captivity. You don't want a visual to give you nightmares at night."

"Do you think it will?" My damn sister glared at me. "I want to see them. I'm not that—"

"If she doesn't want you to have nightmares, it's because she will," Heath growled. "Trust Jacky."

That was when Hisao grabbed me and pulled me away from the group.

"Do you have nightmares?" he snapped.

"Wow." I was really hoping he would hear how incredulous I was because it was better than being pissed off. "That's not your business."

"But the fucking werewolf knows?" His nostrils flared, a sign he wasn't just upset, he was pretty pissed off.

And I had no way to fire back.

"Because he and I went through a lot, I've told him on occasion," I admitted. "It's not frequent enough to be a problem. Sometimes, it's the vampires, sometimes, Carey getting hurt. It's normal shit, Hisao. It's not every night or even every week. It's just...sometimes." Shrugging, I dismissed it. It didn't seem like a big deal to me and didn't impede my normal life.

"My apologies." His grip softened as he nodded. "I wish you talked to me or anyone in the family about it. I think I might be jealous of this friend of yours. I'm your brother, and you know I've seen things, yet you don't talk to me about these nightmares."

My heart ached.

Oh. He...he wants to be my brother.

"Do you have them? Nightmares?" I asked softly. We were far enough away from the group, my sister couldn't hear us. Heath probably could, but I didn't know if Hisao would have a problem with that.

"This conversation isn't about me," the Assassin answered stiffly.

Oh, yes, it is. It's been about you since you dragged me away from the group. I'm not the one with the problem.

"Okay. I'll consider your offer next time." I tried to step away and found Hisao's grip wasn't that loose. His dark gaze was overbearing as he nailed me with it again.

"Some of us don't like how close you are to that werewolf, Jacky. I recommend you do more than consider it. We're family." His eyes flicked toward Heath, then back at me. "He might be a strong ally, but he should not be the first person you call for help—"

"I didn't plan to bring him. He knew the Russians could be involved and offered his services—"

"How did he even know Everett called you?" Hisao asked.

"I was having dinner with his family..." I was caught. "I understand. I'll...I won't put myself in that position anymore."

"With everything going on and those human organizations sniffing around him, I recommend you don't. And please, call your damn family when you need help," Hisao growled. "One, it's safer. Two, we want you to. We want to help you, Jacky. We would never leave you hanging out to dry. This is your twin, and she needed help. We would have respected your need."

"I thought..." Shaking my head, I knew it was worthless to tell him what I had thought.

"Did you think Father would be angry? Because I can tell you, he's angry you didn't reach out sooner."

"I didn't want to pit Hasan as the Tribunal werecat against a werewolf pack," I explained. "Hisao...We could accidentally start a war."

That made a difference.

"Ah... yes," he agreed softly. "Don't worry. We have no intention of taking action as a family. I...I understand your reasoning and will pass it along to Father. I'm certain it will cool his temper."

"Really?" Now, I was really disbelieving.

"I've often done things to stop the very same thing," he said softly. "Things Father can never know about, and he knows that. He worries about you at your age more than the rest of us. We can talk more about it later. I hear Mischa's truck."

I listened, wondering if I could catch it. Once my brother was silent, I could hear the rumble of an engine. We watched in that direction, and two minutes later, it showed up in the tree line and came down a dirt road. My sister was standing in the passenger's seat, waving. I didn't know who was driving.

"Welcome!" she called out.

Hisao and I went back to Heath and Gwen, ready to meet the wild, gorgeous sibling that was Mischa. Her blonde hair caught in the wind, left to fly around loose. Her blue eyes were noticeable at twenty feet, practically glowing. Even in the wilderness, she wore designer brands and looked like she could step off a magazine cover or a runway. In a sense, the Russian beauty and Hisao matched. As she jumped out of the truck, she adjusted the long designer trench coat she was wearing as Hisao walked toward her. She smiled as she caressed his cheek. They looked beautiful together, the same height, both around five foot nine, his dark hair and eyes versus her splash of color.

And I was wearing the same t-shirt I had left home in two days earlier with a pair of old jeans and tennis shoes that wanted to fall apart from the abuse I had put on them.

When Mischa turned to me, the smile didn't leave.

"Sister," she greeted, leaning in to kiss both my cheeks. For a moment, she hovered and whispered in my ear. "Don't ever say I don't love you."

Then she was gone, shaking Heath's hand, then Gwen's.

"It's good to see you again," Heath said with politeness I was certain was an act. There was something tense about him, but I didn't think my siblings would notice.

"You and your Talent," Mischa said with a wary eye at my werewolf. "It throws me when I can't smell people, Heath Everson."

"You get used to it," I interjected before the conversation could take a turn. "Mischa...this is Gwen."

"I know Doctor Duray. Hisao told me what you learned. I was the one who told her to stay away from you. Isn't that right, Gwen?" Mischa turned on my twin and grinned, all her teeth showing in a dangerous display.

"It is," Gwen agreed, nodding. "I didn't see another option."

"Not killing a werewolf or trying to meddle in their pack was an option. You just didn't take it," my werecat sister snapped. "Definitely twins. Both of you can be downright foolish."

I felt that. Like a slap, it struck me and threatened to put me off balance, which was what Mischa wanted. She was trying to take control of the group and making sure none of us would feel like we were in the right place to fight her. I thought it would continue, but when I looked at her again, daring to see what was coming next, Hisao was by her side.

"Sister—"

"No, Hisao. You might have a soft spot for Jacky after everything she's been through, but this needs to be said. Only a band of idiots tries to test their will against a pack as strong as the Russians." Mischa leveled her gaze on Heath. "And you. You could have told Jacky just how powerful they are. Are you trying to let my sister walk into her death? She seems to find trouble—"

"He tried to convince me to stop before it ever really started," I snapped, stepping between her and Heath. "He's here because I would have done it all without him, and he knew that."

Mischa's hard blue eyes were like ice. We stood at very nearly the same height, able to glare at each other.

"And what are you so angry about?" she asked softly. "Is this about Gwen?"

"Damn right, and your current attitude. You want to be mad? Be mad at me. I'm the one who fought contacting the family. I'm the one who decided I would stay and do whatever was necessary to protect my twin. Heath was just along for the ride and trying to help me. He has contacts and information I needed." I stepped closer to her. "You should be grateful. Without him, I would have done this all on my own, and there's a chance I could be dead already. If there's anyone you shouldn't be mad at, it's him."

"We'll talk about *that* too," she hissed. "Get in the truck."

I stomped around her, grabbing my twin as I went.

"She's awful," Gwen mumbled as we climbed into the bed of the pickup.

"She's upset," I countered, "for her own reasons. I understand all of them. Doesn't excuse her behavior right now, but she's not a bad person."

"If it doesn't excuse her behavior, then stop trying to make excuses," Gwen snapped.

Rolling my eyes, I realized I couldn't please anyone today. Gwen hated both my werecat siblings. Both my werecat siblings felt threatened by Gwen and Heath.

Hasan was mad at me. Russian werewolves had my human family, and there was no way in hell I would give them what they wanted.

As Heath got into the truck, I took solace, there might be one person who wasn't angry at me—just one. His grey-blue eyes were full of concern when he looked at me.

Hisao didn't get into the bed of the truck with us, Mischa did. As the truck started moving, I held on to stop from being bounced around.

"So, let me make something very clear as we enter the village. You do not talk to the locals unless they speak to you, and you will not put them in danger. I've protected them from the Russian pack for centuries, and I won't have you jeopardize that." She looked away from us. "A werewolf hasn't entered the village in eight hundred years. They were attacked once during the War, and it was the last time I scuffled with the Russian pack. Alpha Vasiliev and I were known enemies, and he didn't toy with me. This Sergey, I don't know, and that bothers me." When she looked back at us, she glared at Gwen. "You upset the power balance and have put people in jeopardy."

"I did what I thought was right," my sister retorted.

"And yet you failed to see the bigger picture. You'll get your family back, and you'll go home. I'll be dealing with the consequences of this for centuries if Sergey can hold the power. He might not understand why Alpha Vasiliev gave me the space I demanded. He might not understand why these humans are protected—"

"Everyone should be protected." Gwen held firm.

"You have favorites, and I don't care about the reasons. I stopped a monster from continuing his brutal rule, and I won't back down. I did the right thing. If you knew—"

"I did know," she growled. "I told Jacky the same thing. I knew what the Russian pack was doing. We'll talk more about this once we're secure."

I knew Mischa wasn't done with us, but this discussion didn't need to happen in the back of a pickup truck. It needed a round table and alcohol. She was keeping something from us, and I had a feeling it had everything to do with the village we were about to enter.

23

CHAPTER TWENTY-THREE

The village was small, probably three to four hundred people. Everyone waved at Mischa as we drove by. They didn't wear fancy clothing but weren't destitute, either.

In the center of the village was an actual castle. Out of place and out of time, it shouldn't have been there, which meant it belonged to the reigning immortal of the village. The truck pulled in front of the great stone structure, and Mischa hopped out.

"I had it built years ago," she explained at my questioning look. "I enjoyed the sort of homes Niko and Davor were buying and renovating. It's fully modern on the inside. I only made the outside look like this. It's really just a mansion with a cute look."

"Wow." I shook my head in disbelief as I helped Gwen out of the truck. Heath jumped out on the other side and waited for us. He was too good a politician to be uncomfortable, knowing his place was to wait for everyone else.

"It's extravagant, I know. It helps the village, though. I employ a lot of them, teaching them skills and languages during the harsh winters when farming is impossible. Some of the youth become my employees at my restaurants and stores all over the continent."

"Sounds like you raised this village by hand," I pointed out, looking around. Everyone was so familiar with her.

"I did. Hisao, take Alpha Everson and Doctor Duray inside."

On cue, Hisao ushered them both away. Mischa had purposefully used titles, a border of familiarity and professionalism. She didn't want to be personal with them, but when she looked at me after waving to another human, I had some guesses why.

"What's the story here?" I asked softly.

"This village was founded by a wonderful man, his wife, and her extended family. I was always around from the very beginning. Once, this had been my territory. I guarded the village even then. I had to. I would never let my son start a small homestead without keeping him close and protected."

"Mischa—" I wanted to apologize. This was her family. I was so damn stupid. I wish I had known, but none of my siblings ever talked about their lives at any great length.

"He was born between me and a human, The human...I never married. He was passing by, but the son? I loved the son. I loved him with everything I had in me, and when I asked him to let me Change him, and he said no? My heart broke. He had fallen in love with a beautiful human woman and wanted a normal life. He didn't want the life I could give him. He knew everyone, of course, but he didn't want it."

"Like Dirk, except Dirk was adopted."

"Same difference," Mischa snorted. "I don't understand how humans can adopt children and not love them. To me, a child I decide to rear is my child. That's all there is to it. Not the discussion, though. Back to the village."

I nodded slowly.

"He had children. His wife's parents passed on, and the siblings moved away, but my son had children with his beautiful human wife. They left and met their own spouses, but they always came back. They wanted their children raised by their grandmother—me—as they had been, and their father had been. The village slowly grew. Outsiders were allowed to move in if they married into the family. Eventually, the branches of the family grew so much, some moved away and never came back, which is why I started my businesses, actually. So I could give them starting places in new areas. Some work for our siblings. But this village? This heart? This will always be the home of my son. The Russian pack attacked once during the War. In retaliation, I destroyed their compound. I must have killed hundreds of wolves over that year of grieving. Alpha Vasiliev realized I was not one to be toyed with. I was hunting him, but he was always a step ahead of me."

"Of course he was," I whispered, looking at the village with new appreciation. This community was built and shaped by Mischa. No wonder it was different from what

I expected. No wonder they all knew and loved her. "You're a rogue, but you said this was your territory."

"When my son died, the grief was too strong. My grandchildren and great-grandchildren understood I needed to take some time away. I always come back, but I can never stay. Not anymore. Not since he died. There's a statue of him based on my description and paintings, on that cliff." She pointed off into the distance. "One of my distant grandchildren went to art school and made it for me. My son's gravestone was falling apart, and that sweet young man brought my son back to me in that statue. I visit it whenever I'm in the region. It's the first and last thing I see every visit."

"Thank you for...for trusting me enough to see this," I said, meaning every word. "Thank you for telling me about this beautiful place."

"It's yours, too," she murmured, turning back to me. "These people are your family. They love Hisao because they see him the most, but I keep paintings of all of you in my entryway, so the villagers can see your faces. That way, if you are ever in need and one of them sees you, they will reach out and help you. Just ask them who their grandmother is if you want to be certain. The answer will always be *okhranyat*."

"Why?" I would have thought they would just say Mischa.

"My son taught it to his children as my title in the family, and it stuck. Now, it's a way for the family to know these humans are those I expose my greatest secrets to. It means mother, origin, protector. I am all of these things for them."

"And none of them have tried to out the family?"

"No. Why would they?" Mischa shrugged. "They love me, and I love them. I don't give them everything they want, but I give them what they need to achieve their goals. I give them a safe haven. They give me love." She grabbed my hand and slowly squeezed. "And aside from needing to know because you're family, I'm telling you this because if your twin's actions lead to them getting hurt, I will kill her, and there is nothing you can do to stop me."

She released me and walked away, heading for the front door. Before she went inside, she stopped.

"Feel free to wander the village for a little while. I'm going to show Gwen and Heath their rooms. It might not be a long stay, but I will abide by the rules of hospitality. When you come in, Hisao will find you and show you the room I keep here for you."

You won't kill them while they stay with you. Thanks, sis.

"I'll be in soon," I promised.

With her gone, I took the time to enjoy a moment alone. I brought up my phone and looked at the picture again. My parents looked ten years older than they should have and afraid, holding each other, my father keeping my mother somewhat behind him as if he wanted to throw his body in front of a bullet for her. My niece and nephew were scared and had red rims around their eyes that told me they had been crying. Daniel wasn't scared. My ex-brother-in-law was brave, holding his kids from behind. They had to have been posed for the picture. Daniel looked as if he wanted to shield his children but couldn't. He held them possessively, his eyes daring the person with the camera to even try to hurt his babies. He would fight to the bitter end.

It wasn't supposed to go this far. You have to believe me, it was never meant to turn out this way.

Twelve years and this was the first time I was seeing what they were becoming. I thought about my parents, what they could possibly think, and what they would say when I went to get them. Would they be angry? Would I finally make them proud? Would they hate me for not being human? They had never liked werewolves and didn't want to believe magic was real, something they passed on to Gwen and me.

Daniel and I had been friends, but not close. Did he wonder where I disappeared to? He'd always been more accepting of Shane than my sister. I never met their children, but I saw Daniel's eyes had passed down to both children while my nephew had Gwen's hair and nose.

Family. I was protecting mine. Mischa was protecting hers. It always...always came back to the community a supernatural belonged to—who was worth killing for and who was worth dying for. It was the same for good and evil. It always came back to the community.

I put the phone away and took a deep breath of the fresh air. I saw the appeal, why my sister kept coming back to this place. It was beautiful.

"Are you well?" an elderly woman asked as she walked by.

"I am trying to be," I answered honestly. "How are you?"

"Very good. It's nice to have *okhranyat* back home, and I love when she brings family. You are...Jacqueline." The woman's English was good, though it was marked by a thick accent. I wondered if she had ever left the village a day in her life.

"I am," I confirmed.

"She loves you. Says you remind her of herself." She patted my hand and kept walking.

"Wait. What do you do? Who are you?"

"Ah, I am the head of her house. I manage the home and keep it clean during her travels. I keep the appointment book for her. I need to go now. My grandchildren want to see me." She waved and kept walking, her steps supported by a cane.

I went inside the out-of-place castle and found Hisao waiting at the front door, sitting on a bench beneath several paintings. The warm glow of the lights made his face seem soft.

"You met Yelena. She's a sweet woman," he said softly. "She should have retired a decade ago, but the replacement she was training was lost in a winter storm, and she's been reluctant to find someone else."

"Is she hoping for..." I didn't want to finish because it felt crass to ask.

"Mischa asked her, and she said no. She's just... stubborn. She has been since she was a child." He stood slowly, stretching like a cat waking up from a nap. "So, Mischa told you."

"Do you have a secret family, Hisao?" I asked, crossing my arms. "Because honestly, I'm getting really tired of everyone in the family knowing every little detail of my life and being scrutinized every day. I would like to be able to turn that around. If y'all want me to be honest with you, I feel I deserve the same, and I'm not getting that."

"It took her a century to show Niko," he murmured. "He didn't even get a picture in this hall for fifty years. As for me, I've had many names. No families. I already told you who my progeny are."

"Other assassins you've trained. Yeah, I remember." Sighing, I looked at the portraits. They were well done, very classical. It was odd seeing myself on the wall. It was too modern for the type of painting. I was standing in Hasan's inner courtyard garden in jeans and a tee, smiling at whoever took the picture. I remembered the moment clearly. Hasan took it, the only photo of me once I was immortal. He said something about how I would never be able to take one again and to just let him.

Next to me was a woman I had never seen before, but her positioning between me and Niko told me who she was. It could only be Liza. She was beautiful with raven black hair, skin white as a ghost, grass-green eyes, ethereal and somewhat gothic in her grey gown. I couldn't pinpoint her location.

"You're the first person who didn't have to stand for a painting," Hisao explained. "Which is why you didn't know about it, I'm guessing. There was a lot of tension in the family after you were Changed. None of us had been ready, and Father had never broken his own rules before and Changed someone he didn't raise as his own. Davor was the angriest. You were unprepared for all of us, and we were all angry with Father and unprepared for you. It was too soon after Liza for most of us, not that it was your fault."

"So, Hasan took a picture of me to give to Mischa and her painter."

"Mischa is the painter."

To him, it must have been a small detail, but to me, it was a big revelation. I looked at all the paintings with new eyes. Hasan was leaning on his desk, smiling indulgently. Zuri was dressed like a Queen, giving off the same attitude, but there was humor in her expression. Jabari was a little annoyed in his painting. Hisao was patient and calm. I had a feeling he didn't twitch at all. Davor was frustrated. Niko was emotional, but maybe it was because Mischa was finally sitting him down. Liza was just beautiful, peaceful in a way none of the rest of us were.

Then there was me, happy. I hadn't been happy like that since I left Hasan's home only four years into my immortality. Even then, there was something in my expression that wasn't happy. I was finally moving on from Shane, but his absence was still affecting me.

Mischa hadn't captured our likenesses. She captured her family.

"How angry is she?" I asked. Hasan, I could deal with on another day. Mischa was the battle I needed to survive right now.

"Let me show you the room she's prepared for you. After, we'll meet everyone for dinner."

I'm not sure whether to be terrified or elated that he didn't answer the question.

I followed him away from the entry hall of portraits to the second floor. I was the last room on the right on the eastern half. The inside of the castle was understated, but most definitely modern, with cream colors invading every space.

But when Hisao opened my door, it was in my colors. I loved grey neutrals, the coolness of them, and Mischa had realized it.

"She bribed the interior designer who did your home to come here and make a room to match. Don't be offended. She's done something similar for everyone. Mischa loves visual representations of people."

"Sometimes, when I miss someone, I go to the room I keep for them here," she said behind us as I dropped my bag on the king-sized bed. "Your twin and your werewolf are in the dining hall. Let's go eat and discuss what to do next with your human family and the pack. Bring whatever the werewolves want," she ordered, leaving the doorway and disappearing.

24

CHAPTER TWENTY-FOUR

Hisao showed me how to navigate the mansion and led me into the dining hall. He pulled out my seat on the other end of the large table from Heath and Gwen, then sat across from me. Mischa sat at the head of the table on my left.

"Why are they sitting down there?" I asked, nodding down the table. There were four seats between Gwen and me, and Heath was on the other side of her. It didn't make much sense.

"Because I will feed them at my table, but that doesn't mean I want them right next to me," she answered.

Three people walked out of a side door and put plates down in front of us. I didn't look at the food, even though I knew I *needed* to eat.

"Let's talk—"

"You'll eat first," she growled softly, looking down at her plate. "Then we'll retire to the next room for coffee and talk. Hisao told me you didn't eat on the plane. Have you eaten at all since you left Texas?"

"No," I admitted softly.

When she looked up, there was fury in her eyes.

"Have you thought to? Have you taken a moment to take care of yourself, or have you let your twin drive you like a slave to keep her alive?"

"I just never..."

"Have you thought to feed her or Heath?" Mischa's interrogation continued.

"Why are you acting like this?" I didn't like being railroaded every time one of them had the chance to.

"Because you are highly intelligent and driven, yet sometimes, I wonder how you can be so stupid," she snapped. "The werewolves gave you seventy-two hours to make a decision. It took just over twenty-four for you to get here. It's a ten-hour drive from here to their compound for a trade. You've had time to take care of yourself. If you had been just a little too weak, you would have gotten yourself killed in that fight." Mischa stopped and looked at Hisao. "She doesn't see it. She has no fucking idea—"

"No idea of what? Damn it, one of you fucking talk to me—"

"You are going to get yourself killed, and I won't have another Liza!" Mischa screamed, slamming a hand down on the table so hard, it broke off the corner in an explosion of splinters and chunks of wood. Only one person screamed and jumped away from the table, and that was Gwen. Three of us held up a hand to tell her to stop moving—me, Heath, and Hisao. She just did her best impression of a boneless chicken instead and fell to the floor.

None of us moved from our seats as Mischa breathed hard. She glared at the broken table then looked at me.

"You don't know the pain this family had to go through when we lost her. You just keep throwing yourself into danger. Jacky, how can you be so careless with your life? Don't you understand what it does to us? You can't even make sure to take care of yourself while you go out and do these things." Mischa's rage turned into pain and desperation. "And for what this time? To save some strangers?"

I looked down at the food and wanted to cry. Mischa had made one of my favorite meals, hamburgers with broccoli as a side, along with macaroni and cheese. It was my comfort food meal.

"Eat," Hisao whispered. "Mischa, come with me."

She growled, and he snarled back. They left the room together.

I did as he asked, ignoring the two people down the table from me. Gwen eventually made it back to her seat, and I looked down at her to see her eating slowly. Heath stared at his plate as he ate but looked up and captured my stare.

Another moment where I wished I could talk to him, but the things I wanted to say weren't something others could hear. I felt adrift, alone. I couldn't even speak openly to my one friend.

When Mischa and Hisao came back in, my blonde sister sighed.

"I'm sorry," she whispered. "You didn't deserve that."

"Forgiven," I said honestly. Her outburst had hit home.

We ate together, a peaceful silence coming over the room as the tension eased. When everyone was finished and the dishes were cleared, Mischa beckoned us to follow her into the next room, where a fire was going, and plush couches were arranged—a meeting room, a place to discuss art, politics, and religion. A place to teach and to learn among peers.

"This is where I meet with the city's council to talk about changes while I was gone or changes they want to implement," she explained, sitting down.

"They know you're a werecat?" Heath asked, obviously curious on a professional level.

"Only this village," she said, smiling. "You must know a thing or two about that. Did you often work with the city you were based in?"

"And the state of Texas and the United States government," he said, nodding as he sat down across the room from me.

"You were a member of the North American Werewolf Council," Hisao said, positioning himself oddly close to Heath. "That council of yours was why Hasan never tried for a bigger presence in the country, and none of us moved there. When he Changed Jacky, she was a native and went back, but I don't think we've ever looked at North America as a place to be, the way you have."

"I fought for the colonies against the British Empire," Heath said, shrugging. "It's home. Most werewolves born or Changed in the U.S. don't have strong ties to other areas of the world. We spread quickly, too. I can see why we were able to take the 'New World' before you." He quoted that the way most supernaturals did. There was nothing 'new' about North America.

"Hasan had plenty of opportunity to claim it, but he was in love with the wildlands of his mate, and it was too far from his place of birth," Mischa said casually. "What do you do, now that you aren't in any sort of position? Isn't that something most werewolves crave once they have it?"

"I want to raise my daughter. There will always be a need for me when I claim or create a new pack."

"Such confidence," Mischa purred. "Well, don't worry, we're going to get you back to your daughter and son." She turned to me, and I didn't like the expression on her face. "Do you have what those damn werewolves want?"

I fished the USB out of my pocket, where I'd kept it since we walked off the jet. I had no intention of giving it to anyone unless I knew it would make its way to the Tribunal, and the Russian werewolf pack would pay.

"Are we going to talk about how to get Gwen's and my family back?" I asked, holding it up. "Do you know how to get this to...Callahan and Corissa?" I looked at Heath, who nodded. I got the names right.

"We'll discuss how to get your family back. I'm not going to discuss those two." Mischa opened a hand. "I'll also need your cellphone."

"Excuse me?" I pulled the USB back and eyed Hisao, who was standing much too close to Heath. He stepped closer to the werewolf, and Heath was smart enough to stand and prop himself up by the fire.

"Let's make this easy," Mischa said softly. "I know you

want to save the world, Jacky. We all do. Your sister wants to save the world. Fine, she can. You can't."

"What?" I stood as she did.

"I'll clarify since you're having such a hard time understanding. If Gwen wants to risk her life and the lives of your human family to expose a werewolf pack who will see her dead in a day, then she can. *You can't.*" Mischa kept her hand out. "We're going to make the trade. That's the family's call. I'm only telling you what every other person in our family will."

It was a slap in the face of everything I believed in. A heartbeat after her words, I was shocked. Reeling, I stepped away from her again.

In the second heartbeat, I got angry.

"No," I growled. "We can do this. We can save them and expose the pack."

"No, Jacky, we can't," she said softly. "For one, this is now a family matter. They know about you, and the first thing they will do if you go into their compound and try to free your family by force is say you acted against them, and it will start a war. Isn't that something you were worried about? Why you tried to keep us out of it?"

"What about them taking my family?" I demanded. "Mischa!"

"They took Doctor Duray's family. We never publicly said the two of you were related, so they couldn't reasonably know it. Aside from that, your sister acted against them. *She* antagonized *them*." Mischa pointed across the room at Gwen. "Then she dragged you into it, knowing full well who you're related to. Knowing full well the position you hold in our world. Do you really think she called you because she loves you? She used you!"

I looked at Gwen, who shook her head, but I could also see the tears in her eyes.

"Did you?" I asked softly. I was split. There was a chance. I didn't want to believe it, but I wasn't stupid enough to completely ignore the chance.

"I didn't think of it that way. I really didn't know who else to call, and I did know who you were, but..." Gwen wiped her eyes. "You're *my* sister. You were the one person I thought I could trust to have my back. I had no one else who would understand."

There was no lie in her scent. I looked back at Mischa, who sighed.

"We can't, Jacky. If we could, I would have tried years ago. Why do you think I protect my people here so viciously? I know what the pack does, I do, but the last thing we need is another war we will *lose*. We don't have the numbers, and their population has exploded. They will destroy us. We can't risk that."

I refused to believe we only had two options. The world couldn't be so black and white.

I shouldn't have to decide between my human family and my werecat family. I shouldn't have to choose who to save.

I shouldn't have to make this choice.

I tried my best, running in circles in my head to find an argument. There had to be some argument that would work, that would sway my werecat family to my side.

"So, we're cowards?" I asked softly. That made Mischa straighten up, her body tensing as her eyes went wide. "We'll allow a werewolf pack to dictate the terms to *our* family? Our family is the ruling family of the werecats. Hasan is on the Tribunal. He's the strongest werecat alive. We're going to let some fucking sick werewolves tell us how this is going to happen? No. I refuse to believe this family is so weak, we don't want to cause any fucking trouble. They took people who belong to *me,* and the moment they realized they had, they should have given my family back. They should have given me all of them back. I don't care if they knew it or not. I highly doubt they didn't. The entire damn hospital was in on it, Mischa! How do we know Sarah didn't fucking tell them? She based her entire fucking plan on the retribution aspect, the threat that others would—"

"You just...called our family cowards," Mischa said, finally catching up. I really didn't think she would get stuck on that.

"Damn right, I did," I growled.

"After everything our family has been through, you would call us *cowards*?" I had never pissed off my Russian sister before, and now, I knew not to.

She shoved me, sending me into the wall a few feet behind me, causing it to crack. The air flew out of my lungs, and I tried to gasp for air. As I slid to the floor and got away, a piece of drywall fell onto the hardwood floor.

Before I was on my feet, Hisao had her on the other side of the room, snarling at her.

"We don't fight," he hissed. "You know the rules, Mischa. We do *not* fight in this family."

"That's because you could kill any of us," she retorted with a growl.

I brushed off my back, waving away Gwen, who tried

to come to my side. She didn't need to be in the middle of this.

"It's fine, Hisao," I said softly. "It's fine. I apparently crossed a line."

"Yes, you did," Mischa snarled, trying to pass our brother to get back in my face. "We've fought wars. We've saved our kind from extinction. We've watched our children die to protect our people. Your moral high ground and naivety are as stupid as they are honorable."

"Fine, I'm naïve," I agreed, lifting my hands. "I won't give up my convictions for my safety, though. I won't give up and leave people to be hurt because it's convenient for the family. I can't and I *won't* do that."

"And you can't," Heath said from across the room. Everyone turned to him. He'd been silent the entire time. When he didn't continue, Mischa waved him on, glaring.

"You have an opinion, werewolf? Say it."

"If you take the trade, you have no problems now, but you put Jacky in a bad position with the new Alpha." He pushed off the wall, walking toward us. "I don't know how many of you grew up with a human family, but maybe that's why none of you thought of this. I've been thinking about it for a while, but since I'm not welcome, I thought someone would have considered the obvious."

"None of us had or have a human family except this village, which is distant, and the werewolves know not to fuck with them. We were all adopted by Hasan when we were children as orphans," Mischa answered, her glare turning into a frown. "But Jacky has a human family, and that somehow changes this?"

"He'll know he can get whatever he wants out of her

by threatening her family—Jacky Leon, daughter of Hasan, in his pocket until the leverage is finally gone. Gwen's children are young. They could live a hundred years and with technology, even longer. Imagine how much damage a werewolf Alpha could do with that sort of pull over her."

"Like you?" she asked. I hated the way she said it.

"Jacky has pull over me, not the other way around," he countered. "And there's no malicious intent, only my daughter's protection. Smell the truth on me, Mischa." He spread his arms, and his scent drifted across the room. I caught the scents in it, the frustration about the situation, but I couldn't smell a lie. Mischa sighed, and Heath nodded politely, the truth acknowledged.

"So, you trade the files for her family—no wars today with the werewolves. Now, you'd just have a new werewolf Alpha—who is over twelve hundred years old, who has seen the War, who has seen the shift into the Tribunal, who doesn't like the Tribunal—and he has everything he needs to keep Jacky right where he can use her. 'Jacky, go kill this werecat, so my pack can move into the area. Do it, or I'll kill your family.' It's easy, Mischa. When a supernatural has human family, especially close relatives, ones they grew up with, it's so easy to hold that supernatural in a net, they can't escape."

"So, we have to," she said, looking unhappy with the idea. "I'm amazed we missed it." She directed that at Hisao. He shrugged and shook his head, then walked out of the room. When she turned to me, there was something different about her expression. "I'm an idiot. I wanted to be mad at you for getting into another disastrous situation and forgot the obvious. I've done this before."

"During the War," I reminded her. "Your response back then was expected. We've been at peace for eight hundred years."

"But we're not at peace. They took your family." She turned on her heel to follow Hisao. Before she left, she hit the door frame a couple of times, then turned back to me once again. "I should have let Zuri talk to you. She offered to fly over, and I told her I could handle it. She wouldn't have shoved you or ignored what you were saying. This time, I mean the apology."

Mischa left the room, leaving me feeling like I had whiplash.

"Does this mean we're going to rescue our family?" Gwen asked softly.

"It means we're going to try, but not you." When I looked at her, she wore this amazingly confused expression. "You're human. This isn't the place for you. If I have my way, it'll be me, Heath, and possibly Hisao—a small group that can get in and out."

"Oh, yeah. I wouldn't know how to do this, would I?" She half chuckled, and I could only guess why. A fear response? A drop in adrenaline finally taking over? I didn't know.

"They really wanted to be angry with you," Heath whispered as I walked toward him. "Mischa is probably understating it. I think they all really wanted to be angry with you."

"Really?"

"I think forcing you to make the trade instead of what

you wanted...wasn't just because it was a good political choice. I think they meant to use it to remind you that you are the youngest in the family, and you need to learn to follow directions."

"Werecats don't have Alphas," I reminded him softly, looking at the door my siblings left through.

"That doesn't mean they don't have some loose power structure, which you should be at the bottom of," he pointed out. "Everyone follows Hasan. Zuri and Jabari are the next most respected. Mischa and Hisao, each a little different for their own reasons. Davor and Niko are always talked a little down to by their older siblings. Then you, the baby, who lives on her own program and doesn't get into line like everyone else. I think your family is tired of you doing whatever you please."

"You don't think Mischa had a point about me always trying to get myself killed?"

"I think that's why they are trying so hard to get you in line," he murmured. "If you fall into the place where they expect you to be, they can keep you out of danger."

"Did you ever do this with your children?"

Something dark crossed over his face.

"I said something to Landon I'll regret for the rest of my life because I was scared for him," he admitted. "It's one of the reasons he tells so few people about himself, but it's hard to hide when everyone can smell every bodily reaction someone has."

"Oh, Heath," I said, breathing out his name. "How long ago?"

"That I said something stupid? I think I do every day, but that? Around 1900," he answered. "But that's not the point. I think you need to keep your eyes and ears open to the fact your family wants to bring you in line, and they're failing. It might explain how some of them act around you and how you might be able to handle it."

"Thanks. I always appreciate your advice," I said, meaning every word.

He shrugged, but for a split second, I thought he would do something else.

25

CHAPTER TWENTY-FIVE

We sat in that room for an hour until a human walked in and looked at me.

"Okhranyat would like you to follow me," he said, all professional. He was even dressed like a butler. I nodded and jumped up from the couch, waving goodbye to my sister and Heath.

I didn't know where I was going, but I knew what I would find. Mischa and Hisao had left to talk to our family, and I was finally getting invited to the conversation. It was like being called to the principal's office, except I didn't feel the dread I might have in school. I got more pissed off every step, following the nameless, distant relative of my sister.

When Mischa and Hisao had left, their intention was clear, but I was left waiting. An important, long discussion was about to happen in the family, and I was left out. Just like I was when they learned my sister worked at the hospital and never told me. They had made all of those decisions on their own—just like they made a decision on how to help my family all on their own.

We went to the basement, and the butler left me at the door, which I didn't stop to knock on. I stormed right through the door into an office with a massive screen. Hisao and Mischa were sitting on a couch with a camera pointed at them. From the video feed that showed everyone, it could see the entire couch but not me.

"Come sit down, Jacky," Mischa ordered, leaning over and clasping her hands.

"I can see everyone from right here," I said, closing the door and leaning on it. "What's the verdict? How much trouble am I in this time?"

"We don't need the attitude," Hasan said patiently. "Sit down where we can see you."

"No," I snapped. "You're all pretty used to having discussions about me without me around. Just pretend like I'm not fucking here. That's probably easier."

The silence I got in response was long and awkward.

"Yeah," I said evenly, finally walking over to the couch, but not sitting. I leaned on the arm, making sure I was in camera. "Who wants to tell me why I was never told about my sister? Hmm? Maybe this situation wouldn't have fucking blindsided me if anyone had thought to mention that. 'Oh, your twin works for the supernatural hospital. We need to talk to her about what's allowed and what's not.' Instead of just telling her to stay away and never contacting me. Thanks for that fucking awkward moment where I was standing in Everett's house, staring at her, unable to fucking process how it even happened. Really appreciated it."

"We made the wrong call," Zuri agreed softly. "Not all of us voted in favor of that decision."

I looked at Zuri and Jabari, sitting together. Neither seemed comfortable, but then, I could understand that.

"I don't have the same relationship with her you two have. That relationship was poisoned years ago, but thank you for considering me." Once, we might have—before hormones and teenage years, before the resentments on my end could build, and she grew a superiority complex I had to suffer with for over a decade.

"Relationships ebb and flow," she said in return, smiling a little. "You think Jabari and I have always been close? We have our bad decades."

"It doesn't matter who agreed with it or not. We made a decision," Hasan said evenly. "Jacqueline—"

"No, you are the last person who is allowed to talk to me right now," I growled. "Secrets, Hasan, always with the secrets. There was Shane. I'll remind you I disappeared from this family for over six years because of that, and now my sister?" I was hurt. This wounded me in an all too familiar way.

"I thought I was doing what was best. You wanted no contact with your human family after you Changed, even after you left my household."

"That doesn't mean I shouldn't know one is becoming entrenched in the supernatural world. Did I want to talk to her? No! But that doesn't mean never tell me about her at all."

"I see that now," he said, looking down at something on his desk. "And you can hold that against me and continue to rage at me at a later date. I extend my apology for not properly judging what you needed or wanted when it came to your human family."

I hated that. For years, he was unapologetic for never telling me about Shane. He had deep and dangerous secrets when it came to Changing people like me over Shane and more. That I understood.

But he apologized so quickly, it reminded me that Hasan wasn't perfect and even he knew that. This man ruled a sizable portion of the supernaturals and led the werecats to peace. He wasn't perfect, and he was sorry, just like that.

I just wanted to keep being angry. I looked at everyone else on the screen and saw the same apology reflected in their faces.

"Were you all going off what Hasan felt I wanted?" I asked softly. "That I never wanted to speak to them or know about them ever again?"

"We were," Niko said softly, nodding. "But the circumstances changed things, and we should have recognized that."

I cursed under my breath and slid onto the couch, sitting next to Mischa.

"Well, if you're all going to put it that way," I muttered. "I don't like being the topic of conversation when I'm not in the room."

"Mischa needed time to calm down," Hisao said softly. "We haven't been talking for very long. You riled her up."

"Heath's point was a good one," Zuri said, leaning on her brother, making an executive decision to change the subject. "We don't know this Alpha, and we don't know anything about how he's going to run the pack. The death of Alpha Vasiliev changes everything in the region."

"He took Jacky's family the same way Mischa's family was attacked," Davor pointed out. "How different can he be?"

"He's more politically minded," Hasan countered. "And that makes him a danger to the Tribunal."

That confused me. We all waited for him to say more. Hasan never talked about the Tribunal with me, and by the looks of it, he didn't talk much about his business there with most of us.

"Father?" Hisao asked softly. "Are you going to call in an Executioner or an Investigator? Because I can give you recommendations."

"I think I'm going to approach Callahan and Corissa about an Investigator, but first, we need to extract Jacky's family. If this is a move to trap Jacky and get favors out of her—"

"Blackmail her into doing his bidding," Zuri corrected.

"Yes, that," Hasan agreed, nodding. He was too patient, I decided. He was always way too patient with all of us. "Then he's probably looking to cause me problems. That I can take to Callahan, and he'll have to act."

"I'm amazed none of you thought about this earlier," I said softly, leaning back. "The whole 'using my family against me' thing." I hadn't thought of it either until Heath said something, but that was because I had never considered making the trade with Sergey.

"We were all pretty pissed off," Davor muttered,

looking away from his camera. "Here we go again. Jacky's gone and gotten herself into something, there's no winning. There's only a less terrible outcome than others. Fantastic."

"I don't get into trouble that often," I fired back, glaring at his face on the screen, which probably looked odd to them once I considered what I was doing.

"No, you just don't follow conventions," Zuri reminded me. "You broke the Law, and we had to step in. You got into a fight with some vampires, which was more you and Jabari, and it's not a problem, but it's a lot of action in less than six months for a werecat who had just entered the public in a big way. Then there was letting Alpha Everson and his family move in. That upset a lot of people. And when we tried to clean you up and give you something productive to do, that just pissed off some unsavory werecats, who were just looking for an excuse because they had been watching just as closely as we had. You..."

"I?" I waited, but she never continued.

"You're a wild card. That's the saying, Zuri. A wild card." Niko chuckled softly. "Damn, you need to get out a little more."

"Oh, stop. I can't know every single saying in every single language," she snapped back, but it was lighthearted ribbing between them. "But that's what I was looking for. You're a wild card, Jacky. You don't do what the rest of us have done or would do, so when you call Father and tell him, 'I killed some werewolves and by the way, my twin is involved,' then hang up, we don't know what's going on, we don't know why it's happening. Once again, we're in the dark, just like we were when you were oath sworn and called to Duty. You left us wondering what terrible thing we would have to clean up, and hopefully, it wasn't going to be your body."

Heath had been right.

"So, when you discovered there was another way for me to get in a lot of trouble..."

"We immediately jumped on the idea of making you take the trade to get *part* of what you want. It was convenient politically and ended this entire mess faster than it began," she confirmed.

"And clearer heads made us see the problem with that." Hasan rubbed his temples, and I saw how much he hated every moment of this. He didn't want to do it, didn't want to say what I figured he had to say. "So, Jacky, you will get what you want. You and Hisao will rescue your human family—"

"Heath should go too," Hisao said. "A werewolf with a strong nose, he'll give us the edge the werewolves will have on us."

"Accepted. You, Hisao,"—a deep sigh—"and Alpha Everson will go get your human family. It will be dangerous, but I have faith in you to do what must be done. You will leave the new Alpha and as many werewolves as you can alive. Once you confirm to me you are cleared of their compound, and they aren't pursuing, I will contact Callahan and tell him everything, from the beginning to the end, leaving out how your sister...killed Alpha Vasiliev...if I can," he stressed that part at the end. "Hopefully, Callahan and—"

"Try Corissa," Zuri said, tapping a finger on her chin.

"Female. She'll be more willing to see Jacky and Gwen's point. Callahan would understand why you would never trade with a lower wolf, but hopefully Corissa will have the righteous fury on the side of the wolves to excuse Jacky for being involved."

Hasan's blank face said a thousand words, particularly 'Yes, Zuri, I know all of this.'

"I was going to say, hopefully, Callahan and Corissa understand and will talk reasonably with me. I don't and will never contact Corissa directly. She and Callahan have been mates since before I met them. I would never tread on Callahan's toes by going to Corissa privately."

"Ah. Good old-fashioned casual sexism," I said, nodding wisely. Old supernaturals were the best at it. It was something I tried to knock out of Hasan when he Changed me, but he was only a very mild offender and only on rare occasions. He couldn't be much more than that with Zuri and Mischa.

Oh, the look Hasan was trying to level at me through the cameras was terrifying in a comical way. When Mischa snorted next to me and covered her face, I knew I'd won my Russian sister back to me, and we would be okay in the long run.

"Why is Mischa staying?" Jabari asked, trying his best to keep the family on topic. "It's her region, and she knows it the best."

"Hisao knows it next best to me because he visits more often than the rest of you," she replied. "I will stay and protect my village from retribution and protect Gwen. I'll provide a place where they can come back to with hot food and sleep quarters once Jacky has returned with her family."

"Does he know how to get to the werewolves?"

"Oh, yes," he confirmed. I glanced his way and saw a small, cold smile form. "I've always known. When they built this new compound thirty years ago, I went to see it. I know the way."

"You'll be going in blind. Be careful," Jabari ordered. "Father?"

Hasan looked into his camera, then away, the glow of the screen hitting his face at a different angle, making him seem harsher, more angled.

"Be safe," he whispered. "Jacky, leave the files with Mischa."

I took it out of my pocket and handed it to my sister without complaint.

Hasan hung up, followed by the rest of my siblings.

"He hates when we have to fight," Mischa said softly. "He's willing, and he's always been very good at it, but he always hates it."

"He's dedicated his life to peace," Hisao reminded us. "Being one of the remaining first children of the first werecat, he's seen the violence since our creation. He's tired, and he wants peace."

"What?" I frowned. "What do you mean? I knew he was Changed by the first werecat, but you make it sound like he was Changed to be a soldier to fight..."

"He was," Mischa said softly, standing. "We've lived a relatively peaceful existence for eight hundred years. It's been a good run. I would blame it all on you, but it ended with Liza's murder. Before the Tribunal was established...

the war all over Europe eight hundred years ago was just a reckoning. Tensions had been too high, and we've always clashed in personality with werewolves. One human died, and the fragile coexistence fell apart, but we had been fighting for far longer. Hasan says since the day the first werecat and the first werewolf were created. Probably even before they were created."

"Were we made to hate each other?"

Mischa looked at Hisao, who met her gaze.

"This isn't something he tells us when we're young," she said, asking an unspoken question. "Do you think he'll be mad?"

"I think we need to help our sister understand our father better," he said, equally uncomfortable.

"Yes, little sister, we were."

They all knew the origins of the werecats and the werewolves.

"Can you tell me any more than that?" I asked.

Mischa opened her mouth, nothing came out, then she coughed violently.

Hisao chuckled. "Sister, you know better than to try to fight that spell." He looked down at me, a little sorry but also humored by Mischa's coughing fit. "Sorry, little sister. There's only one person who can tell you the origins of the werecats. It took two hundred years for me to learn and be placed under the same spell, a spell only that person can remove." He patted my shoulder as he went to leave the room. "We don't intentionally keep secrets, but you must understand. You're young, and some of these take time. We can't rush it. Neither can you."

Mischa nodded while pointing at Hisao with one

hand and covering her mouth with another. Once it looked like she was okay, she took a deep breath.

"What he said. I can try all day and end up no closer to telling you. I don't know why I even tried."

"Who put the spell on you?"

"Can't tell you that either," she said. "We can talk about this another time. We need to get to work. The sooner we get moving, the sooner we're done, and the better Father will feel."

She walked out with Hisao, leaving me alone. Hasan hated violence, had been Changed to fight for the first werecat, to fight an eternal war to extinction versus the werewolves—even though he now hated violence and worked so hard to keep the peace.

"You could make an army," I whispered.

"Daughter," he murmured, running a hand over my head. "I already have."

They'd had literally ages to create their mysteries and hide their secrets. I had ages to figure them out.

So, I stood from the couch and walked away, leaving thoughts of armies and soldiers behind and focused on the task at hand.

26

CHAPTER TWENTY-SIX

"We will leave by truck in six hours, which will give Mischa and her village time to get the necessary supplies ready," Hisao said to our group. "That also puts us on schedule to be there at nightfall. They're south of us, so they'll have a proper night at this time of the year, unlike this village."

"It's also nearly seventeen hours until we get to them," I pointed out. "Right before we landed, we were down to forty-eight hours left. If my math is right, and it's probably a little off, we've got forty-four left. Another seventeen hours leaves..." I did the quick math, but it was slow. The time zones had already made my head spin, and now simple subtraction was hard. "Twenty-seven or so? Then another ten-hour trip back...I want to get there faster."

"The time limit the werewolves gave you is fine. It won't matter by the time we have your family," Hisao pointed out. "Forget the time limit, it's not a concern for us. We'll be in and out well before they have a reason to hurt your family. I'm more worried about chaos in the compound, thanks to the change in regime. It's going to be okay, Jacky." He was kind with that last line, lifting a hand to make a gesture that told me I needed to bring my anxiety down.

Gwen stood beside me, holding my hand tightly. Heath stood further around the circular table with Gwen between us, his face frozen in a severe expression as he concentrated on the map. Mischa and Hisao were directly across from me.

"We take the truck halfway since we'll have the road that far, then proceed in animal form. It turns off at a bad place. We'll have a bag for clothing for Heath. He's the only one of us I want in human form once we leave that truck and make it to the compound."

"How do we get our family back with no ride on a five-hour run?"

"I can hotwire," Hisao said.

"So can I," Heath added. When I looked at him like he'd grown a second head, he shrugged. "It's a useful skill that can mean life or death, and it comes with learning how to work on your own car. It's not hard. Just a few minutes if the vehicle is old enough and the wiring isn't a complete mess."

Hisao was the only person in the room who gave Heath an appreciative nod of respect. I was still a little shocked to find out the good werewolf father knew how to steal a car.

"It will be an old truck," Mischa said, drumming her fingernails on the table. "Luxury cars are only for the rich, but a good truck out here just needs to be easy to fix and strong enough to handle rough treatment. The pack will have several old things you can steal. If they don't, I'll be surprised."

"So, we drive them back to our original vehicle, then switch, leaving the pack's vehicle," Hisao finished, still pointing at that one spot on the map. "It's not a smooth plan, but it will see us through."

"You didn't talk about how to free our family," Gwen pointed out, her hand squeezing mine.

"There's not much to say. We need to track them down in enemy territory, where there are two options if we fail—be killed on sight for Jacky and me or be captured, which will be Heath's fate. It's not something we can plan since we don't have satellite imaging," Hisao explained. "We have to follow our instincts and our experience to get us in and out. Getting out will be the harder task, with two elderly humans and two children who are prone to making a lot of noise. Don't worry about the details. We'll either succeed and tell you, or fail, in which case everyone will know as soon as the werewolves can confirm our deaths."

"They'll blast your deaths on every channel where supernaturals get their information," Heath said softly. "And they'll try bargaining hard with Landon for my release, something he won't fall for. He knows the rules."

"Let's not talk about the dying or captured thing, please," I mumbled. "So...we have a plan."

"We have a plan," Hisao confirmed, nodding once. "You can all go and clean up, change, take a nap. Mischa?"

"Three hours. A truck will be out front in three

hours." She left first. Heath, Gwen, and I left next. I dropped Gwen off at her guest bedroom, then headed upstairs to my room, which had a small bathroom attached. I went to start a bath when someone knocked on my door.

"Come in," I called.

I was surprised to smell Gwen, then see her come into the doorway to the bathroom.

"I wanted to talk to you," she said, swallowing.

"You could have said something before I left you in your room." I was genuinely confused.

"I...I thought about it for a second, then came up after you. Hisao pointed the way when I saw him in the hall."

"Ah." I went back to checking the temperature of the water.

"Jacky—"

"What happened between us?" I asked softly. "I remember...being very close to you. I have memories from when we were fourteen, and it was beginning to fall apart. I don't remember much else from my childhood, but I know the feeling. I used to trust you implicitly. What changed?" She had come up to talk to me, but I took over the conversation. I sat on the edge of the tub and watched her.

"Well..." Gwen shrugged, then jumped up to sit on the counter, her legs hanging down. "I don't know. I just remember...something changed. We entered high school, and you had so many friends while I was getting better grades. Not that your grades were bad—"

"I graduated high school in the top ten of our class. No, my grades weren't bad," I snapped. "You would get a ninety-nine on something, I would get a ninety-two, and I was treated like I amounted to nothing. Like I was stupid," I huffed. But something else she said stuck with me after that outburst. "I didn't have that many friends."

"You were one of the most popular people in school," she said impatiently. "You were so cool. All I had were my grades and being Valedictorian. You knew how to talk to people and make them see you. They didn't ignore me, but the only reason I was student class president was I was Valedictorian and your sister. You didn't run—"

"So, you used me to campaign." That I definitely remembered, allowing myself to chuckle.

"I've always been certain they voted for me because they thought I was you," she said, laughing. "I said you were good with people. You are. You always have been. I don't know what your life has been like since Shane died, and I can't begin to imagine how much everything has changed you and not just in a werecat sense. You could talk your way out of trouble with anyone. Our parents knew it, and I knew it, but everyone else? They just let you get away with everything. Remember when you cursed at a teacher?"

"He was an asshole to students," I said, going down memory lane.

"Yeah. He didn't write you up, but that news flew all over school. Our parents found out and—"

"And said 'why can't you be more like Gwen?'" I tilted my head and gave her an expectant look.

"Yeah..."

"Yup, that memory is just fine," I said, looking at my half-full bath. "What's your point?"

"They kept telling you to be more like me, but...I was actually jealous of you in high school," she admitted so softly I thought I imagined it. I saw her lips move and the sound come out, but I didn't believe the words. "You stood up for people, fought for them. You talked to the smart kids, the sports kids, the drama kids. Clichés didn't exist for you. You walked into high school and decided in a weird way, you were above that bullshit..." She shook her head. "I was jealous of you. Jacky, I was the person who told our parents about the story. The school wasn't going to. They were getting on to me about how I needed to do something more than be smart. I needed to learn an instrument or join another club, and I just fired out with, 'Be happy I'm not cursing at teachers like Jacky.'"

My jaw dropped.

"I think...I think it was my fault," she whispered. "I think I'm why we lost touch, and the rift grew. I was never a people person. I was driven by ambition, the ambition our parents wanted us to have. You know they wanted us both in medical school, but did you ever really want it?"

"I could help people," I answered. "It gave me the chance to keep helping people."

"You should have been a lawyer," she said, smiling a little. "I always thought it would be a better fit for you."

"That's insane," I said, shaking my head. "I couldn't—"

"Look at you earlier. You were pleading your case and brought witnesses. You stopped, and I could see you do what you always do. You consider your options. How to talk your way to getting what outcome you want. You maneuver and manipulate like the best of them."

"I don't. This was a one time thing—"

"I heard you pleaded your case in front of the Tribunal so well, you convinced Hasan to take your side. He's a member, but apparently he's never held himself or his family above the Law. He even allowed a werewolf pack to deliver justice to the werewolves who murdered his daughter, and because they had done it before he could, he took no further action. He didn't go after anyone else because that was against the Law. He didn't rampage the way a father should. No, instead he disappeared—"

"For over a century until he came to defend me," I finished for her. "I know."

"Why did he do that?"

"Because I explained to him I felt like I was upholding my honor and the Duty by continuing when the Law said I needed to stop. It was a problem of two conflicting Laws and ideologies, and it needed to be changed," I answered softly. "He ended up agreeing with me."

"See?" She sighed. "You were always great at this. You know how to think about social things. Maybe that's why you became a humble bartender."

I rolled my eyes.

"And you're friends with werewolves, something no one really believes is true, but now I've seen it. You and Heath would die for each other. I can see that. You defend each other to the death, and he's literally walked into a lion's den to back you up." She smirked, probably at her own little joke. Werecats weren't lions, but I wasn't going to burst her bubble. "Maybe you shouldn't have been a lawyer. A politician might have been a better choice."

I smiled in return. “I don’t like politicians.”

“Of course not. You never did. They were always too slimy and corrupt for you,” Gwen whispered, her smirk staying.

“Yeah.” I chuckled, remembering the rants I had as a college student when people told me I needed to vote. I was so cynical about politicians, I never voted during my human life and would never be able to now. Something felt peaceful in the bathroom. I turned the water off and leaned over, putting my elbows on my knees. For the first time in a long time, I voiced something I carried for years.

“I was jealous of how much our parents loved you. They were always looking for my flaws, but you were so golden and perfect.”

“I think I was what they expected and wanted, while you wanted to make your own path. I’m sorry I never supported you.”

“We were kids,” I murmured, staring at my hands. “We were kids and...it wasn’t your fault they were never satisfied with me. I’m sorry for the way I used to treat you...still treat you. I’ve resented you for a long time.”

“Is that why you cut us off?” she asked.

“It played a role,” I admitted. “But it wasn’t the only reason. I thought you were too toxic to be my family. A lot of the way you treated me and the way my...other siblings have is pretty similar. I’ve always been the bad kid, I guess.” I shrugged. “So, it wasn’t that. It was just the realistic pain I knew I would have to go through. And exposing all of you to this world? It’s dangerous, as you can see, and easy to get a lot of people hurt, easy for things to go sideways.”

She nodded, and we settled into silence. I really wanted to take my bath, but I couldn't tell her to leave. She had come in here to talk to me.

"What did you want to say when you came in?"

"I wanted to talk to you about this," she said, smiling a little. "Though I expected to be the one apologizing, not hearing one from you."

"I'm all ears," I teased, but the seriousness on her face made the humor die as quickly as it had come.

"I started seeing a therapist after Daniel left me," she said softly. "She asked me why I was angry and upset over Daniel leaving me when I never spent time with him. I'm sad Daniel left, and it still hurts, but she was right. I never saw him. I told her...I was most upset that my perfect life fell apart. It was so perfect, and my kids were going to grow up, getting everything they wanted with well-adjusted, normal parents who were still together. Then I didn't have that. My perfect life was gone, and...our parents did what they always did and were angry with me for not being perfect."

I wondered what point she was trying to make.

"Once I could admit that, the loss of perfection, my therapist asked me why I needed to be perfect. I told her it's because it's the reason our parents loved me," she said quietly, sliding off the counter and looking at herself in the mirror. "They never acted like they loved you. They were so hard on you, which made me need to be perfect because I didn't want that from them. At the same time, I was jealous of you, speaking your mind, doing what you believed in. You had a fire. I think it scared our parents, really."

"Gwen, I'm glad you went to therapy, but I'm not following." I lifted my hands in defeat, hoping for some clarity.

"It's all steps," she said, shrugging. "So, when we talked about you and how jealous I was of you growing up, my therapist said something interesting. She said jealousy was one side of the coin—jealousy and admiration, a two-sided coin like love and hate. I was jealous of you, but it was rooted in admiration. So, I stopped going to therapy after that, knowing...I loved Daniel but not enough. I just wanted to be perfect for our parents, who always demanded it. I thought perfection was the only way. And my jealousy of you was my admiration that you didn't feel the need to be perfect. You only felt the need to be you and to do what you felt was right. You were good with people, and you didn't lie about your flaws. You fought against our parents, whose expectations were always too high and unreasonable."

"I tried to reach them, too," I mumbled, looking down.

"But you still fought when you thought they were unfair," she pointed out. "I always wished I could do that, and I lashed out at you. If I could convince myself you were wrong, maybe I wouldn't feel the way I did. Maybe I could finally be perfect because I would believe the same thing our parents did. I'm sorry for treating you that way when I admired you so much, and I didn't know how to handle that."

Tears welled up in my eyes.

"Then I discovered who you are now and what you've been doing." Gwen sounded choked up. "And I admired that. Life threw you one hell of a curveball, and you were still fighting. I decided I wanted to live up to you."

"Then Alpha Vasiliev happened," I whispered. "Gwen..." I was both touched and horrified.

"I know it's crazy. I know I should have never done it the way I did, but I'm glad we're going to help those women. They need someone to help them. I've realized what you meant about Sarah. She really did play me, and I feel so stupid—"

"Don't beat yourself up. It's not your fault," I said, shaking my head and lifting a hand, trying to stop her before she said something she regretted.

"Then you showed up with Heath, talking about politics and how you couldn't do this or that, and it felt like a slap in the face. You weren't the sister I remembered."

"And you weren't the sister I remembered," I said in return. She really wasn't. "I'm going to bathe, then probably get something more to eat. We're going to get them back, Gwen. I promise."

"Um...Well, that's another question I have. What happens when you do?" She seemed scared. "They'll now know about everything, and Daniel...we're not married anymore. He's the father of my children. And my children are going to need therapy..."

"We'll figure it out," I promised. I was certain there was something we could do—magics I didn't know well enough that someone could offer or even just money to help them adjust and install security. "Worry about that after we get them back. There's always a way in this world."

"How did you do it? How did you adjust to learning all of this and how dangerous it can be?"

"I didn't have a choice. I wasn't human anymore," I said, shrugging. "In the beginning, I was just thankful to be alive and grieving because I lost Shane. I had Hasan, a father figure who guided me. He and I had a falling out about four years in. Took us another six years to really begin talking regularly. My new siblings? I didn't start talking to them regularly until about a year and a half ago. If you ask any of them or Heath, they'll tell you I never really adjusted. I just made my own type of life and went with it. You probably know more about other supernatural species. I've only ever met a handful of fae and only met one witch or half-witch as far as I know. I've run into vampires." I sighed as I checked my water. It was still warm, but I needed to give up on the bath idea and just take a shower once she was gone.

"Do you really see them as your family?"

"Yes," I answered, looking up at her again. I saw the hurt there. She didn't like the truth, but there wasn't much I could do about that.

"They don't treat you very well," she accused, looking out the bathroom door.

"Neither did our parents," I reminded her. "Look, I know it's strange, but I feel...a connection to Hasan. He gave me immortality and treated me like a daughter from the moment we met. I'm not saying we're perfect. No family is perfect, but...when I've been in trouble, they have come to my side."

"But we're..." She waved a hand between us. "Related."

"Families aren't always about blood," I countered. "And I won't let you or them make me choose. If you want to talk to me and be a part of my life, I'm more than willing, but it won't come at the cost of the relationships I've been building with my immortal family. That goes both ways. They can't tell me I can't talk to you if I decide I want that moving forward."

"You're undecided? I thought..." Gwen stepped away from me, shaking her head.

"I haven't had the chance to even think about it," I admitted. "But we'll talk more. I can promise that."

"Okay, I can accept that. I mean, you're right. We were never really good to you, and it's something we need to repair. It can't be perfect just because we cleared the air." Gwen smiled and tapped the door frame as she looked away. "I should go and let you get ready."

"Yeah...Get some rest, Gwen. Clean up, put on a change of clothes. Do something to make yourself feel a little better."

She nodded once more and left.

I drained the bath and opted for a hot shower, feeling as if a weight was finally off my shoulders.

Maybe we can have a relationship going forward. There's a lot we need to do before we can get there, though.

27

CHAPTER TWENTY-SEVEN

"Time to head out!" Mischa called through the house on an intercom system I hadn't realized was installed.

I left my bag in my bedroom and pulled my hair up into a ponytail as I walked out. Heath left his room as I passed it, and we stopped to stare at each other. For a moment, I wanted to lean into him and take some level of comfort. Here we were, heading out on another dangerous task. This time, there was no mystery to unravel like in Washington. There was no reveal in store for us as there had been in Dallas when Heath learned who was leading the coup against him.

There was just us and the goal to free my human family.

He checked the hall, his eyes darting left and right, even looked over his shoulder and checked the corners for cameras.

Then he boldly reached out and cupped my cheek,

his thumb tracing a line over my cheekbone. The hand was gone quickly, but the moment of tenderness and wanting remained, beating between us like a drum. I knew it was going to be a small moment I thought about for years to come. No one, not even Shane, had ever touched me with such care, with so much hidden emotion.

There was nothing we could say, not safely, but Heath's eyes told me how much he hated the unending but necessary silence between us.

I wish I could talk to you. I wish we could sit down and talk about all of this, and you could kiss me like there's no one watching. You're my anchor right now, and I can't tell you that. It feels like my life is falling apart, Heath, and I don't know how to do the right thing anymore. How do I keep everyone happy? How do I keep everyone safe? How do I stay true to myself without hurting everyone around me?

We walked downstairs together, the silence all-consuming.

"You two ready to go?" Mischa asked as we found her at the front door, a handheld microphone in her hand with a wire going to the wall. It was an old school intercom system, probably not using wifi for safety reasons. Old, landline type technology was safer than most internet-based stuff, but it surprised me to see the old model looking brand new in her hand.

"Yeah," I answered. "Heath?"

"Ready to go. Tired, stressed out, but ready."

"You'll have another few hours to sleep during the first half of the trip," Mischa said in a friendly way as she thumped Heath on his shoulder. "Take it." She walked to the front door with the obvious expectation we'd follow. "You know, I was a little pissed off when I heard Jacky was in danger with you *again*, but you're not a bad werewolf. Get some sleep on the drive, and don't die. You've got your own family to worry about."

"Thank you for the consideration," he said, nodding politely. "You know I mean you and your family no harm."

"Oh, I know. You seem to be a lot of things, Heath Everson, but none of us have ever thought of you as a fool." Mischa's smile was wicked and dangerous. "Hasan thinks you've gotten too powerful for what you are, actually."

"He and I have discussed it," Heath admitted softly, which surprised me. I turned to him, and he shook his head. "I'll tell you the story on the drive," he promised.

Mischa snorted as she pointed at the truck. It was old with a military look to it.

"It'll get you there and back with enough space for the entire family to sit. It's not protected from the wind, so we put in a dozen blankets to keep people from getting too cold. You two can ride up front with Hisao or in the back on the way there. I don't care either way."

She went back inside, leaving me and Heath to stare at it.

"You ready?" he asked softly. "And I mean, are you really ready for this? Be sure, Jacky."

"I am." I didn't have the option not to be. "Do you think we could talk for a minute?"

He looked around and shook his head, then headed

for the truck, looking at everything that was loaded. Hisao came out next and jumped into the driver's seat. I didn't see Gwen before I climbed into the back, but she came out to wave as Heath got in after me. I waved as the truck started to move.

The road leaving the town was smooth, but it became bumpy quick, around thirty minutes into the trip. Groaning, I laid back and noticed Heath chuckling silently, his shoulders moving.

"You okay?" he mouthed.

I shrugged. "Did you get a chance to talk to Carey and Landon before we left?"

"I did. What about Oliver and Dirk?"

"I texted them and Carey. She didn't tell me if you had called, but it was nice talking to her. She's worried about us. Dirk and Oliver had already been briefed by Davor. They were a little upset with me for not getting in touch sooner."

"Maybe you should do better at keeping in touch with them," Heath pointed out, friendly advice I didn't need. It was a flaw I knew I had.

"I'm not used to having to call in every move I make, and it's barely been like two-and-a-half-days since we left...I think. The time zones have me all fucked up."

"Of course."

An hour in, I moved to one of the benches and let Heath have the space to pass out in the blankets on the floor. We had six hours before we left, but stress exhausted some people, and we had a long night ahead of us. I couldn't blame him for wanting to grab some sleep.

Two hours in, I went up front to see Hisao, climbing through the back window, letting Heath sleep alone. My brother concentrated on the road and hadn't spoken for the entire trip. I wanted to keep him company.

Three hours in, and I finally said something to him.

"Thank you for doing this for me," I said, looking out my window.

"It's my pleasure," he said just as quietly. "May I ask you something?"

"Sure."

"Why have you been avoiding Heath?" he asked softly.

"I..." I almost said I wasn't, but the lie would be obvious. "I haven't wanted to give people the wrong impression. He's my friend and my ally, but I know if I lean on him too much, people will be upset."

"Like our family?"

"And other werewolves and werecats. He knows. He's been doing it to me, too. We have to ride a fine line between allies and friends. We can't let many people know we're actually friends."

"Correct," Hisao agreed. "I just wanted to make sure there was nothing else wrong. I understand why our kinds dislike each other, but I've learned one thing in my job. No group is all good or all evil. There are werewolves I would be honored to work beside, and there are werecats I would be okay killing. I have no problem with you being friends with Heath. In fact, I think the friendship is an important step toward lasting peace."

"You're an assassin, and you want peace," I whispered. It seemed contradictory.

"I'm an assassin for our family because one was required, and I take the art and skill of killing seriously. That doesn't mean I want to do it all the time, and it also doesn't mean I want to fight a war. I go after bad humans in my free time. It's a personal decision, one that doesn't have anything to do with Father or his position. It's my way of helping the world continue moving forward." He reached out and ran a hand over my head the same way Hasan did. It sent shivers down my spine and not in a good way. "I know I make you uncomfortable. I make Davor uncomfortable, as well. I was never close to Liza because she was scared of me." His hand moved back to the steering wheel. "But I'm not so cold or dangerous, I would never hurt people without good cause. Everyone forgets that."

"You're somewhat of a boogeyman," I pointed out. "I know there are werecats afraid to cross Hasan, even in a minor way, because they fear you showing up on their doorstep."

Me included.

"That's on purpose, but I never intended the family to feel that way." He gave me a sad look. "So, yes, I want peace, so I can walk among my own family and they won't fear me. And I see no problem with you and Heath being friends and allies. I wish I could have something similar."

"Have you ever had a friend? Really?"

"No. Outside of family, I've never had a friend," he admitted softly. "I've raised young people to become better than me, and I consider them somewhat children, but I rarely speak to them once they leave my training, and none of them were friends. They were scared young people who needed to learn to kill if they wanted to survive. That's not a conducive environment to build friendships. Everyone else is only scared of me."

"That's lonely," I said, looking away.

"Hmm."

We went back to silence, but I felt like I learned more about Hisao in that one conversation than I had in years.

As the drive continued, my thoughts turned to my family. Experience taught me how to distract myself when I had a chance, but as we neared the midpoint of the trip, my thoughts turned to the captives I had to free. People I hadn't seen in over a decade, scared and trapped by werewolves they didn't know. They probably didn't even know why they had been taken. My parents, Daniel, and those two kids I had never even met. What an introduction they were about to get to their aunt.

"What can we do to help them once we free them?" I asked. "My family. The kids are going to need therapy, and they'll know our secrets. What do we do about that?"

"We can find someone to replace their memories," Hisao offered, looking at me. "If you want to. They don't need to agree because they won't remember the need. The severity of the memories can't be fully erased, but they can be masked. It's highly regulated magic, and there is illegal memory manipulation but in this case? I think we can have someone do it."

"That's...good," I whispered. Hopefully, that would save them from the trauma and ensuing nightmares.

A yawn behind us was the only signal that Heath was waking up.

"Are we there yet?" he asked in a bleary, childlike way.

I laughed as his head came through the window, and he looked between us.

"Are you doing your best impression of Carey?" I asked as he pulled his head back through the window.

"I was. Figured a laugh was necessary."

I looked back to see him moving around and rearranging stuff and remembered what he said in Washington. He liked making heavy moments lighter. He believed in laughing and smiling when he had the chance, and something made him feel more comfortable.

"How long have you been awake?" I asked.

He only shrugged, which gave me the answer I needed. He had been pretending to sleep when Hisao and I talked about friends and enemies, war and peace. Hisao wouldn't judge the chance to make a friend laugh and think it was something more.

I hoped, anyway, or Heath was going to get us into trouble. I didn't know if Hisao had a line he drew for the mingling of werewolves and werecats.

At hour five, right on time, Hisao parked the car off the dirt road.

"From here, we run," he said, unbuckling and jumping out.

"It's going to be a long run," I mumbled.

Hisao continued as if I hadn't spoken.

"We'll be there shortly after sunset. Stay with me and at my pace. We can't slow down. Feel free to use your magics to communicate."

We Changed one at a time, letting Heath begin first, so we could put his clothing in a bag. It wasn't a silly fanny pack like Hasan had made us use, but a high-quality pack for animals that hung over the back. Once Heath was fully in his werewolf form, I strapped it to him with one belt around his trunk. Once again, I found myself wondering if his werewolf form was getting bigger.

"Heath, you should be able to shift back into your human form with that on," Hisao explained. "I've done it countless times, back and forth."

Heath nodded his big head and backed off, so we could Change as well.

Hisao and I raced through it much faster. We left our clothing in the truck, intending to put it back on once we came back.

"Will anyone steal this?" I asked when we walked away.

Hisao shook his head, but there was no way for him to explain why he felt that way. I just had to trust him.

"There's a symbol on the side of the truck. Does that mean something?" Heath asked from the back.

Hisao bobbed his head in a nod, telling me that Heath was directing his thoughts to both of them.

"Does it mean no one should steal the truck or what's in it?" I asked.

He nodded again, then looked back at us. Hisao's expression, even in feline form, said, 'Please stop asking questions,' then he took off at a jog, and we followed, keeping the easy, long-distance running pace.

"Finally, we can talk again," Heath said in my head. *"You might not know how, but it is possible to have private conversations using this. At least wolves can."*

I concentrated on him and tried it out. I never got to

use this ability, so I never knew what I was doing. Sometimes I screamed, and it went to everyone.

"Are you sure?" I looked at Hisao, who's pace didn't change. I looked at my brother and decided to try something. *"Hisao, can you hear me?"*

He nodded.

When I looked back at Heath, I asked an important question.

"Could you hear that?"

"I didn't hear anything after you asked me if I was sure."

"Awesome!" I grinned. *"I bet I've done it before without meaning to, but I've never really tested this thing. It's been a year and a half, and I never really considered figuring out all the nuances."*

"A very 'you' thing to do," he teased. *"Being in Mischa's house was the worst. Being around your family is really hard when I know they'll rip my arms off if they found out I was..."*

"Yeah, I get it, but it seems like Hisao is cool with us being friendly. We don't have to act totally weird."

"Yes, we do. You tend to give everything away in your scent, and I haven't wanted to put you in the position where your feelings are exposed."

"This is the cost we have to pay, right?" I sighed in my head, letting him hear it. *"We're not supposed to like each other, Heath."*

"I don't let other people tell me how I'm allowed to feel. I'm an Alpha. I'm the ruler of my own body."

"No, you just hide it all, so they never find out."

"Yes."

"Well, so you know, I've missed being able to talk openly

with you, too. It's been really hard not being able to work out all of this with you."

"Well, we have five hours. Feel free to tell me whatever you need or want. I'll be listening."

I got the feeling if he could have kissed me right there, he would have.

CHAPTER TWENTY

Five hours was a long run for anyone, including werecats and werewolves. We all managed, and as the sun crept down, Hisao finally slowed. I wanted to fall on my face and not move another inch, but indulging the feeling was out of the question. We had to breach a werewolf compound, get out five human prisoners, and escape before daybreak, hopefully, without a massive fight.

Hisao changed into his human form and sat down on a log.

"Stay in those forms," he said. "I just wanted to be able to speak with both of you before doing this. We're two miles outside their patrol range—"

"How do you know?" I couldn't stop myself from asking.

"I've visited the compound several times to make sure they weren't sending werewolves in Mischa's direction. The last time Mischa and this pack fought was during the War, and I took it upon myself to make sure the werewolves never considered it again. That's not the point. Now, the new Alpha could extend the patrols, but he also might be too busy securing power."

"He probably won't assume we'll attack him at his home base." Heath laid down and panted, which should have been weird, but he was a wolf, and I was panting, too. Neither of us could sweat. *"That's why he'd keep them here to begin with."*

"And because he would want to show off to the pack how he got Hasan's family to take his deal, and that he knew our family's weaknesses," Hisao added. "Is that enough for you, Jacky?"

I nodded. I knew there had to be a good explanation, but I always wanted to hear it. I didn't want to trust my family blindly.

"We're going to get in and try to pick up your family's scents. We can track them from there. If we don't find their scents, we'll search for where they keep prisoners. From the picture, it looked like they were in a proper cell, so hopefully, they won't be in a highly-populated area of the compound."

"We're going to get caught, aren't we?" I asked.

"There's a strong possibility," Hisao confirmed. "We knew that before we got here."

There was a difference between knowing and accepting the information. I was just beginning to accept how dangerous the mission was. A full compound of werewolves hostile to us. Two werecats in the middle of it. Our scents would get picked up. Heath's wouldn't stand out as much, but they would smell us on him, thanks to proximity.

I was afraid, but I couldn't leave my human family in there, and I couldn't make my werecat family vulnerable. I could also never forget the pack in question was rotten to the core, allowed female werewolves to be raped, beaten, and killed, and oppressed its submissive members and hurt them.

I had to balance the needs of both my families and hopefully, see justice for those in this pack who were being crushed by its leaders.

A lot was riding on us.

Hisao looked between us.

"Let's go," he ordered, then dropped down and swiftly Changed back into his werecat form. We moved silently, following his every step.

"I can smell a patrol," Heath said ten minutes later. *"We need to be careful."*

I had no idea what we would do if we were caught before we even made it inside. I knew we'd be found out eventually, but we needed to find my family first.

Once the compound was in sight, Hisao and I stood and watched as Heath Changed and put his clothes on, breathing hard even in his human form. We gave him a minute to relax and get used to his human skin after so long. Every werecat and werewolf knew the toll it took when we stayed in our beastly forms for a long period. It was just hard and normally made us want to sleep for several hours. Extended periods were normally kept to full moons. We didn't have that option.

"I'm ready," he whispered. "It doesn't look much like a compound, just a village."

I agreed. It was much like Mischa's village, the sprawling wilds with a bit of civilization in the middle.

Hisao snorted, and we started to walk as a unit. Heath wore all black, and someone had put a ski mask into the bag to cover his face. Hisao was near all black in his werecat form. I was the only one not completely built for stealth at that moment, so I stuck close to my brother, using him to help block anyone from potentially seeing me.

We entered the village off the road, through two small ramshackle houses, probably homes for lower-ranking wolves. No one was on the streets, and there was an eerie quiet over the village, a direct contrast with the liveliness of Mischa's home village. There was a heavy weight to the air. I could smell the fear that permeated and the undercurrents of anger.

"This is bad," Heath whispered.

"How bad?"

"It feels like this pack is going to go into a full-scale civil war any minute now," he murmured quietly and fast. "That smell in the air? That's because the inner circle and those loyal to them are keeping everyone down. How could they let this fester? How could they do this to their own wolves?"

I couldn't give him the assurance he obviously needed. There was nothing I could say that would make the smell go away, nothing I could do to fix it. Not until we freed my family.

There was such a heavy scent of werewolves everywhere, I had to keep my eyes peeled for any signs of movement. Lights were on in many of the houses, but I saw no one inside them. It was late, and I hoped that was the only reason for the quietness of the village. Maybe people were relaxing on their couches, trying to watch television. Even as I thought about it, lights went out in a few of the houses, and I saw people moving inside. The sign of life made me relax a little, and some of the eerie nature of the village dissipated.

Heath stopped and pointed down a small walkway. Hisao and I were behind him, but I could see the guard standing at the corner of the pathway and a stone-paved road, with some sort of assault rifle.

"What is he using?"

"AK-47. They can be used with silver bullets," Heath whispered low. "Let's find another way."

Hisao and I nodded as Heath turned onto another alley between the rows of houses. There were no streetlights, the only light coming from the occasional glow from the windows. Hisao and I kept as low as we could without dragging our bellies on the ground. Heath crouched to stay under the windows.

We moved slowly, but it was the safest option. Every time we had to turn, I grew more anxious about finding my family. Was there a jail in the village? Would they keep my family there at night, or was the picture just to scare me and Gwen?

Heath stopped dead in his tracks and lifted his head, then started moving again, motioning with his hand for us to hold still. He went through a small wooden gate and crept up to a doorway. We crouched, waiting as he went to a window and peeked inside. He was sniffing so intently, I could hear him, tracking whatever scent it was.

Finally, he went around the house, and I couldn't hear him anymore. After a minute of not seeing him, I tried to move forward, but Hisao blocked me.

There was a thump inside, and the front door opened. Heath had a hand over a male werewolf's mouth and moved him outside. He forced the wolf to kneel in front of Hisao and me.

"Do you speak English?" Though he was speaking quietly, the growl in Heath's words were a threat.

The werewolf nodded, his eyes wide with fear.

Where are the humans?" he demanded. "You smell like humans, but I bet none live here, so you're going to tell me where the humans are."

"Heath, he might scream," I said, knowing how badly this could go wrong.

"Will you?" my werewolf asked. "We're not here to hurt the pack. We're here to rescue the family of Jacqueline, daughter of Hasan. Do you know who Hasan is?"

The werewolf nodded quickly, hampered by Heath's hand.

"Good. So, you know how bad it can go for your pack if those humans are hurt."

Another nod.

"Will you scream when I remove my hand to let you speak?"

This time, the werewolf shook his head. Heath moved his hand, and the werewolf gasped for air. It wasn't a particularly loud noise, but it felt too loud in the perpetual silence of the village.

"There's a building near the main house where they

keep prisoners. I'm just a guard, sir. Please, don't hurt me."

"I don't plan to," Heath promised, going down on a knee next to the wolf. "What would you do if I told you we're rescuing her family, so we can expose the pack for what it's doing? I can smell just as well as any werewolf. This isn't a happy pack."

"My cousin is kept in the female barracks," he said, swallowing. "I wouldn't care what you do or have planned for the high-ranking wolves. Just know most of us are good, and we try. We treat the smaller injuries and keep our heads down. We're not strong enough to fight the old ones and their followers, but we do what we can."

"Do you have the internet or..." Heath let his confusion show.

"No, we're not allowed phones or any contact with the outside world, and no one is allowed to come here. We can watch what they put on the TV, listen to the music they provide, but that's it. I had a phone...before I was Changed about five years ago. Me and my cousin, at the same time. The females are blackmailed with a family member, and the family members...we stay in line because causing trouble draws too much attention to the females."

"I'm sorry," Heath whispered, touching the werewolf's shoulder.

"You're an Alpha," the werewolf said in a hushed, almost fearful way. "Will you be fighting Sergey?"

"No. I plan to get Callahan and Corissa involved. They'll be able to help the most. They outrank Sergey far more than me."

"I don't know..." He looked down. "You and Sergey seem...similar. I could leave his pack and join yours, and he wouldn't be able to take me back."

"Heath?" I was confused now. First, his werewolf form was massive, and now some wolf was saying Heath and Sergey were similarly dominant? And could Alphas steal werewolves from each other?

"You must be mistaken. I am an Alpha, but I'm not that old, nor have I run a pack this large. Let's stay on topic. We're going to do what we can to fix things here, but first, we need to rescue the innocent humans being kept here. We can't leave them. Some of them are much too vulnerable."

"There's a little girl in the group," the guard whispered, his eyes going wide. "I'll show you." He nodded vigorously. "Yeah, I'll show you, but you have to promise you're going to do something to help us."

"We will. We have all the evidence we need to help you, but we have to make sure Sergey can't kill those humans when we take it to the Tribunal."

The guard got to his feet with Heath's help and started walking. We followed, Heath staying close to him. The guard was smart, leading us through the small alleys.

"There's a curfew," he explained. "It keeps us from running since we can't be out of our homes at night. There's only one patrol out there, and they only catch people trying to run. People still escape, but never for long. They're either killed or brought back before they do anything."

"Full moons must be hard," Heath whispered in return.

"They are. The high-ranking wolves get to run. We're kept indoors by the loyal ones who are looking to get ahead. Those are the males who treat the women wrong."

"So, you've never run under a full moon. I'm so sorry," Heath said kindly. "What's your name, young man? I didn't ask, and for that, again, I'm sorry."

Damn, he's so fucking attractive when he's being a leader, a caregiver, and just...Heath. He thrives when he's trying to meet the needs of others.

"Iosif," he answered. The smile on the young werewolf's face was bright. "Now, we must be quiet. We're almost there."

Heath nodded and let Iosif lead the way. We were only a block away from a large mansion in the center of the village, and Iosif pointed to a guard at the door to the small building we needed to get into.

"The cells are underneath," he explained, gesturing down.

"Are there any guards inside?"

Iosif shook his head. "Just one outside. No need for many guards here."

Heath nodded and started walking, holding up a fist to tell us to stay. He went straight up to the guard whose back was turned as he looked over a shadowy area, obviously bored with his job. It happened fast. Heath grabbed the guard from behind, got the door open, and pulled the man inside. Iosif followed next and went inside. I looked back at Hisao. Were we supposed to follow? He went, and I followed him, slinking low to the ground. Once we were inside, Iosif closed the door.

"That was fast," I said, looking at Heath who held onto the wolf and ignored me.

"You have two options," Heath growled at the struggling man. "Cooperate or die."

The werewolf growled, and Heath made the call. With a sharp twist, the neck was broken. Heath lowered him slowly to the ground and sighed.

"We can't take chances," he whispered. "Keys?"

Iosif grabbed them from the wall and tossed them to Heath. Then all four of us walked downstairs.

"Can you free Ivan?" the young werewolf asked.

"Who is Ivan?" Heath asked, frowning.

"Ah...He's the beta who stabbed Alpha Vasiliev."

"Was he Devora's brother?"

"Ah, yes!" Iosif nodded a lot, in a quick, excited way. "Him! You know Devora? Is she okay?"

"She was murdered at the hospital by the high-ranking wolves who followed her and Ivan there," Heath said softly. "I'm sorry."

Iosif only sighed and leaned on the wall. "These are the cells. Please take Ivan. They've been beating him."

Heath looked at me, not Hisao. He wanted to. I could see the desperation to take not only Ivan but also Iosif, an Alpha werewolf who had the need to protect a pack and weak wolves. As a beta, Ivan might have really hit a nerve as well. I knew something about betas really made werewolves want to help them...or rule them. I would need Heath to clarify it later.

"I'm okay with it. If you think we can take them both with us...We'll already be pissing off the pack by taking my family."

Hisao shook his head, though. I didn't know his

opinion or what repercussions he might be thinking about, but he obviously had something he wanted to say because he growled softly.

"Let's get your family first," Heath whispered. "Iosif, we'll consider it. We don't know what we can get away with here. Taking Jacky's family back is within our rights, but we might lose our case with the Tribunal if we take any of you. But we'll think about it."

"That's okay. Think but don't take too long. I don't know how they haven't realized you're here yet."

"Could you lead us to a truck when we get everyone free? We might be able to give you two a head start to get away on your own."

Iosif only nodded once, then Heath unlocked one of the rooms in the underground bunker-like prison.

When he pushed it open, he revealed my family. They were behind more bars, two layers of security keeping them contained in the werewolf prison.

I didn't try to speak to them, letting Heath continue with his phenomenal leadership. He walked in, with me prowling behind him, and knelt as he unlocked the bars. Daniel was the only one awake when we opened the door, and he glared at us.

"Now there's fucking monster cats? I don't know what—"

"I'm Alpha Heath Everson from Texas. I'm here to help you. You're Daniel Miller, right?"

Daniel's glare shifted to a frown. "Yes, I am. Who sent you?"

"Gwen and Jacky," Heath answered. I couldn't see his

face, but from the tension in his voice, I wondered if he had that tight smile.

I tried not to look at Daniel or the kids sleeping with their heads on his lap or my parents huddled together in the corner, holding each other. There was no missing Daniel's expression, though.

"Is Gwen okay?" he asked. I didn't take it as a personal insult he didn't ask about me. Daniel was asking about the woman he had loved for years.

"She's safe," Heath promised. "Let's wake everyone up and get moving. We can't be here long. This isn't freedom, this is an escape."

Daniel nodded and began to gently shake the kids, whispering to them it was time to escape and that they needed to be quiet. When the bleary children moved, Daniel got out from underneath them and went to my parents, shaking their shoulders until they woke up.

"This is Heath Everson. He and..." Daniel looked at Hisao and me.

"Friends. They're friends, not wild animals. We'll need them if the wolves catch us, so please hurry." Heath unlocked the gate in the bars and slowly opened it.

"Daniel, what if we can't trust this man?" my father asked, glaring at Heath as he stood. He made no move to go through the gate, moving so my mother was behind him.

"Figure out something to tell them."

Heath shot me a glance, asking me in one look, 'Why don't you talk to them?' I didn't make any effort. We didn't want them freaking out that much.

"You're Michael Duray, and your wife is Helene

Duray. You've lived in Minnesota for fifteen years, moving there once your children went to college. Jacky and Gwen are actually Jacqueline and Guinevere, names neither of them particularly like using. You've been taken by the Russian werewolf pack. They control what used to be the Soviet Union and expand even further than that. I'm from Texas." Heath stepped up to the door. "And we don't have time for you not to trust me."

The kids were just getting to their feet when my father nodded. Heath sighed in relief and turned to Iosif.

"I'll get Ivan out of his cell. Can you go out and find us a truck?"

"Yes, Alpha." Iosif jumped into the action.

"I want all of you to stay with...these two," Heath pointed at Hisao and me as he spoke. "I need to free one more person."

Heath was nearly out of the room when a gunshot rang out above the building and echoed down the staircase.

29

CHAPTER TWENTY-NINE

"*Go get Ivan,*" I ordered Heath, my heart pounding. *"We can try to save one of them."*

Iosif's fate was sealed. That was the only explanation.

He walked out of the room with a sense of great urgency. He was back quickly with a beaten and starved werewolf, whose large, dark eyes seemed hollow.

"You've been a brave wolf," Heath whispered to him. "I just need you to be brave for a little longer, okay?"

Ivan's blank stare was heartbreaking, but I couldn't imagine this werewolf had much hope anymore. His sister was dead. After surviving being beaten nearly to death, she was then murdered by her own pack. This man had taken revenge into his own hands, and it changed nothing for them.

Don't worry. We're going to fix this, Ivan. Devora is lost, but not all hope is.

"Let's go," Heath said softly. "Hisao, if it needs to

happen, I want you to run and find a vehicle. Everyone, follow the black cat. He'll get you out of here."

Hisao growled, looking between Heath and me.

"I'm fine, brother. Sergey will know I'm in the group, but he doesn't know who you are. We can't let him learn that Hasan sent the Assassin on this mission."

Hisao nodded and agreed, but the next growl told me he hated the idea of leaving me and Heath to meet the werewolves.

"Let's go meet the werewolves," Heath said softly.

"Do they talk to each other?" my mother, Helene, asked.

"They have a simple understanding of growls between them. They have human forms, but those wouldn't be helpful for this mission. If we get out, you can ask them any questions you like," Heath answered. "Let's move, everyone. We can't hide down here and get trapped."

Heath went up first. Hisao and I followed as a wall of power between our enemies and the vulnerable prisoners. I looked back as he climbed up the stairs. Daniel was carrying his son, and my father was carrying his granddaughter. My mother reached out and took Ivan's hand, pulling him along as she whispered to him.

"You can stay with us, young man. We won't leave you behind," she promised.

She had always had a gentle soul when it came to strangers. I was glad to see that one positive was shining in this dark place.

Heath went through the door first. I could smell the blood and knew the scent.

Iosif.

He had been a great help. My fury turned cold as I followed Heath outside and saw the young werewolf with a dark spot between his eyes.

I'm sorry. I'm so sorry. They'll pay for that, Iosif. I promise they'll pay for it.

I looked at the group assembled in the yard in front of the prison. Sergey stood in the middle, with werewolves behind him in a semicircle. I could only assume they were his inner circle, newly formed since he took power.

"When my patrol caught your scent, I decided not to raise the alarm and make my pack anxious at the idea of an intruder," he explained, smiling coolly at us. His eyes lingered on Heath, then flicked a glance at me. There was a bit of a shock when he looked at Hisao, a massive, dark werecat, built for the kill. "I knew where you would go. I never thought you would convince one of my werewolves to betray me, but that's easy to solve." He nodded to someone behind him, who came forward and grabbed Iosif's ankles, dragging the body out of the center of the group. "String him up as a warning, then tell everyone to leave their homes and come see what we do to traitors and intruders." Three werewolves peeled away, and Sergey looked back at us, smiling.

"It didn't need to be like this," Heath said, standing strong at the front, Hisao and me flanking him. I bared my teeth in warning, just a show of strength and a willingness to fight.

"I'm a new Alpha. It has to be this way. I'm certain you understand. New Alphas cannot tolerate any test of their control or power. In the beginning, we need to rule with an iron fist, beginning our time as Alpha with strength, not weakness."

"Have you smelled the air in your village? You didn't need to beat or kill any of them. You just needed to start treating them better than Vasiliev did. Obviously, you want to maintain his legacy, instead of creating your own."

"You American werewolves are so soft," Sergey said softly, shaking his head. "You want to take care of them. They are supposed to serve you, to see your goal through—"

"Being an Alpha isn't a one-way street, Sergey. You have to provide for their needs as well."

"And I do. They have food and shelter." Sergey shrugged. "If they're so weak, they need a hug because we've hurt their feelings, they do not need to be in this pack."

"Then let them leave instead of killing them," Heath pressed. "And let us leave."

"Why should I? By the looks of it, you've brought me not one but two werecats to keep. They can be good bargaining chips with Hasan, or they can die to my pack and further advance the projection of our strength. One day, we can take Callahan and Corissa down, and there won't be anyone to stop the dominance of my pack."

I wondered for a moment if Heath was afraid. I was, but the werecat body didn't give off emotional scents the same way as a human one. It would be masked. Heath's scent was just gone, as it had been for days. Sergey wasn't just trying to keep his pack strong the way Alpha Vasiliev had built it. He was trying to expand their reach and rule and dismantle any powers that might stand in his way.

Suddenly, his ability to blackmail me if we took the trade went from dark to downright villainous.

Behind him, a post was put up and on it, Iosif's body, wrapped in rope to hold him. It dropped a couple of feet as if it had been fitted into a hole and held straight up, showing everyone. A male speaking in Russian came over an old intercom system. Lights turned on in the houses beyond Sergey and werewolves shuffled out of their homes, guards shoving them to keep them in line.

Sergey wanted us to see this. Maybe not me or Hisao, but he was definitely rubbing salt into Heath's wounds. Heath's strong profile was shadowed and angry as the werewolves were led to see Iosif's body. A woman's scream filled the night, rising over the shuffling of feet and angry orders from the guards. The scream pierced ears, a deathly wail of grief and pain. A sound no one needed to hear in their lives.

Sergey spoke sharply in Russian.

A gun went off, and the screaming ended.

Iosif's cousin had just been murdered.

Every second that rolled by looked more hopeless as grief and anger swirled in the night air and not even the breeze could send it away. It saturated into the very ground and the surrounding buildings. It was the essence of this place.

These werewolves needed to take the anger they had and fight. If anyone could change the very essence of this place, it would never be an Alpha like Sergey. Every single werewolf with him probably saw his vision as a grand thing.

But the werewolves looking at Iosif, the others huddled around a woman's dead body? They could change it. They needed to change it. They needed to rise up. They needed to be defiant. They would never survive in this world if they didn't fight for themselves.

Gwen, you said I would make a good politician. The mark of any good politician is the ability to move a crowd. Let's see how good I am.

"Heath, Hisao...I'm going to do something insane. Iosif knew English, and I think a lot of people here might."

His breathing changed, but I didn't look at him, focusing on the crowd. Hisao shifted his weight between his front paws but made no other movement.

I needed to get my family out. I needed to see Sergey and his werewolves go down. I needed to see another sunrise for Mischa because, apparently, she cared more for my life than I did.

And Heath—I needed to get Heath back to Carey.

"Werewolves of Russia!" I called out mentally. *"You have been oppressed for too long!"*

Sergey's eyes went wide. He looked around, wondering who was speaking, then turned slowly back to my group.

"What is this?" he demanded softly. The gun in his hand lowered just enough in the shock of what was happening.

"You've been subjugated and beaten. You've been chained and whipped. You've lost the rights you have as living,

breathing werewolves and humans. You've had your lives stolen from you! And you're angry!"

"Which one is it?" Sergey demanded, waving his gun between Hisao and me. "Which one?"

"Werecats can't speak mentally," Heath whispered, reminding Sergey of what every werewolf knew. "That's pack magic."

Sergey stepped forward another few feet, closing some of the distance. He lifted his gun and pointed it at Heath. I had to fight my instincts to react to the threat.

"Tell me," the Alpha growled.

"Fight back! Defy the powers that be and prove you have your own!" I roared in their heads. *"Don't let there be another Iosif! Don't let there be another Devora and Ivan! Now is your chance!"* I roared and leapt forward, landing on Sergey as his gun fired, sinking claws in his chest. I felt fire on my side, but I had come for Sergey at an angle, so whatever he hit wasn't my center of mass. The bullet also wasn't silver...a wonder. Was it too hard for them to acquire here?

A deafening roar of the crowd followed suit as I ravaged Sergey's body.

"Hisao, get my family out of here!" I ordered mentally as I jumped for another of the high-ranking werewolves near me, who were too surprised to lift their weapons. I didn't have much of a chance. The crowd was now rowdy. Guards were being tackled to the ground and assaulted. Some were firing back, taking out the uprising of the younger, lower-ranking werewolves.

With a second werewolf dead, I lashed out at a third, scoring his leg with my claws and exposing his femur. He screamed, and I reached out, biting down on his arm, yanking until I felt tendons and muscle rip, and a joint pop out of socket. I tore his arm off and threw it to the side as he screamed and fell to the ground. Gunfire and screams of both victory and pain were all I could hear. The wave of rage I had unleashed was all I could smell.

I dove into the crowd, taking down werewolves, trying to control my instincts to kill all of them. I didn't want to kill the innocent.

Teeth entered my back leg. I turned and swiped at whatever was back there, hitting a werewolf in wolf form, sending it flying into a mass of people, who beat it to death. I was able to separate my friend from my enemy as some cheered me as I prowled in the fight, while others raised their weapons on me. I leapt for a guard and landed on him after another werewolf was able to yank his gun away.

That werewolf didn't last very long underneath me.

Finally, a hand touched me, and I nearly lashed out, but I saw grey-blue eyes when I turned.

"We need to go. Hisao is getting a truck ready for us." He was practically yelling to be heard over the crowd.

I nodded and created a path out of the madness. Once we were free of the riot, he began to jog, and I followed, finding Hisao naked as he hotwired an old truck.

"Let me finish," Heath said, patting my brother on the shoulder. "Change back and cover our exit."

Hisao jumped away and started his Change without missing a beat.

I turned and saw a group of werewolves running for us. I didn't know if they felt we needed to die or if they were following orders from Sergey before he died, but they were coming on four legs, ready to fight.

I blocked my brother and family from them and met the first head-on. With a hard bash from my paw, a skull was crushed. One latched teeth in my shoulder. I shook hard and tried not to fall from pain as something dragged the wolf off me, its teeth taking some of my flesh.

A truck started up behind me.

"Let's go!" Heath yelled. "Let them chase, but we need to move!"

"Go!" I screamed, directing it at him, so only he heard it. *"Just go, Heath!"*

The sound of the truck slowly started to fade. Hisao and I fought hard, dispatching werewolves as quickly as we could, then started running before another group of them could come after us. We got out of the village, trying to catch up with Heath and the truck. My shoulder screamed in pain, and I was bleeding in more than one spot, but the pain wasn't enough to stop me. I needed to run.

Howls filled the night air, overriding the sound of chaos in the village. As we ran for the trees that were our way home, a large pack ran out of the very woods we needed to enter. There had to be over a dozen wolves.

All I could think was that this was the patrol, waiting for us to try to leave. They didn't know what the chaos was in the village. They had their orders, and now, they could use their mission to earn favor with the werewolf who took control once the revolt was put down.

Or they just saw two werecats and escaping prisoners

and wanted to stop us. Sometimes, things were just that simple.

Hisao and I picked up as much speed as we could while Heath simultaneously slowed down and let us pass him. We launched into the pack and started tumbling, trying to kill all of them, so Heath could get through without risking the members of my family.

It was bloody but effective. They tried to dogpile us. Hisao was cleaner and more efficient, bigger and stronger, but I held my own, tearing limbs off when I got a hold of them.

The truck passed us as Hisao raced after the last werewolf and crushed its life in his fangs. We followed the truck, running behind it, our noses to the air, waiting for more to follow us.

An hour later, none came, and we were home free. Hisao and I ran behind the truck for the entire journey. My legs were on autopilot, even as my injuries healed. I couldn't ask Heath to stop and let me in because we needed to be vigilant. If another group of werewolves somehow pursued us, Hisao would need help. None of my injuries were bad enough that I needed to worry about losing too much blood. They just made me sore and my muscles stiff.

I was limping at the end. My body was depleted, and the pain was gone, but only because I had run until my legs were numb. When the truck we had taken from Mischa was in sight, I nearly collapsed, my body trying to give out a little too early. Heath pulled up beside it, and I went around to my clothes.

Next to my ride home, I began to Change, not

thinking about anything but potential sleep. I didn't think about the humans in our group or the werewolf, Ivan, though I could smell all of them.

I finished the Change and sighed, unable to stand, so I leaned against the truck, legs stretched out. In my human form, I could feel how much the run had torn up my feet. I looked at my hands and saw the scrapes and raw sections on my palm and fingers. My shoulder was on fire again, but I was too tired to think about it. My ribs stung from that initial gunshot.

A gasp made me look up. Helene Duray was standing in front of me, her mouth agape, her face pale.

"Hey, Mom," I whispered or tried to.

A scream was my lullaby as I fell to the side, unconscious.

30

CHAPTER THIRTY

I woke up in a bed. My body was stiff, and I felt like a mummy as I tried to bend my limbs and met resistance from tightly wrapped bandages. I could smell someone in the room with me and blinked, trying to wake up more and clear my vision.

"You and Hisao slept the whole way home," Mischa said with a touch of humor. "Heath called, using the satellite phone I gave him, telling me everything that happened. Since then, Father has been talking to Callahan and Corissa. No decisions have been made yet since they want to speak to you, Gwen, and Heath."

"Does it look good?" I asked, hating how dry my throat was. "Water?"

"It looks good, better than you, for sure." Her voice was closer this time. Grabbing my wrist, she guided my hand to a glass.

Once I had it in hand, I tried to drink and realized I was still flat on my back. I dumped water all over my face, making me shoot up, which sent more pain through me, but Mischa laughed.

"Works every time," she said, all too pleased with herself.

"You do this often?" I asked, glaring at her.

"I did it to Hisao not but an hour ago," she said with a grin. "You've been back for just over an hour. I did it to him in the back of the truck."

"You are evil," I accused, shaking my head as water dripped off me.

"I've been told this before," she said, taking the glass. She put it down on the side table and grabbed a second glass. "Here."

I chugged the glass of water, with Mischa holding it for me, her free hand on the back of my head. It was tender and loving, something I didn't expect after the prank she had just pulled, but I appreciated the sentiment. I felt like a child, but not in a bad way. She was my older sister, and she loved me. I had just been through something hard, and she wanted to care for me. That was all.

"Thank you," I whispered. She kissed my forehead and backed away, her smile fading.

"So, what do you want to talk about first?" she asked.

"Well...when do I see Father?" I asked in return.

"After you have a proper meal," she said. "I told him I wanted you and Hisao to have half a day to rest and continue healing. Heath as well. He drove back, with no help from either of you. He only got to sleep when he got here. He got out of the truck and nearly fell off his feet. My people had to get him inside."

"Thank you," I said again, so grateful for how much my family really cared. We didn't agree about much, ever, but when one of us was down, we cared. It felt like I was always the one down, and recently, that was the case, but I knew from their histories, they had all probably done this for each other, and one day, I would probably do it for them. Not that I wanted trouble for them, but it was inevitable.

"We need to talk about something else," she said, sighing as she sat down on the bed next to me.

"Them," I guessed.

"Yes, them." She nodded and licked her lips. "They're in the entertainment room, talking to Gwen. From my understanding, things are very tense. I know they saw you on the trip back."

"My mother watched me Change, and I said hello. Then I passed out," I explained, groaning. "Oh, I can only imagine how she felt. Actually, I kind of know. She screamed. I remember her screaming."

"Okay, we can handle this. Do you want to talk to them?"

"I think I need to," I whispered, rubbing my hands together and chewing the inside of my cheek. "Yeah, I'm going to talk to them. The sooner, the better, right?"

"If that's what you want. I'm more than okay with hiding you from them."

"No...I need to do this." Standing, I smiled sadly at my sister. "For closure."

The pain I saw reflected back was too intense. Standing, she grabbed my hand.

"Then let's go. I'll take you to them, my brave little sister."

She led me through the house. Hisao saw us at one point, and Mischa told him where we were going. He only gave me a solemn nod of respect before going into his room. Mischa took me down two flights of stairs into her basement and stopped at a set of double doors.

"They're in there."

I listened, not moving, barely even breathing.

"Gwen, I can't believe you kept all of this from us," my father said, his tone the same as I remembered—hard, strict, and a bit overbearing. He didn't have the soft, gentle patience of Hasan. Maybe he used to, but I knew this Michael Duray, the one who was hard on his daughters because he 'wanted what was best for us.'

"I couldn't tell you. You would have had me committed. And I don't regret any of it. I don't regret working for the supernatural species. I regret so many things in my life, but that isn't one of them."

I smiled as I grabbed and turned the handle, slowly opening the door to give the people inside time to realize I was coming. Gwen was the first person I saw, and her smile was bright.

"Jacky! It's good to see you awake."

"It's good to be awake," I replied as she met me halfway. The hug was tight, metaphorically bone-crushing. "I'm happy to see everyone is here, safe and sound. I couldn't stay awake to see the rest of the journey home."

"You did great, sis," she whispered, her arms refusing to budge. "You were so amazing."

"Thanks. It means a lot to me to hear you say that." I lowered my head to her shoulder and just held her. Twins torn apart by life and change, brought back together by the weird ways of the universe.

I'm not letting you go, sis. Not again.

When the hug finally ended, Gwen turned back to our family, moving an arm around my shoulder as we looked at the family.

"You..." My father was still trying to process what he was saying. Looking at my mother, I noticed she was pale again. Daniel said nothing, his eyes narrowed on me. His kids were asleep on the couch next to him. I still, after everything, didn't know their names. I would ask Gwen the moment I had the chance.

"I'm a werecat," I confirmed for the room. "Shane and I got into a car accident on our honeymoon. Through sheer luck, a rich man on the island, who often hung out with tourists, found our vehicle and us still inside. Shane didn't make it, but the man made the decision to save me. He Changed me right there." I pulled away from Gwen as I stepped closer to them, clasping my hands. "Twelve years ago, I made the decision to cut off contact with all of you because I was going to have to live a new life. I don't age anymore. I haven't aged since that day. I'm...immortal unless something kills me. I thought it would be easier to never go home. I didn't want to watch all of you..."

"Grow old," Gwen finished for me, her tone giving away the step after that. She stayed back, but her presence was supportive.

I didn't want to watch all of them grow old and die.

"You were always doing your own thing," Helene said,

looking away. "I never thought you would become a..."

"A monster?" I asked, feeling the blow cut open my wounded heart.

"Yes. You knew how we felt about werewolves, witches, and faeries. And you..."

"What did you want me to do, kill myself?" I lifted my hands in defeat. "I did what any sane person would do. I made do. I learned. I adjusted. I continued on with my life, except now, I don't lock my door during a full moon. I'm the reason people should. And let's get to that. We're not monsters. We don't attack people at random for no reason. There are some cases of werewolves losing control, but there are...thousands of good werewolves. Things are going to happen, so let's put the misguided prejudice to the side for a moment." I wanted to rant at them, but cut myself off before I let it go on too long.

Heath. Landon. Iosif. Devora. Ivan. Ranger. Sheila.

I didn't need to fight for them, but I wanted to. I never knew my mother believed werewolves were heinous monsters, but it was clear in her scent.

"I...I can't deal with this," she decided, standing up.

"Mom!" Gwen stopped her from leaving. "We can finally have Jacky back!"

"You can, but I can't condone this—"

"You literally saved a werewolf's life!" I snapped, turning to her. "Ivan, that poor beaten boy? He's a werewolf, Mom. He was beaten because he tried to rescue his sister from being abused. He killed a man as revenge when they killed her. He was a hero who fought for his family, and they beat him regularly. And he's a werewolf. What? You can touch him, but you can't talk to me?"

She turned to me. "Which one were you?"

"Which werecat? I was the tawny, striped one, smaller than the black one."

"Ah. You looked back while we were going up the stairs," she said, nodding slowly. "So, what now? You're a...werecat. Do you have a job, a business, money? Was all of this your fault?"

"I have what I need to get by." I wasn't telling them about the family fortune. "No, none of this was my fault," I promised, looking at Gwen for a minute.

"I just told them they were kidnapped to get back at you and me," she whispered. "They'd been asking so many questions, I didn't have a chance to flesh out the details."

"We'll need to fix that," I said, eyeing her, then going back to my mother. "Gwen called me and asked for help. The werewolves who took you didn't know she and I are related. They didn't know until shortly before they put you on the plane to Russia. Or so the story goes. It doesn't matter anymore when they knew. I never acted against them, Gwen did. So, they had no reason to come after me." I sighed at the end as no one said anything for a minute. Daniel was quiet, listening but not really. This wasn't his family.

"This was *Gwen's* fault?" Michael was pissed, but I didn't wince as I would have when I was human. His fury and disbelief didn't scare me anymore. I had Hasan, whose quiet nature made his fury more terrifying. I had Hisao, who was a proficient killer. I had Mischa, who could do real damage.

No, I wasn't scared of my human father anymore. His

reaction, his disbelief that his perfect daughter was the one who caused this was the last cut I could take, though. He had *wanted* it to be my fault. He had been hoping Gwen couldn't fall more, and this was all something that I did.

I wondered for a moment what I ever did to make this father unable to love me once I started growing up and becoming my own person. Then I realized it didn't matter anymore.

I have a father. He holds me when I cry. He believes me when I speak. He gets frustrated, but he cares. He doesn't expect perfection, and he allows me to make my case. He apologizes. He's not perfect, but he's a good father.

And his name is Hasan.

Privately, staring at Michael Duray, I let go of the pain and rejection I had felt in my human life. I had my werecat family. It would never be perfect, but it would be, and always was, better than this.

"Gwen," I whispered, turning my back on the family. "If you have anything you want to tell them, anything at all—stuff you've always wanted to say, but feared how much it could damage your relationships—now is the time."

"Why?"

"Because I'm going to have their memories wiped of everything that's happened—the kidnapping, being hostages, me, all of it. My family will get the right people to do it, and it'll be better for them in the long run. Your kids should be able to have normal lives."

"You don't want to see us anymore?" She took my rejection of them as a rejection of her.

"Not you," I promised. "I think I figured out the root of our issues. Them. They're the problem. It was never us."

"You can't do that," my mother said, looking between us. "You can't blame your mistakes on us, and you can't wipe our memories without our permission."

"I can do both," I said with a tight smile. "You won't remember, and it's for the best." I wanted to laugh as I gave that line. "Do you really want to remember any of this? You'll never be able to go back to a normal life. We'll have to manage you, keep an eye on you to make sure you don't expose our secrets. And if you did expose us? Being my human family wouldn't stop a werecat or any other supernatural from killing you in retaliation. It's dangerous. Don't be a fool." Now I was ranting. "And as for blaming you for our mistakes? Gwen and I were equally good kids. We loved each other, and we loved you, but you two were awful, and we ended up turning against each other. Dad just proved it. Gwen's at fault, but he wants to blame me. I don't know what I ever did to upset you two, but you hate me, and that's okay. Fine."

"You caught him cheating on me," my mother hissed, glaring, her green eyes like acid. "At ten. And even when I told you I didn't want to know, you felt like you had to tell me. You confronted your father. You tried to break our family because you thought your dad was a bad person. I loved your father. I have always loved your father, and I do not believe in divorce, so we worked it out. Then you had the gall to ask me why I would want to keep a bad husband. You created more problems in our family than any of us could have ever dreamed. It didn't end there, either. You started acting out after that. You always think the world needs to be the way you want it to be. You didn't listen, didn't understand the world didn't work that way, so you acted out."

"You two resented me," I whispered. I didn't remember being ten.

The overwhelming silence that filled the room was broken when my niece screamed in her sleep and started kicking. Gwen and Daniel rushed to her, helping her up and whispering that everyone was okay, and they were free and going home soon.

When I looked back at my mother, I glared at her.

"Take the memory wipe. If not for me, then for them." I tilted my head to my niece and nephew. "Because they don't deserve to grow up like that."

I turned on my heel and walked out, closing the door softly to keep from scaring the children. Mischa was waiting for me on the other side.

"Closure?" she asked, then opened her arms and waited for me to either speak or grab her.

I'm strong. I have a family, and it's not Helene and Michael Duray.

I truly believed it.

I opened my mouth to tell Mischa the same thing as tears welled up in my eyes. She wrapped her arms around me as I leaned into her shoulder.

I cried away my human parents one last time—a final goodbye.

31

CHAPTER THIRTY-ONE

Not even a day later, most of my human family was gone. Hisao put them on his jet, and they left for Japan. When Mischa and I talked to Hasan, he knew a person who would manipulate their memories of the event.

"They'll be on vacation," he promised. "The memories will always be there, but they can be buried and covered with something else. With humans, the manipulation is normally very strong, hard to break. Children are a little different. It could root in their subconscious permanently, but if they start having nightmares, therapy is useful. They should be healthy as they get old and just think of them as childhood fears."

"Thank you," I whispered. "Are you okay with...?"

"You and Gwen can stay in touch. It could be good for you to have a connection with your twin. Jabari and Zuri certainly think so. However, I'd recommend not exposing yourself to her children. That could be a trigger that snaps through the magic done on them."

When I was done crying on Mischa, Gwen and I had talked again, just the two of us, wanting to keep our rediscovered sisterhood. I wanted to repair everything, and so did she. As an adult with long-term exposure to the supernatural, she couldn't get the same treatment as her children, ex-husband, or our parents.

So, we exchanged numbers. She promised she would keep me up to date on whatever she planned going forward. She was unemployed now.

"What's next?" I asked, looking at my father on the screen.

"Someone will be coming to open a door for you to come into the Tribunal's space. All four of you. We'll be talking to Callahan and Corissa. We need to wrap up the issue with the werewolves, then you can go home."

I smiled happily at the idea.

Exactly twenty-four hours after I had woken up, the group of us saw someone who didn't belong come through a door. Some fae no one knew just stood there, watching us, waiting for us to go back through the door with him.

"They're really good at this pocket space thing, aren't they?" I asked my sister, frowning at her.

"I always hate when they have to do it in my house," she said, shaking her head. "But they are really good at it."

We walked into the dark doorway, and it didn't lead to the closet it was supposed to. We entered a room dripping in ancient wealth. Ancient artifacts sat on a mantle over a crackling fire. One wall had a collection of ancient texts, another had a set of dining ware, all gold.

Hasan was seated with his back turned to us, opposite two werewolves I recognized from my last run-in with the Tribunal, Callahan and Corissa. Behind them were eight werewolves, probably all ancient as well, dressed like security guards.

"Welcome," Hasan greeted us, looking over his shoulder. "Why don't you all take a seat. We'll try to get through this quickly."

"There have been stories of chaos coming from the Russian pack. Another Alpha dead," Callahan growled. "We need that region stable, Hasan."

"Maybe he shouldn't have taken my family," I muttered. The Alpha werewolf glared at me, but Corissa reached out and patted his hands.

"She's right," the female said. "Alpha Sergey took her family hostage. Hasan and his children have never allowed anyone to put them in a place of weakness. Their move to take their family back was justified. If Sergey tried to stop them, he got his due. We would expect the same action from any of our children."

Callahan didn't seem pleased by his mate's words but didn't say any more until after everyone was seated.

"So that's it? You ruin a long-standing pack in Russia, and we need to let you walk away?"

"Well...there are those files," Hasan pointed out. I hadn't seen it walking in, but there was a laptop in the center of the room on top of a coffee table between the two main couches.

"Yes..." Callahan stared at the laptop. "We've reviewed them, and I heard the story of how they came to be."

"Those are what I want to discuss as well," Corissa

said with a tight smile. "Doctor Duray, would you care to give testimony on Devora's state when you met her?"

Gwen stood and began to speak, using medical jargon and describing every detail of Devora's injuries and the nature of the girl's story. When she was done, she sat down.

"Now, Alpha Everson, I want to ask you something." Corissa turned to him. "You are one of our more exceptional Alphas in North America. We were sad to see you retire, and the events around your retirement were regretful."

"I'm having a good time raising my daughter..."

"I'm certain you are, but for some reason, everyone keeps finding you following Jacky Leon around," Callahan growled softly. "Want to explain that?"

"The NAWC gave me an open-ended job description, sir," Heath growled back. "Be a representative between the council and the werecat daughter of Hasan, who resides in North America. I have tried to use my loyalty to the werewolves and my respect for her to stop fights and foster communication. I introduced Jacky and Alpha Lewis in Seattle, which led to us having the ability to dissolve suspicion that the pack had killed the werecats, or the werecats had killed the missing werewolves. I came on this trip with Miss Leon in an effort to keep her and the Russians from going head to head. Sadly, the opportunity never arose, and I ended up assisting in the freedom of her human family."

"Why?" Callahan's suspicion of Heath was obvious. "And when did you get dominant enough to look me in the eye? No one in the NAWC is that old or strong."

Heath's eyes dropped quickly. "I helped her because she had done it for my family, not just once, but twice. Jacky has put the safety of my children before her own safety, when both times, the danger to her life was real. I wanted to give that back to her. My growing dominance could be explained by the fact the NAWC has repeatedly requested I move out of her territory and cut off contact, but I don't find that in the best interests of the werewolves in the long term. I want to see us progress, not keep the status quo we have existed in for centuries."

"Hmm."

"Callahan, let me speak to him," Corissa ordered gently. "Don't ever overtake one of my conversations like that. You know how much I dislike it."

Callahan visibly winced. "Sorry, my love. I'll do my best."

"Alpha Heath Everson, you were known to memorize intel during your time on the council. You liked to know things. Tell me, what is the current knowledge the North American Werewolf Council keeps on the Russian werewolf pack? Or current while you were there? It's been nearly two years since you left the council, but you probably have contacts that keep you informed.."

"We knew there were issues between submissives of the pack and the higher-ranking wolves. That became clearer when Alpha Vasiliev drove a beta to stab him. We heard rumors of bad living conditions and abuse. We never had any hard evidence for the charges, however. We could only continue to keep our eyes and ears open until we had what was needed to bring to both of you."

"And...did any of you ever meet Alpha Vasiliev? Or visit Russia?"

"No, Alpha."

That surprised me. I had no idea Corissa was an Alpha in her own right.

"Who did?"

"Their Alpha sent members of their inner circle to tour North American packs. My son and second, Landon Everson, met with their seconds. He also had a handful of encounters with Alpha Vasiliev, but they never amounted to much. From his testimony, the Alpha was rude, outdated, and hated all things different. For my son, that's dangerous. I never exposed my son or my pack to the Russians again after the last one was argumentative because Landon was losing his patience."

I couldn't imagine Landon losing his patience, but it was Heath's story, and I didn't see Landon nearly every day in every situation.

"So, no one visited Russia..." She hummed. "You know, the representatives from every werewolf council in the world have told me the same thing. None of you ever visited. Why is that?"

"It was made clear to us we weren't wanted."

"So, who checked in on the pack?"

"Alpha Callahan of the Tribunal." Heath swallowed, and I noticed his face begin to lose color.

Corissa stood, nodding slowly. "I have already reviewed all the files. I apologize to all of you for seeing the worst the werewolves have to offer. I'm also thankful for your willingness to work with us and would be honored if this information stayed in this room."

I didn't say anything. Hasan nodded politely beside me as Heath continued to lose color. Now, he looked like a glass of milk.

What does he know that I don't?

Corissa turned on Callahan, who tried to stand with her as they stared at each other.

It was like a lightning crack. Corissa slapped Callahan so hard, he fell sideways on the couch, looking like he had just seen the face of God.

"Don't come to me tonight. You will keep your head low for as long as I want you to, mate. You let those females be abused because you were protecting yourself from the instability that would be caused by fixing the problem. You were more worried about staying prepared for another war none of us want than you were about the lives of our most innocent people!" She was screaming at the end.

"I'll fix this," he promised.

"No, *I* will fix this. I will go to Russia and clean this up. I will teach those wolves it doesn't matter what's between their legs, they all die the *same*. You will begin planning an initiative you will launch worldwide for all werewolves to honor and strengthen our females and submissives by getting them educations and wealth of their own. All of this will be done so they no longer need to be dependent on a mate or an Alpha in case they find their mate or Alpha to be abusive. You will do this, or you will find yourself alone for a very long time. Am I clear?" She screamed at the end again.

I sank into the couch with each word. Hasan reached out and took my hand, and I grabbed Gwen's. Mischa wrapped an arm around Gwen, holding her. When I looked at Heath, he was on his knees, dropped by the dominant power that was Corissa of the Tribunal, his eyes wide with fear. This was the power of an Alpha that could not and never would be denied.

The beautiful woman took a deep breath and sighed.

"Forgive me for the outburst. Alpha Everson, you did good work exposing this. Hasan, you have a wonderful daughter with an eye for those who need her and for trouble. Good luck. I feel only more trouble for you will come from her. The best children are often the ones that make us worry the most."

"Have a good evening," Hasan said, standing and nodding respectfully at Corissa, which she mirrored back.

He led all of us out of the room, and we ended up in his office.

"Sorry, Mischa. You can go back in and take a shortcut home."

"It's fine," she said, sitting down on the solitary couch. "She's still everything she was in the War."

"Corissa is still the dominant power," my father agreed. "Heath, are you okay? Brandy?"

"Please," my werewolf croaked. "I knew she had set him up, the moment she started asking about who goes to Russia. It was only ever Callahan."

"Did you know she was the dominant Alpha?" Hasan asked, obviously curious. He was testing Heath in some way. I knew the look on my father's face well.

"When she made Callahan wince, I figured it out. That's not public information."

"I thought the Tribunal members were all equal." I kept my volume low, almost afraid to speak.

"For everyone except the werewolves," Hasan said, smiling at me. "Heath, how many Alphas can rule a single pack?"

"One."

Hasan pointed at the wolf, still looking at me with his sly smile.

"It's always fun to see Corissa put her reactionary, aggressive husband in his place. She was a force to be reckoned with during the War, but she was more amenable to peace when it was offered. She doesn't like seeing her werewolves die, for any reason."

"Well, this is all fun, but I would really like to go home," I declared.

"Certainly. Why don't you take Gwen and Heath on a short tour of my island as I prepare the flights for all of you?"

They followed me out of the room, all of us ready to escape. With that meeting, it was finally over.

I showed them the island, even stopping to point out the spot where Shane and I had gone over because it was important. I showed them the beaches and the markets. People waved at me, recognizing me as the daughter of their patron and their greatest secret. Like Mischa and her village, Hasan fostered knowledge and trust with his local humans, though he wasn't related to them.

I stopped on the beach as Gwen and Heath walked with me.

"What are you thinking about?" my twin asked.

"Nothing. Just enjoying the view."

32

CHAPTER THIRTY-TWO

JUNE 30TH, 2020

I sat in my kitchen, reading a text from Gwen as the sun came through my windows.

Gwen: Found a new job already! Joining a non-profit to help survivors of domestic abuse.

Jacky: That's amazing. Oh, and happy birthday!

Gwen: Do you celebrate our birthday anymore? Well, then. Happy 38th birthday!

I put the phone down, smiling—my birthday. I didn't celebrate it anymore, but she gave me a reason to at least acknowledge it. I was now thirty-eight, and in July, I would have been a werecat for thirteen years. Where had the time gone?

I didn't do anything special. For weeks, I had taken

solace being home again and seeing Carey. Heath had been respectful of my space since the day we came back. He didn't try to get me alone or anything else. He waved at me from his truck or his front door during Carey exchanges. I knew what he was doing. I was always desperate for alone time after being away from my territory. Instead of being worried, this time, he just accepted it.

But when he moved around in my territory, I always wondered if he would turn my way.

I was cooking dinner when I next caught him moving around. Landon wasn't with him, and I had spent time with Carey only the day before. He turned in my direction, and I felt him come closer and closer. He slowed down when he reached my bar, having to go on foot now. I went to my front porch, glad my dinner could go in the oven and be forgotten. I waited for him as he came out of the woods and smiled.

"It's not very romantic if I can't sneak up on you," Heath said, grinning as he showed me the flowers he was holding.

"Yes, it is," I said softly. "Come in. I'm making dinner, and you can tell me what the flowers are for."

He jumped up the steps, and I raced inside to keep from getting caught in his web of sexual energy on my front porch. I went into my kitchen, and he came up behind me, putting the flowers down by reaching around me. He sneakily kissed my cheek.

"The flowers are for your birthday."

"I should have known," I said, feeling a little stupid for not thinking about myself. "I haven't gotten a gift in years. I figured you would have picked up last year that I don't really celebrate."

"I decided you shouldn't spend it alone this year," he murmured as I turned around, and our bodies brushed together. "If you want me to go, I can. You can keep the flowers, of course."

The heat was palpable.

"You should stay. I've been thinking about something I've wanted to say for the last few weeks." I needed to get it off my chest. "You know, when this started, I was worried about so many things. I didn't know if I was desperate, I just wanted something I couldn't have, or if I was just a passing fad to you—"

He growled softly, his eyes getting hard. I smoothed out his wrinkles with my fingers, then brushed my fingertips over his lips. As my fingers left, I leaned in and kissed him softly.

"Let me finish," I whispered, then pulled away, creating distance between us. I needed to speak, not just kiss him. "I didn't know what we were doing or why, and it scared me. Then the whole Russia thing happened and helped me put things into perspective. I love talking to you...about everything. Our problems, our secrets, our families. If I could sit and talk to you for years, I would. I realized I never once thought about Shane, I only thought how much support you were giving me. I realized there's no way someone risks their life for a passing crush or attraction.

"There were things you said...that touched me. They scared me when I heard them, but by the time we made it home, I was different. I've been thinking about them for weeks now and waiting for you to come by, hoping I had this chance to say...I want to be with you. Trouble be damned. Fuck werewolf and werecat history. Our feelings aren't wrong. Nothing that inspires the connection we have and the lengths we go to for each other could ever be wrong." I reached out and picked up the flowers, chuckling. "But I need you to say it because I've been wrong before, and I've been burned by people I care about, like my own parents."

"You are not a passing fad for me. All those things they don't like you for, I adore." He spread his hands. "They want you to fall in line, and I love seeing you break the mold. They want you to temper your expectations, and I love to watch you shoot for the stars. They want you to stay out of trouble, and I say to hell with them. You do what's right, and it's inspiring and..." He trailed off, taking a deep breath. "Your parents found reasons to dislike you, and those reasons are all the ones that have caused me to fall in love with you, Jacky Leon. I don't need you to love me back, not right now. I fell hard and fast for you. When you're in danger, I want to protect and help you. When you need someone to lean on, I want to be that person."

"You can't be my Alpha," I whispered.

"I don't want to be your Alpha. I would never chain you like that. I love you because you're free from all of it. Pretending to try to be your Alpha is just a good laugh." He reached out and took my hand. "I know you'll never back down from me because you want to keep me as your status symbol." The earnest expression on his face told me how much he wanted me to accept what he was saying. "You will always do what you want or need to do.

With Gwen, I started out unsure, but I trusted you and couldn't let you do it alone, so I stuck with you. I'm glad I did. I was right to trust you. Gwen did one stupid thing, but in the end, it helped us save so many. Ivan is getting a new life. Corissa and her inner circle cleaned up Russia and saved over three-fourths of the pack. There are still problems, but problems come when change does." He chuckled. "Off-topic now. Russian werewolves and your twin aside, I know you will always stand up for what you believe in and not once has that led either of us astray.

"So, Jacky Leon, I love you. Now, do with me what you will."

I pulled my hand away and turned off the oven. Dinner could wait.

I launched myself at Heath Everson, who met me in a strong embrace and a passionate kiss. The world and its problems melted as this werewolf held me.

His hands roamed my body as he pushed me against the counter. My shirt didn't last long. I don't know what it was about this encounter with Heath, but he knew what I meant when I leapt into his arms. This time, there would be no cold water thrown on the fire between us. Tonight, I fully intended to stoke the flames.

My bra came off next, and his mouth found my breasts. As he played with me, my head fell back in ecstasy. Lifting one of my legs to wrap around his waist, he pressed himself closer, growling in pleasure as I responded to his every movement.

I had taken the leash off a wild animal. Heath—beautiful, wonderful, kind, patient Heath—was a wild animal I had let loose. I had forgotten for a moment that he was a werewolf. I had never had sex with another supernatural. His intensity wasn't what I had expected.

I hadn't expected my response, either. My pulse skyrocketed, and my breathing came faster. My body needed to be touched, and I wanted to touch him. I wanted this to be rough. I grabbed his shirt, forcing him to stop the insane thing he was doing with his tongue, and yanked the shirt off, tearing it in the process. He chuckled as I threw it across the room, letting it land somewhere unseen.

"Well, if that's how it's going to be," he growled in a taunting, sensual way that made my knees weak. Reaching down, he didn't unbutton my jeans, just popped them open, sending the button ricocheting around the kitchen. He tore the seam at the base of the zipper down the center and slid his hand down and pushed a finger inside me.

It was hard and fast, that first orgasm, as he took great pleasure in driving me high and sending me over the edge. Once the tremors ended, he lifted me, wrapping my legs around his waist. He carried me up the stairs and checked each door to find my bedroom, not bothering to just ask me.

He laid me down and ground between my legs. Our pants went next, then our underwear. Grabbing his wallet, he pulled out a condom.

"Really? Do we have to worry about that?" I asked, half laughing.

"Better safe than sorry. Don't worry, it's not ancient. I started carrying them after you kissed me the first time."

He positioned himself over me and claimed my mouth as he pushed into me.

It was rough as we moved together. He was a taskmaster of a lover, demanding, pushy, wanting to wring every moan and sigh from my lips. He growled happily as I screamed his name and arched proudly as I clawed his back. He tore my sheets as he held onto them, and the bed banged against the wall. I was in sensory overload as he bit my neck, speeding up, his every movement powerful and consistent.

I screamed one last time as I came, and he groaned, following me. We were left panting as I held him to me, my legs quaking. He rolled to the side, and I went with him, keeping one of my legs over his waist, refusing to lose the vital contact I had with him.

We laid there for what felt like an hour, listening to each other breathe. It was bliss. I had found something extraordinarily special.

"Can I stay the night?" he asked, kissing me softly as he wrapped his arm around my waist. His other arm ended up under my head, a good place for it.

"You can," I whispered happily. "You know, the world is going to make this hard for us. We're going to have to ease them into it, keeping it a secret for a little longer. Are you okay with that?"

"I am," he assured me. "Are you?"

"The world can go to hell," I answered. "It can burn."

"Hmm." He leaned in with a smile and kissed me again. "You need to stop picking fights with the world."

"Why? The world is the one who needs to stop being wrong," I retorted, smiling. "Because this isn't."

"No, it isn't," he agreed. "But that wasn't the point. I think you need to stop because I find it too damn attractive." He kissed me again and rolled us, laying me on my back again.

"I don't see a problem here," I said, laughing as he kissed a trail down my body. "Oh, while I have you here, do you think you can start teaching me all this stuff I don't know about supernaturals and stuff?"

He laughed as his head went between my legs.

Hours later, I looked out my window and admired the peaceful night, thinking about what I was doing. I turned back toward the bed and saw Heath sleeping and smiled.

I was defying everyone to be with this one man.

And it was worth it.

~

Keep reading for more information about the next release, special news, and more.

DEAR READER,

Thank you for reading!

Now, normally I put some teasing information into these dear reader pages. I don't know what to say this time except...

Jacky and Heath sitting in a tree...

You know the rest. Now, I know there's many people out there who don't like sex in their books and that's totally okay. For future clarification, there will probably one or less sex scenes every book, so if you could tolerate that, then we'll be fine.

Also, those mentions of Mygi Pharma? And that prison outbreak Jacky was ignorant of? Read my **Kaliya Sahni** series to figure those out.

Now, onto the best news, I'm going to start telling you here in Dear Reader when the next book should release.

JACKY LEON BOOK FIVE

FEBRUARY 16, 2021

If I still have you, head over to my website to get the latest updates on the next book in the series. Head over to my website and sign up for my mailing list! There are exclusive teasers for those who are signed up: Knbanet.com/newsletter

Also, I have a Patreon, where I write a monthly short story or novella. You can check that out here: Patreon.com/knbanet

And remember,

Reviews are always welcome, whether you loved or hated the book. Please consider taking a few moments to leave one and know I appreciate every second of your time and I'm thankful.

THE TRIBUNAL ARCHIVES

The Jacky Leon series is set in the world of The Tribunal. Every series and standalone novel is written so it can be read alone.

For more information about The Tribunal Archives and the different series in it, you can go here:

tribunalarchives.com

ACKNOWLEDGMENTS

I'm very bad at giving really public praise. I shower people in praise in private. But that's not everyone's love language and that's okay.

So this little page shall now be dedicated to everyone who helps me get these books from the concept to the release and beyond. From my PA, to my editor and my proofreader, to my wonderful friends helping me through the hardest moments. To my husband, who doesn't read my books, but loves that I write them and is willing to listen to me talk about them for hours.

And to you, the reader, for without you, I wouldn't have anyone to share these stories with. I'm a storyteller at heart and you have given me the greatest gift of listening.

I love all of you. Thank you for continuing to go on this journey with me.

ABOUT THE AUTHOR

KNBanet.com

Living in Arizona with her husband and 5 pets (2 dogs and 3 cats), K.N. Banet is a voracious... video game player. Actually, she spends most of her time writing, and when she's not writing she's either gaming or reading.

She enjoys writing about the complexities of relationships, no matter the type. Familial, romantic, or even political. The connections between characters is what draws her into writing all of her work. The ideas of responsibility, passion, and forging one's own path all make appearances.

facebook.com/KNBanet
instagram.com/Knbanetauthor
bookbub.com/authors/k-n-banet
amazon.com/K.N.-Banet/e/B08412L9VV
patreon.com/knbanet

ALSO BY K.N. BANET

The Jacky Leon Series

Oath Sworn

Family and Honor

Broken Loyalty

Echoed Defiance

Shades of Hate

Royal Pawn

Rogue Alpha

Bitter Discord

Volume One: Books 1-3

The Kaliya Sahni Series

Bounty

Snared

Monsters

Reborn

Legends

Destiny

Volume One: Books 1-3

The Everly Abbott Series

Servant of the Blood

Blood of the Wicked

Tribunal Archives Stories

Ancient and Immortal (Call of Magic Anthology)

Hearts at War

Full Moon Magic (Rituals and Runes Anthology)

Made in the USA
Monee, IL
18 October 2022